Also available

#gaymers
Status Update
Beta Test
Connection Error

Out of Uniform
Off Base
At Attention
On Point
Wheels Up
Squared Away
Tight Quarters
Rough Terrain

Frozen Hearts
Arctic Sun
Arctic Wild
Arctic Heat
(September 2019)

Also available from Annabeth Albert

Trust with a Chaser
Tender with a Twist

Treble Maker
Love Me Tenor
All Note Long

Served Hot
Baked Fresh
Delivered Fast
Knit Tight
Wrapped Together
Danced Close

Resilient Heart
Winning Bracket
Save the Date
Level Up

To my amazing beta reading team, especially my Alaska readers. You all helped make this book something I'm truly proud of, and I can't tell you how much I appreciate your time and patience with me.

ARCTIC WILD

ANNABETH ALBERT

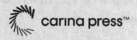

carina press™

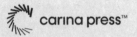

carina press™

ISBN-13: 978-1-335-00690-5

Arctic Wild

Copyright © 2019 by Annabeth Albert

PLEASE RECYCLE
THIS PRODUCT IS RECYCLABLE

Recycling programs
for this product may
not exist in your area.

www.CarinaPress.com

Printed in U.S.A.

ARCTIC WILD

Chapter One

"What do you mean she's not coming?" Reuben tried to catch his breath after the long dash from the security checkpoint to the gate for his flight. While waiting for Craig to explain this turn of events, he slipped off his suit jacket. He wouldn't ordinarily wear a suit for a long day of travel, but after an early morning meeting ran late, he'd had no time to change.

"She just called. Someone leaked the Henderson Motors buyout news, so now they're having to work double time to both get the deal done and find the source of the leak. Heads are going to roll, and she's on the warpath. You know Leticia. Damn it." Craig looked both impressed by his spouse's reputation and ready to kick something. "And now I've taken a week off to spend time with my wife—no offense, Rube—and she's going to be in meetings while I'm four time zones away with no cell coverage. Fuck this. Last three vacations we've planned have all either been canceled or turned into working trips."

"I know." Reuben wasn't sure what else to say. This whole trip had been Craig's idea. Ever since another partner at Reuben's law firm had returned from seeing his adult kid in Alaska, Craig had been full steam ahead on the idea of going on an Arctic wilderness adventure and had settled on Reuben's impending birthday as an excuse to drag him along. The argument that Reuben and Leticia worked too hard at their law firm was an old one, and Craig had made a passionate case for the trip. He'd also lobbied for Reuben bringing someone along, but that plan had fallen through when Dan broke up with Reuben around Passover. Still smarting from that dismissal, Reuben had no desire to bring someone just for the sake of not being a third wheel. And zero time to date. That too.

"I seriously don't know what to do anymore. We never see each other, and when I do see her, she's shackled to her cell or laptop." Craig rocked back and forth on the balls of his feet. "My marriage is crumbling, and hell if I know how to save it."

Reuben was the absolute last person to hand out relationship advice, but he tried for a sympathetic tone. "Do you want to just forget the whole thing?"

"You'd love that, wouldn't you?" Craig's eye roll was worthy of Reuben's teen daughter, not a fortysomething corporate event planner. Unlike Reuben, he was dressed more casually in a pullover and khakis and his rumpled hair suggested he'd spent more time that morning worrying about his wife than his appearance. "More time to work for you. But, no, much as I want to run after my wife, we can't completely cancel. This is the family company that Vale's kid's boyfriend works for. They're counting on our business, and it would be beyond rude if all three of us back out. And it's your birthday in two days. Come on, Rube, you seriously want to turn what… forty-eight this year in an office with a stack of papers in front of you?"

"Eh. It's just another day." Reuben shrugged. And really, it was. He wasn't a big sentimental guy. Amelia, his daughter, had made noises about skipping her end of the year eighth grade field trip to spend the day with him, but he'd insisted she go with her class. It was simply another number on the calendar for him, but Craig loved making productions about holidays. And unlike Reuben, Craig was obsessed with how close to fifty they both were now, something Reuben really tried not to stop and think about. "And I'm not saying to cancel for *me*. You're going to be miserable. If you stay, at least you can try to see Leticia when she's free, maybe go out to dinner, catch a show with your time off. Staycation or whatever. Try to talk to her, maybe."

"You're not wrong." Craig slumped against a nearby concrete column. "I really do want to save this thing before it's too late. But I know you. If I say I'm not going, you're going to back out as well. And then you'll be at your desk on your birthday."

"Priority boarding for flight 435 to Seattle-Tacoma should begin shortly," a female flight attendant announced over the loudspeaker. Fuck. Not much time to argue with Craig, who was clearly spoiling for a fight.

"Let me worry about my birthday. If I say I'll go ahead and go, would that help?"

"You'd really do that? Go to Alaska without either of us?"

"Is it really that big of a deal?" Reuben didn't like Craig's implication that he'd be helpless on his own. "Sure, it's a long flight, but I did Brisbane and Tokyo last year, Jakarta the year before. Did Europe with Natalie back when we were together, more than once. It's not like I'm a stranger to travel. And there's a guide, right?"

"Yeah, but this is roughing it. Bush planes and national parks."

"Which you were all for even a few hours ago," Reuben reminded him.

"Yeah, I was. And I'm still pissed to have to miss it. Damn Henderson news. So you'll do it?" Craig didn't bother to disguise his skeptical once-over, eyes traveling over Reuben's suit and his leather carry-on.

True, Reuben wasn't exactly dressed for Alaska, but he drew himself up to his full height and gave his friend his best hard stare, the one that usually sent first-year associates scurrying for their desks. "Sure."

Now going felt almost like a point of pride. If Craig really thought he wasn't up to the task or would chicken out, something ridiculous, he'd forgotten who Reuben was. One of the most sought-after corporate lawyers in the tristate region, a fixer with a reputation he'd honed for twenty-five years now. Partner in a large firm with an impeccable reputation for getting the job done. He didn't shy away from challenges. Sure, he'd rather do almost anything other than fly to Anchorage today, but he was perfectly capable of going, making Vale happy— which might give him an ally in the current management drama at the firm—and proving Craig wrong at the same time. Win-win.

"Okay. *Okay*. Thank you." Craig smiled for the first time since Reuben had shown up, but it was a tentative grin with none of his usual confidence.

Reuben clapped him on the shoulder. "I'll handle this. You handle your relationship. I've got faith you guys can get through this." He tried to put conviction behind his words. Granted, his own relationships seldom survived his career, but he did believe Craig and Leticia were good for each other. If anyone could make the never-ending work and life-balance thing work, it would be them.

"Yeah. And who knows, maybe this will be good for you. A nice escape on your own. Tell me you're not bringing work."

"Just for the flight," Reuben lied. He figured with a string of boring nights ahead of him, he could get through a backlog of document reading as long as he had power. But Craig would scoff at that plan.

"Socialize. Chat up the guide. Hike. Enjoy yourself."

"Now boarding for our first class and priority members for flight 435 service to Seattle-Tacoma."

"That would be me," Reuben said, mainly to avoid more life advice from Craig. "Take care of Leticia."

"Okay, will do. I'll message the guide, tell him it'll only be you."

"You do that." Reuben forced himself to smile and not grimace at the sudden realization that he and this tourist guide were about to be stuck with each other, like it or not. Probably some grizzled old mountain man pilot, older than Reuben, like those guys on the reality show Dan had made him watch an episode or two of. Maybe he'd be the strong but silent—please God *silent*—type and leave Reuben to his reading in peace. Yes. That would be perfect. If the guide kept to himself and didn't expect much out of him, maybe this whole thing wouldn't be so terrible.

"So, the bear is like *right* there, staring us down, near the doors to the plane, and we need to take off soon to get the folks back in time for their flights home. And what you think we did next?" Toby deliberately widened his eyes and leaned forward, enjoying how the two other patrons at the hotel bar did the same thing.

He hadn't yet figured out whether the two young out-of-towners were brother and sister, friends, or a couple, but he did love a captive audience, and they were an excellent distraction while he waited for this week's client to show. Client, singular, because apparently one of the other two was some high-powered super attorney who'd bailed on the Alaska vacation at the last possible minute. And knowing how lawyers loved to nickel and dime people, he had no doubt the missing two would suggest that a refund was in order. A personalized private bush plane tour wasn't cheap, and Toby had been counting on his percentage of the take from three tourists, not one. One who was late at that.

"Drink?" The bartender asked a well-dressed man walking up to the bar area right as Toby was about to continue his story. Given that the dude certainly looked like he could afford Toby's services even as his pricey duds hardly looked ready for the backcountry, Toby got off his stool and moved away from the eager duo.

"Not yet. I'm meeting someone." The guy had an East Coast accent with a tone that said he was used to being listened to. He looked around, distracted, eyes scanning right past Toby. *Typical.* Thousand-dollar suit and not the sense of a reindeer.

"Mr. Graham?" Toby stuck out a hand. He was wearing an official Barrett Tours polo—new this season because his boss was never going to stop dreaming up expansion plans—and clean jeans but he still felt decidedly unkempt next to this guy's smooth elegance. He supposed some people would call the guy a silver fox—older, distinguished face, well-trimmed facial scruff and full head of silver-tinged hair—but silver *bear* might be more accurate, given his height, broad shoulders, and overall bulk. Older didn't usually do it for Toby, but he had to admit the guy was hot in that aging-movie-star, rich-dude sort of way. "I'm Tobias Kooly, your guide. Glad you made it."

"Call me Reuben, please." He shook Toby's hand—nice firm grip, large hand, the sort of confidence Toby associated with a guy who got things done. "This is supposed to be a vacation. I can be Mr. Graham back in the office. And since it's just us, we might as well be informal."

"You've got it. My friends mainly call me Toby. And speaking of friends, I'm sorry yours couldn't make it. Man, passing on a vacation to stay in the office. Can't imagine doing that. But lawyers, right?"

Reuben did a slow blink, the sort of thing that immediately told Toby he'd screwed up. "I'm a lawyer too. And yes, these things happen. Way too often, actually. Millions—possibly billions—are on the line in the deal Leticia stayed behind for."

"Oh, sorry." Fuck it. He didn't usually suffer from foot-in-mouth disease, but he'd clearly gone for the wrong tone here. Not the start he wanted. "Didn't mean to be flip. And I thought my boss said you were an events planner."

"No, that's Leticia's husband." Reuben's sigh made Toby feel like he hadn't done a good enough job listening to Annie's rundown of the clients. "And good that you mentioned *boss* as I suppose you have some paperwork for me? Waivers and such? We might as well get that over with."

"I do." Toby grabbed his folder off the bar. The guy

sounded like Toby was offering a colonoscopy, not a week of fun, which meant Toby was going to have to work harder than usual to make a good impression. "But you're probably starving. Let's grab a table. It's dinnertime here, but you're a bunch of hours ahead. We usually tell people to come a day or so early to get acclimated to the time change."

"We didn't have that kind of time." Reuben followed Toby to a nearby table, but cast a glance over his shoulder at the other tourists. "You don't need to finish up with your...friends?"

Damn it. Not that Toby had been doing anything wrong, having a soda to kill time and getting a little bit of flirt on, but Reuben made him feel like he'd been goofing off on the clock.

"Nah. Let's get you some food." He did spare a smile and a little wave for the other tourists though, just to prove he wasn't a total ass, raising his voice to say, "Sorry. Business calls." The duo waved back and returned to their drinks.

Reuben had the sort of distant but respectful manner with the server that Toby had come to expect from rich people, fussing over the wine list but not dipping into rude territory. Toby stuck with his soda and ordered the burger he always got when meeting clients at the hotel. He could expense his food, but he tried not to take advantage of that. He'd leave the steak and garlic mashed potatoes to Reuben, who also ordered a red wine with a name Toby wasn't even going to try to pronounce.

"Thanks for suggesting food." Reuben cut his meat into small, precise bites. "The options on the plane were decidedly lacking."

"Your friends did tell you that most of the meals on

the trip are fairly rustic, right?" Toby didn't want him getting his expectations up that all meals would be this nice. "It's all small local lodges and simple but hearty meals. Some of the lodges have wine or beer, but the selection is usually limited."

"I'll be fine." Reuben waved Toby's concern away. "I grew up in Brooklyn on very basic fare. I'm not a picky eater."

"Good." Toby pulled out the paperwork Annie had sent, glancing down at the itinerary before handing it to Reuben. "I'm planning to stick mainly to what we worked out for the three of you, but you can tell me if you don't want to do something, and we can change it up."

"Excellent. I'm sure Craig and your boss came up with a good plan, but I don't mind more downtime. I brought plenty to keep me busy."

"I can't guarantee Wi-Fi at most of the stops." This wouldn't be Toby's first corporate client who couldn't disconnect from work, and explaining the limited cell and internet service was never fun.

"I expected that. I preloaded plenty of reading on my laptop, which has a long battery life."

"That should be okay. Most places have electricity." Personally, Toby couldn't see the value of bringing a stack of work on a once-in-a-lifetime vacation. And why look at a laptop instead of the scenery? But he nodded anyway. He knew better than to argue with a client. If Reuben wanted to work the trip away, so be it. "We leave first thing in the morning—it's an early start, which is why we usually meet up the night before. But you did have a long trip in. Do you want me to try to push the flight plan back?"

"Don't be ridiculous." Reuben's stare had a hard edge

to it, a man who would not stand for coddling, which Toby could respect. The look also made his insides heat, an unexpected spark of arousal—commanding didn't usually turn his crank, but as he was in the midst of something of a dry spell, he supposed even hot, older, presumably straight silver bears could get his motor humming.

"Sorry." He looked away, not wanting to reveal his line of thinking—this was not a guy who would take kindly to being Toby's eye candy for the week.

"I'm used to long days. As long as there's coffee, I'll be perfectly fine."

"There will be time to grab coffee before we head to the seaplane," Toby assured him.

Dinner almost finished, Reuben took a long sip of his wine. "Now, about that paperwork? I really should think about checking my email."

The man had to be exhausted and in dire need of sleep, but Toby had a feeling this guy would never admit such mundane needs. So Toby focused on getting him to sign the necessary waivers. Exactly like every other lawyer Toby had ever met, Reuben took his sweet time reading the waivers, frown lines deepening with each page until finally he let out a mighty *harrumph.*

"Not your doing, but your boss needs better boiler-plate." Reuben shook his head.

"I can't take you up in the plane unless you sign." Toby had been down this road before with clients who wanted to cross out sections or write in others. Someone please save him from the rich and picky.

"Fine. Guess I'm putting my life in your hands." Reuben signed, and Toby's insides did a weird shimmy, like maybe he didn't want that responsibility, didn't want the possibility of letting this man down.

"Thank you." Toby took cell pictures of the signed documents for Annie and returned them to his folder so she'd have a hard copy for her records.

"So…" Reuben sat back in his chair, not in the apparent hurry to get up to his room that Toby would have figured. "How does the story end? What did you do to the bear?"

Damn it all to hell. Reuben *had* heard that part of Toby's story. And ordinarily, it wouldn't be that big of a deal and he'd give Reuben the same dramatic ending he'd been planning for the young tourists, but there was something about this guy that simply kept him from lying or showboating. It wasn't the suit or the expensive shoes and haircut—Toby had told tales for many a rich client before. Maybe it was Reuben's intense stare—the one that said he was listening, really listening and didn't want to be disappointed. Or the set of his jaw, like he'd recognize a lie for what it was and judge it accordingly. Whatever it was, for a change, Toby didn't feel comfortable with his usual bragging.

"Not a thing," he admitted, truth spilling out. "Made the tourists wait behind me, and we gave the bear space, let him lumber away. You don't mess with bears. We were late taking off, but I made up time in the air, and they still caught their flight home."

And they'd tipped well, happy to have such an exciting adventure and close call with nature that they could tell their friends about. Boring, predictable ending, but when it came down to it, Toby would rather keep the clients alive rather than have a moment of glory. Of course, he was damn good at editing in those moments of heroism when picking people up or when a group needed a good story. But Reuben didn't need to know *all* his tricks.

"I see." As it was, Reuben raised a manicured eyebrow, narrowed eyes saying that he knew Toby had been planning a different ending for his audience earlier, but he didn't call him on it, continuing with a more casual tone. "I'm good with letting the wildlife have its space. Not big on animals."

"All animals? No pets?"

"No." He shrugged, showing off his broad shoulders and the way the expensive suit fabric clung to them. "Never had the time or the inclination, really."

"That's too bad." Toby had a sudden vision of Reuben with a big old mutt of a dog, tracking mud all over everything. Yup. That image just didn't fit this cultured man at all. And why that made Toby a little sad, he couldn't quite pinpoint. Reuben didn't have a wedding ring on, and the idea of him going home alone to a quiet house every night simply didn't sit well. Toby needed some chaos to feel truly at home himself.

"I really should get to checking my messages, see what can't wait." Reuben stood, and after making arrangements to meet at the front desk in the morning, Toby let him head to his room under the email pretense. Honestly, though, he hoped the guy slept. Tomorrow was going to be a long day, and a grumpy, tired lawyer who already kept looking like he'd rather be anywhere else was only going to make Toby's job that much harder. And without the other two paying clients, Toby really did need to score that tip at the end, try to offset the possible loss in income if Annie ended up giving a refund to Reuben's friends. It might be a long week, but one way or another, Toby was going to win Reuben over, get him to enjoy himself. He'd tackled far bigger challenges than one prickly lawyer.

Tory Temptation

"Any minute," Toby was going to retire, since even on his holiday he felt like he looked little more than a prickly overripe.

Chapter Two

Reuben had been a morning person most of his life, so even with the time change screwing with his sleep, he was up and ready at the appointed time to meet his guide. His far too young and far too talkative guide. His wish for a silent guide had died a quick, brutal death the moment he'd met Toby, who was the sort of guy who clearly styled himself as a charmer, what with his smooth delivery and easy, joking manner.

His eyes though told a different story, dark brown with a sort of emotional depth that Reuben usually associated with people twice the guy's age, the type of thing one only got with a lot of lived experience. The contrast between his intense eyes and casual demeanor intrigued Reuben, way more than it should. He'd learned his lesson with Dan—younger men were trouble he didn't need, and Craig's encouragement to chat up the tour guide hardly applied here. Reuben wasn't going to have much in common with the guy as it was, and having watched Toby flirt shamelessly with the young female tourist at the bar, he could pretty much predict that the guy was straight.

No, better he just concentrate on making it through the week, use it as chance to get caught up on reading he'd been putting off. To that end, he kept his phone out, intending to do a last-minute email check from the hotel lobby while waiting for the guide to show. But Toby surprised him by already being in the lobby, two cups of coffee in his hands. He held one out to Reuben, cream and sweetener packets balanced on the lid.

"Morning. You said coffee, but I wasn't sure how you took it." Toby's grin was way too wide for the early hour. His dark hair was damp, like he'd rushed a shower, and he wore another polo with the logo of the company he worked for—last night's navy, today's reddish orange. He was probably somewhere around thirty, so not a kid, but still, Reuben felt a little guilty admiring the way the shirt clung to his broad shoulders and lean torso.

"Thank you." Reuben accepted the coffee, added a sugar and discarded the creamer in a nearby trash can. Trying not to be frustrated at the loss of email time, he pocketed his phone. Through the lobby doors, a bright morning waited to greet them. "Wow. Still not used to the idea of such an early dawn."

"Oh yeah. Sunrise was around four thirty this morning, and we'll have light until eleven or so tonight. That's part of why we leave so early—might as well take advantage of the sun while we have it." Toby led the way to one of the hotel vans. "We take the shuttle to the airport, then we're off in my seaplane. Today's itinerary has us flying over the Kenai Peninsula—the area where our company is based—with several scenic stops for you, then overnight is at a lodge near Katmai National Park. There's a good chance we'll see bears and other wildlife, so be sure your camera is ready and batteries fresh."

"I didn't bring one," Reuben admitted as they waited for the driver to load their luggage.

Toby frowned and looked like he was about to say something, then swallowed, face going more neutral, tone upbeat. "Well, hope your cell has a good charge then. There's plenty of things you're going to want a picture of."

"I'm not really one for pictures." He didn't like how grumpy he was coming across, but he wasn't someone who did a lot of sightseeing and touristy stuff, even when abroad for work.

He and Toby weren't the only ones on the shuttle and ended up in different rows, which gave him a chance to finally check in with his phone. The office knew he'd be out of range but he still had several key emails to respond to and was just finishing up when his phone buzzed. Ordinarily he wouldn't be so rude as to answer in close confines like a plane or bus, but it was Natalie. If there was a problem with Amelia or something else critical, he needed to know now, not in a few days.

"Yes?" He kept his voice down at least. "I'm on a shuttle—"

"I'll keep this brief." As always, Natalie's tones were as clipped and precise as the tailored suits she favored. "I know you're in Alaska. Alone. Leticia filled me in. You don't have to do this, you know. You're hardly the outdoorsy type. No one would fault you coming home."

Why did the world seem intent on telling him that he wasn't fit for this experience? Hell, even the guide had seemed doubtful. All those assumptions had him bristling, needing to prove them wrong. He might not have a *good* time, but he wouldn't be admitting that to anyone, Natalie especially, and he was more than capable of surviving the trip.

"I'll be fine."

"Of course you will." Natalie's tone was just this side of patronizing. "And honestly, the time away may be good for you. Maybe it'll give you a chance to think about the restructuring vote."

He should have known that was the real reason she'd called. "I'm not taking a buyout or retirement or however else you want to frame the restructuring you and Forthright are so hell-bent on."

"At least think about it." Natalie had positioned herself as managing partner at the firm. Years ago, they'd been ruthless associates together, and the fact that they worked together had probably kept them together far longer than it should have. They'd had an amicable divorce as far as these things could ever be pleasant, but recently Natalie had seemed to chafe at his presence and was encouraging him to take the buyout package the firm was offering to several senior partners. But he was far from convinced that accepting the offer was the right course of action for his future. He'd worked too long and hard for this firm to be squeezed anywhere he didn't want to go. Sure, he'd been fortunate with his investments, and he could undoubtedly take his talents to another firm, but why would he want to start over at his age? No. Not happening.

"There's nothing to think about." He kept his tone measured, not wanting to be one of those idiots arguing on a cell phone in public. "Now, how's Amelia? Everything all set for camp?"

"Yes, the nanny purchased everything on the list that Camp Flint Rock sent. She'll be ready for you to take her. Thank God drop-off is on your parenting time, not mine. I don't envy you the drive."

"It'll be all right." Truth be told, Reuben was dreading the drive to the Catskills, but more because he never knew what to say to Amelia, how to get her off her tablet and talking with him. He was a master negotiator and could close multinational deals, but all it took was one fourteen-year-old to reduce him to a bumbling fool who couldn't even talk with his own kid. "Any ideas as to something I could bring her from Alaska?"

He wasn't usually the souvenir type of father, but something about Toby's expression when he'd said that he didn't do pictures had him feeling strangely guilty, as did the thought of having nothing to say to her. Maybe if he greeted her with a present—

"Like a stuffed animal?" Natalie's voice was light, but he could hear the scorn there too. "Please don't bring a dust catcher. She's too old for that stuff anyway. Just make sure there's money in her commissary account, and she can get what she wants at camp."

"Sure." Reuben ended the call more than a little unsettled. Lately, Natalie always seemed to get under his skin like this, and he hated it. Maybe the best thing would be to take the buyout package, but hell, the other partners contemplating taking the deal were a good twenty years older than him. Savings cushion aside, he had plenty of years of usefulness left, and after giving two decades to the firm, he simply wasn't ready to say goodbye to something he'd poured so much of himself into. In any event, the choice was his, not Natalie's, so he returned to his email, trying to regain his sense of balance.

"We're here." Toby tapped him on the shoulder as the van came to a stop. "Let me get your luggage."

"I've got it." Reuben was used to people catering to him, but certain things he preferred to do for himself.

Besides, his main bag rolled, so it was hardly a hardship to drag it along.

"Do you want a brief tour or overview of the seaplane airport? This is the largest one in the world, and a lot of our clients enjoy hearing about the different types of planes and seeing examples on our walk to our slip."

"I'm good." If he were being honest, he was a little nervous about going up in the little plane. Whenever one heard about plane crashes, it was usually noncommercial planes like this. Even corporate jets made him antsy, not unlike a conversation with Natalie. And even if it was safe, he wasn't a small man, and he'd stopped flying coach as soon as he could afford better. Being crammed in a tin can with wings wasn't his idea of fun, but he wasn't telling Toby that. Besides, he still had a decent signal, and he could scan messages while he walked.

"No problem. I do usually do some commentary over the com headset while we fly, but if it gets to be too much, just let me know." As it had been last night, Toby's tone was affable, that of a guy who was easy to please, but his eyes had briefly flared with irritation before his expression returned to a welcoming smile.

Reuben refused to feel guilty for being a difficult customer. Craig had already messaged him to tip the guide well at the conclusion of the trip, and he'd do that even without the reminder. He might be grumpy and particular, but he wasn't an asshole. And if he wanted to turn down unnecessary chatter like a tour of the airport he didn't need, then he would, no guilt allowed. They made a brief stop at a small building for Toby to check in his flight plan before continuing onto the planes.

At the edge of the large lake, he reluctantly switched his phone off and stowed it when Toby came to a stop by a red plane parked next to a short dock. It was one of many planes parked along the shoreline, with structures of varying sizes by each dock.

The plane was even smaller than Reuben had expected. If Leticia and Craig had come, there would have been room for the three of them in the cabin, behind the cockpit where Toby would sit, but not much else, and quarters were decidedly cramped, even by the awful standards of commercial flights. Following Toby's instructions on how to climb up, he accepted the headset he handed him and tried to find a position that didn't have his knees around his earlobes. So much for hoping he could balance his laptop while they flew—there were no tray tables nor any room for a carry-on, which Toby had stored behind him before he could grab it back. With the phone off and laptop out of reach, he was at loose ends while Toby circled the plane, checking this and that before sliding into the cockpit and talking into the headset, presumably to the tower. Reuben was both ready to get underway and dreading takeoff. He prided himself on being a rational, logical man, and he tried to remind himself how many aircraft came and went from this place every day without issue, but his stomach still insisted on churning.

"Doing okay?" Toby's voice crackled across the headset. "It'll be a few minutes before we get clearance, but if you watch out your window, you'll see some planes coming in. Breakfast is going to be at our first stop, at a lake near Seward. We'll be going across the Kenai Peninsula, and with today's clear skies, you should have good views of the mountain passes and other features."

"Fine, fine." Reuben stopped short of telling him to get it over with. He honestly wasn't sure he'd be able to eat, not with the acid currently burning the back of his throat, but he'd deal with that, assuming they lived through the flight. Which they would.

His mother's voice echoed in his head, warning him against borrowing trouble. She'd taught him to be pragmatic, not dwell on negative emotions, and he tried to follow that advice as he took some deep breaths. God knew she'd be laughing at him now, shaking her head the way she'd always done. He'd been doing a terrible job at pragmatism that morning—and with everyone assuming that he'd be miserable, it had been easy to give in to a black mood, prove them right. But no more. He'd clawed his way to the top of his profession, to the point where he could give Amelia so much more than his own parents had been able to. He could handle one short plane flight, no matter how rickety the craft.

However, even telling himself all that, his stomach still fluttered as they pulled away from the dock, joined the line of planes waiting for their turn to race across the smooth surface of the lake. And even the sensation of moving across water at slow speed was different than the tarmac—bouncier and less predictable.

"Here we go." Toby's voice sounded in his ear, and as they picked up speed Reuben braced his hands on the arms of the seat, like that could help. The roar of the plane was so much louder than he'd expected.

The plane lurched, tilting up, leaving a good part of Reuben's composure behind them as they lifted off. Takeoff felt so much more…personal in a small plane like this, just him and the pilot, thin tin separating him from the sky. His breathing sped up, fingers digging into unforgiving plastic. He'd give an awful lot for the distraction of work right then, the need to be back on familiar ground almost overwhelming. Survival. He just had to survive this week, find a way back to his pragmatic center, then he could get back to the business of being the person he knew he was, not this anxious wreck with his eyes squished shut, already counting down until they landed.

Huh. Toby had not expected the cool, calm, and collected businessman to be a nervous flyer, but his last glance at Reuben before takeoff had revealed a decidedly uncomfortable person—stiff body, pale face, shuttered expression. Ordinarily Toby would try to reassure him, but Reuben had made it clear that he wasn't one for idle conversation. Instead Toby had to hope the smooth skies coupled with his usual spiel about what they were crossing on their way to the island lodge near Seward would settle the seriously anxious vibe coming from behind him.

For himself, he couldn't recall a time when he had been anything less than excited to fly. Even in terrible weather, he trusted his skills, trusted his plane. And in good weather, like this, there were few greater pleasures in life than being aloft, the land he loved beneath him, spring fully arrived at long last, true summer not far behind it. Up here, he could truly relax, let his guard down and simply *be*. His commentary about the Cook Inlet and the Turnagain Arm was something he'd delivered countless times and didn't cut into his pleasure at flying, even when Reuben stayed silent.

"Headset working?" he asked as they traversed parts of the Chugach State Park and National Forest, giving some spectacular views of Prince William Sound off in the distance beyond Whittier. "Any questions for me?"

"Yes, I can hear you fine. No questions." The strain in Reuben's voice was unmistakable.

"There's an air sickness bag under your seat if you're feeling ill. I'm going to dip down, give you a nice look as Esther Island before we turn for Seward."

"Not ill." Now Reuben sounded annoyed, which Toby supposed was better than white-knuckle panic.

"Good. Now we'll be landing on a lake near Seward where we'll pull up right next to a little lodge with the best biscuits and gravy in Alaska." He had a feeling that Reuben was looking forward to landing and solid ground more than food, but without him admitting to feeling poorly, Toby had little choice but to stick to his script. "They'll knock your boots off, but there's plenty of other choices too."

"Boots off, huh?" Reuben released a promising if shaky laugh. "Sounds interesting."

"We'll circle to set up our approach and then taxi across to the lodge. Stay buckled until I open the hatches, okay?"

He did one of his best landings on this lake, barely skimming the surface, bouncing not too harsh, barely a jolt as they touched down, but he still made out a muffled curse from Reuben.

"How about a walk before we eat?" Toby asked after securing the plane and opening the doors. Experience with other travelers had shown him that fresh air might be more of a restorative than his company or conversation.

"Fine." Reuben's expression was resolute as he disembarked, mouth set in a thin, determined line, eyes hard.

"Hey now, I'm only suggesting an easy trail by the shore, not a trek up Denali. Or a frog eating contest."

He added that last bit simply to see if he could get a smile out of Reuben, which it turned out he could not. Oh well. "Listen, I'm going to level with you. You hated the flight, right? And the idea of exploring feels like another burden?"

"I didn't *hate* it." Reuben bristled at this, shoulders pulling back to emphasize his taller height. "This whole trip is something outside my comfort zone, that's all."

"Exactly." Toby offered what he hoped was an encouraging smile. "So, what I'm trying to say, is this is your few days. You want to go back, hole up in the hotel with your work? I won't tell anyone other than my boss that you only did the one flight. Or do you prefer a land tour? We do those too. To be frank, the plane tours are the big-ticket, luxury items for our business. We do group photography and hiking tours mainly by van. If you'd want to go by land, I'm sure Annie could do something about the price of the tour for you."

Toby was being honest—much as he loved to fly, Reuben's comfort mattered to him, and they could do plenty of exploring via vehicle. Might mean massaging the timetable and accommodations some, but better a happy client than a shitty few days for both of them.

"I don't need special accommodations." Reuben's mouth pursed, eyes flashing with irritation. Toby wasn't sure exactly what type of lawyer Reuben was, but man, he'd be freaky intimidating in a courtroom, all glowering and pacing, eyes ready to burn those in his way to ash. "Whatever Craig and your boss worked out as an itinerary is fine. I'm sure I'll get used to the flying parts."

"You will." Toby resisted the urge to clap him on the shoulder, reassure him further. "But I don't want you merely enduring. This is supposed to *fun*, so if there's anything we can do to get you having a good time, just tell me."

"Will do." Reuben gave a sharp nod that had Toby wondering if he would speak up even if he were truly miserable.

"So a walk?" Toby led the way from the dock to the path that skirted the shoreline. "Or straight to the food? And I've got some motion sickness pills you could take with your food, might help."

"Walk is fine. It might settle my stomach enough to enjoy those biscuits. I'll think about the pills." Reuben drew in a deep breath, like he was making a decided effort to be more social, and indeed, his tone was more upbeat, less grumpy. "But I might be slower than you'd like. I've never hiked much, outside of camp as a kid. It's always seemed more efficient to work out indoors, where I can read or listen while I do the elliptical or whatever. However, lead the way, and I'll do my best."

"That's the spirit." Setting a moderate pace, Toby headed down the trail. It was a nice, easy paved one that summer bikers and day-trippers enjoyed with an impressive view of the snow-tipped mountains surrounding the valley. Boats dotted the far side of the lake, and above them, a red and white Cessna circled. The crisp air licked at his cheeks, the sort of early June day that always made him feel lucky to be alive. But he swore he could almost feel Reuben counting down until he could drag out his phone.

"See the kayakers?" After they'd been walking in silence a few minutes, he pointed at the blue and orange dots on the water. "Your friends wanted to try that— it's on the agenda for day three. You ever been in one? Or a boat at all?"

"Does a ferry count?" Reuben easily kept up with him, long legs matching his strides. "Growing up in Brooklyn, I did the ferry a fair bit. Then canoes at camp, but that's been...years."

"I bet it's like riding a bike. Your old canoe skills will help, and the kayak outfitter will give you a lesson too." Toby was glad Reuben hadn't turned the experience down right off. And honestly, he was happy Reuben hadn't taken him up on his offer to take him back to Anchorage so he could commune with that damn phone. He'd had tougher clients, and work was work. He'd make the best of this.

"Do you kayak too?"

"As a guide, I pretty much do everything along with my group—fish, bike, hike, boat and so on. Only thing I don't do is hunt because of restrictions on certain seasons on the amount of game you can bag—I leave that to the clients, but I go along, help them find good spots." Toby also had a personal bias against trophy hunting that he didn't want to explain. It was fine for the clients, but he'd been raised to value subsistence hunting. He enjoyed getting the occasional moose for his family, but he tried to stick to their values when he did so. "Ditto photography. I'm not a pro by any means, but Alaska has so many once-in-a-lifetime shots, and I enjoy helping clients capture them."

Sure, he was bragging, but he was damn good at what he did and took pride in the experiences he delivered.

"That's nice. A personal touch." Reuben nodded as they turned back toward the lodge. "This was a good idea. I'm feeling more like I could eat, so thank you."

"No problem." Toby didn't like how warm the unexpected praise made him. Pride was one thing, but the last thing he needed was an attraction to Mr. Hot-Older-and-Unattainable, who was already grumpy and probably wouldn't appreciate his interest. "And we can walk again after we eat—we don't have to head right back to the plane."

If he had it to do over again, he might have picked up on Reuben's unease back in Anchorage, offered to take him directly to the lodge in Katmai. However, since they'd come this far, sticking to the day's plan seemed like the best option, but he still wanted Reuben comfortable.

"Worried I might puke in your plane?" Reuben's laugh was deep and rich and way too welcome. Cranky was far easier to deal with than this inconvenient urge to flirt.

"Nah." Toby had to laugh too as he led the way into the restaurant at the lodge. "Okay, maybe a little. But you wouldn't be the first, I promise you."

The server knew him from all the tours he brought through, and she gave them a table near the large window overlooking the lake. Not that Reuben seemed ready to enjoy the view—he was already getting his phone out, and his preoccupation with work was a good killer for any flirty impulses. Toby got his usual omelet, while Reuben looked up long enough to order the biscuits.

"I suppose I should see if you're right about them being good. I don't often eat pork sausage—holdover from childhood when my grandmother would make me feel all kinds of bad for looking at bacon."

"Ah. Jewish?" Toby guessed. He'd had other tourists who were, including a family last year that kept kosher.

"Yes. My grandparents were stricter than my parents, who were pretty lax about most things outside of the major holidays, but my grandmother gave us all grief about our eating habits, and it's funny how even forty years later I still hear her voice whenever I indulge in food like this." Reuben glanced down at his phone as he finished his story. "Oh, look at that, we do have a signal."

Toby wanted to hear more about Reuben's childhood in New York, a place he'd never been but had always been intrigued by, but he could tell Reuben really wanted to mess with the phone from the way his eyes kept drifting back toward it. "It's okay. Take advantage of the signal. I should probably check my own messages too."

More or less to be social, he fished out his phone and scrolled through a few updates of upcoming tours from Annie. And since there wasn't a message from his sister, he quickly dashed one off. These months were always his busiest time, and he needed Nell to be reliable this summer more than ever.

Did Dad get his morning meds? I'll likely be out of range until late tomorrow, but I'll check in when I can. Call Annie if anything pressing comes up.

The reply came right as their food arrived, Nell studding the message with a flood of emojis. A row of eye-rolling smileys greeted him. We're *fine.* And you'll be happy to know I've got a lead on a summer job. Might even get an interview before you're back. TTYL!!! Happier dancing emojis ended the text.

He did a fast return text before eating. Happy for you! Let me know if you need anything. He shoved down the urge to remind her that Dad came first and to not leave him alone too long while she job hunted. She knew full well how Dad tended to overdo things if on his own too long, and both of them would only bristle at Toby's reminders. Still, he couldn't help the sigh as he put the phone away and tucked into his eggs.

"Everything okay? Bad weather coming in?" Reuben finally spared a glance for the window, where clear skies still beckoned.

"No, no. Nothing like that. Just a family thing." He never talked about his home life with clients if he could help it—this was work, but it was also his escape, the time he got to be Toby, the freewheeling tour guide, and not Toby, the big brother and son.

"You said you're from this area? Your family too?" Reuben had the expectant look a lot of tourists got when they wanted to ask questions about his origins but didn't want to be rude.

"I grew up near Ninilchik, a village south of Kenai and north of Homer on the peninsula here. My family background is a mix, but mostly Athabascan from Ninilchik and Kenai. Also some Russian, Dutch, German thrown in." He gave the same condensed version he always did—it wasn't on him to educate tourists on the diversity of tribes and cultures within Alaska and he sure as hell wasn't producing a family tree, but he'd long since learned that tourists were inevitably curious and had some serious misconceptions about native peoples.

"I see. Interesting. My family had a long history in the same working-class neighborhood in Brooklyn but were originally from Poland. And much to my grandmother's unhappiness, I never picked up much Hebrew or Yiddish. Are you bilingual?" Reuben asked his follow-up while cutting his biscuits into more of the same precise shapes he had done with the steak last night, and his tone was conversational, not probing, which Toby appreciated.

"Not really bilingual, but I do speak some Dena'ina and have picked up some Yup'ik from friends and other native dialects here and there. Thanks to my guide work, I actually speak a fair bit of Japanese too—our company is super popular with tourists from all over Asia, and I've always had a quick ear for languages."

"Now there's a skill I don't have." Reuben laughed and paused long enough to eat some more of his food. "Okay, you were right. This is great stuff. Well worth the indulgence."

"Hey, it's your vacation. Enjoy it."

"Maybe." Reuben gave him something of a bemused expression before returning his attention to his food.

Fuck. Had that come out too flirty? Toby often found himself encouraging clients to enjoy themselves and didn't usually censor himself from being playful, but somehow things were different with Reuben. Maybe because it was a solo trip or the hot silver bear thing, but whatever it was, Toby hoped he didn't have to spend the whole trip walking this strange tightrope between friendly and professional.

And funny enough he found himself hoping for good cell reception for Reuben—grumpy guy obsessed with his phone was easier to not like, and not liking meant fewer chances of things getting weird between them, which he definitely didn't want.

Chapter Three

We're not going to crash. Planes are safer than cars.
Reuben tried some positive affirmations as Toby did a
round of checks after breakfast. Which had been all that
Toby had advertised, fluffy biscuits and rich gravy and
strong coffee. Because of all his business lunches and
dinners, Reuben was usually a breakfast-optional sort
of man, focusing on his coffee and getting work done
before the day got too crazy. But he had to admit he did
feel better—something about the combination of the
food and the fresh air had revived him after the stress of
the flight. And checking in with the office had grounded
him too, made him feel less adrift in this strange place,
distracted him from the coming next leg of their itinerary.

But now that he was back in the plane, his nerves
were getting the better of him again. He trotted out the
calming device he hadn't used since high school, since
he was usually able to produce more than enough confidence on his own for any given situation. Strange too,
how he hadn't thought of his mother much recently, but
her advice about good attitudes making a difference kept
creeping into his head today.

"All set." Toby's voice came over the headset. "This

next leg will take us over the southeastern part of the peninsula, right into the heart of the Kenai Fjords National Park. I'll be making several passes so that you get some hopefully impressive aerial views especially of the Harris Bay area, then we'll head to the tip of the peninsula before coming back up for lunch and exploring around Halibut Cove."

"Sounds good." Ever since Toby's offer to return him to Anchorage or change to a land-based trip, Reuben had been trying to be more social. He appreciated the offer but didn't need special treatment. Surviving this trip with his dignity intact had become a point of pride for him, and he refused to admit defeat after one short flight. He *would* make it through this trip, prove his friends and Natalie and even the tour guide himself wrong.

This time he was ready for the bouncy sensation as Toby taxied across the lake, picking up speed until they were airborne. Unlike the steadiness of commercial flights, the small plane experience was more akin to a roller coaster. His breakfast stayed put, thank God, and he forced himself to keep his eyes open, more out of a need to not be a nervous wreck than a desire to sightsee. But to his surprise, the view was more than enough to distract him from unpleasant thoughts. Below them, the lake region gave way to towering mountains with rivers meandering through.

On the headset, Toby pointed out the town of Seward and other points of interest, but the contrast between the mountains and the water really captivated Reuben. He'd flown over the Rockies before, but at twenty thousand feet or so, and his only real mountain experience was the Catskills, but those were mere rolling green hills compared to this craggy terrain.

"Doing better?" Toby's voice was kind, and Reuben couldn't help but enjoy the way he really did seem to care about whether Reuben was miserable or not.

"Yeah. I am. Thank you." And he could admit that he'd used his phone at the restaurant in part to avoid staring at the handsome guide—a trick he'd used before to keep from revealing more than he wanted to. Because Toby truly was that attractive with those soul-deep dark eyes and chiseled face and lean body, and the more time he spent around him, the more Reuben found himself caught up in his charms. He had to keep reminding himself that arousal was every bit as unwanted as airsickness.

"We're turning into Harris Bay now. You should have a good view of the glacier field."

Field turned out to be something of a misnomer, as it was more like undulating rivers of snow and glaciers. The whole region reminded Reuben of a giant bowl, only the walls were granite and lined with hanging glaciers and impossibly tall. It was like something out of a movie, and for the first time, he understood why Craig had been so keen on coming. The scenery was unlike anything he'd seen before, and he'd seldom felt so small and insignificant as he did when confronted with the vastness of the landscape. He was more used to feeling like the gear in the center of a machine, everything else rotating around him. These sensations of having shrunk and being a speck in time compared to eons of ice were more than a little disconcerting, but also riveting at the same time.

Although he kept up with Toby's commentary, he was still startled when he realized they were circling for a landing in a small bay where other planes were al-

ready docked. After another brief hike, this one up to
an expansive viewpoint for the bay, lunch was a choice
of a couple of different seafood choices, and they talked
easily about what they'd seen and about what would be
upcoming.

"Do you want to try to see bears or other wildlife
when we land at Katmai? I know a good, safe trail that's
fairly easy, but it has a great chance of wildlife spotting."
Toby's tone was encouraging, but not pushy. "The other
option is for you to settle in early at the lodge, but with
it being light so long, most people like a late dinner with
a hike beforehand."

"Hike sounds fine. And no need to slow yourself
down on my account—choose a trail you like." He forced
an optimistic tone, because he didn't want Toby thinking he needed easy options like some eighty-year-old.
The same part of him that wanted to prove his doubt-
ers wrong wanted to impress Toby, but that urge carried with it an undercurrent of wanting to show off for
the attractive guy, an urge Reuben hadn't had in years.

"Hey, it's your vacation." Toby offered him a lazy
smile, the sort that made Reuben's insides feel decades
younger. "But sure, I'll show you some of my favorite
vantage points. It's not a short flight, so we'll have plenty
of time for exploring."

Reuben liked the sound of that, especially since most
of the next leg of the trip was over water with less scenery to distract him. However, Toby kept up a nice if
crackly commentary, pointing out little dots in the water
that were whales, and providing a history of the Katmai National Park and Preserve with its lava fields and
unique landscape and the lakes and rivers of the region,
and when they touched down on a lake, he'd almost sold

Reuben on the idea of trying fly fishing in the morning as a not terrible endeavor. Apparently, the lodge had all the equipment they'd need for borrowing, and Toby's enthusiasm was infectious.

"Now I'm really wishing Craig and Leticia had come," Reuben joked as they came to a stop, before Toby had a chance to jump out. "Leticia with a fishing pole would be a sight worth seeing."

"I bet." Toby waited until he'd opened the hatches to speak again. "Wait till you have dinner—you'll want to brag on that too. This is one of the best food stops on your trip, which is why we do two nights here. I let them know you're a wine drinker, so the chef should have done some nice pairings for you."

"Now that sounds wonderful. But first we hike?" While not exactly eager, Reuben had to admit he was falling into the rhythm of the trip more, less uncomfortable than he'd been at first.

"Yeah. They'll take our luggage up to the cabins by ATV, and our hike will circle back to the main lodge in time for the dinner. There shouldn't be too many other guests as it's a fairly exclusive place." Toby set their bags on the dock right as a young woman rode up on one of those squat motorcycle-like things with the fat tires, pulling a little cart.

"Hey, Toby." She had a big smile for him and one for Reuben too. "We put your client in cabin four, near the sauna, and you're in your usual one. Don't be late for dinner!"

"We won't." Toby gave her a grin that made her cheeks go pink before he turned toward Reuben. "Your cabin has electricity and heat, and that sauna is totally worth a post-dinner try."

"I'm not usually much on recreational sweating." Reuben realized too late how that sounded, and Toby's rich chuckle said that he'd caught the unintentional joke there.

"Well, that's just too bad." Toby's tone might have been called flirty if they'd been in a bar, but out here just seemed like more of his natural charm. "Trailhead is this way."

The lodge was located in something of a valley, a strip of land jutting into the lake, so the hike was fairly level, but hardly boring with changing views of the water and wooded terrain both. They didn't see bears, but they did see some moose in the distance. By the time they reached the lodge for dinner, Reuben was famished in a way he hadn't been since his high school and college basketball playing days.

Toby hadn't been lying about the food—the meal opened with asparagus in puff pastry and only improved from there. Toby, naturally, made friends with the other guests and seemed to know the fishing guides, everyone seated at a massive dining table that invited easy conversation and lingering over courses.

Everything was pleasant right up until a woman in a red apron came out and knelt next to Toby. "Annie told me one of your guests was having a birthday. Is it this one or one of the cancellations?"

"Depends." Toby gave her a wink. "What did you make?" To Reuben, he said, "I forgot to ask you about the birthday. Is it yours?"

It would have been exceptionally simple to lie, but while Reuben would own up to his faults, lying easily wasn't one of them. "It's mine. Day after tomorrow. No need to go to any trouble, no matter what Craig arranged."

"Hey, now. Not so fast. There might be cake or pie." As he leaned forward, Toby's eyes sparkled. "Marta does incredible pies."

"Thanks." The chef twisted her apron. "But with berry season later in the summer and early fall, no pies today. I went for a dark chocolate torte with some of my own cloudberry preserves as garnish. We don't have to do the singing, but I've got a lovely port to accompany desert if you're interested."

Not wanting to disappoint Toby, who seemed genuinely eager for the treat, Reuben nodded. "That sounds nice. Just a small slice for me."

"I'll skip the port, but chocolate sounds amazing." Toby grinned, waiting until the chef had returned to the kitchen before speaking again. "Any special requests for your birthday that maybe your friends didn't think to put on the itinerary? And don't say high-speed internet access."

"I wouldn't turn that down." Joking with Toby made his chest feel like a hot air balloon—warm and light at the same time and more than a little unsteady. "Seriously though, don't go to any trouble."

"It's not trouble. And if your friend arranged more cakes for you at the other stops, I'm all for sharing that bounty."

"Sweet tooth?"

"You know it." Another easy, whole-body-warming smile. And damn if Reuben didn't find himself smiling back. He might be far too old for hopeless crushes, but his body seemed determined to loudly disagree. Ignoring that clamor from his underused libido might be equally as challenging as the terrain.

* * *

The early June trout season always made Toby happy, almost as happy as king salmon season, and he was glad he'd talked Reuben into some morning fishing. There wasn't much better in life than Marta's cinnamon rolls and aggressive early season trout making easy pickings for novices. It was also another chance for him to show off, and he prided himself on his ability to teach newbies. But why he particularly wanted to show off for Reuben was a question probably better left unasked. And it didn't help matters that he had to touch Reuben to show him the best fishing stance, and stand close enough to him to smell his herbal shampoo—something expensive no doubt, with a clean, fresh undercurrent.

It was a great time of year for sight fishing with dry flies, and it didn't take long before Reuben had his first success.

"Well, would you look at that? I guess I wouldn't starve out here after all." Reuben gave him a lopsided grin that made him look far more approachable.

"We're doing catch and release today since our dinner will already be waiting for us, but yep, you got a good one there." Toby helped him to free the fish from the line so it could happily swim away, seeking the schools of fry populating the river.

"Can I admit that I like this more than the flying? Which I'm rather surprised at, frankly."

"Careful there. You might find yourself actually having fun if you don't watch it." Toby liked teasing him, far more than he should have.

"Never know, I might like that." Reuben's tone was just as teasing as Toby's, which was a little jarring. Were they flirting? Toby could almost always tell when someone was interested, but something about Reuben made him a difficult read. Maybe it was his smooth sophistication when he wasn't out of his element. Like last night at dinner, how he'd effortlessly pronounced the wine names and remarked on their qualities with an ease that spoke to years of experience. And Reuben more relaxed, like he was this morning, was infinitely more appealing than him nervous and grumpy about flying.

Breathing deeply, Reuben tilted his head up, seeming to absorb the sunshine at a deep, cellular level that made Toby want to be the thing that put that look on his face, made him that relaxed.

"Man, I wish Amelia could see this." Reuben gave another easy smile. And just like that, icy water rushed over Toby's growing attraction. Reuben didn't wear a ring, but that didn't always mean a lot.

"Amelia? Wife?"

"No. My kid. Her mother and I have a…complicated relationship. We divorced five years ago, but we still work together."

"I'm sure you're a better dad than you think." Toby kept the conversation going in part to cover his relief that Amelia wasn't a significant other. "Plenty of kids survive divorce."

"I never know what to say to her." Reuben studied the water, restlessly moving his pole in a way that wasn't going to get him another fish. "She's fourteen now, and it's gotten worse, not better. She'll be off to boarding high school in the fall, and… Heck. You don't need to hear all this."

"Sure I do." Toby was used to clients unloading on him. Something about the time away from their ordinary lives and the close quarters made them forget that Toby wasn't a longtime friend or therapist. He'd learned more than a few secrets over the years, and honestly, he didn't mind people telling him stuff. Kept things interesting, and he enjoyed hearing people's stories. He didn't usually volunteer anything in return, but something about Reuben's earnest worrying loosened his own lips. "I've got younger sisters. Teens are hard. Don't beat yourself up so much."

"Yeah. I know. Everyone says teens are difficult, and I get that. But she's pretty much all the family I have left, and it bugs me that we're not close anymore."

"Ah. You didn't remarry?" Yeah, Toby was fishing even without being already hip deep in water, holding a pole.

"Over the winter I was seeing a nice guy who's in-house counsel at an energy firm, but he didn't stick around very long."

"Oh, you're bi?" Given the couple of looks that had passed between them, Toby wasn't all that surprised. And he really, really shouldn't have been pleased, like the knowledge could benefit him personally. Despite his thing for casual hookups, he wasn't one to fish off the company pier, so to speak—he might flirt, but he did try to maintain a certain level of professionalism. But he had to work to suppress a grin, because damn if Reuben didn't challenge all those ethics.

"When I was younger, I thought I was probably gay but never came out, and dated women here and there. I met Natalie, and we were such good friends at first, and we had some happy years together. Then after we broke up, I started dating men openly for the first time. There I go, rambling again. Sorry. Anyway, I suppose *bisexual* is the most accurate label for me even if most of my attraction has been toward men."

"Fuck labels, man. Accurate and otherwise. People aren't supposed to fit in boxes. I sure don't. But I'm the opposite of you, though." Oops. Toby had forgotten himself again, shared more than he'd meant to.

Reuben's eyebrows went up, curiosity clear in his eyes. And there was something else there, a sly little smile that made heat unfurl in Toby's stomach. "Oh?"

"I've mainly dated women but had the occasional hookup with guys or nonbinary people as well." He'd already revealed so much, he might as well keep going. "If people ask, I usually say bi, but really, labels suck."

He didn't add that the question didn't come up all that often. His family knew, and close friends. Generally if he was interested in someone, he went for it, but given how informal most of his hookups were, his sexual identity wasn't something he needed to give a lot of deep thought to.

"Is it hard being open out here?"

"Not sure." Now it was Toby's turn to look away. Damn it. This was why he usually kept his personal life to himself. This level of self-reflection wasn't something he did very often. And he wasn't entirely sure he liked how easy it was to open up and share with Reuben. "I can't speak to others' experiences. For me, I'm just not a good liar, never have been. If people have issue with the fact that I hook up with all genders, they can go fuck themselves."

"Amen to that."

"I mean, sure, I've had my share of ignorant comments over the years, and my family's something of a mixed bag as far as acceptance goes, but I've seen how

staying closeted eats at people. I made the decision to
not apologize for who I am or who I fuck, and that's
worked out for me so far."

"I respect that." Reuben nodded. "I wish I'd been that
kind of brave at your age—"

"Stop making yourself sound ancient. I get it, you're
older than me, but you are undoubtedly aware that you've
got the whole silver bear thing going on." Clearly the
icy water had seeped inside his waders, frozen his brain
cells because he'd just said *silver bear* aloud.

"I've got what?" Reuben turned toward him, which
made the water ripple around them. Fuck. Toby really
was going to have to explain this.

"You know. A lot of guys your age get called silver
fox. But you're kinda taller and broader than a fox…"
Could he really dig himself any deeper? "But…uh…
still hot. You know?"

"I see." Reuben's voice had the sort of gravitas that
made Toby's insides tremble. "If I had time for hookup
apps—which I do not—I should put that on my profile.
Silver Bear. Like a fox, but bigger and hotter. Think it
would get me clicks?"

"Dunno. Put a clip of you pronouncing wine names
and it might." Toby's tongue appeared to have a mind
of its own right then.

"That's hot, huh? Syrah, Malbec, Aligote, Vranec,
Aidani…" Reuben's tone wasn't especially flirty, but it
also wasn't all business either. They'd definitely wandered into new territory, away from the more abstract
discussion of sexual identity to something more personal. And dangerous, but hell if Toby could resist keeping this going. The whole way-too-personal conversation
felt way better than it should have.

"Showoff. And seriously? You've never used a hookup app?"

"I've got better uses for my time than deciding whether to swipe right. Besides, I'm something of a serial monogamist. I like relationships. I'm lousy at them, but one-night stands have never appealed much to me."

"Really? Again, I'm the opposite. Relationships don't do it for me." Better he get that out front right now. If he was going to be honest about his life, he might as well own up to that part too. And it wasn't like Reuben was asking him to start something or even would *want* to start something, and Toby absolutely should know better than to go there too. Nevertheless, he felt he owed it to them both to be clear about who he wasn't.

"That's too bad. Bet you change your mind someday." Reuben's smile was warm and his tone friendly, flip almost, but something about it grated on Toby.

"Bet I don't." Then, because snapping at a client was always a bad idea, he added in a light voice, "You ready for a snack? There's another spot I want you to try afterward that I think you'll really like."

Better they get back to dry land and safer conversation topics for a while before Toby had the urge to share more. He'd had plenty of clients he liked, on multiple levels, so he wasn't sure what it was about Reuben that totally got under his skin. But he absolutely did, and that could hardly be a good thing.

Chapter Four

Trying to remember his resolve to enjoy himself more, Reuben eyed the plane while Toby got them ready to load for an afternoon flight to Brooks Falls—a location within Katmai National Park apparently renown for bear watching. As it was only a twenty-minute flight, he had no reason for the return of yesterday's nerves.

"If you liked the fishing, you'll love this," Toby assured him as he opened the hatch. "It's not unusual for us to see a dozen bears or more, especially in July. With it being June, there may not be as many, but I bet we'll see a few. And it's an easy one mile walk to the viewing platform. Buckle up."

"I didn't hate the fishing," Reuben agreed as he climbed into the plane. Far from it actually. A few holiday seasons ago, Craig and Leticia had gifted him a massage at a locally renowned spa. Reuben had felt honor bound to use the certificate, and the experience had been pleasant. However, this morning, out in the sunshine, frigid water lapping at their waders, catching and releasing trout, he'd been far more relaxed and at peace than even that skilled massage therapist had managed.

And he really had missed Amelia, in a way he hadn't in a very long time, missing the little kid who'd been so happy to do things with him, with her exploring, inquisitive side unmarred by whatever sullen transformation the past few years had wrought. That kid, the one he remembered, would have been bouncing up and down in her seat waiting for takeoff to see the bears and would have loved trying fishing, would have laughed at his failures and cheered his successes. He hadn't been lying—he wasn't the picture-taking type, but he'd found himself wanting to share the experience in a way that startled him.

Even if he couldn't show Amelia, sharing the day with Toby was hardly terrible. He was good company, getting Reuben to open up about his parenting worries in a way that not even Natalie or Leticia could get out of him. Toby was equally adept at comfortable silences as he was sharing stories of other fishing trips and tours, keeping Reuben more than entertained. And okay, Reuben would be lying if he didn't admit that the subtle flirting and knowing that Toby was bi wasn't hurting anything as far as his enjoyment was concerned.

Not that he was going to *do* anything with that attraction, but simply the low thrum of attraction beneath the surface was invigorating—like a workout for his rusty flirting skills.

"Here we go." Toby's voice crackled over the headset as they skated across the small lake, airborne in what felt like seconds, impressive vista beneath them, and he'd barely had time to take in the lava fields along with the many small lakes dotting the terrain before they were landing again.

Brooks Falls was apparently a popular tourist spot with planes from other touring companies already docked and plenty of tourists along the short hike. They stopped twice to greet rangers and fellow tour guides who Toby knew, and Reuben was a little impressed at how well respected Toby seemed to be by his peers. He'd already known Toby to be charming, but seeing how others responded to him made Reuben value his expertise a little more.

As they walked, Toby told him about the archaeology of the area and the nine-thousand-year-old artifacts that had been found nearby. His reverence for the spot further impressed Reuben. He envied that deep connection to the land and its history. And he enjoyed listening to Toby talk on a level that surprised him even more than the spark of attraction had—he genuinely enjoyed being around Toby in a way he hadn't had in a long time, even with his friends.

The falls were a wide swath of rushing water spanning the width of the river. With the trail ending at the wooden viewing platforms, tourists were prevented from going down to the riverbank. At first, Reuben didn't notice anything other than the pristine beauty of the surroundings.

"Look to your left, about ten o'clock. In the foliage." Toby advised.

"Is that…a *bear*?" A fuzzy round shape was barely visible through the dense vegetation. The bearlike shape was larger than Reuben had expected, even from this distance away.

"Yup. Now if we wait, it may come out, and it might even have friends or babies with it."

Yesterday, Reuben would have been tapping his foot, ready to move on, but something had shifted inside him in the past twenty-four hours. Waiting was no hardship now, not with so many details to take in—logs rushing over the falls, more intriguing shadows that could be wildlife on the banks, gorgeous contrast between the deep blue river and the baby blue sky.

I've missed this. He didn't realize that he'd actually voiced the thought until Toby smiled at him and nodded.

"Funny how so many people get too busy for nature and almost forget it's out there." Toby's tone was understanding.

"Yes." Memories came rushing back to Reuben— camp as a kid, summers on the Jersey shore in college, brief trips and vacations since then, but somehow along the way, he'd lost touch with the kid he'd been when he first stepped off the bus at camp, in awe of the endless expanse of trees and all the different smells and sounds. And maybe that was what he meant—not that he missed this, a place he'd never been before, but that he missed that younger version of himself, missed the joy he'd once taken in the outdoors.

As he contemplated this, the shadow from the banks lumbered out of the trees, a large, brown bear, and sure enough, Toby had been right that it was accompanied by another, slightly smaller bear. They made their way into the water.

"They're so big. And it's amazing how they stand the water." The small amount that had seeped into Reuben's waders and splashed on his skin had been icy. No way could he swim in that.

"They're used to it. And see how they play?" Toby pointed to how the larger of the two was poised on the top of the falls now, directly in the path of the rushing water, balance sure and steady. "They're looking for dinner, but they have fun too."

Reuben could sense that—the creatures carried a

strong air of contentment with them. Not that he wanted to get any closer though and test how friendly they actually were. "Are we dinner?"

Toby's laugh at his weak joke hit Reuben square in the chest—he had a great laugh, rich and deep, and his eyes crinkled with good humor. "Not tonight. The rangers keep this place patrolled and safe. In general, if you stay away from the bear, it stays away from you, but there are things you can do to protect yourself too."

"Like what?" Reuben was surprised at how much he cared about the response. He was no longer simply being polite, and continued to ask follow-up questions about bear safety as they made their way back to the plane. Toby shared several stories of close encounters various tour groups had had over the years, and by the time they were back at the plane, Reuben had forgotten to be nervous about the short flight back to the lodge.

And once they landed, instead of being eager to try for a cell signal, he found himself reluctant to part from Toby.

"Do we have time before dinner?" he asked.

"A little. Maybe not enough for a nap, but plenty of time for a shower or to check out that sauna or the hot tub on the main lodge's deck."

"Maybe the hot tub," he allowed. "How about you? Do you ever use the amenities here?"

"I have on occasion," Toby said slowly.

"Care to join me?" Reuben realized too late how forward that sounded, his voice lower than he'd intended.

"I shouldn't." Toby's laugh had an uncomfortable edge to it.

Reuben had run into the boundary between them— this wasn't the start of a friendship, no matter how pleasant it felt. Toby was paid to be this nice to everyone, and he really didn't need a come-on from an old goat like Reuben.

"I'm sorry," he said quickly. "Didn't mean to imply…"

"Nah, it's okay." Toby waved Reuben's concern away. "I've got to call Fishhook, confirm our plans for tomorrow. But it's not…not that I'm not tempted, you know?"

"I get it. Guess I'll head to my cabin."

"Sounds good." Toby gave Reuben a searching look, one that felt like he could see deep inside him, and something passed between them, a brief sizzle of heat, an unspoken acknowledgment of mutual attraction that made warmth surge to Reuben's face. But regret was there in Toby's eyes too.

And Reuben got it—the guy had ethics, but that didn't mean Reuben wasn't a little disappointed as he made his way back to his cabin alone. He had to laugh at himself. Wouldn't Craig find this hilarious? He'd told Reuben to enjoy himself, but even he probably hadn't meant pining for the tour guide like a kid with a crush on a camp counselor.

But you're both consenting adults… Reuben could almost hear Craig's reply. And yes, yes they were. Ethics were great and something Reuben could respect, but he still felt the warmth of that look. Something was there, brewing between them, and whatever it was, it made the rest of the trip suddenly a lot more intriguing.

Toby had almost said yes, almost joined Reuben in the hot tub, and even now, the morning after, he still wasn't sure he'd made the right choice. He hadn't wanted to make things any more awkward between them, and as good as it felt to flirt with Reuben, he was reluctant to cross that line. Reuben was a lawyer, someone with a clear code of conduct, and Toby wanted to…well, *impress* made him sound desperate, which he wasn't, but he supposed he did care about Reuben's opinion of him, didn't want Reuben assuming that he hooked up with clients on the regular.

But now, wader deep in the river, watching Reuben fish like a seasoned pro instead day two of lessons, he was regretting his choice because Reuben discovering he was competent at something was almost addictively attractive. Reuben's seemingly innate confidence and take-charge attitude had been tempered by all the uncertainty of being in an unfamiliar place, which Toby had found more than a little endearing. But now that he had his bearings somewhat, Reuben had transformed from cute to devastating.

"I think I see why people like this so much." Reuben offered him a grin with no trace of hard feelings over the previous night. If he'd been disappointed, he'd done a good job of hiding it, being professional and friendly both at dinner and again this morning. In fact, they'd spent a long time talking after dinner, Reuben asking more questions about bears and other wildlife and charming more stories out of him. There was something just so *easy* about hanging around Reuben, something that made Toby want to keep sharing, long past when he'd usually put the brakes on, keep things fun but impersonal, more distant.

"You want me to push back departure time? We're not on commercial flight schedules here, so I can just let the lunch stop know that we're taking our time. We'll have plenty of daylight, so we can go at our pace. And it's your birthday—you really should do what you want."

Toby had already messaged the Fishhook lodge to confirm a cake had been arranged. Mr. I-Don't-Celebrate
could deal. Toby wanted cake, and birthdays were meant
to be enjoyed. He'd make sure Reuben had a good day
even if he had to push a little. "There's some wind, but
I'm expecting the weather to hold either way."

"Hmm." Reuben's thoughtful noise made blood rush
to Toby's groin. Fuck. He might've had resolve last night,
but he wasn't sure he could count on willpower for the
rest of Reuben's stay. "Maybe another few catches? I
don't mind a later lunch."

"We're going to make a fisherman out of you yet."
Toby clapped him on the shoulder after loading a fresh
fly on the line. "Watch it because before you know it,
you'll be back next year, frying up your catch, asking
me for all the good spots…"

"Dream big." Reuben shook his head like Toby was
too much, which he probably was, teasing the guy like
this. As if he'd ever want to make a return trip. This guy
had one-week wonder written all over him, and he'd be
back in what was undoubtedly a corner office this time
next week. But he'd been better at breakfast—talking
with the other guests and not looking at his phone, so
maybe, if nothing else, Toby was providing him with
a much-needed break. And to that end, Toby kept him
out on the river long enough to see some bears fishing
downstream and to get a few more successful catches.

The wind had picked up further, but all the weather
reports had rain holding off until later in the day, and
Toby had flown in plenty of worse wind conditions.

"Might be a little bumpy," he warned Reuben as he
did his final check before takeoff. "We'll be passing
Lake Clark then the Nancy Lakes area, and over the

Hatcher pass before landing at a lodge near Fishhook. If the weather holds, we'll explore the Matanuska and Knik River areas via air after a late lunch."

"And if it doesn't?" Reuben frowned. Toby already had his number as someone who didn't wait well, and the promise of board games at the main lodge wasn't going to do much for Mr. All-Business.

"Pretty sure the lodge has cell reception and Wi-Fi for the cabins with a code. These cabins are newer and pretty luxurious—our clients all love them."

"Oh good. If it rains, I'll just check in with the office."

"Let's hope it doesn't." Toby gave him what he hoped was a stern look and not too flirty. "Surely the office can live without you for another day."

Reuben muttered something under his breath that Toby didn't quite catch, then gestured at the hatch. "We leaving?"

"Yup." Toby shut the plane doors, then performed the last of his safety checks before takeoff. He gave his standard spiel about the lakes they passed, but the wind was requiring more concentration than usual, so he found himself saying less as the skies darkened.

"Is it going to rain?" A rare question from Reuben came over the headset.

"Think so. We're not too far from Fishhook now though, so don't worry even if you start seeing some drops. I've flown in rain a bunch." He hated it, but weather was simply a fact of life for a small plane pilot. He tried not to end up in conditions where visual sight rules became difficult or impossible. As the weather shifted, all his senses became hyper-focused on the rapidly changing conditions. Visibility was his primary concern, but the wind was no joke either. The need to press on for the lodge had to be balanced against doing an unscheduled landing, waiting out the storm.

Company rules stated that they didn't fly when winds were over thirty-five miles an hour, and while conditions had been decent when they took off, the wind now bounced them around, turbulence worse than he'd experienced in a long time. The storm closed in, and he had to pick his way forward, visibility severely compromised. Around them, the sky started crackling with lightning.

Time for plan B. His avionics included alert systems to help his situational awareness, but there was no substitute for intuition, and even without the avionics' help, he made the call to look for the nearest landing spot. He'd flown in all sorts of weather conditions over the years, but lightning was nothing to mess around with.

Rivers and lakes were never in short supply in this region except for right now when he desperately needed one. Hell, he'd take mudflats at this point, but beneath them, the terrain was craggy and uneven. They were too far out for turning back to be an easy option either. His attention was also on his engine—impeccably maintained but not infallible, especially in quick-changing weather.

He didn't like the noises the plane was making one bit. Checking every gauge on his instrument panel, he started going back through his preflight checklist—he'd been focused as always. Had he missed something? Right as he looked again, every gauge went wonky—nothing pegging, not even pressure or oil. Was the lightning causing equipment malfunction? *Fuck.*

"I'm looking to set us down, wait out the worst of this," he told Reuben over the headset. "Landing's likely to be fast and rough, so brace yourself, but no need to panic."

Yet. He left that part unsaid as he flipped off the channel with Reuben, visibility decreasing further, every bit of sense he had saying that he needed to set them down *now.* Didn't matter how close they were to Fishhook, they weren't going to make it unless he took decisive action, listened to both his instruments and his intuition. He made sure his emergency transmitter was on, went ahead and issued a mayday distress call. Plenty of pilots he knew would try and press on, but the conditions were fast deteriorating and he wasn't taking any chances.

There. Finally, he spotted something of a valley, a hint of water. In the distance, there might have been a sliver of road, but his visibility was too compromised to tell for sure. The valley was his best shot, so he dipped low, preparing to line up. Another gust tossed them around, disorienting him temporarily.

"Fuck. Fuck. Fuck." His curses filled the cockpit as the plane dropped precipitously.

True fear hit him, stomach bottoming out right along with the plane. This wasn't just wind tossing them around. Wind he'd dealt with hundreds of times. Whatever it was, lightning or equipment failure, things were going from not good to worst-case as he struggled to control the descent. He'd done all he could, and the only thing left was to try to control the landing. But it might not be enough, not if they were losing engine power.

We're going to crash.

He tried to deny that thought as his mind raced, trying to find the best way to land that would sustain the least damage. But there was no arguing with the reality that he was losing control of the plane. He could only hope his efforts would save them, but was not at all certain of that outcome.

Chapter Five

"Brace for impact." Toby's voice, usually so light and charming but filled with serious intent now, crackled over the headset.

Chills raced through Reuben's body. He'd known something was wrong when the usually chatty Toby had gone silent for a long stretch. This was exactly Reuben's worst fear about flying in a small plane—being at the mercy of the weather. The lightning had almost made him need the airsickness bag.

And he wasn't someone who felt fear easily—no nerves walking into big meetings or signing important deals. Hell, he'd never even had test anxiety in college and law school. He regularly drove on snow in the winter, and he was known for being good in an emergency. But this sort of life-or-death terror was new, almost paralyzing in its intensity.

Come on, think. Think. Years of halfheartedly listening to preflight safety checklists came filtering back, and Reuben tried to remember what *brace* meant. Lean forward. Feet on the floor. Arms tucked in. Hell. He hoped he was doing this right. The plane lurched again, but he didn't dare lift his head to look out the window.

Dear God, please let me live.

When had he prayed last? When his father passed away years ago? When Amelia was born? *Amelia*. He couldn't die, not yet, not when he still hadn't figured out how to talk to her, not when he'd failed so spectacularly at parenting, not when he hadn't seen yet who she'd become. He couldn't go out this way. He saw everything in stark clarity in that instant.

God, I'll do whatever it takes to be a better father. Better man. Just let us live.

Bump. His prayers came to an abrupt halt as the plane went from bouncing in the wind to connecting with something real and solid. Not water.

Boom. Rattle. Thud.

The next few seconds both dragged on like an eternity and went by in a jumbled blink, plane getting tossed around, him jolting from side to side like a pinball, seatbelt digging into his thighs. The awful sound of rending metal filled the air, but he also caught a few muffled curses that weren't his own.

Then silence. Nothing but silence, eerie and awful as the world went gray, then black.

"Reuben? Reuben?" A strong hand shook his shoulder. It took him more than few moments to realize that he was still in his seat. And alive. His arm and leg muscles burned, and he figured that dead would feel more floaty, less urgent. He took one shaky breath after another, heart racing like it never had before. Yes, he was definitely alive.

"Toby?"

"We've got to get out of here." Toby loomed over him, tugging at his seatbelt, pulling at his shoulders. "Smoke. Fire. Come on."

"Smoke?" Even as he said the word, the air was caustic with the scent of fuel and rent metal—a dry, bitter odor that carried with it a sense of doom. Fire. There could be fire. He shook his head, trying again to make sense of the impossible. The smoke hampered his ability to see Toby clearly.

"Front hatch is too damaged. Gotta climb out through the rear. I need to get the emergency kit before it blows." Toby yanked on him again, and this time, Reuben got his body to cooperate.

Get out. Get out now.

Not the most limber on the best of days, he pushed the seatbelt Toby had already unbuckled away with trembling hands and struggled to turn himself so that he could follow Toby's orders. Finally extricating himself, he tried to navigate the awkward drop to the ground. Felt too good to have dirt under his feet again, relief coursing through him almost disorienting in its intensity. He stumbled clear of the plane. Toby was busy throwing items from the plane—their luggage, a nylon pack with a red cross on it, sleeping bags.

"What can I—" He never got to finish the question as the wing of the plane, already at an awkward angle, gave a sickening screech, breaking free and crashing into Toby, knocking him off the plane, and trapping him under it. Toby didn't have chance to react—neither of them did, no chance even to scream a warning before it was over, Toby on the ground, wing and debris over him.

"Toby? You okay?" Reuben rushed over, forcing his voice out past his panic. Silence greeted him, but he had to know. *Please don't be dead.* Another useless prayer sent up. *Please don't let me be alone here.* Hell, he could almost hear God laughing at such a selfish request. But he meant it, didn't want to be alone. And he *liked* the guide, liked his easy smiles and charm and ability to banter without taking shit from anyone, liked the growing sense of closeness they'd shared, even beyond the flirtatious moments and heated looks, and he refused to contemplate a world where all that vitality had been snuffed out.

Toby's upper half was free of the debris, but he had a nasty bump on his temple that was already turning purple.

Fuck. "Toby?" Reuben reached out, shook his shoulder gently.

"Unnngh." Toby gave a mighty groan, then blinked twice. "Fuck. Hurts."

"I know. You took a nasty blow."

"Reuben." Toby blinked again, as if he was trying to place where he was and who he was with. Not a great sign. Reuben's stomach, already uneasy, lurched. They needed a medic. An ambulance. Something.

"We crashed. You saved me. Saved both our lives. But now, we've got to get you clear of the plane before there's a fire."

"No." Toby groaned again, this sound decidedly pained. "You go."

"Nothing doing." Somehow Reuben summoned the voice that got shit done at the office. "We've got to get you free."

"Hurts."

"I know." He touched Toby's hair with what he hoped was a gentle hand. "Can you feel your fingers and toes?"

Hell. Reuben might not know much medical jargon, but he did know not to try to move a suspected spinal injury. Not that he might have much choice if there was fire.

"Head. Aches. Wiggle...yeah. Fingers. Toes. Moving." Toby sounded like each word was a struggle.

"Good. What hurts?" God, he hated this helpless feeling, not knowing how to make this right, what the right course of action was. But he did know he couldn't leave Toby.

"Leg. Trapped. Pretty sure it's broken." Toby's grimace made Reuben hurt on a deep, primal level, wanting to take his pain. He'd been injured trying to save Reuben, *had* saved Reuben. Hell, he'd most likely still be passed out in there if it wasn't for Toby.

"Anything else?"

"Shoulder. Right arm. All fucked up. Get...yourself... clear."

"I'm not leaving you." Using both hands and all his strength, he heaved the wing debris off Toby, enough to pull him free, then knelt, trying to pull Toby into a fireman's carry.

"I'm too heavy. Not gonna work." Toby's eyes flickered shut briefly then opened again. "Take emergency supplies. Emergency beacon. Help should come."

"I'm no lightweight." Reuben made his voice stern. Truth be told, he had no clue what he was doing, but he wasn't letting Toby know that. "And yes, it's probably going to hurt. Sorry. But I'm going to move you. You come first."

"Okay." Toby took a deep breath, like he was trying to find energy or gumption or maybe a little of both. "Let's do this."

The scent of fuel was stronger now. Precious seconds ticked by while he tried to figure out the best way to lift Toby, ending up dragging Toby onto his shoulder, wincing himself from Toby's pained yell.

Damn. Toby was heavy, but Reuben hadn't come this far to give up now. He staggered away from the plane, making it up a little hill until he decided they were clear of immediate fire danger. Setting Toby down under a tree, he tried to be gentle, but still got groans from Toby. From the hill, he could see a small lake some distance beyond the plane.

"Now I'll get the emergency supplies." He tried to project confidence.

"Don't take stupid risks." Toby sounded a little more with it now, voice not quite as thready, but each word still sounded like it cost him.

"Got it." The rain, which had tapered to a mist, was possibly the only thing keeping the plane from becoming a fireball, so he tried to work fast, gathering the supplies Toby had already tossed clear. He brought as much as he could carry to the tree.

Hiss. The plane made a weird rumbling noise, smoke rising into the cool air. Shit. They'd gotten out just in time.

"Run," Toby yelled, and Reuben did just that, dragging the luggage to their spot right as flames engulfed the plane. The rain sizzled as it hit the fire, a nasty chemical smell filling the air.

"Fuck." Sweet hell. His hands shook and his stomach threatened to upend itself. If Toby hadn't shaken him awake, if Toby had been injured sooner or worse, then Reuben would still be in the wreckage, burning alive right now. They'd barely made it to safety, and he owed most of that to Toby's quick thinking.

Utterly spent, he collapsed next to Toby and watched the fire and rain duel it out in the steaming pile of wreckage.

"If we're lucky, rain will keep it from spreading." Toby's eyes were squished shut, and Reuben wasn't sure whether it was pain or not wanting to see his plane burn.

"Maybe it will work like a smoke signal." That was a thing, right? If his limited knowledge was correct, rescuers could find them easier with a fire.

"Ha." Toby started to laugh, then gave a pained cough. "Oof. Bad idea. Yeah, could help."

"You said something about a beacon?" Reuben desperately needed to cling to hope of rescue.

"Yeah. Emergency transponder. I hit it. Should help them find us. Second one used for hiking in the emergency kit."

"I'm on it." Reuben dug through the stuff, finally finding a bright orange device on a carabineer clip with an SOS button. "Will this let us talk to someone?"

"Nah. Not that fancy." Toby sounded sleepy, which gave Reuben pause.

"How's your head? Dizzy?"

"Yeah. Feels like a hangover." Wincing, Toby glanced away.

"Stay with me. Keep talking. No sleeping." That right there was pretty much the extent of Reuben's knowledge of concussions.

"Trying. Hit the button on the device."

"That's it?" Reuben did as instructed, and a light started blinking near the SOS button.

"Yeah. Should be." Toby had to pause to groan, a low noise that made Reuben wish for a pain drip even more than for the emergency beacon to work. "Never had to use one before. No way to know if it'll work, especially on this terrain, but worth a shot."

"Anything is." He had to believe help was on the

way. Both because he didn't want to spend a night in the mountains and because Toby needed medical attention far beyond what Reuben could provide. "Now what about your injuries? What can we do?"

"You're injured too." Toby tapped his temple, and Reuben did the same, fingers coming up bloody. Hell. And his shoulder ached, both from carrying Toby and from the rough landing that had slammed him against the plane's interior, but he didn't think anything was seriously broken. He might be a little banged up, but it was nothing compared to what Toby was going through.

"I'm fine. Should we splint your leg? Would that help?" Fuck. Why hadn't he gone to medical school like his parents had suggested? Not that they'd been too put out at law school, but he'd give an awful lot for some medical knowledge right then.

"Maybe. Gonna hurt like a fucker though, moving it at all. Keep accidentally moving arm and…fuck. Did it again."

"Okay. Two splints then."

"Knee…hurts too. Messed it up."

"All right, we'll do a long splint for the leg." Almost pleased to have a purpose, Reuben set to work finding four sticks that could work. At Toby's direction, he used Toby's pocketknife to trim the side branches off, and then sliced up one of his own shirts into sloppy strips to secure the splints.

"Oh, *fuck. Owwww.*" Toby let out a keening moan as Reuben straightened his leg for the splint. God, he hated hurting Toby like this, even if it ultimately would help. Trying to think like a doctor, he used multiple points to secure each splint, not wanting to cut off circulation, but wanting to immobilize the injuries enough for the splints to help with the pain. By the time he finished, Toby's eyes were squished shut, and Reuben couldn't tell whether it was sweat or rain that coated his face. The tree was sheltering them somewhat, but they were both rather damp, and Reuben's shirt clung to his back. Cold and wet seemed like a bad combo, especially if they had a wait for rescue.

Shelter. They needed some sort of shelter. His memory flashed back a million years ago to his summer camp days. They'd made a lean-to once. His recollection of the specifics was hazy, but it started with more sticks. Gathering the longest ones he could find, he made a pile next to Toby.

"What are you doing?"

"Need to make something to keep you dry."

"Too late." Toby gave another laugh that ended in a whimper. "Damn. Ribs hurt too."

"If I lash these together and lean them against the tree, it might work. Need something to cover them with."

"Use space blankets. Heavy tape in the emergency kit."

"Good call." After shoving the sticks in the ground and getting a workable angle, he tied the sticks together with more pieces of his shirt, then used tape to secure two space blankets. Finally satisfied with the shelter he'd built around Toby, he straightened. "Now, fire, right? And to get out of the wet clothes."

"Any other situation and I'd think you were eager to get me naked."

"I'm not. Not my intention," he sputtered, too quick with the denial.

"Relax. Just joking with you. Trying to keep awake."

"Well, in that case, joke away." Reuben knelt next to

Toby, studying his eyes and the multiple bruises on his head as if that would give him some clue as to the severity of his injury. "And keep talking. Tell me what to do to make a fire to warm up."

"Gonna be hard with the drizzle. It already reduced the plane fire to smoldering. Let's wait it out a bit, see if it clears."

Reuben didn't like this advice, didn't want to wait, wanted something meaningful to do, and hated that their best option appeared to be dry clothes and huddling under the lean-to until they were rescued. If they were rescued. *God, please let the beacons work.*

He'd prayed more in the past hour than the thirty years prior, but he meant every syllable. He hadn't survived the plane crash only to die out here. He wasn't going to let Toby's efforts to rescue them be in vain. And it was more than merely survival at stake—he wasn't letting Toby down either, was going to make sure he got the rescue he deserved.

Toby was in way too much pain to appreciate watching Reuben struggle out of his wet clothes and into dry ones. Any other circumstances and he'd be appreciating the view of fuzzy chest, but right then, he was way more concerned with the incessant throb in his leg. Changed, Reuben ducked under the lean-to to cut Toby out of his own sodden clothing without disturbing his splint job.

"Watch the knife." He wasn't joking that time. He really didn't fancy one more injury on top of all his others. Judging by the way he'd hacked at the branches, Reuben was a newbie with knives and not much better with the scissors from the first aid kit either. But he clearly meant

well, fussing over Toby's wet shirt and chilled skin like
that was the worst of their worries.

"There are easier ways to get me naked, you know.
Jack and Coke works better." Okay, that one was a joke,
one that made Reuben's pale cheeks pink up.

"I didn't..." Reuben swallowed hard, and Toby felt
a little bad for messing with him under such circumstances. Fuck, their flirting back at Katmai seemed decades ago now, that moment when they could have acted
on the attraction a hazy mirage lost in the hell of the
present moment where it was either tease or give in to
the despair threatening to swamp him.

"Relax. Just having you on because it's easier than
cursing this pain out."

"Curse if you need to. Or joke. Whatever gets you
through this. But you're going to have to live with the
naked thing because I don't think we're going to easily
get new clothes on you." Reuben tucked one sleeping
bag around him, which honestly wasn't that bad of an
idea—the sleeping bags tended to work better at keeping in heat with less clothing on anyway.

"Living is good. And this works."

"Good." Wrapping himself in the other sleeping bag,
Reuben finally settled down. The lean-to was cramped,
their bodies squished together, shoulders rubbing. Reuben had arranged things so that he was next to Toby's
less injured side, which Toby was grateful for. A few
hours ago, he would never have predicted that Reuben
would cope this well stranded in the mountains. Not that
he'd expected hysterics, but Reuben had doggedly attacked each problem as it presented itself, first getting
Toby safe, then addressing the need for shelter and dry
clothes, all while the plane continued to smolder, a chill-

ing reminder of how very close to death they'd come. Through the opening in the lean-to, Toby looked beyond the plane for the first time.

"Fuck. Lake is so close."

"That's what you were aiming for?" There was no censure in Reuben's voice.

"Yeah. But engine stalled. Couldn't control the descent and glide in. And my visibility was nil. I tried though…" He had to stop and catch his breath, the enormity of what had happened catching up to him.

"I know you did." Reuben surprised the hell out of him by wrapping an arm around Toby. "I'm not blaming you. Hell, you undoubtedly saved our lives getting the plane down as well as you did. And then you saved mine again, coming for me, waking me up."

"You might have a concussion, way you were passed out. But thank you." It was a gift, Reuben not being angry. Most lawyers Toby knew would already be planning their litigation. And maybe that would come later, but for right now, he'd take Reuben's kind words.

"I mean it. Don't waste time beating yourself up. I saw the weather come up out of nowhere. You did the best you could and saved my—our—lives."

"Says the guy who pulled me away from a smoking plane." Despite the ringing in his head and ache in his limbs, joking felt far better than giving in to emotions that threatened to overwhelm him.

"I did, didn't I?" Reuben sounded mildly bemused, like his heroics had even surprised himself. "Maybe I just didn't want to be alone out here."

It was a moment of bald honesty, and Toby repaid it by reaching down and squeezing Reuben's thigh with his good hand.

"Me either. And we *are* getting out of this." He tried to put all the conviction he could summon in his voice, trying to convince himself along with Reuben. "If nothing else, the lodge at Fishhook will notice if we fail to arrive tonight. We'll be found."

"Hope so. When the plane was going down, all I could think of was Amelia and all the ways I've failed her."

"What's she like?" Toby asked, needing a distraction from the pain.

"Typical teen, I guess. Moody. Attached to her electronics. Thinks she knows everything. But then again, she was kind of born like that—endless questions and testing of rules."

"I've got a sister like that. Nell. High spirited, my mom called it." Fuck, but Toby did not want to think about his family right then, not when he would have traded anything to be with them again, to reassure them that he was okay.

"Yeah, high spirited. That's it. And when she was younger, she was such a cute kid in many ways. Always exploring, making secret hideouts, dreaming up imaginative games." Reuben paused, swallowing hard. The love he had for his daughter was obvious from the sheen in his eyes before he looked away. "I'm probably not the best dad. We both work a ton of hours, making partner. We always make sure she has good nannies and the best schools, but… I miss a lot. Feels like I blinked and she's gone from four to fourteen."

"That's how it goes." He shifted, which made the pain spike and he had to groan before continuing. But forcing out complete sentences kept him from letting the hurt pull him under. "Feels like just yesterday Nell was trying to goad me into playing Barbies with her, and now she's almost twenty. Still headstrong."

"You sound like a good big brother." Reuben's voice was soothing, something about it hitting a tender place in Toby's chest that he'd forgotten existed.

"I try. I missed a lot, like you. Working. Trying to keep the house and family together."

"You raised Nell?" Reuben sounded curious, but also nervous, like he too was trying to not give in to pain and despair.

"Sort of. Long story."

"We've got nothing but time, and I need to keep you talking." The edge to Reuben's voice increased as wind whipped past them, rain picking up again.

"It's a family thing." Toby sighed, knowing the whole story was about to spill out. But like Reuben said, they might as well talk. It wasn't like there was any point to keeping his fun-loving, freewheeling facade up any longer. He'd already shared more with Reuben than a decade's worth of other clients. He didn't know what it was that made Reuben so easy to talk to. The stuff about Nell had simply spilled out, right along with everything else Toby had shared. *Nell. Dad. Hannah. Fuck.*

He groaned again, both from pain and frustration. "And fuck. That's why we are *not* going to die out here. The beacons will work. My family needs me too much for me to not make it back."

"Tell me about them." Reuben's voice was gentle, not demanding.

"It's just me, my dad, and my two younger sisters now. Mom died of meningitis two years ago. But really, it all started with my dad's accident. When I was twenty, I was in college in Anchorage when I got the call that my dad had been severely injured in a snow-machine accident. I dropped out to help the family while he recovered. He ended up with partial paralysis and lasting health problems. He tries to do as much as he can for himself, but he still relied heavily on my mom, and now she's gone."

"I'm sorry. That's awful. Both of my parents are gone now too, but they were far older."

"Thanks. Anyway, I promised her I'd take care of Dad and see my sisters get through college. And I try, but…"

"It's hard, that kind of responsibility." Tone understanding, Reuben touched Toby's good arm. "I get it. And we'll get you back to them, promise."

"Not gonna be much use to them in any event." Toby gestured at his injuries. He didn't even remember the wing coming loose—one second he'd been hyped on adrenaline, trying to save Reuben, and the next he'd been flat on his back, pinned to the ground. Beyond the immediacy of needing rescue lay a deeper worry about what would come next. And fuck, the prospect was almost more than he could bear, and his breath hissed out.

"Easy." Reuben patted Toby's hand. "You'll heal. And they'll be happy simply to have you back, I'm sure." Voice going thoughtful, Reuben licked his lips. "I hope Amelia feels the same way. When we were out on the river yesterday and today, I wished I could share the experience with her."

"Told you. We're going to make a fisherman out of you yet." His voice trailed off to a mumble as keeping his eyes open suddenly became a challenge.

"Hey." Reuben nudged his shoulder. "You getting sleepy?"

"Yeah." Toby couldn't hold back the yawn.

"You can't sleep, remember?"

"Wake me. Every twenty to thirty minutes." Another big yawn escaped. "Can't stay awake. Sorry."

"Don't be sorry." Reuben pulled him closer, giving Toby his broad shoulder as a pillow, natural as if they'd done this a thousand times before. "I'll wake you. And I'll try not to be so boring after your nap."

"Not boring." Toby's words slurred, and he wasn't sure how to tell Reuben that far from being bored, he liked talking to him more than he had anyone in years. Telling him about his family situation had felt strangely right and instead of awkward, he felt warm. Seen. Understood. Like Reuben got him, got what was important to him, and didn't try to pity him or jolly him up with platitudes. And as Toby drifted off, he pulled that warmth around himself, used it to reassure himself that they would get through this. Rescue was coming. It had to.

Chapter Six

The quiet brought with it a chilling wind, seeming to drop the temperature another ten degrees when Toby drifted off, leaving Reuben alone with his worries and thoughts and the rain falling on the back of their lean-to. He liked holding Toby though he wished it was under different circumstances. It had been a while since someone had fallen asleep on him, and he'd forgotten how good it could feel, being trusted like that, feeling all warm and protective watching the other person sleep. However, he wasn't anywhere close to sleep himself. Too much post-crash adrenaline, too much worry about Toby's possible concussion and other injuries, too much fear of what it might mean to survive the crash but not get found in time.

Behind the adrenaline was also an unexpected feeling of satisfaction. He'd worked hard, getting Toby to safety, getting their supplies, building the shelter, and he'd felt truly useful for the first time in ages. Reminded him of when he'd been at an earlier stage in his career—drafting his own contracts and briefs, staying up all night working out the details of deals, getting in there, making stuff happen. The past few years had been endless meetings, other younger, hungrier subordinates doing the bulk of the hands-on work. He missed that work.

The burn in his muscles from carrying Toby and building the shelter also took him back decades ago to the college summer he'd worked for a friend's father, helping remodel a beach house on the Jersey shore. At the time, he'd been primarily concerned with networking, hoping to get into the same Ivy League law school as the homeowner, but there'd been something deeply satisfying about the work, digging up the backyard, laying tile, painting, and such.

It had been such an idyllic summer in so many ways—working all day until he was sweaty and sore, then hanging out with other young people on the beach late into the night, the last summer he'd been truly free. *I want that again.* Not that he wanted to fuck around or to work construction, but that feeling, both being useful and free at the same time, was something he hadn't even realized he missed. But now that he thought about it, he missed that wide-open sensation, the future stretching endlessly in front of him, all possibilities open. He'd had that at camp too—arriving as the city-bound scholarship kid whose most intimate experience with nature was a nearby city park that was more concrete than grass, eyes wide, everything a new experience.

When they'd been on the river fishing, little prickles of awareness had raced through his body. Some of it was Toby's nearness, the spark of attraction that kept persisting there, but some of it had simply been the setting, long-lost pleasures of being outdoors returning to him with each activity they tried. Of course, he'd give an awful lot to be indoors right then at a hospital preferably, Toby getting the treatment he needed.

Every so often Toby would stir, pain obvious in every movement and soft moan. Reuben wanted to take that from him, wanted a way to shoulder his burdens, be useful beyond merely being a human pillow. Eventually he decided enough time had passed—his battered cell phone had no signal, but the clock still worked—and he gently shook Toby.

"Toby? Can you wake up?"

"Uh-huh." Toby blinked, a sleepy, vulnerable expression on his face that made Reuben's heart contract. "Hurts."

"I've got headache-strength painkillers somewhere in my luggage, but I don't think we should give you anything until you see a doctor."

"Doubt they'd do much good anyway." Wincing, Toby straightened, and Reuben felt the loss of his warmth and closeness, even though he was only inches away now. "Stomach hurts too. Meds might make me puke. But you hungry? There are protein bars in my bag."

"I'm not eating if you can't." Worry chased away any hunger in Reuben's gut, filling him with a cold dread. God, he hoped Toby didn't have any internal injuries in addition to everything else.

"You need to keep your strength up. We could be in for a long haul—sun will set around eleven, which will help searchers have more daylight today, but it could easily be morning or beyond before they make it to us. Rain will play a role for them too." Toby ended this pronouncement with a low groan. God, they needed medical help and soon. Toby's condition couldn't wait for days.

"Fucking rain." Outside their little shelter, a steady drizzle kept up, skies still gray. Not the sudden downpour of earlier, but enough to make thoughts of a fire futile and probably enough to mess with rescue efforts. If anyone was even looking for them yet, but Reuben had to have faith they were.

"You're hot when you curse." Toby gave him a bemused, still-sleepy smile.

"And you're delirious." Reuben felt his forehead, not surprised to find it warmer than his own.

"Hey, I speak truth. Maybe you need to rethink your stance on hookups. Remind you that you're still hot as fuck, not all ancient. Shake things up."

"I'm pretty sure falling from the sky counts as a big enough shakeup for this year," Reuben replied, keeping his voice dry, not giving in to the urge to laugh at Toby's undoubtedly feverish suggestions. "And something tells me that you tell that to a lot of your tourists…"

"Calling me a manwhore?" Toby's laugh was closer to a cough, but still a welcome sound. "Tourists, sure, but not as many of my own clients as people probably think. I do have *some* ethics."

"I know you do." Any sting Reuben had felt at Toby's subtle rejection the day before had faded. And whatever misconceptions he'd had about Toby at the start, those too had been replaced by the reality of the guy he'd gotten to know. Who really did seem to be an upstanding guy—well respected, devoted to his family, and with a strong backbone. Maybe even stronger than Reuben's own, truth be told. "I married a colleague, so I'm not really one to judge. And *fuck*."

"What?"

"She's still my in-case-of-emergency on a lot of forms. Which means her and Amelia finding out about this, maybe even today. I hate the idea of Amelia all scared and worried while Natalie's trying to figure out the business implications."

"Hell. Right with you there. Nell is with my dad right now, and I don't like worrying either of them. Or my boss, Annie. Doubt she'll fire me over this, but the loss of the plane is going to suck for the business."

"Surely they have insurance."

"Fucking insurance," Toby scoffed. His voice was stronger again after his nap, but he still winced with every shift of his body. "They'll find any excuse to not pay. Health insurance gave us hell after Dad's injuries, claiming he'd been involved in dangerous, exempt activities by using the snow machine like every other Alaskan does every single damn winter. Thought about trying to sue the manufacturer, but the lawyer we consulted said there wasn't a case and wanted big bucks for the consultation. That on top of all the lawyer wrangling with the health insurance. No offense, but your profession sucks sometimes."

"You're not wrong there." Reuben sighed. "I wish I could say something noble like how I went to law school wanting to crusade for good, but the truth is, it promised good, steady income that would let me help my family, get me out of the old neighborhood, into the nicer digs I coveted. I went in wanting to make a lot of money, and I did. And I don't usually apologize for that, but I do admire the public interest lawyers who put people first. Wish there were more of them."

"Nothing stopping you from being one of the good ones now." Toby's voice was pragmatic, like he already knew Reuben wouldn't make that change. And damn if Reuben didn't want to prove him wrong.

"Point taken. And even before this crash, I've been

wondering about my future direction," he admitted. He hadn't wanted to face that before now, but it was true, and maybe it was part of the reason he'd agreed to this trip in the first place. He'd been restless ever since the breakup with Dan, and uncharacteristically uncertain ever since the buyout offer was presented. "They're restructuring the firm and a retirement package is on the table. Natalie wants me to take it, and I… I guess I'm no longer so sure what I want. I don't want to be one of those guys who works himself into a heart attack ten years from now and *then* gets his wakeup call about priorities and all that jazz."

"I've seen that happen a time or seven. Some of them come here post-big health scare, throw themselves into the whole tour thing."

"Exactly. And maybe this could be my wakeup moment. Not sure exactly what I'll *do* with all these realizations, but I do know what you're saying."

"Maybe simply thinking on them is something. And sometimes life hands us a new direction when we're not looking. Like, I never set out to be a tour guide, but then my dad had his accident, my mom still had two kids at home, and the family needed income fast. I loved to fly—my major was going to be aeronautics technology, and I already had a pilot's license from working my tail off for lessons the summer prior. So I started running cargo and short-haul flights for Annie, but it wasn't too long before she trusted me with tourists. And soon I'll have been doing it for a decade. Fuck. Really hope I still have a job after all this is over."

"I bet you will." Reuben wished he could promise him more definitively. "You're good at what you do. They'd be fools not to want you back. But you've never thought about going back to school? Finishing your degree?"

"Nah. Family needs me, even now. Nell's still pretty young at almost twenty, still figuring out what she wants to do. And Hannah's in medical school now. She got a lot of scholarships, but there's stuff they don't cover. I promised Mom I'd see them graduate."

"That's pretty noble of you." Reuben was humbled by Toby's commitment to his family. And strangely, that dedication made him far more appealing than his easygoing, flirty tour guide persona.

"Hell, I'm no prince. It's just what family does."

"Yeah. I still remember the day I was able to move my mother into a better place. It felt like I'd really made it, both as a lawyer and as a man." Reuben shook his head. "Can't believe I'm sharing all this with you."

"Hey, what else are we going to do? And you're a good distraction. Tell me something else, something no one else knows about you and how you tick."

"Like a secret?" Reuben couldn't keep the skepticism from his voice. He wasn't in the habit of sharing—or keeping—many of those.

"Exactly. Who am I going to tell? And honestly, I'll probably forget it after they shoot me full of painkillers."

The reminder of how much pain Toby was in had Reuben wanting to help, even if only as a distraction. "Honestly, I work hard not to have secrets—I don't like the stress of hiding stuff. But let me think... I cried when Amelia was born. I'm not sure even Natalie knows that—she was pretty out of it, but they handed me this little bundle and she was so small... I'd never felt that helpless."

"That's sweet." Toby got a dopey smile that was probably half delirium from the pain and half sentiment. "I think you're probably a better dad than you think you are. What else though? Tell me something juicy."

"Juicy? Are you angling for sex secrets?" Reuben had to blink. "Sorry to disappoint, but I don't have those. No kinky dungeon or anything like that."

"Damn. You arrive looking like walking suit porn and no Fifty Shades of Reuben in your repertoire?"

"Afraid not. Weirdest thing about me is probably the thing that drove Natalie nuts over time and Dan too after a while."

"Oh? Now I'm curious."

"I…uh…" Geez. How to explain this without sounding like a total idiot? "I like taking care of people. A lot. Doing things for them. That sort of thing."

Toby's head tilted. "Like you're a submissive? You like serving people?"

"No." Reuben's skin heated. "Not that there's anything wrong with that, but I like being in charge, both in bed and out. It's more… I like giving people what they need. Giving them pleasure and making them happy. Natalie was—is—super independent, so me wanting to take care of her caused a lot of friction. And Dan used to joke, call me a service top, whatever that means, but he was more…adventurous in bed, wanted things rougher, I guess. Said I was too sweet. Not sure what he meant by that."

"Some kink is overrated." Toby's laugh was warm, not like he was poking fun at him. "And nothing wrong with wanting to see to the other's person's pleasure or whatnot. I'm more used to taking on that role myself, not used to having someone take care of *me*, but I'm…

intrigued, I suppose you could say. Sounds kind of nice, actually."

I'd like to show you. Reuben bit back the words. Toby was injured, and this conversation was supposed to distract, not titillate, so he didn't need a come-on. Instead, Reuben said lightly, "It can be. Anyway, that's my big dirty secret. Not sure I have others. Maybe you should tell me some of yours."

"I—" Toby opened his mouth like he was going to speak, then abruptly swallowed, face frowning. "Do you hear something?"

Ears straining for any sort of noise that might signal rescue, Reuben couldn't help the surge of hope flowing through him. "Let me check."

He scrambled out of the shelter. Finally the rain had tapered off. Scanning the sky, he looked for signs of a plane or helicopter. *Anything.*

"I'm not seeing... Wait. There. It's far off though. Come on, come on. Over here." But the speck didn't listen, getting more distant, not closer. "Damn it."

"It's good though." Toby's voice was far weaker than Reuben liked. "They're searching. They'll find us."

"Yeah." Reuben wished he was as sure. He really didn't like how pale Toby was all of a sudden. Then Toby lurched, coming half out of the shelter, chest heaving as he threw up.

Oh fuck no. Vomiting. Possible head injury.

This was *bad.*

Something was wrong, that much Toby was sure of. And checking his vomit for signs of blood was hardly what he wanted to be doing right then. Fuck. It sucked not knowing whether his queasy stomach was adrenaline drop or something more serious. Not that a probably broken leg and fucked-up arm were exactly minor, but at least he could see those injuries, quantify the pain. And yeah, the pain, which kept coming in waves, some more severe than others, was undoubtedly playing a role in his nausea.

"Do we have a water bottle?" Reuben stopped scanning the sky and riffled through their stuff until he came up with Toby's emergency canteen, then held it to Toby's lips. "Here. See if this helps."

"Okay." Toby took a small sip. "At least the rain is letting up."

"What do you think is on the other side of the lake?" Frown deep, Reuben's voice was as serious as Toby had heard it. "Any chance of there being a trail? Something I could pick up?"

"You're not going anywhere," Toby said firmly.

"I've still got a little cell power left. Figure I should try to get to reception, and the terrain looks higher on the far side."

"No. Power down the phone. We've got the beacons, and checking the time is just pointless." He punctuated his words with a wide yawn, talking exhausting him now.

"Are you about to doze off again? I need it to remind me when to wake you." Reuben sounded like he was close to begging Toby to stay awake as he squeezed back into the lean-to, and Toby hated that he couldn't even give him conscious company, but he couldn't deny the weight of his eyelids, the fuzziness of his brain.

"Sorry. Everything hurts. What a fucking birthday for you. Sorry."

"I know. And quit apologizing." Reaching out, Reu-

ben brushed the hair off Toby's forehead, hand gentler
and more lingering than if he was checking for fever.
His fingers drifted down, stroking Toby's cheek, and for
a heartbeat, he thought Reuben was about to kiss him,
but then he straightened, eyes going wide. "Wait. Now
I hear something."

A distant drone, barely audible over the regular forest noises of wind and rustles caught Toby's attention
too. "Not plane or helicopter."

"Damn." Reuben's disappointment was so palpable
that Toby gave him a pat with his good hand.

"Listen. Getting louder." Despite telling himself to
not get his hopes up, Toby's pulse still galloped. "ATV
maybe…"

Remembering the sliver that could have been road
that he'd glimpsed during their rapid descent, he let himself truly wish for the first time that they were closer to
civilization than he'd calculated. *Please. Please. Please.*

Right as he was about to chalk up the noise as mutual
hallucination, dark shadows appeared at the tree line opposite the crash site.

"We're here!" Reuben scrambled out of the shelter,
waving his arms. "We're alive!"

Yes, yes they were. And Toby intended to stay that
way, even if it meant fighting the pain and the urge to
sink into the buzzing in his head, louder even than the
ATV engines. And that's what they were, ATVs, draw-
ing closer, helmeted riders wearing what looked like
ranger uniforms.

"Oh thank fuck," he breathed, whole body going tingly. And for the rest of his life, he was going to remember the look on Reuben's face of stark relief, mouth slack,
tears in his eyes.

"The beacons must have worked." Reuben kept waving at the rapidly approaching duo.

The vehicles pulled up between the crash site and their shelter, and the two rangers dismounted, pulling off their helmets. The male, probably late thirties, looked like an ad for the park service with his rugged looks, and was barking into a radio. A similarly aged woman with short dark hair had a smile that reminded Toby of his mother. He had to chew on his lower lip, trying to hold back a weird surge of emotion.

"Well, are we happy to see you!" The woman swiftly walked over them. "Alaska Air National Guard requested our assistance—they received notice of a distress call from a small plane, but thick clouds and this wind are hampering the helicopter search efforts. Luckily for you, you crashed within park boundaries, and we were called out to patrol potential crash sites. Now, what's the injury situation?"

"Toby's hurt badly." Reuben led her over to the shelter. "Possible broken arm and leg, and I think he's got a concussion. Confusion. Sleepiness. Vomiting."

"You sound like you're auditioning for a medical drama," Toby complained. "I'm okay. Just get us home."

"Quill?" The woman called to the other ranger as she knelt next to Toby. "Tell them we've got significant injuries. We need whatever they can do to get a bird over here. I don't like the look of this, don't think we should attempt land transport."

Toby wanted to argue with her, tell her that he could ride on the back of the ATV, but he hurt too much. Even words hurt, almost like the pain had been holding off for this, waiting for their discovery before swamping him, arm and leg throbbing in tandem with his head.

"Don't leave me," he said instead, fear rising right along with the pain. He didn't want to be alone with all this hurt, didn't like how vulnerable and open he felt. Weird, but he almost missed the closeness they'd had in the lean-to, the distraction of Reuben's stories.

"Not a chance," Reuben answered, crouching down next to the ranger and grabbing Toby's good hand. "We're going to get you out of here. Man, your hand's like ice."

The ranger tsked. "You're both probably chilled through. You did a good job with this little shelter though. But I'm worried about hypothermia for both of you—it's not that warm today and with the wet and possible shock, we need to get you warmed up."

"I'm not cold. Feel hot." Toby couldn't keep the edge of panic out of his voice, not sure if he could trust his own body anymore, and not liking her grave tone or expression as she checked out his injuries, making his pain spike with each gentle touch. "F—ow. Ow."

"It's okay. I'm right here," Reuben soothed, not dropping his hand, apparently unconcerned what the ranger might think of that.

"We've got a collapsible stretcher in our gear. We'll do our best to get you ready for transport while Quill tries to get a helicopter here."

Transport. Oh fuck. As in he was going to have to *move*. He hadn't thought that far ahead yet, and now that he had, fresh worry bubbled up. Fuck. Just like how he'd held his hope at bay, so too had he pushed aside fully realizing the extent of his injuries and the logistics ahead.

"Reuben. Man. Promise me you'll call my boss, Annie. Tell her to tell my dad—"

"You'll tell them both yourself." Reuben squeezed his hand.

"It hurts." He hoped he wasn't whining too much, but it did, and fuck but he didn't want more pain when they moved him. Or maybe it was the realization that he wasn't walking away from this one. No, he was going to be carried out and laid up who knew how long. His dad. His family. His income. Fuck. He might have lived through the crash, but unlike Reuben who'd apparently had some sort of new age epiphany as a result of the crash, all he knew was dread, not hope.

Everything was screwed now. Everything. And he'd seldom felt as alone and helpless as he did, lying there, listening to the others discussing rescue options, so he clung to Reuben's hand like the lifeline it was. Something had shifted during their ordeal. Maybe he'd feel this way about anyone else he'd been stranded with, but he felt an odd connection to Reuben, one that went beyond mere physical proximity. Deeper. Like he trusted Reuben to make this hurt less, to make the coming hours less hellish. Reuben had saved his life, gotten him this far.

And right then, Toby was grabbing onto him, searching for something in his eyes, something to find hope and reassurance in. And when Reuben said again that he wasn't leaving him, Toby relaxed slightly. He wasn't alone. He had Reuben. And that was something.

Chapter Seven

Reuben wished there was more that he could do other than hold Toby's hand. His condition had visibly deteriorated, especially since their rescuers had appeared. The female ranger, who'd told him to call her Hattie, had clearly had some sort of first-aid training. Checking Reuben's splint job for Toby, she clucked over the injuries as she adjusted the position of the fabric. She pulled back the sleeping bag to reveal several nasty bruises blooming along Toby's ribs that Reuben hadn't noticed before.

"Possible broken ribs," she called to the other ranger, Quill. Funny name, but take-charge sort of guy, with the sort of attitude that immediately commanded respect. Frankly, Reuben would have been happy with any rescue, but something about this duo settled his nerves, made him trust in their skills.

"They've got a medic on board the chopper," Quill said as he came over to them. He unrolled some sort of collapsible stretcher, which he and Hattie lay next to Toby. "Key is going to be whether they can land. They're aiming for that clearing by the lake."

"You let Quill and me get the stretcher," Hattie ordered. "You focus on keeping yourself warm and keeping your...friend calm."

Her pause before *friend* gave Reuben a start. Were they friends now? More than merely guide and client? They'd been through hell together, and the way Toby clung to his hand certainly seemed to indicate something deeper than a passing acquaintance. And while he'd do anything to take Toby's pain away, he'd be lying if he didn't admit that he liked the way Toby seemed to need him, the way his presence seemed to soothe the otherwise stoic man.

"I'm...calm." Toby's voice was thready.

"We're going to move you onto the stretcher now," Quill told him. "Curse all you need to."

Toby managed a weak-sounding laugh at that. "I don't...*fuck*. Ow."

His face contorted with pain as they moved him onto the stretcher, and Reuben felt his hurt all the way down to his soggy socks. Reuben had dropped his hand so the rangers could move him, but when Toby flopped his good hand around as if he were looking for him, Reuben grabbed it back.

"I'm here," he assured Toby. "Not letting go."

"Good." Toby's eyes fluttered shut as they made an awkward shuffle toward the clearing. A helicopter roared in the distance, but it circled wide, not coming close enough to land.

Quill barked into his radio before reporting back, "Damn wind. They're going to try again, but we may only get a single quick shot at this."

"You're going to need stitches too," Hattie said matter-of-factly to Reuben. "And I wouldn't rule out a concussion for you as well. They're going to attempt to take you both to an Anchorage hospital if the weather cooperates."

Reuben's collection of aches and pains and scrapes hardly seemed significant next to Toby, but he nodded. "Good. Him first though. I don't want to leave him until he's with a doctor."

"I understand." She gave his arm a sisterly pat. "We're going to get you guys out of here. The crash investigators will probably want a statement from you as well, but first priority is medical assistance."

The helicopter circled back into view, and Reuben found himself again in the unexpected position of praying. *Please let this work. Let Toby get help.*

"Here we go," Quill shouted over the drone of the helicopter as it lowered into the clearing. The next few moments were a rush of movement, a team of personnel rushing out of the helicopter, transferring Toby to yet another stretcher and loading both of them up with frantic commands, taking off again so fast Reuben scarcely had time to register that he was on board. He didn't even have a chance to say thank you to Quill and Hattie. He managed to return to holding Toby's hand while the medic checked him out.

It was weird, being in the air again, and his stomach kept hopping in time with the helicopter's lurches. Realistically, he knew the chances of crashing twice in twenty-four hours were slim, but that didn't help when the turbulence kicked them around. But finally, civilization came back into view, blessed buildings and homes and roads. He'd never been as relieved as when they touched down at a hospital helipad, a team of medical people in scrubs greeting them.

"You're going to need to let go," the helicopter medic said to him gesturing at where he still held Toby's hand.

"I promised—"

"It's okay." Toby's voice was a bare whisper. "Go get your stitches."

"I'll be back to check on you," Reuben promised even as a stately nurse with a long red braid led him away. But keeping his promise turned out to be harder than he'd thought as getting checked out himself took forever. He kept asking for updates and the kindly nurse obliged, but she couldn't share much—first Toby was being examined, then he was off for an X-ray and tests on his head and apparently there was nothing yet to share.

"Do you want to talk to your family? If so, I can hunt down a phone charger for you," she said after the doctor finished the stitches on his temple. They'd wrapped him in thick, warm blankets and said he'd probably be kept for observation even after the stitches were in, which was not news Reuben wanted to hear.

"That would be great," Reuben said even as he dreaded hitting dial. One of the military personnel on the helicopter had revealed that both Toby's employer and Reuben's family had already been alerted, so he had to contact Amelia and Natalie. The nurse brought him a charger that worked with his battered phone. Funny how he hadn't even once during their ordeal thought about the office, about what was happening with his cases and deals. Telling too, and it underscored all his swirling thoughts about his life and where it was headed.

To his surprise, it was Amelia who answered Natalie's line. "Dad? Dad, is that you?"

"It's me. I'm safe. I'm so sorry for worrying you and your mother."

"They said your plane crashed." She let out a strangled hiccup that hit Reuben square in the chest. "But they said there was some kind of distress call, and to not give up hope, but I was *worried*."

"I know you were." Reuben's skin went warm at her emotional reaction, more touched than he would have thought. "But I promise I'm fine. I'm at the hospital—"

"Hospital? Are you hurt?" Her voice escalated again.

"Just some stitches and precautionary observation. My…pilot was hurt pretty bad though, so I got lucky."

"Send me a picture of the stitches," she demanded. "I need to see how bad."

"Amelia—"

"Dad. *Please.*"

"All right. I'll do it in a moment here. But I'll see you in person soon enough and you can see for yourself—"

"Oh, of course, you wouldn't want to miss the camp drop-off." Bitterness dripped from her words, making Reuben slump against his hospital bed pillow. Here they went again…

Except. Wait. Weren't things supposed to be different now? Hadn't he resolved out there in the wilderness that things *would* be different?

"Don't you want to go to camp?" he asked, trying to keep his voice gentle, not give in to her antagonizing tone.

Her reply was a loud sigh. "Does it matter?"

"Of course it does. You don't *have* to go."

"The nanny's going back to Germany at the end of the month. And despite the fact that I am *fourteen*, Mom doesn't trust me on my own. Says I need rides to see my friends and someone to cook. Like I even *have* friends. And like I can't use the microwave. And besides, summer is supposed to be *you*, and you're paying for camp, right?"

How had Reuben not known that she had friend issues? His heart contracted yet again for all the distance between them. The hospital was too damn chilly. He tucked the blankets more firmly around himself as he struggled with how to respond.

"Forget what I'm paying for. And the nanny." He didn't want to be this kind of dad anymore, the kind Amelia seemed to expect, who wrote the checks and not much else. If he'd been granted a second chance to make things right, then maybe he should start here, with Amelia. "What would you say to me taking some time off? Us spending the summer together?"

"You don't mean that." Her sigh was world-weary.

"Yes, I do," he said, voice firmer now.

"Well…at least you'd be better than the girls in my cabin last year. God, if Emily Whitborn is back…" Her voice held all the drama of a teen girl and less suspicion than a few moments ago, which he'd take as a win. "But… I bet you'd miss work in three days. The whole summer off?"

"I'll take that bet," he said with more confidence than he actually felt, determined to prove her wrong, to show her that he could make up for all the times he hadn't been present earlier in her life. Other than this trip and a few weekends here and there, he hadn't taken a nonworking vacation in years, hadn't a summer off since college. Part of him worried Amelia might be right—maybe he couldn't truly disconnect from the office.

But another part of him remembered what Toby had said about people coming to Alaska after health scares and other wake-up calls. Maybe this was Reuben's wake-up call. He still wasn't sure exactly what to do with the realizations he'd had while stranded about his priorities.

However, if Amelia needed him, maybe this could be a start. A chance to be a better person for the one thing in his life that truly mattered.

"What'll we even do? I kind of hate your condo. And forget three days—twenty-four hours and you'll be sneaking back to the office just to check on something."

She wasn't wrong. Reuben might have the resolve to spend the summer with her, but he knew the distractions of the office would be powerful if he were mere blocks away. Besides he'd had another realization the past few days about how much he missed being outdoors.

"We'll travel, maybe. Rent a vacation house somewhere pretty where it's not so easy for me to get sucked back into work."

"I don't like travel. Or outdoors. Or—"

"I bet you're wrong. I was fishing yesterday, and I kept thinking how much you'd like it."

"Fish guts? Uh no. And you want me to go to Alaska? That state nearly *killed* you. And you want to take me *there*?"

"Maybe." He was surprised by his own answer, but yeah, Alaska was definitely on his short list of places to take Amelia. Despite everything that had happened in the past twenty-four hours, he didn't feel done with this place, had this weird feeling that he was supposed to be here. And he wasn't one who usually believed in karma or luck or whatever other new-age substitutes for hard work and determination hippy types cooked up, but he couldn't deny the overwhelming feeling that the world was trying to send him a message. "Might be more fun than say the shore. We could hike and fish and explore—"

"At least the shore would have Wi-Fi," she grumbled. "And I'm not getting in one of those planes."

"You wouldn't have to. There's plenty we could do on land wherever we go. But what do you say? Me taking time off work, us together? I want to do this. Especially if you hate camp. I don't want you doing anything you hate for weeks on end."

"Nice of you to worry about that *now*." Ah, they were back to the sarcastic kid he knew and loved. And that was okay. He'd take the time to show to her that he was a better man than she thought. She exhaled hard again before continuing. "And anything's better than camp." It was hardly a ringing endorsement, but it would have to do for now.

"So should I tell Mom the new plan? And that I'm okay?"

"She went to lie down with a headache. Said to wake her if there was news, but she had *that* look. I bet she says no to your plan."

"I'll handle her. Take her the phone," he instructed, listening to the sound of Amelia's steps on the stairs and her rapping on a door before she talked to Natalie in low tones.

"Reuben?" Natalie sounded sleepy when she came on the line. "You're alive?"

"I am." He recounted more of the tale for her than he had for Amelia, summarizing the crash and aftermath, and ending with "I'm fine. A few stitches, but I'll heal."

"Good. Are you coming back tomorrow? Amelia was beside herself with worry. I don't want her going off to camp in this state next week."

"I haven't looked into flights yet." He deftly avoided

that question in favor of more treacherous conversational territory. "And about camp… She doesn't want to go."

"Oh, she says that now. She'll get over it."

"I don't think she should have to." It was one of the few times he could remember contradicting Natalie about a parenting thing, but he kept his voice sure and strong. "I want her to spend the summer with me. She was all I could think about when the plane crashed."

"With the kind of hours you work? Be realistic, please. I get that you've had some sort of near-death experience, but you can't leave a bored kid alone that many hours. Especially one who refuses to get any sort of meaningful hobby."

"You wanted me to take time to think, right?" he countered. "Do you still want me to take the buyout?"

"Well… I'm not sure this is the best time to talk about *that*."

"Let's." He used the tone he usually used with junior associates, not her, but he didn't like her carefully calculated tone.

"Okay. Fine. Yes, I think the buyout would be best for everyone concerned, you included. That hasn't changed."

"Then let me have a few weeks' leave of absence to think about it, come to a final decision. And in the meantime, I can spend the time with Amelia. Since you're always on me to spend more time with her, that should make you happy, along with me seriously considering the buyout you're so keen on."

"She's not an easy kid," Natalie warned. "She went back downstairs, so I can tell you that. Boarding school this fall can't come soon enough. You'll be begging me to come back to work inside a week."

"How about you let me handle that? After all, our custody agreement is clear that I get summers. And while we've done camp the past few years, I want my time now."

"Fine." Her tone was exactly as long-suffering as Amelia's had been, and it was rather clear that she didn't think he was capable of the sort of changes he wanted to make. "Email me more about this leave of absence once you have a chance to rest tonight. I'll send out a firm-wide message that you've been found safe, but you'll probably want to call Craig and Leticia yourself in the morning."

"Will do." He ended the call, stomach churning as he hunkered down into the blankets. What the hell had he done? Agreed to a whole summer without work? And with Amelia? Perhaps he really did have a concussion like Toby...

Toby.

How had he forgotten about the other man while talking to Amelia and Natalie? A fresh bout of worry made his neck and shoulders tense as he craned to look for signs of the nurse. Forget Natalie's admonishment to rest—he wasn't going to be able to relax until he knew that Toby was safe and out of danger.

Toby had never been a huge fan of drinking or party drugs because he'd seen too many friends go down bad paths, and he liked having a clear head for things like driving and sex. But right then he was all about writing an ode to painkillers, the soft, fuzzy feeling keeping him from the pain lurking at the edges of his consciousness. He had vague awareness of doctors and nurses attending to him, but mainly he simply floated, hearing them talk about things like concussions and compound fractures and ligament damage but not really registering it on a deep level.

"Your friend is asking about you," a kindly female voice said, but Toby couldn't even be bothered to open his eyes. He'd lost all sense of time, unsure whether it was the middle of the night or not, and not really caring enough to figure it out.

"I'm okay," he slurred, tongue too fat for his mouth.

"Actually, you're off for surgery soon. Thank goodness your brain CT scan came back negative. You gave everyone quite the head injury scare."

"Sorry." He still couldn't be troubled to open his eyes. Surgery. That sounded bad, but his reactions were blunted, bad news hitting him like cotton balls, not sticks.

"Anyway, no visitors until after surgery for you. But do you have a message for your friend? The guy in the crash with you?"

"Reuben." He blinked at last, but lights in the room were low and he couldn't seem to make his eyes focus on the woman in scrubs next to him. "Tell...thank you."

He wasn't so far out of it that he'd forgotten about the crash or about how Reuben had carried him away from the plane, kept them both safe, held his hand during the rescue when Toby had had that weird attack of nerves. But hell if he could find words for all the emotions butting up against the blurry neurons.

"I'll tell him. You rest now."

Like Toby was capable of much else. Conversation done, he let himself drift again, floating on clouds that smelled a lot like Reuben's shampoo, and the next time he came to, the room was colder and brighter and his awareness crisper than he would have liked, pain seeming to increase with each breath.

"Ungggh." He tried to speak and failed.

"Oh! You're awake." Another voice, also kind, this one female with a hint of Southern accent to it. "And from the sound of it, not doing so hot. Let's hit your pain pump, shall we?"

"Don't like…meds." He swallowed, mouth feeling like someone scrubbed it out with steel wool. His eyes were similarly raw, but he blinked until he could focus anyway. The nurse was older with a big head of blond hair and efficient movements.

"And here's a water for you. Sip slow." She held out a cup with a straw in it. "They had to do your IV on the left, so you're going to have to let me hold it for you for now."

"Right arm…what did they do?" Glancing down at his body, his eyes burned for a whole different reason. His right arm was heavily wrapped and strapped to some kind of board. From what he could see peeking out of the blankets, his legs were in even worse shape, left one in some kind of plastic boot thing that kept squeezing at weird intervals, and the right one elevated and in some sort of cast-like contraption. "And leg?"

"Those are great questions. And lucky you, here's Dr. Yamamoto to explain your condition more fully." She gestured at the door as a slight young man in a white coat entered the room. He was around Hannah's age, maybe a little older, which probably made him a resident of some sort.

"Doctor." Nodding hurt, but it wasn't like they could shake hands.

"Mr. Kooly. You are indeed a lucky guy. Lucky to

be alive, that's for sure." Like a number of Hannah and Nell's school friends, he had a casual, almost surfer-guy way of talking that seemed at odds with his doctor garb. "What we're dealing with is a couple of different injuries—displaced fractures to your wrist and radius both, and then in your leg, you fractured your knee cap, tibia, and did significant ligament damage. But the truly good news is that you escaped with only a mild concussion. Your limbs will heal—brains are far trickier, so you dodged a bullet there."

"When...when do I go home?" That was the only question that really mattered.

"Well..." He rubbed his jaw, and Toby could already tell he wasn't going to like this. "I hear that your family is on the way. When they brought you in last night, you were in pretty rough shape. Worried a lot of people. So I think you'll be good to have visitors very soon—"

"Home." Fuck. He wasn't happy at all to hear that his family was on the way. Either Nell had left Dad, or she was dragging him along on the drive, neither of which sat well with Toby. "When can I walk?"

"That's another good question." The doctor smiled encouragingly, but Toby felt anything but uplifted. "A lot is going to depend on your setup at home. Home health care or someone to take care of you, whether there are stairs..."

"My room's upstairs." The long flight of wooden stairs with worn carpeting that he'd done almost every day of his life flashed in his brain. He could almost feel the treads squeaking under his boots, feel his worn comforter under his fingertips.

"Ah. Okay. Well, like I said, home health care is an option. Rented hospital bed, that sort of thing."

"Living room is tiny." Toby groaned at the thought of trying to squeeze a bed in there. "Couch'll be fine. Just tell me when I can go. I'm needed there."

"Hold on a sec." The doctor held up a hand. "You've had some very serious injuries. It's going to be several weeks before you can put any weight on the leg, and because of your arm, crutches are going to be a challenge. You'll be able to start physical therapy soon, though, and it will help you gain back some mobility. But patience is going to be key here."

Toby could only growl in response to that.

"I'm going to level with you—a lot of patients in your situation end up doing a stay in a rehab facility. We can't have you spending weeks on end on a narrow couch or something suboptimal like that. That leg's been surgically repaired, and if you're patient, do the physical therapy, let it heal, you'll eventually get a lot of your range of motion back, but you push things, go too fast, and you could end up with more permanent limitations for that leg. Not to mention your arm."

"No, no rehab. Those places are crazy expensive." He knew that from his dad's recovery. And he couldn't be in Anchorage that long, away from home and all he had to do there. Not to mention the loss of his summer income—this was when he made the bulk of his money, and the last thing he needed was costly rehab on top of that loss. "I'll make do."

"Mr. Kooly…" Frowning, the doctor trailed off as there was motion outside the open door. A person. No, not just any person. Reuben. He was lurking right outside the door, in way cleaner clothes than Toby had seen him in last time, with a concerned look on his face.

"Reuben!"

"I... You're with your doctor. I'll wait."

"No, come in. You can explain to Dr. Yamamoto here that I can take care of myself. I don't need any talk of a rehab hospital facility."

"If the doctor thinks that's a good idea, maybe you should consider it." Reuben came into the room, and simply his presence had Toby relaxing. He did really like how Reuben could fill a space so completely, bringing his energy and personality with him, even when not saying much.

"You know I can't." Toby shot him a look that he hoped was pleading and not pathetic. "My family needs me home, but he's saying how I need someone to take care of me and can't camp out on the couch with all this." He gestured with his hand that had the IV in it, which pinched. "Ow. Just tell him to drop this rehab idea. I'll figure something out."

Reuben's mouth twitched, and he was silent for a long time, probably figuring out how to agree with the doctor without pissing Toby off. Fuck. He'd hoped Reuben might do the whole scary lawyer thing, get the doctor off his back, not make things worse.

"Never mind—"

"No, no never mind. You can stay with me. I'll take care of you."

Huh. The pain meds must have kicked in again because no way in hell did Reuben—hotshot silver bear attorney just say *that*. All Toby could do was blink.

Chapter Eight

"You'll do what?" Toby looked like he might be about to pop out of his hospital bed, so Reuben moved to put a hand on his shoulder. Damn, but Toby seemed all kinds of vulnerable, lying there all wrapped up and in a white hospital gown. And honestly, he'd surprised even himself with his proposal, but like a lot of things lately, including his decision to take the summer off, as soon as he'd said it, it simply made sense.

"It fits with my new plans. I'm going to spend the summer with Amelia. I was already making a list of potential places we could go. I want to be close to the outdoors again, and it wouldn't be that much more trouble to find a vacation rental here where you could come recuperate as well."

"No." Toby's chin took on a stubborn tilt.

"How about we worry about your post-hospital plans later?" The young doctor had a too bright voice, but Reuben supposed he was used to trying to pacify difficult patients. "Let me finish my check here, and then I'll leave you guys to work things out."

The doctor examined Toby quickly, movements efficient as he looked into his eyes, then at his arm and leg. Reuben's back muscles tightened at the sight of how injured Toby really was—it was one thing to have splinted him up in the middle of nowhere and another to see the results of his early morning surgeries. The doctor tried to explain about why they'd had to do surgery—something about pins and displaced fractures, but Reuben had had a hard time listening beyond his own worries.

"Will he heal?" His throat was thick as he forced the question out.

"Oh, yeah. As long as he listens to us about *rest*." The doctor offered a winning smile. "Maybe you can convince him of that. Overdoing it now would be a recipe for permanent problems."

"I'll do my best." Reuben already felt guilty about whether carrying Toby and his splint job had made things worse. Not to mention the fact that Toby had been injured saving *his* life. No way was Reuben letting him risk long-term injury when he had a shot at fully healing.

"You do that. I'll be back later, Mr. Kooly." With that, the doctor exited the room, leaving Reuben with Toby, who was glaring at him like Reuben had stolen his breakfast. He'd do well in the corporate world with that entertain-no-idiots expression.

"Did they check you for a head injury?" Toby demanded. "Because that's one hell of an awful idea."

"No concussion. Amelia doesn't want to go to camp. I want to show her places like the national parks, maybe take her fishing. Hiking. See the stars." He didn't think the plan was *that* crazy.

"You don't have stars back east? And this is summer. We don't get stars until very late."

"I mean metaphorically. I'd already decided to take Amelia someplace where we could explore nature. And Alaska would work well for that. Maybe I'm supposed to be here." Reuben wished he could explain the hold this place seemed to have over him. Sure there were plenty of scenic places all around the country, but something about the idea of summering here got his pulse speeding up. Even with the crash, he wasn't ready to move on, felt like there was some greater purpose to his being here. And yeah, he knew it sounded like a bunch of spiritual woo-woo stuff, but he couldn't help it. Something had changed in him, and he felt honor bound to explore that further.

"Won't you miss your job?"

"I'm taking a leave of absence." Reuben tried not to sound defensive. But everyone he'd spoken to so far had expressed doubt that he could live without work, which just had him that much more determined to prove them wrong.

"So, your plan is to rent a cabin and hopefully not get yourself stranded again as you explore with your kid?" Toby shook his head.

"Well, see, that's where you could come in." Reuben started to seriously warm to his impulsive offer. Because maybe he didn't have the first clue of what to do to keep a fourteen-year-old happy, but Toby did. Hell, not only did he have sisters, but it was his job, one he was very good at. "I know you'll be limited in what you can do, but you could help me plan day trips with her, tell me which hikes to do and so on."

"A bed-bound tour guide?" Making a scoffing noise, Toby gave Reuben a hard stare. "I don't need your pity. Or charity."

"That's not how I meant it." Reuben stepped back from the bedside so he could hold up his hands. "I like you and genuinely enjoy your company. I'd like to be friends, and I'd make this same offer for any friend. I've told you I enjoy taking care of people—"

"Hate to disappoint you, but I'm probably not going to be able to put out anytime soon."

"It's not a sexual thing." Reuben couldn't help the offended tone this time. He got that Toby was hurting, but this plan wasn't *that* absurd an idea. They could help each other out. "I mean, I'm not going to deny being attracted to you. But I'd never expect some sort of…barter. I want to help you because it feels like the right thing to do. And because you can help me with Amelia, make sure I give her some good memories."

If Reuben was being honest, he really did like the idea of another person in the house, someone to buffer all that togetherness if things went south and Amelia stayed sullen all summer. He wanted to help Toby, but he wasn't kidding when he said Toby could help him too.

"I'm a tour guide, not a nanny. And I'm needed at home. I can't be away from the peninsula that long."

"We could find a rental close to your family. I'm not all that picky. I liked the parts of the Kenai Peninsula we flew over. It would make a decent home base for me and Amelia." He pulled out his phone, ready to see what the rental market was like in that part of the state. He might be taking a break from work, but he was still used to getting things done and getting his way.

"I don't want to owe you for helping me. I'll figure something out." Toby still had the defiant look on his face, eyes narrow, nostrils flared.

"Maybe you should think about it. No need to make big decisions right yet." He was more than used to complex negotiations and knowing when to back off a little to find a better bargaining position.

"Says the guy who somehow decided to uproot his life in less than twenty-four hours." Toby gave a harsh laugh.

"Point taken. And really, I came by to see how you were—you can think about the offer. Oh, and I wanted to warn you that the crash investigators will probably be by to speak with you. I already had my interview this morning. I told them you did everything you could to avoid the plane going down."

"Thank you." Toby nodded sharply. "I appreciate that."

"It's the truth." Reuben didn't hold any secret grudges against Toby for the crash—the weather truly had come up out of nowhere, and he knew Toby had done the best he could with an awful set of circumstances. "And I hope your boss sees that too."

"Boss sees what?" A striking older woman with a long gray braid and no-nonsense demeanor came into the room.

She was followed by a man who looked like an older, frailer Toby with short, dark hair shot through with gray, and chiseled features that spoke to their Native heritage, leaning on a walker. A young woman trailed after them, wearing a T-shirt advertising a band that Amelia had several posters of in her room.

"I'm Annie Barrett, Toby's boss. This is his sister Nell and father, Paul. You must be Reuben Graham."

"I am. And I was just telling Toby he did everything he could to avoid a crash, and I hope you hold his job for him while he recovers."

"Of course we will." Annie sounded offended that Reuben would even suggest otherwise. "He's one of my best guides. And he's practically family. Honestly, I was more worried about whether you were planning on suing than whether Toby might need time off."

"No, I won't be suing," Reuben reassured her. Despite his profession, it hadn't crossed his mind to blame the tour company for something caused by an unlucky bout of weather. "And I was just leaving. Toby, I'll be back by later."

"Okay." Toby's hard eyes boring into Reuben's said that he wasn't planning on changing his mind. Which was fine. Reuben could afford to wait him out. And even if Toby didn't want to stay with him and Amelia, Reuben would still help him however he could. Reuben wasn't going to let Toby go it alone, not after all they'd been through together.

As Reuben left the room, Toby's brain was a mess of emotions—frustration at Reuben for his surprising offer, happiness at seeing his family, worry over how his dad was coping, and gratitude at Annie saying he'd still have a job. And damn Reuben for saying he'd be back, like Toby might change his mind. Which he wouldn't. The last thing he needed was anyone's charity. Or pity, including his family's and Annie's. They hadn't even spoken much, but their faces all held the same horror and sorrow that Reuben's had as they took in his condition.

"Oh, *Toby.*" Nell's shiny eyes looked dangerously close to tears. "What did you do to yourself?"

"I'll be okay," he said gruffly. "Doctor says I'll make a full recovery." He left off the part about the risk of re-injury or making things worse. What mattered was calming Nell down. He'd deal himself with the questions of where and how he'd recover. And right then, his concern was more with her and Dad. "Tell me you didn't drive all this way with Dad."

"I could do it. I wouldn't *like* it, but I could do it." She waved her hand dismissively, purple nails glinting in the fluorescent light, like their father's difficulties with long drives were nothing. "But Annie flew us."

"I knew you wouldn't want Paul doing a long drive." Annie crossed the room to rest a hand on his shoulder while his dad settled himself into one of the visitor chairs near the bed.

"*Paul* is just fine. You don't have to talk like I'm not here. I'm perfectly capable of coming to see my son." As always, his father's speech was slow but firm, deliberate. He might have to fight for each word, but he had a way of making each count. "And dang, Toby. You really did a number this time."

"Sorry." His eyes stung, hating knowing he'd let all of them down.

"Don't be sorry." Annie rubbed his shoulder with a gentle touch. "You heard your passenger. You did everything you could. And I know that's what you'll tell the crash investigators. You don't have to worry one bit about having a job. You just need to get well."

"Thanks." He had to swallow hard.

"And I don't want you fretting about the stairs at your place. You can come stay with Roger and me while you recover."

"No, thank you." He was somewhat kinder in his reply to her, but no less firm than he'd been with Reuben. She was recently remarried, still in the honeymoon phase with her husband, who had health issues of his own. Not to mention it was their busy time of year, and she was trying to help her son Griff with his cabin project. He didn't need her adding taking care of him to her list of burdens.

"Toby. Be reasonable."

"I'll figure something out." And he would. He'd come up with a way not to put anyone out.

"You could have my room. I could try the stairs. Or the couch." Dad's face was serious, but Toby wasn't having it. Dad had a long history of thinking he could do more than his body would let him, and Toby's job was keeping him safe.

"No way. Last thing we need is you falling or in some sort of flare-up. Seriously, guys, this isn't as bad as it looks."

"Well, it looks bad." Nell was never one to mince words.

"Tobias Kooly?" Two well-dressed men and a woman in a smart suit poked their heads in the already crowded small room. "We're with the crash investigation team. Do you have a moment for us?"

"Yeah." It wasn't like he could put them off forever, and he might as well get this over with before he ran out of what limited energy he did have. "Hey, Annie? You think you could take Dad and Nell to get coffee? And maybe ask the nursing station when I get food?"

"No problem." She gestured at Nell and Dad to follow her out.

"Thanks." He didn't need to further worry his family with a retelling of the accident. And it would be easier to talk without Annie there either, without worrying whether she was judging his actions, finding them lacking. An experienced pilot with decades of flying under her belt, Annie was someone Toby looked up to as more than simply his boss. He was already second-guessing himself enough as it was. Had it been the lightning or had he missed something? He honestly wasn't sure, and that worry gnawed at him.

But as he answered the investigator's questions, he tried to have confidence in his answers, knowing that his pilot's license and Annie's insurance claim might rest on his performance here. They painstakingly walked him through every aspect of the crash, from preflight checks to the fire after Reuben rescued him. By the time he'd answered the nine millionth question about the weather and wind, he was exhausted, breathing harder, forehead sweating.

"Almost done. Just need you sign this release for medical records so we can see the toxicology reports from last night." The female investigator held out a clipboard for him to do an awkward left-handed signature. Thank goodness he had nothing to worry about in that area, but from their frowning faces, he gathered they wouldn't believe it until they saw the evidence.

"We'll be in touch if we have more questions. But we'll let you rest now," one of the men said on their way out of the room.

Ha. Like he could rest easily with his head churning about what conclusions they might reach. And with interruptions every few minutes from nursing personnel for vital signs and his family coming back in. He tried to keep up with their conversation, but eventually a fitful sleep claimed him, and when he woke up, the room was empty. A clock on the far wall said that it was early evening. Weird how he'd lost most of a day what with surgery and sleeping.

"Toby?" A hesitant voice he'd recognize anywhere sounded from the door.

"Hannah Banana, what the heck are you doing here?" Her latest rotation had her serving at a hospital near Fairbanks. The medical school program she was in was based out of the University of Washington, but let her take almost all her clerkships in Alaska. Her latest one—which she had just started—was in emergency medicine, an area she eventually hoped to specialize in.

"I caught a flight as soon as I heard. Annie helped me find one. And Nell wasn't kidding about you being banged up." Tears glistened in her brown eyes as she sank into a visitor's chair. "I've already talked to my program chair. I can come home for the summer, help nurse you through this. I'll bunk with Nell, like old times. We'll put the couch on the porch—"

"We will not." He struggled fruitlessly to sit up. "You worked way too hard to get this internship. You can't take the summer off."

"Sure I can." She shrugged her delicate shoulders. She was smaller than both Nell and their mother, and there had always been something about her almost elfin face that called to all Toby's protective big brother instincts. "Besides, we might not have enough money for the fall—"

"Don't worry about that. You will not have to delay school. I promise you that."

"Toby. Be reasonable."

"That would be a nice change." Dr. Yamamoto bustled into the room. "I hear you've been terrorizing the nursing staff. And I'm here to take a look at your incisions before I sign off on you having some real food, so be nice to me or it's liquid diet for you." He laughed at his own joke as he looked at Hannah with unchecked curiosity. "And you are?"

"Hannah Kooly. Tobias's sister and a med student at WWAMI. Tell me about these injuries."

The two of them talked medical jargon for a few minutes as Dr. Yamamoto showed Hannah all his incisions and discussed the severity of his injuries like Toby was a car he was restoring. But Hannah hummed and nodded like she understood all the medical terminology. She beamed at the doctor, admiration clear in her eyes.

Oh fuck. Usually it was Nell he had to worry about with guys. But Hannah getting a thing for his doctor would be just the perfect cherry on this shit sandwich of a day. And of course, she tried to use the doctor to advance her position.

"Tell my brother to let me take care of him." She glared at Toby.

"That's not a bad idea." The young doctor scratched his chin.

"It would mean her postponing an internship. Tell *her* she can't do that." Toby wasn't above using the cute guy to get Hannah to cut this nonsense out.

"Oh." Dr. Yamamoto's eyes darted between Toby and Hannah, clearly torn.

"Toby. You've had serious injuries. Were you listening to the doctor just now? And I intend to take care of you, make sure you don't re-injure yourself. Unless you're willing to do a rehab facility, this is probably our best option."

"It's not." Unbidden, Reuben's face flashed before his eyes. Damn it. He did *not* want his help either. But the idea of Hannah giving up school was absolutely unbearable. As was the expense of a rehab facility and being that far from Dad. "You missing school isn't the only option."

"Oh?"

"I've got a...friend. Former client, really. But he offered to help, let me stay with him. As did Annie. I'll get this covered, Han. Really."

"I don't like the idea of strangers taking care of you."

"And I don't like the idea of you dropping school commitments. You know Mom would hate that." It was a low blow, playing the mom card, but damn it, he had not come this far with her education for her to sacrifice it for him now.

"We'll see." Her glare turned positively lethal, but her defeated tone said he was close to winning this battle. Which meant Toby really was going to have to rely on Reuben or Annie, and of the two, at least Reuben wasn't his already overburdened boss.

Fuck my life. He barely suppressed a groan. He wasn't looking forward to having to eat his harsh words toward Reuben, ask for his help. And right on cue, as the doctor left, in came Reuben looking way too good in a crisp white shirt with the sleeves rolled up and khaki pants. Either their luggage had been retrieved or he'd been shopping.

"Oh, I'm sorry. I saw the doctor leave and thought you might be alone." Reuben backed toward the door.

"Nah. Don't go. It's been a revolving door here all day. You. My family. Annie. The crash investigators. Doctors."

"Speaking of family, I should probably go meet Dad and the rest of them for dinner in the cafeteria. We'll all come back up later." Hannah kept glancing at Reuben, clearly waiting for an introduction.

"Hannah, this is Reuben. He's the client I was telling you about."

"Oh." Her mouth made a perfect circle as her eyes went wide, rapid calculations apparent. She never had been much of a card player. "You're the one who said Toby could stay with you?"

"I am." Reuben shot Toby a questioning look.

Damn. Could this get more awkward? Did Reuben already regret his offer? "If you've changed—"

"No, no. Of course not. I've already got a list of suitable rentals."

"Because of course you do." Toby wasn't sure whether to laugh or groan.

"Do you have any medical experience?" Like Nell and their mother, Hannah wasn't one to back down from a challenge. "I am perfectly prepared to take the summer off—"

"Which is why I am taking Reuben up on his offer." Toby cut her off before she could go down that path again, and tried to tell Reuben with his eyes that he needed him to help with Hannah.

"We'll manage fine," Reuben assured her, neatly side-stepping the medical experience question. "Toby's going to help me come up with activities to do with my daughter. It'll be fun."

Fun. Strange word coming from Mr. All-Business. And *fun* it would definitely not be, but Toby could only nod. He *needed* Hannah back at school, doing her internship. And he needed to be close enough to at least check on Nell and Dad. This might be his best option, but that didn't mean he was looking forward to it.

Any way he looked at it, it was going to be one hell of a long summer.

Chapter Nine

"I can't believe some random guy is going to stay with us." Amelia removed her headphones after the captain asked that electronics be shut off for their descent into Anchorage. This meant she had to stop the phone game that had occupied her during both flights, and allowed her to focus her ire on him again. "Mom says he could be a serial killer. And to call her as soon as I want to go back to camp."

"He's not a serial killer. And he's injured. Your room is upstairs and his is downstairs, but if it makes you more comfortable, we'll make sure your door locks." Reuben's stomach jumped, even though the skies were relatively smooth. Flying was never going to be stress free again for him, and part of him would have preferred to have Amelia fly out here without him going back east to fetch her. But he'd had things to wrap up with the office and to get set for a summer in Alaska, and he didn't want to be the sort of dad who had her fly as an unaccompanied minor just because he had a sudden fear of flying himself.

"And going back to New Jersey?"

"If that's what you want, sure." They'd already been over this territory a bunch in the last few days, and he had to work to keep a patient tone. "But you said you'd keep an open mind."

Her sigh was loaded enough to blast through concrete. Her long, curly hair was even more unruly than usual, and her cheeks were pink with indignation. "Mom thinks you've lost your mind though."

"She'll get over it." Reuben tried very hard to never argue with Natalie in front of Amelia or to talk bad about her. And even if Natalie didn't always play by those same rules, Amelia really didn't need to know how hard Natalie had tried to talk him out of this plan and into something "saner and simpler." But once his mind was made up, he was all-in on accomplishing his goals. He didn't do things by half measures, including near-death wake-up calls.

If he was going to be a better person, better father, then he wasn't going to do it hanging around the office, giving in to the temptation to fall back into old patterns. And despite her reluctance, Amelia needed a change of scenery as well. She'd done little other than complain about school and her lack of friends since he'd returned, and she didn't seem all that pumped about boarding high school in the fall. Not that she seemed pumped about much at all, surly for their ridiculously early morning flight for Seattle, getting them into Anchorage around early afternoon.

"You're looking at your phone again," Amelia complained as they waited for the rental SUV he'd arranged to have for the summer.

"Oops. Sorry. Old habits." He was still wrapping up a few cases, assigning tasks to associates and junior partners, and the urge to check on them had gotten the better of him. Again. This was why he needed thousands of miles between him and the office—even yesterday, he'd snuck in a meeting in between making sure Amelia was packed.

"Mom's right. You know it. They're going to *need* you, and you're not going to be able to resist going back."

"We've agreed to the summer. And Toby needs us." Privately, Reuben had to wonder if perhaps he'd agreed to help Toby for just that reason—making sure he couldn't run back to the office at the first urgent email or hard day with Amelia.

"Well, if *Toby* needs us…" Amelia shook her head and pulled her game back out, and she slumped in the front seat as soon as they got in the car, not answering him when he asked if she was hungry.

"Amelia. I asked if you want food on the way to pick up Toby?" It had worked out that Toby was still in the hospital, recovering while Reuben had been back east, but he was finally ready for discharge. "I'm pretty sure we're going to pass some fast food."

"Do they even have real burgers here? Or is it all moose meat?"

"I'm pretty sure the chain places have real beef." He pulled into a familiar franchise's parking lot. "While we eat let's make a list of groceries you want. We'll shop while I wait for Toby to text that he's ready for discharge."

"I can't cook." She gave him another stony stare.

"That's okay. We'll figure it out together." He relied far too much on takeout and business meals himself, but he was determined to do things right here. To that end, he made a long list, and after they ate, they filled the back of the SUV with nonperishable groceries and a cooler with some meat and other refrigerator stuff.

There were grocery stores on the peninsula, but Toby had suggested they might want to do a big stock up in Anchorage.

Maybe it was just Toby being bored in the hospital, but they'd had some fairly long text chats working out the logistics, and straying into other topics like TV shows and food. While Toby could get as irritable as Amelia over staying with Reuben, he seemed to have mellowed into the idea in recent days, and Reuben found himself getting a little thrill with each new message.

Reuben and a progressively more grumpy Amelia made another stop at the home health rental place near the hospital to pick up the order Toby had cleared with his insurance for a wheelchair, shower stool, grab bars and other essentials he'd need. When they arrived at the hospital, Toby was sitting up in a wheelchair. He was dressed in a loose shirt and shorts over his big black leg cast and a matching smaller contraption on his arm. His injured leg was extended on the wheelchair's leg rest, and he held a plastic hospital bag with some papers and belongings on his lap. The need to not bend his leg much was why he was traveling with Reuben and Amelia. A short plane flight might have been easier for him than a long car ride, but the SUV would give him more space for the leg.

"You look ready to go." Reuben wasn't sure how to greet him, especially with Amelia right behind him. Handshake felt way too impersonal. Shoulder clap too close to a hug. In the end, he did nothing more than smile, but the urge to touch Toby was almost overwhelming.

"So ready. They already did all the discharge papers.

And Nell's bringing by more clothes and stuff tomorrow morning. She's happy the place you found is so close."

"The pictures look really nice too." The furnished vacation rental was about halfway between Toby's family and the small town where the tour company was based. Toby would be able to see his family and friends often, and they'd also be close to lots of places for him and Amelia to explore as well. From Reuben's point of view, it was a win-win for everyone.

"There's a lot of wood. Like a ton." Amelia studied Toby as if she couldn't make up her mind how rude to be, settling for an argumentative tone directed at Reuben. He'd shown her all the pictures, hoping to get her enthusiasm up, but she'd complained the log structure was too close to a camp cabin, despite the gourmet kitchen and other nice touches.

"You must be Amelia." Toby stuck out a hand. "I've heard a lot about you."

"Same." Amelia's mouth quirked as she shook hands. "But I thought you'd be old. Like Dad."

"Oh, uh, I'm thirty-one."

"Hey, I'm not *that* old," Reuben protested to both of them.

"No, you're not." Toby's eyes were warm, and the back of Reuben's neck heated. He still had a hard time telling when Toby might be flirting and when he was simply being his usual charming self.

As they made their way from the hospital to the parking lot, Toby turned that charm on Amelia, asking her about the trip and getting monosyllable answers in return.

"Sorry. She's kind of cranky," Reuben apologized as he helped Toby into the backseat.

"I've got younger sisters. I get it." Toby's smile faltered as they arranged his leg as best they could. "F—*ow*. Might need to stop to stretch partway there."

"We'll stop as much as you need. Besides, it'll give us a chance to admire the scenery."

That got a snort from Amelia. "I'm too tired for scenery."

"Then you sleep." Reuben really hoped her attitude improved in the coming days or it was going to be a long summer. Then he caught sight of Toby's face in the rearview mirror and decided that maybe a long summer wouldn't be such a hardship after all. However, he needed to remind the fluttering in his stomach that he was here to take care of Toby. As a friend. A friend who didn't need Reuben's inconvenient attraction.

Toby's leg started aching even before they cleared downtown Anchorage. And Reuben's kid hated him, which was a different type of ache. He was used to people liking him. He'd made friends with plenty of clients' kids of all ages, but this one seemed determined to dislike him. She was playing some sort of game on her latest-model phone, the one Nell coveted, with a blinged-out sparkly silver case. As they left Anchorage, he tried to slip into tour guide mode, telling them about the Turnagain Arm of the Cook Inlet, but it wasn't long before her head swiveled, curly hair swishing against the seat back.

"I'm going to try to sleep now, okay?"

"My commentary that boring?" Toby tried to laugh.

"Maybe."

"Amelia," Reuben warned.

"Hey, it's cool. She can sleep if she wants. Maybe you can find some music? We'll be able to pick up Anchorage stations for a while still and then we'll get the Seward and Kenai stations after the pass."

"Sure. What do you like?" Reuben fiddled with the stereo.

"Not your film scores." Amelia yawned. "Dad has this thing for movie scores. Which is almost as bad as classical. And it's not like he watches a ton of movies either."

"It's good music to work by," Reuben said mildly, but Toby could tell he was working to stay patient with Amelia.

"Try 90.3, KNBA. It's a native-owned station that I love, and they play a little of everything. I listen to that or one of the oldies stations."

"You don't have a playlist app?" Amelia sounded like Toby had just confessed to living in a cave.

"Nah. I've got an older Explorer—I care more about the four-wheel drive than having the stereo talk to my phone." He finished on a groan as a thought hit him. "Nell's going to be happy as she'll get it all summer."

"You'll get back to driving," Reuben assured him as he found the station Toby had recommended and a recent pop hit filled the SUV.

"Hope so." Toby really didn't want to think about his recovery, how long it might be before he was back driving, riding ATVs, flying. All the stuff that had been second nature to him. And *could* he fly? It wasn't simply a matter of the investigators clearing him or Annie saving his job—the more the days passed, the more his doubts mounted. He wanted to believe he would fly again, that the thing he loved so much hadn't been ripped from him, but it was hard.

His insurance had agreed to cover physical therapy,

and someone from a practice in Homer would be driving over to work with him. He'd had an endless parade of therapists and caregivers for Dad when he'd first come home from the rehab facility, so he was somewhat used to the drill and intent on minimizing their visits so that the co-pays didn't sink him.

They listened to music while Amelia dozed—or at least she did a good job pretending. It was a nice, companionable silence, but as they approached the Sterling Highway cutoff, Toby really did need to stretch. His pain level was starting to spike, turning into an insistent ache that made it hard to think, and much as he didn't want to, he'd need to take some of the meds when they ate.

"There's a lodge coming up where we could grab some food," he said to Reuben. "Gorgeous view of Summit Lake too."

"Sounds good. I'm really enjoying the drive so far. Never seen so many trees like this."

"Where is the cranky guy tied to his phone who I first met? Not on a strict schedule now?" Toby teased, voice going flirtier than he'd intended, but Reuben only laughed.

"Oh, I'm sure the office will still manage to reach me in case of emergency, but honestly, I feel…freer than I have in years."

"Mom says it's a midlife crisis." Amelia blinked her way awake as Reuben pulled into the gravel parking lot. Personally, Toby agreed, but no way was he saying that out loud. Reuben did seem different, changed somehow, but Toby had zero faith that he wouldn't flip back into businessman mode at some point soon when he realized he missed all his moving and shaking and big money deals.

"Look. There's an accessible ramp. That's handy." Reuben did better at ignoring Amelia's barb than Toby would have in his shoes. And he was surprisingly good at muscling the wheelchair out and getting it set for him. Ever since the crash, Toby had seen how masterful Reuben was at taking over a situation—from the rental to the medical equipment to this more hands-on help, he seemed to have appointed himself as chief director of Toby's recovery. And what was truly shocking was that part of Toby didn't hate it, liked being taken care of after all these years being the one doing the caretaking.

Oh, he still chafed at his injuries and hated feeling like his independence was being taken from him, but he had to admit that Reuben making it so that he didn't have to worry so much about the little details was kind of nice after years of micromanaging everything to keep his family afloat. Although, he wasn't giving up on his family either—he'd managed to do bills from the hospital on a laptop Nell had brought him, and even one-handed he could still send reminder texts to her and Dad.

"Do you need me to cut the food for you?" Reuben asked as they considered the menus.

"Nah. I'm just getting fries as a snack." Because yeah, eating left-handed had proven to be more than a small challenge, but some things he liked to do for himself, especially in public.

"I already had fries earlier. I'm getting a blended mocha since they've got an espresso machine." Amelia's arch tone dared one of them to object to her order.

"Decaf. Remember it's late back east." Reuben's voice was mild but firm. "You'll probably want to go to sleep as soon as we get settled into the cabin."

"Dad." Amelia made a face before returning her at-

tention to the menu. While her riot of curly hair was far different than Reuben's carefully styled short silver crop, she had his intelligent hazel eyes and a similar broad build.

"Do you play any sports?" Toby asked. "Basketball?"

"Because I'm so tall, right?" she scoffed. "No. I hate sports. Dad played basketball to go to college, so he thinks I should try it. But I don't want to."

"Just trying it in a rec league isn't the same as saying you need a sports scholarship." Reuben's tone was tight, like he was reaching the end of his patience.

"I bet you'll like fishing." Toby tried for a lighter tone. "I didn't think your dad would like that, but he took right to it. Maybe you'll discover something this summer that you enjoy doing."

"Fishing isn't a *sport*."

On that note, the server arrived to take their order. The exterior of the small lodge was typical log building with stairs in front, ramp off to the side, and the dining room area was small and homey. He'd eaten here before, many times, but he could pretty much see Amelia disapproving of everything from the plaid table coverings to the animal trophies on the far wall. And indeed, their snack was a mix of her complaining and Toby trying to keep the peace with some stories of other meals here with tourist groups. If Reuben wanted him along for his guide skills, he was determined to prove his worth, find activities and experiences that Amelia would enjoy, even if doing so proved to be an uphill battle.

After they were in the car again with Amelia immediately feigning sleep, he sent a quick left-handed message to Nell. The text wouldn't go through until they were through the mountains, but at least he'd have it queued up to send before the pain pills kicked in and he forgot.

"Everything okay?" Reuben asked as he turned back toward the highway.

"Yeah. Just making sure Nell's coming tomorrow. I need clean clothes."

"I'm sure I could find you something." Reuben had a warm, rich laugh, one that made Toby want to hear more of.

"And okay, really, I need an update on Dad. It's weird going this long without seeing him. Most of my tours are a week or less." He still wasn't sure what it was about Reuben that had him opening up about his family and his worries.

"I'm sure he's okay." And that right there was probably a big reason why he'd shared—when Reuben said things would work out, something in him was inclined to believe him. Reuben passed a slow-moving RV before he continued. "Can you call him directly?"

"He's never been much for talking on the phone, and texting frustrates him." The past week had been interminably long—Hannah going back to her rotation, his dad and Nell back home, a few assorted visitors as he'd endured a second leg surgery and battled an infection before finally getting the all clear for discharge. His text conversations with Reuben had been a major highlight for him, and talking now, in person, that same sort of comfort had him relaxing more into the seat.

"Well, if he doesn't come with Nell tomorrow, I'll drive you to see him. You'll probably feel better once you see him for yourself."

"Yeah. And thank you. The whole not driving thing

sucks. Why couldn't it have been my left leg? At least then I could have driven an automatic."

"If it helps at all, I keep asking myself why you had to get so injured and I escaped with only a few stitches. I keep replaying that moment when the wing broke loose, over and over in my head. I'd do anything to make it easier on you."

"I don't need you feeling guilty." Toby's body was caught in a weird limbo between warmth at Reuben's admission that he cared and chill at the idea that all this help might be motivated by a misguided sense of obligation.

"I don't," Reuben said, but the reply was too fast and too clipped for Toby to fully believe him. He let out a loud yawn. "Sorry. Long day."

"It's okay. You're still on east coast time. Bedtime for you guys."

"I'm used to it, but I'm hopeful Amelia sleeps for real once we get to the cabin and that she wakes up in a better mood."

"Here's to hoping." Toby wasn't so sure that sleep would be enough to cure her attitude, but he knew better than to talk bad about Reuben's kid to him. They still had another two hours to the cabin, but at least they had plenty of daylight for it. Still, though, knowing full well the risks of sleepy drivers on mountain roads, he made an effort to keep Reuben talking, even as he fought sleepiness himself. Pain meds were starting to kick in, which was good, but now he was drowsy and needed the talking to stay awake just as much as Reuben did.

As with their text chats, their conversation flowed easily from music—they'd lost the Anchorage stations— to Reuben's efforts to wrap up business at the office to plans for the rest of the week. He was actually a little surprised when the GPS directed them to turn in at a long gravel drive leading to a newer log home.

It was a showy place with big picture windows to take advantage of the view, and set up as a vacation retreat what with the hot tub and bikes chained to the deck and welcome message from the rental company on the dining table. Reuben had picked well as the single step into the house wasn't that hard to get the chair past, and the open floor plan inside made easy navigation in the wheelchair while Reuben and Amelia unloaded the SUV.

Not liking to watch them work, he positioned himself at the walk-in pantry and helped put away the food and supplies. Amelia yawned her way through the whole endeavor and was quick to head upstairs, which contained a little loft area plus her bedroom. Downstairs there were two bedrooms, one decorated in pastels with a queen bed and a master with an attached bathroom that Reuben insisted Toby take.

"I don't need the biggest room," he protested as Reuben set up the grab bars in the bathroom for him.

"Yes, you do. The attached bath will be easiest for you. And this room has a nice TV for you as well having the bed at a better height for easier transfers to the wheelchair and your walker."

"But—"

"I've been up over eighteen hours now." Reuben rubbed his eyes. "I'm too tired to argue, and honestly, I can sleep anywhere. Take this room. Please."

"Okay." Toby wasn't going to keep him from sleep even if he felt weird taking a room this nice—big king bed with fluffy linens, nice pine entertainment center with a flat screen TV, hardwood floors with little rugs that Reuben rolled up so he wouldn't trip, and French doors leading to a private deck. Far bigger than his room back home—the whole house was a little intimidating in its luxury. He was used to accommodations like these for his richer clients, but taking advantage of it for personal use felt a little wasteful.

"Night." Reuben hesitated in the doorway, almost like he wanted to say something else but wasn't sure what, eyes uncertain.

"Sleep well." Toby wasn't sure what to make of the suddenly charged air between them. Wasn't like either of them was looking for a good-night kiss or anything silly, but still, there was this…energy with Reuben that he didn't have with other platonic friends. Too bad his body wasn't going to be in any shape to take advantage of a few weeks in proximity to Reuben.

Hell, with his right hand out of commission, even jerking off was likely to be frustrating. Last thing he needed was to go getting a thing for Reuben, go craving kisses he had no business wanting. But even knowing that, as Reuben retreated to his own room, a weird loneliness settled over him. He'd have to be careful to keep from getting too attached to this place with all its little comforts and this confounding man.

Chapter Ten

"Oh. You're up." Reuben emerged from an unusually deep sleep to find Toby fiddling with the coffeemaker in the open kitchen area, stretching to reach it from his wheelchair, trying to get a filter in one-handed. "I thought you might need my help. Dressing and stuff."

"You just want to get me naked." Toby laughed, probably at the flush Reuben could already feel on his face. "These are still yesterday's clothes. I'll try to figure out getting clean and changed after Nell comes. Might get her to help me if she's not too weirded out by that."

"I can help too," Reuben insisted, gently taking the filter from him and getting the coffeemaker set up. "That's what I'm here for. And not to…you know. Perv on you or something. I wouldn't—"

"Relax. I was just having fun with you." Toby's laugh was a little self-conscious. "Better than admitting that I can't even pull a T-shirt on easily by myself right now. I hate needing all this help."

"I know." Reuben rested a hand on Toby's muscled shoulder. His neck and shoulder were tight, and not over-thinking the impulse, Reuben started a light massage, seeking out the knots.

"Mmm. That feels good." Toby stretched into the

contact. "Maybe you can…" He trailed off and pulled away as Amelia padded down the stairs, tone going from sleepy and flirty to what sounded like forced cheer. "Morning!"

"Did you make enough coffee for me?" She gave them both a frown, but if she'd seen Reuben touching Toby, she didn't remark on it.

"How about some breakfast?" Figuring saying no to coffee was a losing battle, he found the cupboard with coffee mugs and got three down. Reuben poured her a scant third of a cup, earning him another glare as she dumped in some milk.

"I don't eat cereal." Her tone said he should know that already.

"We got pancake mix, remember? That can't be too hard."

"It's not," Toby answered before Amelia could. "If you bring a bowl to the table, I'll help make the batter."

Leaving his coffee on the counter, Toby wheeled himself in the direction of the nearby eating area. For needing to operate with only one hand, he was doing remarkably well at steering the wheelchair, giving Reuben an Amelia-worthy look when he moved to help. Reuben settled for bringing him his coffee and a mixing bowl.

"Here." Amelia fetched the mix from the pantry and eggs from the fridge with a minimum of complaining. As Toby gave them instructions for heating a nonstick skillet, Reuben's neck muscles gave a funny little twitch, as if they too were relaxing, sure as if he'd been the one getting a massage. But something about the utter domesticity of the moment hit him right in the solar plexus. Even with Natalie, he'd never had lazy mornings like this three-person effort to make a simple meal.

"Hey, it didn't burn!" Amelia's smile as she flipped the first pancake was worth the whole week of logistics. This was why he'd come back with her. To earn more of those smiles and her genuine enjoyment. Proving she didn't completely dislike Toby, she followed instructions to make him some smaller ones that he could more easily eat left-handed. And typical teenager, she out-ate both him and Toby, pronouncing their efforts "Pretty good" as she helped herself to thirds.

Toby's phone buzzed as they were finishing eating. "Nell and Dad should be here soon."

"Visitors?" Amelia did a shriek more suitable for a spider invasion. "I need to put on, like, real clothes. And do my hair and makeup—"

"You don't need makeup." Reuben squinted, trying to see the little girl who'd worn a unicorn costume for weeks on end and the messy kid who'd had to be parted from her stained favorite sweatshirt in the face of this too mature young woman.

"Says you." She shook her head at him on her way back up the stairs.

"You're doing a good job," Toby said softly as her door clicked shut. "I know she's been cranky, but she's a good kid."

"Thanks." Reuben exhaled hard. "It was easier, having your help with breakfast."

"Anytime. It was fun." Their eyes met, and Toby's expression was soft. Not exactly flirty, but…affectionate. Like he really did get how hard Reuben was trying and appreciated it. And just knowing that, the not-aloneness of having him share these moments made him smile, a grin so wide that his facial muscles protested the unfamiliar movement.

Amelia reappeared in a purple shirt advertising her favorite band accompanied by a cloud of sticky-sweet perfume right as Toby's family arrived. Nell was dragging a large black suitcase and carrying two paper grocery sacks, while Paul navigated the porch area with his walker. Rolling in front of Reuben, Toby made all the introductions for Amelia.

"Dude. You like them too? Cool beans." Nell gestured at her own shirt, the same one she'd worn to the hospital. "We're practically twins."

"Yeah. I like your lip gloss." Biting her lip, Amelia glowed with undisguised hero worship at the compliment from the older girl, who even Reuben had to admit was glamorous, what with her painted nails and shimmery makeup. She had Toby's eyes and his tallness, but where his hair was short, hers was long and glossy, hanging in dark waves down her slender back.

But she had a kind smile for Amelia, commenting on the name of her lip gloss as Amelia looked ready to start taking notes. And with that, the two of them were off on a conversation about makeup brands that Reuben could barely follow, both of them flopping onto one of the white leather couches in the living area just off the front door.

"Nell brought you a suitcase," Paul said to Toby as they followed the girls to the seating area. He had a very deliberate way of speaking—not halting exactly, but it reminded Reuben of his grandmother after her stroke, having to work harder than normal for words. Moving slowly, Paul settled on the other couch next to the pile of things Nell had carried in. "I brought some stuff too. One of my grabbers."

Paul pulled out a stick with a mechanism for opening

and closing a claw on the end. While he showed Toby various accessibility aids he'd brought, Reuben busied himself cleaning up the pancake mess, feeling a bit unsure how to navigate Toby's family. Which was strange because he negotiated with high-powered attorneys all the time and could usually talk to anyone without losing confidence. But somehow it mattered to him what they thought, in a more personal way than he was used to.

Dishwasher started, he couldn't keep up the cleaning pretext indefinitely. He was tempted to check his phone next, see if the office had any questions for him, but even he had limits of how rude he could be with the phone. He went to sit next to Amelia, who was still deep in conversation with Nell, comparing favorite cosmetic vloggers.

"We're going to owe you," Paul said solemnly in Reuben's direction, eyes narrow. He looked to have some years on Reuben, which probably meant he'd had his kids later in life.

"It's no problem," Reuben assured him. "And honestly, Toby's helping us out—got us through making breakfast, and he's working some hikes and activities for Amelia and me."

"I'm not so sure about hiking," Amelia interrupted. "And—"

"You'll give it a try." Reuben cut her off before she could make matters worse by suggesting yet again that they not have Toby with them. She'd been nicer while cooking, but he wasn't sure how long that would last.

"Toby said you saved his life," Nell added, voice far less ominous than her father's. "Carried him away from the burning plane and everything."

"Anyone would have done the same." Reuben shrugged off the praise. "The rangers and the rescue team deserve the real credit for finding us so fast. And Toby's the one who got the plane down without killing us both. And he rescued me first—I was passed out cold when he roused me, and he got all the gear out too."

"Still. Thank you." Toby's dad still sounded rather dour, almost as if he'd already decided not to like him. Which sucked. But Reuben could understand somewhat— he was an out-of-towner who'd more or less swooped into Toby's life, not a long-term friend or boyfriend. Oh. Maybe that was it, too—it was possible that Paul had picked up on the weird energy between them and didn't approve of that either. Not that it was going anywhere. Toby was injured, and Reuben wasn't going to take advantage. Not to mention, he and Paul would probably agree on him being too old for Toby.

"So, you're a lawyer?" Unlike ninety percent of the people in Reuben's life, Nell said it like it was a dirty word, a disease to avoid catching.

"Yeah. Corporate law." Why did this suddenly feel like a job interview and why did he feel like he'd already failed it? "I'm taking leave for the summer, but it's a fairly big firm. I handle a lot of mergers and acquisitions."

"My mom's a lawyer too." Amelia sighed as if this was a fate worse than death, probably to try to impress Nell. "I'm going to be a vlogger."

This was news to Reuben, but then last time they'd talked jobs, she'd wanted to be a mermaid and had been crushed to learn that wasn't a career option. He felt honor bound to reply, "You're still going to college. Videos might be hot now, but there's no long-term job security in them."

"You sound just like Toby." Nell laughed. "Like seriously. 'Nell, makeup isn't a career choice.' All. The. Time."

Her imitation of Toby's deeper voice got a laugh from the whole room.

"And I'm right." Toby looked at Reuben. "Tell her I'm right."

"Well…" He trailed off. Finding no easy way out of this predicament, he had to throw up his hands, which set both girls to giggling. And nicely lowered the tension in the room, allowing for easier small talk until Nell and Paul had to go to a doctor's appointment at a wellness center that had both traditional Dena'ina healers as well as western medicine practitioners. As they gathered up their things, Paul urged Toby to make an appointment for himself with one of the healers.

"I can take you," Reuben offered. He could understand why the family supported a more holistic approach to healthcare, and he wanted to make sure all Toby's needs were met.

"Nell will take him," Paul said firmly, looking away. "And we better hurry now. Don't want to be late."

"Go in with him," Toby instructed Nell. "And text me after."

"Yes, warden." Nell rolled her eyes on her way out the door. "Nice meeting you, Amelia. *You* can text me."

"I will," Amelia promised, then after the door shut, flopped back on the couch. "I'm so *bored*. Already."

Toby clapped his hands, a smile on his face that Reuben associated with him slipping into tour guide mode. "Did you see the bikes on the porch? You and your dad should ride before lunch."

"Dad doesn't bike." Amelia's laugh was slightly bitter, and Reuben couldn't tell whether she was using that as excuse or was genuinely put out by it.

"True, I haven't ridden in…years." Decades more like, but he didn't want to sound even older than he already was.

"You'll remember how. You don't want her going out alone, right?" Toby looked at him expectantly.

"Well…no."

"Then go on. Give it a try." Toby made a little shooing motion with his hand.

"Okay. What are you going to do while we're out?"

"At the risk of sounding like a total slug, probably nap. Trying to take as little painkiller as I can, but I'm not used to this many hours in the chair yet, and my leg's feeling it." Toby frowned, lines around his mouth and eyes deepening. Hell. He really was in pain.

Reuben insisted on helping Toby get settled back on his bed, leg up on some pillows. He tried to keep his touch impersonal, especially with Amelia lurking in the doorway, but Toby's solid flesh under his hands made him shiver in a way that had nothing to do with the cool morning air.

"Come on." He led the way outside, Amelia trailing behind him as if she were headed to the gallows.

"I'm not sure I remember how." She glared at him as she selected a purple bike. Helmets hung from the handle bars, and Reuben put one on as she did the same.

"I taught you." Reuben remembered that much. It had been a Sunday afternoon, no work, day off for the nanny. They'd laughed and laughed, no sour expressions back then.

"Like a million years ago." Amelia stomped all over that memory. "And we never did it together."

"Well, no time like the present." He forced himself to sound cheerful, not hurt as he grabbed a red bike and checked the seat height. "This can't be too hard. There's a reason for the old saying that people don't forget how to ride a bike."

All it took was thirty seconds and he was cursing that adage, wobbling all over the driveway, kicking up gravel and setting Amelia to giggling.

"Funny, huh? You try."

Marginally more successful than Reuben, she made it partway down the drive before she faltered, bike wobbling precipitously before she stopped herself with her feet. "This is stupid."

"You can do it." Reuben tried again himself, wanting to show her that he wasn't giving up. This time went smoother than his first effort, and they both wove their way to the road. "Look at the trees. And how it smells here. Nothing like this back home, right?"

"Dad. Just stop. Stop trying so hard." And with that Amelia rode ahead of him, still shaking her head, leaving him feeling silly and small for thinking she might like this.

If her attitude kept up, she'd be begging to go home soon enough, and he'd feel even more like he'd lost her. He wished teenagers came with a blueprint or study guide or something. Maybe he could ask Toby if Nell went through a phase like this. Toby. Simply thinking about him made Reuben's pulse quicken. Toby might think Reuben was the one doing him a favor, but knowing that he'd get to talk to Toby later had Reuben taking a deep breath, resolving to get through Amelia's latest funk.

* * *

"Eww. You mean I have to *touch* the meat?" Amelia stared at the bowl of ground beef like Toby had suggested she eat it raw. They were making hamburgers for dinner—seemed like an easy bet what with the grill on the porch and Amelia's professed love for beef. But apparently that love didn't extend to actually doing the work. Toby couldn't do it easily without getting his arm cast messy, so he stared her down.

"Yup. Squish, squish. I already added the seasonings. All you have to do is mix it and make burger shapes."

"I might be turning vegetarian," she warned.

"Just wait. I'll have Nell bring some moose meat from our deep freeze. You'll change your mind."

"Eww. Some animals aren't meant to be eaten."

"Tell that to my chili recipe." He gestured at the bowl. "Come on. It's not that bad."

"What's not that bad?" Reuben came in from seeing to the grill outside.

"Toby needs you to make the burgers into circles," the little liar said as she pointed to the bowl. "Can't get his cast dirty."

"Oh, okay." Reuben rolled up his shirtsleeves, revealing muscled forearms that did something to the libido Toby was trying to keep in cold storage. As did watching a competent, confident man work. Making fast work of forming a stack of patties, Reuben loaded up a plate to take to the grill. "Hope I got the grill at the right temperature. It's been years since I did this."

"We *know*." Amelia leaned against the counter. "This whole trip is like…summer camp for you or something."

"Maybe." Reuben's jaw twitched like he was having

a tough time not arguing with her. "But it's fun, right? Like the biking?"

"More like weird. But the biking wasn't *terrible*."

"High praise. Want me to check the grill?" Toby rolled toward the patio doors, more to get away from her bad mood than anything else. Reuben followed with the burgers, getting the door. This part, the cooking with Reuben, was nice. He liked feeling useful, and he'd had fun before dinner looking over maps with Reuben, talking other bike trails he and Amelia could try now that they had the hang of riding again.

While in the hospital and typing one-handed, he'd typed out a list of potential activities and experiences for Reuben and Amelia. They'd reviewed the list together, adding more things and coming up with a rough calendar of activities to try. Being back in tour guide mode felt good, like putting on a familiar sweatshirt fresh from the dryer, and he especially liked the respect he'd seen in Reuben's eyes. Impressing him with his knowledge was a nice little bonus, and a good reminder that he was skilled at this. No matter what nerves he was having about flying again, he still had this, a decade of experience no one could take away from him.

"Can you have a beer with your meds?" Reuben asked once the burgers were sizzling.

"I wish. Better not. I'm going to need to put the leg up after dinner as it is." Great. Now he sounded like the complaining teen, not Amelia. "But you go ahead. You've earned it."

Reuben returned with a large mug of ice water and a specialty brew that made Toby really wish he could drink. "You've got good taste."

"I'll save you one for once you're done with the

meds." Shoulders looser, Reuben looked a lot more relaxed out here and infinitely more attractive as he sipped his beer.

Damn. It was bad enough that Toby's body had decided Reuben was his type back when they'd been client and tour guide. But this, knowing the attraction was probably mutual and not being able to do a darn thing about it, was torture. And unprecedented too—he was far more used to feeling a spark, having a hookup, getting it out of his system and getting back to his life. This prolonged dance they seemed to be doing was as unfamiliar as it was pleasant.

Because Amelia's attitude aside, he enjoyed simply hanging out with Reuben, even with sex off the table. What with his work and family obligations, it had been a while since he'd made a friend, but that's what this felt like—deeper than flirting, laying the groundwork for something he wasn't sure he'd had before.

After a pleasant dinner of only slightly overdone burgers, he found himself wanting more of the good feelings he got from being around Reuben. Amelia escaped up to her room the second the dishes were done, and Toby let Reuben accompany him into the bedroom and set up the pillows to support his leg and arm.

Reuben seemed as reluctant to say good-night as he had the night before, lingering next to the bed. "That work?"

"Yeah. Feels weird being in bed so early. You wanna watch a movie with me or something?" He gestured at the entertainment center across the room.

"Okay." Reuben's voice brightened, as if he too had been looking for an excuse to stay. "You'll have to choose—despite liking film scores, I don't watch a lot of TV, so pick something you like." Dragging a small ornamental chair from the corner of the room over toward the bed, Reuben gave an almost sheepish smile.

"Don't be ridiculous." Toby pointed at the chair. "That chair looks all kinds of uncomfortable. This is a king. Come sit next to me."

"If you insist." An adorable pale pink flush stained Reuben's cheeks as he toed off his shoes before stiffly arranging himself on the edge of the bed, as far from Toby as he could get without being on the floor.

"I do. And relax. I won't bite, promise." Toby managed to use the remote left-handed to browse recent action movies he hadn't had a chance to see yet. "You're probably going to regret letting me pick. I'm pretty simple—give me lots of explosions. Bet you're more into thinky pieces."

"Hey, I like explosions too. I'm not *that* intellectual. Although I do think we had enough real-life adventure for this year. So maybe not that one where they're stranded."

"Point taken." Toby laughed and scrolled to the next choice. "This one's a superhero reboot—you probably saw the original as a kid, but this version looked good in the trailer."

"You calling me old?"

"Hey, you're the one who insists on acting like you're older than this comic book series." Toby made the mistake of glancing over, taking in all the ways that Reuben wasn't the least bit ancient. Those forearms. His worldly eyes. His broad, strong hands that felt so good whenever they touched. His polished demeanor, even in casual clothing. Older had never been a thing for him before, but he had to admit Reuben's appeal, especially the way he seemed far more settled into himself than a lot of the younger people Toby hooked up with.

"At the risk of proving you right, I actually did own toys and books from this franchise as a kid. You know, back in the dark ages. But I'm game for the reboot. Start it up." Finally relaxing back into the pillows, Reuben gave him a fond smile as Toby clicked on the movie. And a weird thing happened as they watched—their bodies seemed to drift closer and closer, until he could swear he could feel Reuben's warmth and smell that herbal scented body product that Toby was fast getting a thing for. He liked Reuben's nearness, but he couldn't hold back a laugh.

"What?" Blinking, Reuben looked over at him. On the screen, the heroes were plotting their next move, a quiet sequence that wasn't exactly a laugh-out-loud scene.

"Nothing." He sighed, already knowing that non-answer wouldn't fly with Reuben. "I was just thinking. Realized that I've never cuddled with a guy before."

"Really? But I thought..." Reuben made a vague gesture that Toby took to encompass sex.

"Oh, I've hooked up. But quickie blow jobs don't really lend themselves to snuggling up after. And even with women, we usually both know the score. Not a lot of hanging out."

"Ah. Well, I wouldn't say I'm a cuddling expert by any means, but you're missing out. And definitionally challenged."

"Come again?" Toby should not like it so much when Reuben trotted out the big words in that deep, cultured voice of his.

"This isn't cuddling. Even I know that much." A smile

tugged at the corners of Reuben's mouth, making him look slightly wicked, the sort of temptation Toby couldn't resist playing with.

"It's not? Maybe you should show me. Give me a better vocabulary or whatnot."

Reuben's mouth quirked, and he started to scoot closer before he abruptly stopped. "Wait. I don't want to hurt you."

"You won't. I've got my pillows of doom here. Surely we can get creative?"

"We shouldn't."

The firmness in Reuben's voice made Toby that much more determined to play. They were in this weird gray area—sort of friends, sort of roommates, no longer client and paid tour guide, and Toby's usual ethics didn't seem to apply. In fact, his brain was doing an excellent job rationalizing his desire. If they were going to be friends or roommates, they might as well be the kind that had a little fun together.

"It's a cuddling demonstration during a boring movie, not an engagement ring. Come on. Show me what I've been missing."

Face serious, Reuben considered him for a long moment, doing some sort of mental calculation Toby could only guess at. "Okay."

Reuben resumed moving closer, close enough that his body was pressed up against Toby's, a sensation Toby didn't realize he'd been craving until he had it—big body next to his, shoulder to shoulder, hip to hip. And Toby wasn't a small man, but Reuben made him feel…well, not tiny exactly. But *safe*, which was a silly thing really, to feel protected by the mere presence of that much warm bulk sheltering his body. But he did, relaxing into the contact, trusting in it the same way he'd believed Reuben when he'd said Toby would be okay. He'd kind of expected Reuben to call it good once he'd moved close enough to touch Toby's uninjured side. But he went a step further, leg overlapping Toby's but managing to stay clear of the leg with the cast. Same for his arm, which came around Toby, not yanking him closer, but *there*.

Secure. That was the right word. He felt secure in a way that maybe he hadn't even realized he'd needed until right here, this moment, this guy. He'd had massages from well-meaning partners that didn't relax him as much as this simple act of closeness.

"Am I supposed to be able to keep watching the movie?" he joked, because joking was easier than the sudden tightness in his chest, and laughing was a good way to cover how his breathing had sped up at Reuben's nearness.

"That would be the point." Reuben's voice was a warm rumble in Toby's ear. "Unless you've had enough of a demonstration?"

"No, no." Toby put his hand over Reuben's when he moved to roll away. "This is nice. Really nice."

"Yeah." There was a wistfulness to Reuben's sigh that made Toby wonder how long it had been since he too had something like this. When was the last time Toby had simply lay with someone like this, no sex in the equation? Definitely not with a guy, and maybe not since his short-lived college days. Ever since his dad's accident, he'd simply been too busy. Sex was the one outlet he allowed himself outside of work, and even that was limited. Few repeats, no relationships, nothing that could distract from his need to put his family first.

But now the universe was laughing at him, ensur-

ing that he had to take this break, and for the first time
in a decade, he could really see what he'd been missing. Little pleasures like this. A not-so-terrible movie, a
warm body, this feeling of security and safety and being
cared for in a way that he seldom let himself. He drifted
along on the goodness of the embrace, paying only the
bare minimum of attention to the movie, eyelids getting
heavier the longer they cuddled.

"You ever fall asleep like this?" Yawning, he snuggled deeper into Reuben's arms best as he could without disturbing his leg.

"Yeah." Reuben's voice held all the same yearning as
Toby's. "But we're not falling asleep."

"No?" Toby held Reuben's arm tightly so that he
couldn't roll away.

"No. Amelia might come looking for me, and it
wouldn't be a good idea for…other reasons."

"Yeah." Toby got it. Them getting involved on anything more than a friendship level would be a bad idea,
given that they needed to make the next few weeks of
proximity work and didn't need any additional awkward-
ness. But he didn't have to like it, and frankly, he was
tired of doing the right thing, the logical thing. So when
Reuben pressed a kiss to his temple that felt a lot like an
apologetic goodbye, before he could extricate himself,
Toby stretched up, found Reuben's mouth with his own.

"Please?" Pausing with his lips a fraction of a mil-
limeter from Reuben's, he let go of him so that the guy
wasn't locked into a kiss he might not want. But Toby
was banking on him wanting this as much as he did,
and he wasn't disappointed when Reuben growled low,
closed the distance between them. And like the cuddling,
it wasn't the sort of hot-and-heavy, get-it-while-it's-good

kiss he associated with hookups. Soft and almost painfully sweet, Reuben's kiss was a gentle benediction, the punctuation mark on the last hour of buildup.

Days, really, as it felt like they'd been working toward this moment from their first meeting. But it also felt like kissing a friend, something he hadn't done in a very long time, the sort of kiss where there wasn't any rush and where mutual affection rode right alongside urgent passion, tempered it so that the pace was more stroll in the park than drag race. And as it turned out, ambling along was another of those simple pleasures, following the kiss to see where it might lead. Reuben's mouth was surprisingly lush, and despite the slow pace, he absolutely knew how to kiss, exploring Toby's mouth with a thoroughness that left them both breathless.

"Need…"

"I know…" But instead of ramping up, moving toward something more urgent, Reuben backed off, soft kisses that retreated until they were nothing more than warm air on his cheek. Resting his forehead against Toby's, Reuben breathed hard for long moments that felt as intimate as the kiss had before he rolled away with a groan. "You're too damn tempting."

"How about I tempt you again?" Toby patted the now-empty space next to him.

"We should go to bed."

"Good—"

"Separately." Reuben's stern voice did things to Toby's already aching dick.

"Not fair. Now I'm all worked up and can't even use my right hand to solve it."

"Is that you angling for a handjob?" Laughing, Reuben sat up and moved farther away. "Not tonight, okay? I'm trying to be good here, not take advantage of you."

"Not tonight isn't never," Toby pointed out. "And it's not advantage if I'm asking for it."

"I don't want you thinking you need to do *anything* simply because you're staying here. And no, I'm not ruling it out, because I'm only human too. I think it's clear there's an…attraction between us. But you should probably sleep on it, see how you feel tomorrow."

"And if tomorrow I want another cuddling demo?"

"Then we'll see." Reuben rubbed the back of his neck.

The pink tint to his cheeks was enough to convince Toby that there would be more kissing tomorrow if he asked. Which he would. Because he didn't feel taken advantage of—far from it, actually. He felt taken care of, cared about. Hell, even Reuben insisting on waiting was caring. Not many people in Toby's experience would put the brakes on when he was giving a clear green light to more fun. But he got it—they needed to both be sure before they went further, because yeah, things could get awkward fast. And this other thing they were building, the friendship thing, that was important too. Accordingly, he didn't push or flirt his way into more kisses right then and there.

"Tomorrow." His voice was every bit as firm as Reuben's. Because there would be a tomorrow, and for the first time since this mess started, he was actually looking forward to it.

Chapter Eleven

"Why are you smiling? It's weird." Amelia glared at both Reuben and the coffeemaker, which was taking its sweet time brewing.

"It's a nice, sunny morning. I slept well. I'm in a good mood." All three things were true, but they were also lies as they had nothing to do with his smile as that had been him replaying last night's kiss for the hundredth time while he'd loaded the coffeemaker. But he sure as hell wasn't telling Amelia anything about *that*.

"Can I have toast this morning? I don't wanna do the whole pancake thing every morning."

"Sure." Reuben found the bread and a toaster and set both on the counter. Even if he was a little hurt that she didn't want to cook together, his waistline could agree that pancakes should maybe be more of a special occasion thing. Toby called from his doorway, which was behind the kitchen area.

"Hey, Reuben, could you give me a hand with the shower?"

"Sure. Let me get Amelia set here—"

"Even I know how to make toast. Go play nurse." Her expression reminded him of her mother when irritated, complete with the heavy sigh at the end.

"Sorry," Toby said when Reuben entered the bedroom. "I meant to have Nell help me yesterday, but then they had to leave. I'm dying to get clean and changed. I'm surprised my scuzziness didn't throw you off the... lessons last night."

"You're not...scuzzy." Unlike Reuben, who would probably have been well on his way to a full beard at this point, Toby looked only mildly disheveled. This would probably be a good spot to remind both of them that cuddling had been a mistake and that they probably shouldn't repeat it. But what came out was "I wasn't put off. At all."

"Good." Toby gave him a grin that started wide, then went tight. "This isn't a ploy to get in your pants either. I hate asking you for help."

"It's why I'm here," Reuben reminded him. "And it's no problem. I picked this house in part because of the shower being walk-in. Do the casts come off or do we need to cover them?"

"Cover. The hospital gave me a few, but I could use help with securing them in place."

"No problem." Working together, they covered both Toby's arm and leg casts with special plastic sleeves before heading into the bathroom, which was wide enough for the wheelchair to easily maneuver. Reuben set up the shower chair while Toby inspected their handiwork.

"I look like a freezer meal ready to microwave. Man, I can't wait until they upgrade me to being able to remove the casts for bathing."

"I hear you. But in the meantime, need help with getting the shirt off?"

"Yeah." Toby's mouth twisted. "Should have gone for a button-down, but Nell didn't bring me many of those. My wardrobe isn't as fancy as yours. I got the shirt on, but it takes me like twenty minutes of tugging to get it off."

"That's what he said." Reuben couldn't resist the tease.

"Hey, now. I'm trying to be good." Toby's laugh was rich and hearty and echoed off the tiled bathroom walls. "You said maybe tonight though..."

"We'll see." Reuben already knew he wouldn't be able to say no to more kissing if Toby asked, but he'd meant it about giving Toby room to think.

"I like the sound of that." Toby grinned at him as Reuben helped him out the T-shirt. His broad, muscled shoulders contrasted with his lean torso with its miles of golden skin punctuated with tawny nipples that pebbled up from the cool air in the bathroom. "All the more reason to get squeaky clean."

"Behave," Reuben said, to himself as much as Toby, trying to curtail his impulse to warm up Toby with his hands and mouth. The bruising around his torso was enough to give him pause as well—he'd ended up without broken ribs, but he still looked battered enough that Reuben wanted to soothe away any lingering hurts.

"Oh, you're enjoying this too, admit it. Come on, what would you be doing back home?"

"Probably a meeting of some sort." Reuben had to laugh, because Toby was right. As it was, he'd had to sneak a few email replies in before breakfast, dealing with some questions that just couldn't wait. Disconnecting from work was proving way harder than he'd thought, and Toby was the perfect distraction. "Not washing down a hot guy."

"I'm hot?" Toby gestured at his plastic coverings.

"You know you are." Reuben shook his head, but when Toby didn't laugh, he added, "You're hot—you. Your laugh, your smile, your voice. Those shoulders. Your injuries don't change that."

"Maybe." Toby snorted. "Can't wait to heal, though."

"I know, but I'm being serious here—your attractiveness isn't measured by how well you recover. I'd still find you hot regardless of any…limitations. Permanent or otherwise."

"Thanks." Toby's cheeks darkened, and he looked away. "Can you do the shower controls? I like it warm but not burning."

"Sure." Reuben adjusted the water temp while Toby wiggled out of the loose shorts he'd been wearing, raising up enough to shove them off without getting out of the wheelchair. Reuben worked hard to avoid glancing down at Toby's groin—much as he wanted to, he was trying to be a helpful friend not the old perv desperate to get Toby in bed. "Do you want me to stick around? Do your hair?"

"Clean hair sounds nice, but it'll get you wet too."

"I can always change."

"And there's one other problem too." Toby's unrepentant grin had Reuben's skin prickling.

"Oh?"

"Anytime you touch me, I'm half hard."

"That's…a problem." Reuben still didn't look, not trusting himself to keep his hands to himself despite his resolve. "Ready to transfer to the shower?"

"Boy. You have some self-restraint." Toby reached out, letting Reuben help him swing from the wheelchair to the shower chair.

"Comes with age," Reuben said dryly. "That and my kid is probably still in the kitchen."

"Okay. That reminder helped my issue." Chuckling, Toby arranged himself under the shower spray. "Damn. That feels good. The nurses in the hospital helped me clean up some, but nothing beats a real shower."

"I bet." Watching him stretch happily had Reuben's own dick taking notice, making him wish he was the one giving Toby reason to make those pleasurable noises. To distract himself, he handed Toby the soap, which was lined up next to other travel size toiletries on a little shelf in the shower.

"Thanks." Working quickly, Toby soaped all the essential parts before rinsing and turning his back toward Reuben. "Okay. Shampooing one-handed might be hard. Guess I'll let you help."

"Sure." Reuben poured some shampoo into his palm then lathered up Toby's dark hair, unable to resist the temptation to massage his scalp.

"Mmm. That feels good." Toby leaned into the touch. "Way better than the nurses."

"Gee, thanks. High praise." Reuben kept the massage up a little longer, then helped him rinse.

"Hey, I'm trying to be good and not ask you to rub… other things with those magic hands of yours."

"When—*if*—we get to that point, I can guarantee you it's going to be for way longer than a two-minute shower jerk-off. I like taking my time. A lot." Reuben turned off the shower before Toby could manage to change his mind about fooling around.

"When. It's definitely a when." Toby grinned as he held out a hand for a towel. "And I'm down for slow.

I'm good at quickies, but I'm not opposed to trying it your way too."

"Good. And I'm not saying quickies don't have their place, but if I get someone I like in bed, I'm not letting them up before they're a sweaty wreck."

"These days getting me into bed isn't the problem—it's getting *out* where I need a hand." Toby laughed as he dried off before letting Reuben help him back into the wheelchair. They worked together to unwrap the plastic from his casts. Then, wearing the towel, Toby rolled back into the bedroom and grabbed clean clothes from the dresser under the TV. "I used Dad's grabbing tool to unpack yesterday. Pretty handy. Speaking of, I think I could use it in the pantry while you guys are out, start a chili for dinner. Tell Amelia I promise no moose this time."

"That sounds good." Reuben helped him pull on a clean T-shirt, hands lingering a little longer than they needed to. The plan Toby had drafted called for him and Amelia to take the bikes to a nearby fairly flat trail that skirted a river.

"Is it bad if I say I hope the ride wears her out and sends her to bed early again?" Toby looked about as hopeful as Reuben's fluttery insides felt.

"Ha. Judging by how bleary she was this morning, she was up with that computer game, not sleeping. But I hear what you're saying."

"Good." Toby's eyes met Reuben's, and judging by the heat there, Reuben bet he wasn't the only one who had spent too much time replaying that kiss. And despite knowing that he should push all such thoughts from his brain and focus on the biking and Amelia, he knew he'd spend all day counting down to the next kiss, hoping that Toby didn't change his mind about wanting a repeat.

Saying he could make chili—a dish he'd made on his own since his early teens—one-handed had been decidedly optimistic. First, he'd gotten a late start on the meal thanks to a post-lunch nap. His pain was doing better, but the combo of meds and poor sleep had him napping more than he had since toddlerhood.

Thanks to his dad's grabbing tool, he got all the cans lined up on the counter. But then he spent the next half hour wrestling the manual can opener. Seriously. It awkward trying to use it with the wrong hand from a seated position. He hated being thwarted by a hunk of metal, but he was about to give up and make an easier meal with the ground beef when his phone buzzed. Nell.

"Tell me you're close by," he said in lieu of greeting.

"Actually, yes. On my way back from another job interview. Why? You need something?"

"It's stupid." He rested his head against the stainless fridge, hating that he couldn't do a simple task on his own anymore.

"I'm ten minutes out. And my very wise big brother always says there are no stupid favors."

"Yeah, but I meant that for *you* and keeping you safe—like when you need a ride back from a party."

"Well, now it's our turn to help you. Whether you like it or not. There in a few." She ended the call, and sure enough, his Explorer pulled into the long drive in short order.

Nell strode into the house, a tight black skirt and white shirt that he supposed passed as interview clothes. "So what is it you need help with?"

"To open some cans so I can make chili for dinner." He led the way to the kitchen area.

"Oh, the sugar daddy has put you to work?" Her voice was light, but Toby's hands still clenched at the barb.

"Don't call him that." Despite knowing Reuben was gone, Toby still glanced around.

"What? I'm just saying…if the designer shoe fits…"

"It doesn't. He's just being a friend. I've made friends with former clients before." He hated how defensive he sounded.

"Sure, sure. But he is into guys right? Because if he's a closet case, he does a really bad job hiding how he'd like to eat you up with a spoon."

"Nell." He gestured at the line of cans. "Help, please. Cut the snark. Yes, he's bi. But he's not… This isn't some sort of *arrangement*."

"Good. He's old."

"He's not that old." Toby couldn't explain why he felt honor bound to defend Reuben.

"You *do* like him." Practically using a singsong voice, she gave a little shimmy as she made quick work of opening the cans. "But seriously, too old, too rich, too out-of-towner. You can do better. I've got friends—"

"Who are, no offense, *kids*. I'm not taking up with a twenty-year-old." Not that Toby exactly made a habit of checking IDs for one-night stands, but he did have some standards.

"Well, and clearly you're not taking up with anyone like this." She gestured at his injuries.

"Yeah." Toby swallowed hard. Reuben had been pretty convincing that morning, saying how Toby was attractive as he was, and the night before his mouth certainly hadn't seemed to have a problem with Toby's banged-up state. But damn it, Nell and her inherent bluntness had a way of making him doubt all Reuben's niceness and worse, his own worth. Not being able to work, to provide for his family—hell, he couldn't even make chili on his own. It sucked.

Teeth grinding, he tossed the ground beef in the skillet along with some onion he'd hacked into uneven chunks earlier. If he'd known Nell was coming, he would have saved that task for her too, because now his cast probably smelled of onion. Yuck. And his noninjured arm was starting to ache almost as bad as the one in the cast from overuse. Working out some of his unease over Nell's teasing, he attacked the meat with a spatula, breaking it up.

"Feels weird, salmon season about to start and you not around. Hannah's going to try to come down for a weekend, help with the catch and the smokehouse. I'll make sure we get the family limit though, even if she can't come." Like most women in their family, Nell was experienced at dip net fishing, taught by their mother, same as Toby and Hannah had been, and for all her love of pretty things, she could gut and prep fish as well as any of them.

"Yeah, it's...different." Even knowing that Nell was more than capable of handling it, he still felt a strange pull in his chest. This was the first year ever that he'd miss fishing. He took a lot of pride in keeping their freezers well stocked with salmon, moose, and other meats to last the winter. Anything that kept down the bills was good, but being out there fishing with his sisters or hunting with an uncle, he felt more connected to their mother's memory. "I'll see if I can at least stop in. There has to be something I could do to help."

"You can help by getting better. You need me to help you change clothes while I'm here?" Managing to sound both helpful and put out at the same time, Nell didn't look up from washing her hands at the sink.

"No. Reuben helped me with a shower earlier." He regretted the admission the second it was out.

"Oh, hello. Sugar daddy has seen you naked and it's still not like that?" She shook her head, long, dark hair swirling about her shoulders. Taller than Hannah and shorter than him, she'd always had a certain innate glamour about her that set her apart from the rest of the family.

"It's not. And if you call him that where he can hear, I'll..." He tried to think of a suitable threat. "I'll take my car keys back."

"Calm down. I'm not that mean. Just having fun with you. Honestly, I wouldn't mind a sugar daddy of my own. Some rich guy to buy me stuff—"

Toby cut her off with a warning growl. "You better not. You need to focus on finishing school. Grades, not guys."

"Yeah, yeah. How about you not give me a hard time about how the spring classes turned out right now, huh? I'm doing you a favor."

"You can't keep switching majors and dropping classes. It's time to get real about your future."

"Being a trophy wife doesn't count?" She batted her eyes at him, but he had a hard time telling how serious she was.

"Get a degree. Then you can be whatever kind of wife you want—preferably the kind that waits until forty to tie the knot—but you know, knock yourself out. After you've graduated."

"You're no fun. And be glad you already got your shower—I might be tempted to turn it on full-blast cold to match your soul."

"Drama much?" This was old territory for them—he loved Nell with a fierceness he couldn't put in words. But he'd been eleven when she came along, a total surprise for the whole family, and they'd been complete opposites in temperament from the very first. Even as a tiny toddler, she'd had the ability to flounce from the room while shooting a scathing look worthy of any diva three times her age.

"I'm just saying. You need to loosen up."

The memory of last night's kiss teased his brain. He'd been plenty loose then. And fun loving. It didn't matter what Nell said about Reuben being too old and rich. Maybe Reuben was exactly what Toby needed. And what he didn't need was his baby sister sticking her nose into his life when her own still needed so much help.

"I'll loosen up plenty when you and Hannah are done with school. Speaking of, make sure you don't miss any fall registration dates."

"Yes, Tobias. Wouldn't want to miss my chance to retake that math class." She collected her black leather purse from where she had tossed it near the couches. "I'm going to get on home to Dad. And before you start in on me with another round of reminders, we've been managing okay. Only had frozen pizza three times last week—"

"Nell."

"Joking, joking. It was twice. And he's fine. I even unclogged the sink without you. You forget that we're capable too." She shook her finger at him. And she did have a point. Their mother had raised her and Hannah both to be strong, self-sufficient women. Nell might tend toward the flighty, but he understood why she chafed at his nagging and worrying, and duly chastened, slumped in his chair as she continued. "You need to relax. Like seriously."

Again the image of Reuben crept into his mind. He doubted he'd ever be able to drop the sense of responsibility he felt for her and Hannah, but the idea of stress relief was very appealing. He'd seldom been more relaxed than he'd been the night before, lying in Reuben's arms.

"I'll try," he said, both thinking of Reuben and not wanting her to leave angry. They both knew how fast life could change, and no matter how much they argued, he always made a point to try to leave things on a good note. "Sorry if I'm coming down hard about school. It's important, but you know I love you, right?"

"I love you too, Tobes. Maybe I'll stop back by when your suga—*friend's* daughter is around, do her makeup."

"That would be nice of you. Drive safe." He saw her out as far as the porch, then returned to the kitchen and the browning meat. As he dumped in the seasonings and the cans of tomatoes and beans, his irritation over Nell's goading faded, replaced by little flutters of anticipation over the coming night. If Nell had a point—and he wasn't willing to concede that—then relaxing with Reuben, setting his worries aside for a couple of hours sounded about perfect. Now to just hope that Reuben was on board with that plan, hadn't decided that Toby was more trouble than he was worth.

Chapter Twelve

Toby had the chili done and keeping warm by the time Reuben and Amelia came through the front door, sweaty and laughing.

"That smells amazing." Reuben's praise was more than enough to make up for the hassle of getting Nell to help and figuring out how to cook from the wheelchair without ending up with a lap full of chili.

"Was it a fun day?" Toby asked as Amelia shook her helmet hair out.

"It was okay." Her crooked smile said that it had been more than okay but that she wasn't about to give Reuben that kind of credit. She was a lot like Nell at that age, more stubborn than sensible.

"Do I have time for a fast shower before we eat?" Reuben glanced down at his shirt, which was looking a little worse for wear. And Toby was all in favor of him being freshly showered for any post-dinner fun, but of course he couldn't allude to that with Amelia right there.

"It's chili. It'll keep," he said lightly, trying to tell Reuben with his eyes what he couldn't out loud.

"I guess I'll shower after dinner. I don't trust this place to have enough hot water for both of us," Amelia complained as Reuben made his way to his room, which like Toby's was located behind the kitchen area.

"Good plan. My sister was by earlier—she said she might stop back sometime in the next few days to do makeup with you. That would be cool, right?"

"I guess." Amelia flopped in one of the dining chairs. "You don't have to be nice to me, you know."

"Uh…" Toby wasn't sure what to make of that pronouncement.

"It's not going to make my dad like you more or something." Her tone was world weary. "Mom's dates are always bringing me books and stuff. Dad's too. That Dan guy always asked about my school."

"Heaven forbid someone be nice to you." Toby couldn't resist a little sarcasm. "And I'm not a date. Just a friend. One who happens to have sisters. But if you want me to tell Nell to forget it—"

"No!" Amelia's eyes went wide, as if she hadn't expected to be called on her rudeness. "She can come."

"And since I don't have to worry about impressing you, I'll be sure and tell her to bring moose meat. Maybe some porcupine or bear if we're feeling fancy…"

"You're a dork." She pulled out her phone, effectively dismissing him until Reuben emerged with wet hair and in fresh clothes.

"Can you help me dish up?" Toby asked. "I can't reach the bowls."

"Sure." Reuben smelled fabulous as he reached around him to get three bowls down. Looking more casual than Toby had seen him, he was in shorts and a gray T-shirt that while logo-less looked softer and pricier than most of what was in Toby's drawers. "Thanks for the idea of that trail—it really was perfect. Not too hard. Amazing vistas. Even Miss Cranky had to stop to take some pictures for her mom."

"Just proof of life for her." Amelia didn't even look up from her phone as she shot down Reuben's enthusiasm.

"Didn't tire you out too much?" Toby kept his voice low even though Amelia was still engrossed in her game.

"Nope." Air charged, their eyes met. Held. Oh yeah. Reuben hadn't forgotten about later or changed his mind.

"Did you know that movie from last night has a sequel already?"

"Does it?" Reuben asked lightly as he dished up the chili, but his eyes were simmering with heat far more delicious than anything Toby could cook up.

"Uh-huh. We should watch it. Tonight."

"We'll see. I need to see what Amelia wants to do after dinner."

Toby groaned, but he also really did admire Reuben's commitment to his kid. "You're a good dad. And I'll be up late. Got a nap earlier."

"I'll keep that in mind." The back of Reuben's neck turned dusky pink.

Taking pity on him, Toby turned off the thinly veiled flirting during dinner, instead asking about the ride. "You want to do another ride tomorrow or should I find you a hike? That's if the sun holds—I saw the weather earlier and there's a chance of rain."

"Ugh. I hate rain," Amelia groaned. "Especially when there's no mall to escape to."

"So that's a yes on getting a fishing license? Or maybe kayaking?" Toby refused to give in to her bad mood. He'd been adding to the plan and calendar for her and Reuben. Having had tougher customers than one cranky teen, he refused to give up on finding *some-*

thing she was enthusiastic for, hopefully more than simply makeup with Nell.

"Anything that gets us out of the house," she snapped.

"Amelia," Reuben warned.

"What? I'm just saying the truth. It's boring as—"

"Language," Reuben said over her mumbled curse. "And we'll hope for no rain."

"Do I have to help with dishes?" Amelia continued the pissiness after dinner.

"Yes," Reuben said firmly before Toby could say *no*. "We didn't cook, so we clean. Do you want to watch TV with me after dinner? There's a cupboard of board games over by the couches too."

"Eww. Dad, no. Board games are for babies. And nerds. I just want to game on my laptop. I'm about to level up, and it's easier on the computer than on the phone or tablet."

"What's the game?" Toby asked as Reuben started loading the dishwasher.

"You wouldn't like it. Part of the *Space Villager* universe. There are ships you can race and planets to explore. The phone part is mainly just managing my colony."

"Sounds cool. You should show us sometime." Reuben hit Start on the dishwasher.

"Dad. You're such a dork." Amelia gave them both a dismissive stare on her way upstairs.

"Glad to know I'm not the only dork. She tried that line on me earlier too." Toby waited for Reuben to finish wiping down the counter before he headed toward his bedroom, confident Reuben would follow.

"I guess we can be dorks together." Reuben laughed self-consciously. Toby transferred himself to the bed before Reuben could come help. Instead, Reuben hung out by the door, some sort of indecision warring in his eyes.

"Come on." Toby patted the bed next to him. "You did the good dad thing. She's occupied with her game. You've earned a little relaxation."

"Is that what this is? Relaxation?"

"Sure. Nell said earlier that I need to unwind." He conveniently left out the part where Nell didn't approve of Reuben. "And you do too. You're here. I'm here. This doesn't have to be complicated."

"So like…a summer fling?"

"If that's how you want to classify it." Toby shrugged. He didn't usually need to spell out the parameters for his hookups. And he wasn't used to this sort of negotiation where something was happening beneath the surface, something more than their words—this wasn't simply about what they called this thing between them. But hell if he knew how to articulate all his churning emotions and wants that he refused to admit, even to himself.

"I don't want to hurt you. Physically or emotionally." Reuben's expression was far too serious, eyes narrow, mouth firm.

"Physically, how about you actually come over here and we see what works? We did fine last night with the pillows." He went ahead and grabbed one, stuck it under his leg with the cast. His leg always seemed to hurt worse later in the day and at night, but the prospect of more alone time with Reuben worked almost as well as a pain pill. And no way did he want to be groggy for this, so he'd avoided taking one with dinner. "I promise to tell you if something hurts."

"And emotionally?"

"Emotionally, I'm an adult. I'm not expecting anything more from you than a good time. And I'm doing this because I want to. Well, that and I need cuddling lessons." Trying to lighten the mood, he grinned at Reuben.

"That you do." Reuben's tongue darted out to lick at his lower lip before retreating. Sexy as fuck. Toby barely suppressed a groan as Reuben finally, mercifully closed the door. And locked it.

Oh, hell yes. Toby's pulse sped up as Reuben made his way to the bed. His feet were bare, and even they were sexy, big and broad and strong. He stretched out next to Toby, but didn't move to kiss him.

"Start the movie," Reuben ordered.

"Seriously? You want to watch something *now*?"

"Background noise in case Amelia comes back down. Also, I meant what I said earlier—I don't like to rush. We're not on deadline here. We'll get there."

Toby was tempted to grab Reuben, tug him over for a kiss that would surely goad him into the fast pace Toby was more used to. But he hung back, finding the remote and queuing up the sequel to last night's movie, some part of him liking listening to Reuben and curious to see where he might lead. He was rewarded for his patience by Reuben scooting closer as the movie started, arranging them so that he was sort of behind Toby, broad chest a pillow for Toby's head, both of them somewhere between sitting and lying down.

"Gonna be hard to kiss you like this," Toby grumbled, even though he really did like lying like this, completely surrounded by Reuben.

"No, it's not." Reuben punctuated his words by dropping a fast kiss on Toby's mouth. "I can kiss you just fine. And I like holding you like this. It feels less likely to jostle your leg."

"Screw my leg."

"Wrong body part. We really do need to up your education." Reuben laughed, then pointed at the screen. "Watch the movie."

"You're mean."

"So Amelia tells me," Reuben said mildly. And it quickly became apparent that he intended to make watching as difficult as possible, running his hands up and down Toby's sides and nuzzling his hair.

"Tell me you're not planning on quizzing me on the movie." Toby stretched, seeking more contact from Reuben's roving hands.

"Nope." Reuben's breath was warm against Toby's ear right before he gently bit it. "No test, but stop trying to drive." He pushed Toby's shoulders down with firm hands, staying his wiggling around. "No bonus points for getting off before the bad guy reveal."

They were lying in such a way that he could feel Reuben's hardness against his back, but Reuben continued his languid assault, seeming in no hurry despite being clearly turned on. But there was novelty in this, in not being the one in charge deciding where the encounter would go next. And Reuben had all but promised him an orgasm, so he tried to relax and just enjoy discovering new sensitive spots that made his dick jump. Like the inside of his uninjured arm and the side of his neck—places he'd never given much thought to before Reuben lit them up with little touches. Ditto his ribs, but when Reuben slipped a broad hand under his T-shirt, Toby couldn't help groaning his approval.

"Shh. We've got the TV on for a reason, remember?"

"No moving, no moaning. You really do want to kill me, huh?"

Reuben's chuckle washed over him like another caress. "I think I lied. I do have a kink. I love this, love edging and making my partner wait and beg."

"Well, as long as one of us is happy…"

"You're liking this, and you know it." Reuben palmed Toby's aching cock through his shorts in a much too fleeting touch.

"Do that again, and I'll like it more," he countered. Reuben wasn't wrong. He did love this, loved the banter and the laughing. And even the waiting, all the delicious anticipation for when and where Reuben might touch him next. Tugging Toby's shirt up and off, Reuben continued to explore his torso, trailing fingers over his collar bones and down his sternum.

"Here?" Reuben gave an experimental tweak to one of Toby's nipples. And while they'd never done much for Toby before, his skin was sensitized enough from the playing that he shivered and hummed his approval. Seemingly emboldened, Reuben started playing with them in earnest, pinching lightly and flicking until Toby went from shivering to panting.

"Please…"

"This?" Using only one blunt fingertip, Reuben teased all along Toby's waistband, dipping almost low enough to reach his straining cock but not quite.

"Come on. Please." Toby was perfectly capable of shoving his own shorts down, but something had shifted inside him, given Reuben control.

"You want something?" Reuben licked at Toby's neck.

"Touch me. Please."

"Hmmm." Reuben made him wait through several more neck and jaw kisses. "You gonna let me do it my way?"

"Yeah. Anything," he promised, breath coming in little pants as Reuben pushed his waistband down. It had been easier to go commando than to try to wriggle boxer briefs over his cast, a choice he was doubly grateful for as his hard cock sprang free.

"No moving. Don't want to hurt your leg. Just let me get you there." Reuben ghosted a hand over Toby's cock, not quite gripping it and not nearly enough contact.

"More."

"Shh." Reuben's free hand rested on Toby's bare stomach, a warm pressure holding him in place. "Let me make you feel you good."

"I do," he gasped, surprised at how true it was, every nerve ending singing for this man. Gradually, Reuben tightened his hand, soft teases becoming more purposeful strokes, but lazy, so lazy. Ignoring the command not to move, Toby stretched his neck, searching for Reuben's mouth. "Please."

Reuben rewarded his begging with a searching kiss, plundering Toby's mouth with his tongue. Welcoming the invasion, Toby sucked hard on Reuben's tongue, earning a low moan from Reuben. Good. Maybe the guy wasn't made of granite after all.

"Want to touch you. Can't guarantee I'm much good with the wrong hand, but I wanna get you off too," Toby babbled as Reuben continued to slowly work him.

"Nope. You said I could do this my way, and I want to focus all on you. Love getting you close, making this last, and left hand or not, you touching me right now would end this in a hurry."

"That doesn't sound terrible." Toby gave a shaky laugh that ended on a soft moan as Reuben did a twisty thing with his stroke that had his back arching.

"No, don't strain." Reuben pushed him back down. "Let it happen."

"Need…faster."

"Like this?" Reuben sped up only to back off as soon as Toby's breath matched his strokes. "This good or you like it slicker?"

"Slick is nice, but I don't…oh fuck, do that again. Don't have anything unless there's lotion in the bathroom."

"I grabbed that earlier." Reuben shifted briefly, then produced a travel-size bottle. "When I showered. I might have had some fun imagining this…"

"Yeah? Did you get off?" Just thinking about that had Toby even more on edge, even before Reuben touched him with a single slippery finger, tracing the length of Toby's cock before he replied.

"Got hard. Didn't come. Told you. I like edging when I've got time to play." Reuben managed to sound almost indifferent to the prospect of orgasm, and his fluttery touch on Toby's dick said he still wasn't in any hurry to bring Toby off.

"I haven't edged like this since I was teen amusing myself with jerk-off games," Toby admitted. "These days I usually just come, get on with my day or with falling asleep."

"That's a shame. I mean, I'll totally admit being too busy to rub one out some days, but I'll happily forgo a little sleep or take an extra five minutes in the shower to make it truly good." Reuben returned to something of a more purposeful rhythm but as before, he slowed as soon as Toby started chasing his fist. "No moving, remember? Don't want you hurting yourself."

"What hurts is my cock," Toby groaned. The lotion

had subtle minty overtones, a scent he was forever going to associate with Reuben and this moment. "Need to come."

"And you will." Reuben bit his ear before adding, "Just not yet."

"Bastard. I think you're right. You are a kinky fucker." He had to laugh even as he complained because this really was the sweetest torture he'd ever had. "Faster. Please."

"That's it. Tell me what you need."

"This. More. You. Please." Pushed beyond making sense, Toby didn't recognize his breathy, needy voice. "Want to come."

"I know." Reuben's voice was soothing, like they truly did have all the time in the world. The slide of his cock through Reuben's slick fist made lewd squelching noises, joining both of their rough breathing in filling the room. On the TV, the movie continued, but all Toby's senses were zeroed in on this guy, on the way he was undoing Toby, seam by careful seam. "Tell me when you're close."

Another stroke. Two. Toby bit his lip to keep from crying out. "There. Fuck. There."

And the fucker backed off. Because of course he did, more of that infinitely patient voice. "Breathe. Breathe. Don't force it."

Toby honestly wasn't sure he knew any other way to orgasm than chasing it headlong like a wave he was determined to ride, hard and fast, tensing and straining—all the stuff that made the good feelings happen that much faster. Waiting patiently for the ocean to reach him simply wasn't his style. But that seemed to be what Reuben was urging, what with his whispered commands and

barely there touches. He was masterful at giving Toby
the sort of driving pace he craved only for as long as it
took for him to be on edge again, then playing and teasing until Toby really was begging.

"Please. Please. Reuben. Need it."

"A little more," Reuben coaxed, finger sweeping
along the top of Toby's balls.

"Oh fuck. Fuck. Do that again."

"This?" Reuben's voice as he repeated the motion
was exactly the hot, dirty whisper Toby hadn't known
he needed. "You want to come?"

"Yes. Please. Get me off."

"You can come." Reuben said the words like he was
sharing a filthy secret, but his pace stayed maddeningly
slow.

"Can't. Faster."

"Yes, you can." Every sensation was magnified—the
rasp of Reuben's stubble and teeth against Toby's neck,
the weight of his hand holding Toby close, the sound of
his voice, the scent of his shampoo and the lotion. His
vision glittered, and blacking out before he could orgasm seemed a real risk. And he opened his mouth to
tell Reuben that, but what came out was a low, keening
sound that Reuben swallowed with a kiss.

After all that, all the touching and teasing and
games, it was the simple feel of Reuben's mouth crashing down on his that finally sent him tumbling over the
edge. Whatever the opposite of strained was—puddled,
perhaps—he did that, collapsing against Reuben, utterly boneless as he came and came. Felt like gallons,
coming so hard his balls actually ached, that he trem-
bled with each piercing aftershock until he was a limp

wreck. Using his last reserve of energy, he managed what he hoped was a smile.

"Fuck. I…never…fuck." Okay, so words were still failing him, the ability to make sense beyond him at that moment. He settled for pulling Reuben in for another kiss, this one slow and soft, and more than a little sleepy, at least on his part.

"Good?" Reuben's voice was smug as he pulled away, using Toby's T-shirt to clean his hand and Toby's stomach. And chin. Because damn.

"Yeah. So good." Toby couldn't hold back the yawn. "Sorry."

"It's more than okay. You sleep. Love knowing I got you that relaxed and spent."

Spent. Wait. There was something missing from this equation, and his addled brain tried again to find words. "You didn't… Let me…"

"I almost did when you finally went over. And now, I'm going to take a second, super-long shower while you sleep, and I'm going to replay that whole thing about five times."

"That hardly…seems fair." He wasn't really making much of a case for helping, what with yawning midsentence and all.

"Oh, it's very fair. Trust me." Reuben dropped a tender kiss on his head, rolling away before he covered Toby with a blanket. "You sleep."

"Tomorrow…"

"Maybe tomorrow I'll let you help."

And on that yummy thought, Reuben was gone with a click of the door, leaving Toby counting down until they could do this again. Really, though, he should take offense at Mr. Bigshot with his "I'll let you…" decrees.

Toby was a full-grown adult and he didn't need the sort of take-charge caretaking Reuben offered. But oh how he *wanted*. Craved. And he should know better than to go craving someone like Reuben, but hell if he could stop it, especially not wrung out like this, falling asleep with the taste of Reuben's mouth still on his lips.

Reuben overslept, which he almost never did. And as it was a vacation of sorts, he supposed it wasn't the worst thing in the world, but it did mean that he missed his chance for a quiet moment with Toby alone. And not just to see how he was feeling after the previous night. While Reuben did want to make sure he hadn't pushed too hard with their play, he also was simply craving a little one-on-one time, maybe some flirting over coffee.

However, when he finally emerged, far blearier than his hours of sleep would suggest, Toby and Amelia were already at the table with plates of toast in front of them.

"Amelia made the coffee." Toby pointed at the half-full pot. "And the cinnamon toast."

"Oh. Uh…thanks." Far be it from Reuben to understand mercurial teen moods and the rare bouts of helpfulness they produced.

"*Amelia* was hungry." Ah. And there was Reuben's prickly princess. "And cold."

"Should I raise the heat?" He went to the thermostat located near the pantry door. The house had central heat, but they hadn't really needed it.

"Yeah, and can you turn off the rain too?" Amelia glared at him like he alone was responsible for the dreary drizzle coming down outside. Unlike the dark skies of rainy days on the east coast, though, the sun was out while it poured, which took some getting used to. Maybe someday Reuben would be able to see rain without remembering those awful hours of waiting to be rescued, fearing for their lives, cold and wet. But today wasn't that day, and a shiver raced through his body.

"You okay?" Toby asked.

"Sure. Just don't like rain." No way was he confessing to either of them that he still had flashbacks to the crash. He helped himself to a cup of coffee, added his usual scant amount of sugar, and almost lost his eyeballs on the first sip. "Wow. That's uh…"

"It's strong." Toby gave him a wry smile that said he hadn't wanted to critique Amelia too harshly.

"It's how Mom likes it. And last year's nanny did too." Amelia's stiff spine and pouting lips dared him to object.

"It's…fine. Like an espresso almost." He discreetly added some water to his mug while making himself some toast.

"The rain wouldn't be so bad except the internet keeps going out and the TV too—must be some sort of dish service thing." Amelia sounded like this was a tragedy of epic proportions.

"Oh no, you might have to talk to us." Reuben faked horror simply to watch her roll her eyes.

"I'm going to go try it again." She stalked off, leaving her dishes behind. He should call her back, but he was loath to get in another battle with her.

"Morning." Toby gave him a much warmer smile once Amelia was upstairs. "Sleep well?"

"Like a tranquilizer dart hit me."

"Darn." Eyes dancing, Toby kept his tone playful even as his voice was low. "I was hoping you tossed and turned, wishing you'd taken me up on my offer to help."

"You were more than half asleep when you offered,"

Reuben pointed out. "And I told you, that was all about you. But don't worry, I didn't go to sleep…frustrated."

"I want to hear all about that later." Toby licked a stray grain of sugar from his lips, sending heat sparking straight to Reuben's groin. "Or maybe you can give me a demonstration?"

"Maybe." Reuben had never been into performing for partners, preferring to focus instead on getting the other person off, but judging by the heat in Toby's eyes, he liked the idea of a show very much. "But I'd rather—"

The clatter of feet on the stairs had him straightening back up and swallowing down the sexy proposal he'd been about to make. Sure enough, Amelia reappeared in a matter of seconds.

"Internet is still out. I rebooted the modem and everything. And I was *this* close to finishing a quest in multiplayer."

"Multiplayer. You play with kids from school?"

"No. Just randos who crew my ship and work my colony. And before you start, yes, I know not to give my name or location or anything like that. And my handle and avatar don't even show that I'm a girl. In the game, I get to be Escape_Velocity badass space pirate, not Amelia, queen of the rejects table."

"I'm glad you're being safe online. Keep that up, okay? But was school really that bad? We chose that middle school because of its excellent reputation."

"All the cool classes can't make up for kids being jerks." She looked far older than fourteen as she shrugged. "Mom says it'll be better at high school. She goes on and on how much she loved that school, but if you ask me, being with the same group of girls twenty-four/seven doesn't sound like much of an improvement."

"You're going to boarding school?" Toby asked.

"Yeah. Me and three hundred of my soon-to-be-besties in the middle of nowhere upstate New York. Should be fun." Amelia's dour tone made it sound like anything but. "But hey, I bet we'll have internet, so win."

"You're super brave," Toby told her. "I don't think Hannah or Nell could have gone off at fourteen. I know I couldn't have."

"Maybe. But my mom did it, and her mom did it, so you know, it's expected." Amelia's world-weary voice pierced something soft in Reuben's chest. But right as he was about to probe further about her friend problems and reservations about school, she looked around the living space. "Anyway, there has to be something to *do* around here."

"Board game?" Reuben figured it was worth offering again. "Are there any movies in the cupboard? I know it's old-school, but I can see if there's a DVD player or something."

"I'll see. I'm going on a hunt before I die of boredom. Maybe I'll find like a secret passage or something." There she was again, a glimmer of the little girl Reuben remembered, an all-too-fleeting phase when she'd loved hide-and-seek, treasure hunts, and exploring new places.

"I hope you do." He had to work the words out past a strangely tight throat. Watching her race around, opening doors and cabinets warmed his chest, like a visit from a beloved ghost from the past. And even when her search took her back upstairs, he stayed quiet, deep in his feelings. And Toby seemed to get that, not pressing him into more talking.

"Hey! Look what I found!" Amelia came back downstairs toting a large plastic box with a handle. "It's a sewing machine. There's a bunch of sewing supplies and beads and other craft stuff in a cupboard under the eaves upstairs with a note to help ourselves. Guess the owners of the house like old-school hobbies."

"Bring it here." Toby pushed the plates aside and patted the table next to him.

"You know how to sew?" Amelia's tone turned skeptical, but she brought the machine over and popped open the plastic case.

"Sure. My mom was a fabulous seamstress. She was well-known for making regalia—ceremonial clothing for gatherings and dances like moose hide jackets and tunics that are made by hand. But she also had a machine and did plenty of everyday stuff like alterations, bags, aprons and stuff like that to sell. It was her business, one that let her stay home. She made sure all three of us knew how to sew, so we could help."

"But you're a *guy*."

"Yup. Didn't matter to my mom. Traditionally, men and women around here are both taught to sew because it could save your life in the wilderness. And trust me, the machine doesn't care what gender you are. Now was there any material up there? Let's try it out."

"Be right back." Amelia dashed up the stairs two at a time.

"Thanks," Reuben said to Toby, chest filling a way it hadn't since he'd eavesdropped on Natalie doing story time for Amelia as a toddler. "You don't have to teach her, but I haven't seen her this enthusiastic in a long time. So thank you."

"No problem." Toby fiddled with the controls and the spool of thread on the machine until Amelia returned quickly with some brightly colored fabric.

"Will this work?"

"Absolutely." Toby smiled at her. "Now I can't do the foot pedal with my cast, so you'll have to do that. Think of it as good practice for driving in a few years—it's sort of like giving the machine gas."

"Okay. I can do that." Amelia pulled up a chair in front of the machine, following Toby's instructions closely as they picked a scrap of material to practice on and got the machine set. Watching them together made Reuben happy in a way that was difficult to quantify. And it made Toby attractive on a different level, seeing him being so patient and kind with Reuben's kid.

"Hey, I'm doing it!" Amelia crowed as she produced a line of neat stitches. "When can I make something for real?"

"Now." Seeming to remember that Reuben was still in the room, Toby turned toward him. "Can you find us some scissors? I think she can do a basic bag, and we don't need a pattern for that."

"I can do that." Grateful to have something to do, he located scissors in a drawer in the kitchen and brought them back to the table where Toby and Amelia were deep in negotiations about bag size and shape.

Sensing he'd become invisible, Reuben dug out his phone, made sure nothing was brewing back at the office that required an immediate response. With each day that passed, he felt more and more removed from the life he'd spent over twenty years building, and seeing no new messages was a bit of a letdown if he were honest with himself. Didn't they need his input?

Hell. Amelia was right. He *was* a workaholic who didn't know when to shut it off. But he was here to change that, so he wandered over to one of the stuffed bookshelves in the living room. As he browsed the paperbacks, listening to Amelia and Toby was like inhaling sunshine—a balm he hadn't known he'd needed. His minor irritations and restlessness faded. He'd sat in many a high-powered meeting, but this right here, rainy day with his kid and the guy he liked, was about as perfect a moment as he could remember. And he couldn't wait until later when he could show Toby how grateful he was to him for giving them this experience.

Chapter Thirteen

Toby hadn't had much time to simply hang out in over a
decade—most of his time spent either working or doing
things for the family. When he had time for friends, it
was often sporadic and hurried, so spending a lazy, rainy
day hanging out with Reuben and Amelia felt weird.
Not bad. But weird. He was supposed to be working.
He should be gearing up for salmon season, for the glut
of tourism that summer always brought to the Kenai.
Griff had sent an early morning text asking questions
about a tour group he was covering for Toby, and the
guilt over not being the one heading out had made it
hard to answer.

Griff had also said they were still waiting on the official crash report so that Annie could move forward with
an insurance claim for the damaged plane. More guilt.
More worrying. What if they took his license? What if
Annie grew tired of holding the job for him? What if the
findings made it hard for him to get the workers' comp
money that his family desperately needed.

His churning brain added to the weirdness of the day
spent trapped indoors, but teaching Amelia the basics
of sewing and answering her endless stream of questions both about sewing in general and about native tra-

ditions surrounding it was a good distraction from his
mounting worries. And he liked the connection to his
past as well—all the memories of helping his mom, the
way she'd always put the family first, even as her business grew. She'd have been proud at how much he still
remembered.

Even after the internet returned, Amelia remained
focused on her projects, which was cool to watch.

"I'm going to need more material." She bit the inside
of her cheek, head tilting as she considered the last of the
fabric that she'd brought down from upstairs. "But I bet
there's not a fabric store around this place."

"You'd be wrong. There's a place in Kenai that Mom
liked. But our garage is practically a fabric store on its
own. I still haven't sorted all Mom's stuff. Just wasn't
ready." He took a deep breath, not sure if he'd ever be
ready to dispose of the last links to his mom. Silly, but
all the plastic totes meant something to him, something
real and tangible. "Tell me your favorite color, and I'll
have Nell bring some when she comes with her makeup."

"Purple," Amelia and Reuben said at the same time.

"Okay. Texting Nell now. She never really liked sewing, but she still does traditional jewelry like from porcupine quills from time to time. If you ask her, she might
show you."

"Cool." Amelia sounded genuinely enthused, which
was a really nice change. Toby wasn't sure he could have
coped with another black mood from her while his own
was so murky.

As he made arrangements for Nell to stop by, he sent
up a fervent wish that she not pick up on any new energy
between him and Reuben as the result of the night before. Much as he was dying for a repeat that night, pref-

erably one where Reuben got off too, he wasn't ready for another round of Nell's teasing and judgment. And staying on the down low with Amelia around made sense too.

Besides, hanging out platonically wasn't as boring as he might have thought. Despite jumping for his phone when his email notifications dinged, Reuben seemed content simply being around them. It was cute and cozy and domestic and made Toby want all sorts of things he had no business wanting. Reuben wasn't staying. Toby was never leaving, and anything more than a friendship would be beyond foolish. Besides, Toby needed to focus on getting back to work quickly, not on the way his pulse danced thinking ahead to later. Repeat hookups weren't supposed to make his stomach flutter like this.

But each heated look or little flirt when Amelia was out of the room had exactly that effect on him. However, Nell's arrival put an end to the flutters.

"Dad didn't come?" he asked as Nell arrived with a sack full of different purple fabrics and her carefully organized makeup case. She appeared ready to settle in for the remainder of the rainy day.

"I left him napping with food for later. He said he was too…tired to come." Nell's eyes darted to Reuben briefly before returning to Toby. Fuck. Unlike most of their outgoing relatives and friends, his father had always kept to himself, and while not surprising, his instant dislike of Reuben was more than a little disheartening. "He sent me with salmon from the freezer though. Said we owed your…friends."

"Thank you." Reuben accepted the fish from her. If he'd picked up on the tension, he did a good job of hiding it. "I'll look up some salmon recipes on my phone for dinner, unless one of you can suggest something?"

"Just don't overcook it." Nell laughed. "Toby's a better cook than me. Ask him how to season it." After she admired Amelia's growing stack of bags and pillow cases, she spirited her upstairs for an impromptu makeover.

Which left him and Reuben to put together a dinner, but it wasn't like they could sneak off for a make-out session, no matter how much Toby craved it. The sound of the giggles coming from upstairs was enough of a deterrent to anything more than some teasing as they got the salmon ready for the oven.

"You'll have to open the salmon package," Toby told him. "I don't want fish juice on the cast. If I stink, you might not want me around later."

"Oh, I'll want you around." Reuben gave him a pointed look that went a long way to chasing out his worries over his dad's disapproval and everything else. "Might have to wash you down, but that's hardly a hardship."

Laughing, Toby took the broccoli to the table. Dicing things one-handed was tricky, but he could handle breaking the vegetable into florets.

"Nell won't do anything…permanent, will she?" Reuben sliced up an onion, already better with a knife than he'd been a few days ago.

"Nah. No bleached hair or anything unless you say okay. She might be as stubborn as Amelia when she wants to be, but she's got a good heart where it counts."

"Good. I appreciate both of you today. You particularly. You've been great with her. Way more patient than I could be."

"Sometimes kids learn better when it's not their parents. I taught Hannah to drive because she was driving my mom nuts. She was the model student for me though, so you never know what's going to work."

"Yeah. It's great seeing Amelia excited about anything. I sent some pictures of her sewing to her mom just to prove she's not on the game night and day here. She's always on Amelia to get a hobby."

"She's fourteen. I'm pretty sure I didn't have many productive hobbies back then either. Cut her some slack."

"I'm trying. She's just so different from me—I was all about grades and scholarships and my basketball team as a means to a good school." After adding the onion, Reuben stirred together the mustard and other ingredients for the sauce for the salmon.

"I bet you were totally a born leader in school. But let her be her. I have to remind myself that with Nell all the time, but you can't change personality. Much as we might like to."

"Very wise." Reuben gave him a bemused smile, but his eyes were thoughtful, like he was truly listening.

Toby was surprised how much he liked cooking with Reuben. It was totally different from trying to get food on the table for his dad and the girls when they weren't at school, which was often a lonely, frustrating enterprise. He could cook, but having someone to cook with made the mundane fun. And he liked the contrast between how take-charge Reuben could be, especially in the bedroom, and how well he took suggestions from Toby when he encountered something unfamiliar like making rice from scratch.

Working together, they had a decent dinner ready right as Nell and Amelia came back downstairs, faces looking more ready for a prom than a humble supper.

But Amelia was positively glowing, so Toby supposed they could chalk Nell's visit up to a huge win.

"Thanks," he told her in a low voice when she took the seat next to his at the table. "You made her happy."

"See? I can be a nice person."

"And humble too." He tried to tell her with his eyes that he really did appreciate her. She'd been every bit as moody as Amelia as a teen, and seeing her morph into something a little more mature was as gratifying as it was scary. She stuck around after dinner long enough to help with the cleanup and to get Amelia set back up with the machine, helping her to cut material for a basic apron before heading home.

"Tell Dad I'll call him," he said as he followed her out onto the deck.

"Good luck getting more than a two-minute conversation out of him." She laughed. "And next time I come, we really should talk about bills."

"Hell. Yes. Bring what you've got or text me pictures of the mail. I'll figure things out."

"Don't stress, Tobes." She patted his cheek before heading to the car.

Don't stress. If only it were that easy—here he was with mounting worries and nothing to do but wait and hope he healed. How was he supposed to relax when he should be taking care of his family? He needed something to do with all this restless energy.

Reuben. Yeah. Sex. Sex was exactly what he needed.

Unfortunately, Amelia industriously sewing rather than being upstairs meant no alone time with Reuben. Which was fine and he was an adult, not some pouty teen.

"I need to get my leg up," he said to Reuben who was

on the couch with his book, some detective novel. His leg had that late-day ache that seemed unavoidable even as he did his best to not need the heavy-duty pain meds.

"Do you need help?"

"Nah." Help would inevitably lead to flirting and wanting things they couldn't have with Amelia right at the kitchen table. "But I'll probably be up awhile, watching some TV or whatever."

He hoped his tone conveyed that he wouldn't mind an interruption later, and judging by Reuben's sharp nod, he got the message. Toby did end up watching TV, actually paying attention to the show, a paranormal drama that Nell had gotten him into. However, he was several episodes in and no Reuben had appeared, so he pulled off his shirt, turned off the bedside lamp and got under the covers for one last episode before trying for sleep. Halfway through, though, there was a gentle tap at the door and Reuben's head appeared, shadowed in the light from the hall.

"Oh. You're asleep." Reuben started to back away.

"No, no, come in."

"I was on my way to bed after Amelia finally finished her project, but I..." Stepping into the room, Reuben shut the door.

"You were horny?" Toby guessed hopefully. "This the roommate version of a booty call?"

"No!"

"Liar." Toby beckoned him closer. Yes, this was exactly what his weird mood needed, easy banter and a healthy infusion of sex.

"Okay, well not *just* that. More like I wanted to say good-night, check on you..."

"And you wanted a repeat. It's okay to own that. In

case I didn't make it really clear today, I'm totally down with more happy fun time together."

"Happy fun time?" Reuben sat down on the side of the bed.

"Yeah, you know, the sort where we both get naked and get off." When Reuben laughed, he added, "So how about you help me out with the naked part—shirt off. Pants too."

"Uh…" Reuben seemed strangely uncertain. And instead of taking off his shirt, he reached for the alarm clock on the nightstand.

"What are you doing?"

"Setting an alarm—it's late, and since you're so hell-bent on us both coming, I figure the chances of me dozing off are high. I want to make sure I'm back in my own bed before morning."

"I like a planner." Rolling toward Reuben, Toby tried to tug him under the covers with him. "But seriously, lose some clothes. You didn't even take your shirt off last night."

"With good reason. Even banged up, your body looks like something out of a swim team calendar. I'm more… dad bod than six-pack."

"I like your 'dad bod' a lot." Shoving Reuben's shirt up with his uninjured hand, Toby dropped a kiss on Reuben's back. "For real. I never thought it would be a thing for me, but I like that you're bigger and taller than me. Love your big hands especially. They felt so good on my body. And I've been dying to feel your fuzzy chest."

"Okay, okay. You win." Reuben pulled away long enough to remove his shirt and strip down to boxer briefs. Even in the low glow from the TV, Toby liked what he saw before Reuben slid under the covers next to him. Broad back, wide chest, strong arms. And he liked what he felt even more, running his hand down Reuben's chest and stomach heading for—

"None of that." Confident, in-charge Reuben was back, and he wasn't having Toby's attempt to go straight for his cock. "I've got plans for you first."

"Oh, do you? Gonna show me what you did in the shower last night?"

"Even better. I'm going to show you what I thought about." Reuben loomed large over Toby, fuzzy chest rubbing against Toby's arm and side before he dipped his head and claimed Toby's mouth with a bold, assertive kiss. It was a kiss that said he knew what Toby liked and that he intended to give it to him—but only on Reuben's terms. And damn if there wasn't something incredibly seductive about that, about letting Reuben have control over his mouth, over the direction of the encounter.

"Much as I loved stroking you off, I spent part of my shower kicking myself for not spending more time discovering what your skin tastes like." Balanced on his forearms, still keeping his weight off him, Reuben licked Toby's neck.

"Fuck. Not gonna complain if you decide to remedy that." Toby used his uninjured hand to stroke Reuben's bare back before shifting to spread his legs more. "You're not going to hurt me if our bodies touch, promise. Want to feel you."

Feeling a hard cock next to his, even through shorts, was still enough of a novelty that the thrill outweighed the logistics of navigating his casts. And when Reuben let himself settle in, chest hair prickling against Toby's smoother skin, cock riding right along Toby's hipbone, Toby exhaled as if he'd been wanting this for decades.

Needing this weight, this pressure to relieve some essential want he hadn't even realized he possessed. Completely surrounded by Reuben made the next meeting of their mouths that much more intense, made it that much easier to just relax into whatever it was Reuben had planned.

And when Reuben shifted again to Toby's neck and shoulders, he let his eyes drift closed, gave himself up to seeing where Reuben's hot mouth would land next. For such a refined guy, he was surprisingly oral. And thorough, kissing and nipping at Toby's shoulders until they were putty, then turning that same level of attention to his chest. He had a feeling where Reuben was heading with this, but for once he didn't feel the need to gallop to the finish line. If Reuben wanted to spend long minutes on his pecs and nipples, then Toby was here for that.

Luckily the TV was still going, cover for the soft moans he simply couldn't hold back as Reuben gently rolled to the side, scooting even lower to pepper Toby's stomach with kisses. It was odd how Toby didn't really associate big, powerful men like Reuben with liking to suck cock—probably said more about Toby and his assumptions than about Reuben, who seemed unconcerned with any expectations as he licked all along Toby's waistband before pushing his shorts down and carefully off over the cast.

"You're much less...demanding tonight," Reuben chuckled against Toby's thigh. "Doing okay?"

"Oh, yeah. More like I had to admit that your way works—the whole buildup and edging thing was pretty awesome. So tonight I'm kinda just going with the flow. I figure eventually you'll let me get off."

"When you ask nicely." Reuben lightly bit his hipbone.

"Oh is that how it is? You like me begging, don't you?"

"Guilty." Sucking gently, Reuben laved Toby's balls with his tongue before continuing. "And you love it."

"Fuck. Do that again."

"Ah, there's the impatience." Reuben laughed, but went ahead and indulged him, spending some serious time exploring Toby's balls with his mouth until Toby's whole sit-back-and-wait plan was in shreds.

"Please. Come on. Please." Awkwardly, he used his left hand to stroke Reuben's short hair.

"Please, what?" Reuben blew warm air across Toby's sensitive wet skin, making his belly quiver.

"My cock. Suck my cock." He wasn't used to asking, not like this, all needy and restless, like he might leap out of his skin if Reuben didn't suck him in the next thirty seconds. And Reuben, damn him, seemed to revel in his state, licking up the shaft of his cock, but stopping just shy of the head before retreating again. Over and over, he licked and teased, lighting Toby up. On the TV, dramatic music played, adding to the rising tension in his body.

"Please. Getting close. Please."

"Yeah? You think you could come just from this?" Reuben ghosted his tongue along the underside of his shaft, finally teasing the crown, still both too much and not nearly enough.

"Keep...going." He tried to laugh but it came out all strangled.

"Mmm. Fuck, you are delicious when you come undone." Big hands coming to hold Toby firmly in place, he at last took Toby's cock fully in his mouth. And even without much ability to rock or thrust, Toby's balls still lifted, every muscle tightening as pleasure circled closer. Unlike last night, he was more ready for Reuben to let him get close like this before backing off to slow slides of his mouth, but it was no less devastating, the build and retreat.

"Let me come. Please. Hand. Tongue. Mouth. Don't care. Need to come."

"Mmm." Reuben humming around his cock was almost enough to get him there, but something in Toby was waiting, hesitating. Wanting—no *needing*—approval.

"Please. Need it."

Reuben pulled back enough to ask, "You want to come for me?"

"Fuck. Yes. Please."

"God, I love it when you beg." Reuben's hand, sure and strong, took over for his mouth. "That's it, go ahead. Come for me."

That. He'd been waiting for that, for that moment of encouragement. Permission even. And once granted, it was as if every cell sprang into action, whole body vibrating with so much energy it was a wonder he wasn't levitating, Reuben's hand on his hip the only thing holding him in place as orgasm rocketed through him. The pleasure was so intense that it made him see a flash of white light before he collapsed back into the mattress.

"Not sleeping," he managed to gasp out.

"Didn't think you were." Reuben's laugh was its own source of pleasure, so much that Toby had to laugh with it, especially as Reuben dabbed at his stomach with what was probably one of their shirts.

"Don't think you're escaping." He tried to be stern, but it came out more breathless than intended. "Come up here, let me return the favor."

"Logistically speaking, we should probably try that in better lighting, preferably when I'm not so on edge." Reuben scooted back up the bed to pull Toby tight against him.

"*Logistically speaking*, most guys don't turn down a blow job." Toby leaned over to bite at Reuben's bare shoulder before stroking his fuzzy chest. "But as long as you get off, I'm happy."

"Good." Reuben shoved his box briefs down far enough to reveal a cock that was impressive even in the dim glow of the TV. Not that Toby got to see much of it before Reuben was stroking it.

"Hey, aren't I supposed to be doing that?"

"No. Kiss me." A hitch in his voice, Reuben's composure finally seemed to crack. Toby had a feeling that Reuben's request for a kiss had as much to do with him not wanting to be watched as with desire, but Toby indulged him anyway. He kissed him soft and slow, letting Reuben's hunger ramp the kiss up.

"Fuck. That was so good. You got me off so hard." Toby whispered against Reuben's lips. Dirty talk wasn't a particular talent of his, but he wanted Reuben to feel as good as he had. He explored Reuben's chest and abs with his hand, discovering that his nipples didn't get a reaction but that stroking his lower stomach made Reuben inhale sharply. "You close?"

"Yeah. God, you're so hot when you let go. Love your sounds…everything." Reuben's head fell back and his hand sped up.

"Trust me, it's mutual. Wanna see you go. And fuck, you're packing. Wanna play with your big cock."

"Here." Reuben grabbed Toby's hand, led it to his

balls, his bossiness making Toby's pulse surge like he hadn't just had the orgasm of his life. "Close."

Toby swept his thumb along Reuben's heavy balls as his mouth came in for another kiss, this one more urgent. Feeling the friction of Reuben's hand brushing against his fingers was an unexpected turn-on.

"Yeah, that's it. Jerk that cock." He supposed he could play with Reuben more, encourage him to edge, but he was too eager to see him come, anticipation tensing his muscles almost like he was about to come again himself. "Come for me."

"That's…" Reuben trailed off as his face contorted into a grimace, shoulders pushing into the mattress as come splattered his stomach, some dripping onto Toby's fingers.

Unable to resist, he brought his finger to his mouth. "Hot. Next time we're figuring out the *logistics* for me to able to suck you."

"Next time?" Reuben cleaned up with the shirt, then gathered Toby close, more of the cuddling that Toby was fast starting to crave as much as more sex.

"Yeah, Rube. Next time. As in the time after this one. There's no reason why we should spend the rest of the summer denying ourselves when this is so damn good."

"I guess not." He didn't sound particularly certain, but he also didn't let go of Toby, which seemed like a win.

"Listen, I'm not saying we go telling everyone our personal business. But this? Late at night? No reason not to go there. Frequently."

"You're incorrigible."

"You like it."

"I do." Reuben gave him a solemn kiss on the forehead then yawned. "I was right. So tired now. You wore me out."

"Sleep. I'll shove you when the alarm goes off."

"Do that." Reuben yawned again, clearly on the verge of drifting off. But Toby lay awake a little longer, the unfamiliar sensation of someone sleeping next to him, being held close like this, both disconcerting and wonderful at the same time. Back in college, he'd always had roommates, making sleepovers difficult, and spending the night had only grown more complicated once he moved back home. So this was an unusual thing, but surprisingly not unwelcome. In fact, the only difficult thing was going to be convincing himself to give it up. Which he would have to do. Someday. But right then wasn't someday, so he pushed that thought from his brain as he snuggled in closer, trying to save up all the good feelings for when he'd need them later.

Chapter Fourteen

"At least it's raining again." Amelia gave Reuben a cheeky smile as he parked the SUV in front of the fabric store. And it wasn't pelting rain as much as sleepy drizzle—the sort of summer rain that cooled things off, but wasn't a major hindrance. And apparently was a boon to teens looking to get out of physical activity. She'd already convinced Toby to change the itinerary from a rock climbing class to shopping with a side stop at a trail. "Bet you won't make me hike on the way home."

"Probably not," he admitted. Even his newfound enthusiasm for outdoor activities had its limits. Much as he'd enjoyed everything Toby had thrown their way with his itinerary planning from easy mountain bike trails to kayaking trips and whale-watching boat tours, soggy from rain wasn't one of Reuben's favorite states and still reminded him too much of being stranded.

And besides, as with most days latterly, he was in something of a hurry to get back to Toby, who had stayed behind because he had a physical therapist coming by and he wasn't sure how wheelchair friendly the store layout would be. Over the past couple of weeks, he had improved at navigating short distances with a walker, which remained challenging with his broken arm, but still he used the chair most often.

As they entered the store, which was in a low-slung, older building, Reuben had to admit Toby had been right—narrow aisles cluttered with sewing notions and bolts of fabric at all sorts of unpredictable angles. Paradise for Amelia and her new obsession, but full of hazards for the mobility impaired. He'd never given much thought to accessibility before, but seeing the world through Toby's eyes was illuminating. And humbling.

"Should I make something for Toby?" Amelia asked, seeming to sense the direction of his thoughts. "Think he'd wear an apron? Or maybe I could do some sort of bag for the wheelchair back? Like a big pocket?"

"That I think he'd love. And that's very thoughtful of you. I know you were…skeptical of this arrangement to start with." He followed her to a display of northwest-themed fabrics with moose, reindeer, and trees featured prominently.

"Eh." She shrugged before picking up a bolt with salmon jumping out of tiny lakes. "He's not that bad."

"I think he'd take that praise. And he might like that fabric. Or maybe something with dogs—he's mentioned the dog he had growing up." Luckily, Toby had mentioned the dog a few times in dinner table stories, and not just in their late-night conversations.

"He has good ideas sometimes. Like the kayaking." For a kid who claimed to hate all things athletic, Amelia had taken to kayaking like a natural, and had forgotten to be sullen the entire trip, marveling over the otters and other creatures they'd gotten to see. "And I like his stories. Like when he talks about his grandmothers and their traditions. Or his sisters growing up. He's fun to listen to."

"He is." Reuben had to temper his response, because his soul enthusiastically agreed with her—listening to Toby talk was one of the true pleasures of this whole trip. He'd enjoyed all the activities Toby had planned for them, but the quiet time around the table, the three of them eating, was what he liked best. "Do they have fabric with food pictures?"

"Food? Sure. But doubt they have Toby's beloved moose meat on fabric though." Her laughter tickled long-ignored parts of Reuben's soul. He liked this new cheerful side to her and liked the purpose that sewing seemed to have given her. Turning to another display, she clapped her hands. "Oooh! Cake fabric!"

"That would work." Reuben didn't really have much opinion on fabric, especially not bright pink fabric with birthday cakes dancing around, but he was trying to be supportive of her new hobby.

"Speaking of cake, you never got much of a birthday, did you?"

"I got rescued. That was more than present enough. Got the chance to spend the summer with you. Met Toby." He hadn't really meant to slip that last part in, but it was too late to recall the words.

"Maybe I could talk Toby into helping me make you a cake. A do-over birthday." She put the cake fabric in her basket.

"I don't need a fuss, but I'm not going to turn down dessert."

"Of course not. Who turns down cake? What's up with you guys anyway?" Seemingly indifferent to his answers, she moved onto to a display of threads and needles.

Struggling to catch up with her mental leaps, he took a minute before replying. He'd been both dreading and expecting this question for a week or two now.

"What do you mean?" He kept his voice neutral. "We're friends."

"Friends." She shook her head at him. Nell had taught her some sort of complicated side twist for her curly hair that she'd been wearing everywhere lately. "Friends don't finish each other's sentences."

"We do that?"

"All the time. Especially when cooking. He'll reach for something and you're already handing it to him. It's cute. And you watch a lot of TV together."

"That's because you ditch us at night for your game," he said lightly.

"*Dad.* He's got you watching superhero shows now. And liking it. Admit it, you guys are a thing."

"I'm not exactly sure we're a *thing*," he hedged. Toby dodged most attempts to talk about what they were doing, brushing it off as fun and blowing off steam and agreeing with Reuben's assessment that this was some sort of summer fling. And really, who wanted to have state-of-the-relationship talks in the middle of an already limited-duration fling?

Except this didn't really feel like any casual relationship he'd attempted before. He genuinely liked Toby—liked dozing off next to him, thought about him first thing in the morning, looked forward to meals together, and the late-night conversations that weren't all just a cover for more make-out sessions. He supposed friends-with-benefits was the closest analogy, but it wasn't one he'd make to Amelia.

"You're a thing. Like you and Dan were a thing. And Mom and that investment banker last spring. Ugh." She pretended to shudder. "He was creepy. At least Toby doesn't talk through his nose, and his eyes are normal sized."

"Normal eyes are good." He had to stifle a laugh because Natalie famously did have a taste for money and influence over looks in her dates. "And okay, if it *was* like Dan and me, would that be a huge problem for you?"

"I guess not." She added a bolt of fabric with small robots on it to the basket. "I mean he's already living with us. It's not like you have to pay the nanny so you can have sleepovers with him. What do I care if you kiss him or whatever? Just like not all mushy in front of me, because that's kinda gross. But if you have to make out with someone, I guess he's not a *terrible* choice."

"I'll take that as resounding approval coming from you. And duly noted about mushy stuff in front of you. I don't think you have much to worry about there. In fact…" He paused, floundering around for how to tell a fourteen-year-old to keep something confidential.

"Keep it on the down low?" Laughing, she put a pack of multicolor bobbins next to the fabric she'd already picked out. "I've got you. I'm not a *baby*. I'm not going to go blabbing." Frowning, she dropped her voice. "Is he not out?"

"That's not it. It's more that we *are* friends, and we're only here for a short time, and some things are private."

"Ooh. Like a secret boyfriend. Some kids at school had those—like everyone knew they were a thing, but they wouldn't admit it to anyone because they didn't want people to make a big deal."

"Something like that." He wasn't sure he liked being compared to how eighth graders conducted relationships, but he also wasn't sure he had any better explanation for what they were. Another thought popped into his head. "Did *you* have a secret boyfriend? Or person?"

"Ew, Dad. Gross. I don't want a boyfriend. Or girlfriend. Or whatever. They have opinions and expect stuff and you have to change to make them happy and—"

"Breathe. If it's the right person, you don't have to change at all." He was surprised at how true that was. But with Toby there weren't any expectations beyond Toby's professed desire for "happy naked fun time," and Reuben didn't feel like he had to change who he was to fit what Toby needed. With Natalie, he'd felt pressure to be the perfect husband and dad and to achieve the kind of success that made her happy. And with Dan and other lovers since, he sometimes felt the need to live up to what they wanted in the bedroom or to fit some image of what they wanted. But with Toby there was none of that, and it made hanging out together among the most relaxing times in his life.

He still missed work occasionally, missed being in the loop on big deals, and missed his old friends from time to time too—lunches with Craig, passionate arguments over contract terms with Leticia, but there was something undeniably calming about being around Toby.

"But sometimes you do change, even if you didn't mean to." Amelia sounded resigned.

"Decent point." People did change. He had. Some nights he lay awake wondering what it would be like when he went back. Was he still the same guy? Did he want to be that guy anymore? He just didn't know. "And if they expect *stuff*, you don't have to go along with it, and that probably means they're not the right person either. The right person will wait—"

"Can we not have a sex talk in the middle of a fabric store?" she said in a harsh whisper. "I meant more they'd expect me to game less, pay attention to them more, be all…squishy-happy-touchy."

"Squishy-happy-touchy?"

"You know. Like couple stuff. Like you and Toby do even if you say you don't. You touch his shoulder or his head, and you sit close on the couch, and you're *nice* to each other."

"Having someone to be nice to isn't the worst thing in the world. In fact, it can be pretty darn wonderful." Doing things for Toby, making him happy, fulfilled Reuben in a way that he hadn't been in years. "Your opinion on relationships may change in the next few years."

"Maybe." She didn't sound particularly convinced and there was something uncertain in her voice, so he put an arm around her stiff shoulders.

"And if you don't, that's okay too, and that's valid. Not everyone is into relationships or wired a certain way. Whatever—*whoever*—you are is more than enough for me."

"Thanks." She bit her lip before pulling away to browse a row of marked-down fabrics. "Do I have a budget here?"

Getting that she needed to change the subject, he nodded and did some fast mental calculations to come up with a number that made her smile but would still force her to make some budgeting choices. He spent the rest of the visit being her assistant, carrying bolts of fabric to the cutting table and trying to soak up her happiness, do better at living in the moment with her, not let himself get carried away with worries over going back to work, fitting in there after a summer here, and especially not letting himself dwell how right Amelia had been—he and Toby did fit together remarkably well. But thinking about his feelings—and their consequences—was a recipe for a bad mood, and Amelia deserved more from him.

They made it home right as Toby's physical therapist, an older woman with ash blond hair and teal glasses, was leaving.

"How's he doing?" Reuben asked her.

"Good. Good. Of course, we'll know more when he has his follow-up in Anchorage with the specialists in a few weeks. I'm looking forward to the doctors giving him the all clear for more weight bearing."

"Me too." Toby rolled his way to the door, sweaty but smiling. "No offense, Connie, but I'm ready to move on from stretches. If they give me a walking cast, that would be a huge step forward."

"Yes, it would." Connie gave him a pat on the shoulder. "And like them or not, keep doing the stretches." She turned toward Reuben, adding with a wink, "Keep him in line for me."

"Will do." Reuben had every intention of giving Toby a nice massage later as a reward for all the physical therapy work, but he wasn't going to say as much in front of Connie and Amelia, even if Connie did seem to assume they were a couple.

"Take care!" Connie headed for her truck.

"What smells so good?" Amelia's head tilted, voice decidedly suspicious.

"It's moose roast with potatoes in the slow cooker. Really basic recipe, but Dad always likes how it turns out. And Nell was nice enough to bring some meat by."

"Nell eats moose?" Amelia's mouth quirked. Her hero worship of Nell had reached epic proportions with her quoting Nell's opinions on hair and skin care frequently. Based on their talk earlier, Reuben didn't think it was a crush as much as a need to have a stylish role model who paid attention to her and made her feel important and worthy.

"She does. Porcupine. Grouse. Clams. Halibut. If Mom cooked it, she'd try it, same as the rest of us. My mom shared the Athabascan belief that women who aren't elders shouldn't eat bear meat, so that wasn't on our table, but everything else was fair game. And porcupines are so easy to hunt, even Nell can bag one for dinner in an emergency."

"I draw the line at porcupine." Amelia gave a comical shudder.

"It's a delicacy," Toby teased. "And she had good news—she's picked up a part-time job at a salon in Homer, working reception for them. I was hoping she'd find something more related to her classes, maybe in an office or something, but she's excited for this."

"That's great." They'd all been following Nell's seemingly endless job search the past few weeks. She had a lengthy list of things she didn't want to do, which made searching harder. "And she'll have plenty of time for offices later. When I was her age, I worked a summer on the Jersey shore. Some of my best memories."

"You? Not behind a desk?" Amelia sounded skeptical, so Reuben told her and Toby stories from that time while they dished up the food. He liked working together like this, Amelia setting the table, Toby telling him how to finish off the slower cooker dish, and the two of them making fast work of a salad and some bread for the side.

We feel like a family. The realization crept into his brain, and once planted, bloomed into a full-fledged longing. It was silly, really, wishing this summer could drag on indefinitely. Time would march on. He'd give the firm an answer one way or another on the buyout, end up back east either way, and Amelia would head off to school, and the summer would fade into pleasant memories, not unlike that long-ago time on the shore. This wasn't real life—simply a pleasant interlude, but oh how he wished it could be a peek into the future instead of a memory to be stored for the lonely days that loomed for him.

"Hey, I have a favor to ask," Toby said as they settled in at the table.

"Sure." All that longing had Reuben in a particularly indulgent mood.

"Day after tomorrow, Nell has a long day of work scheduled, and so I thought I might see if she could drop off Dad on her way to work, then stop here for dinner on the way back. I know I shouldn't be inviting company—"

"Of course, you should. This is your place too. Your family is welcome here whenever. And I know you miss your dad."

"Yeah, I thought it would be nice to hang out with him, maybe watch one of the documentaries he likes, then cook something to celebrate Nell's job."

"Sounds like a great plan. And if there's any other company you want at any time—friends from work or whatnot—you should have them over. Or have me take you to them. I don't want you to feel isolated here." He knew full well that Toby's father wasn't a fan of his—had caught whisperings between Nell and Toby to that effect—but if Toby needed to see him, then Reuben would make that happen for him.

"Thanks." Toby nodded sharply, but his eyes softened. "Appreciate it. And I don't. But it might be nice to get out—maybe if you guys want to bike a flat paved trail, I could come along, see what I can do in the chair. Might be nice just to see the sun."

"Absolutely," Reuben said quickly before Amelia could put her opinion in. The last thing he wanted was Toby feeling cooped up or like he couldn't ask for what he'd like. Maybe this was just a summer fling, but it was important to him that Toby feel valued and supported. Doing nice things for him made Reuben feel great, but this was less about indulging Toby and more about making sure Toby feel like an equal, respected partner in this thing. Because he was, and that was essential to them having any sort of future—

Wait. He had to stop that thought right there. They didn't have a future, only an end date on the calendar. Damn it. However, Reuben could so clearly see now that he wanted one, wanted more of these meals that felt like family, more nights talking and holding each other. A summer wasn't nearly enough time for everything he wanted from Toby.

"I didn't need a babysitter today," Toby's father grumbled from his spot on the couch. "Not sure what you and Nell are about with your worrying."

"Maybe I missed you," Toby said lightly as he queued up a history documentary series that his dad was a huge fan of.

"Ha." His dad gave a mighty snort. "Cushy place like this? Doubt you're missing much."

"You'd be wrong." Toby tried hard to keep from getting defensive. But it was the truth—he had missed his father, more than he would have thought possible. After years living at home, he'd grown used to seeing him all the time, his shows on in the background, his food in the fridge. "And I miss work too."

"Even flying?"

His dad sounded more curious than skeptical, and it was a question Toby had fielded from a lot of different people. So far as everyone seemed to think he'd developed a phobia about flying after the crash. Hell, he asked it himself, every single day. Could he fly again?

He liked to think that he had too many years of loving the sky, loving being up there, in control, to let one rainstorm steal that love from him, but he honestly wasn't sure. He still had nightmares some nights after Reuben returned to his own bed, dreaming about the uncontrolled descent of the plane, the helplessness making him wake up sweaty and confused.

But he couldn't admit any of that to his dad. The family needed him working again. Fast. Bills were mounting, and whether or not he'd have the gumption to get in the cockpit was the least of their worries.

"Yeah. I'll be ready to fly again as soon as they clear me."

"Good. That's the right attitude. Annie's right to hold that job for you." The firm set to his jaw reminded Toby of his dad's quiet expectations that he'd succeed back when he'd been Amelia's age. It was nice having someone believe in him, even if the accompanying expectations did get a little heavy after a while.

"And it's not just the paycheck. I even miss the craziest of our clients. Miss being active. And useful."

Reuben and Amelia were out visiting a wildlife sanctuary, so he felt comfortable confessing his restlessness to his dad. He didn't want Reuben feeling bad that he was bored. And it was a weird thing, being happy with Reuben and his time here, but also itching to get back to work. He loved hanging out with Reuben and Amelia, but it wasn't the same as having that sense of purpose that work gave him. And if there was one person on earth who would get how he was feeling, it was his dad.

"I hear you. Been what? Decade now, and I still miss work. Disability check doesn't replace that wanting to be out there. Your mom used to say that work wasn't a measure of a man's worth, but it's…hard." Tone solemn, his dad looked away, staring out the picture window at the sunny afternoon.

"Yeah."

"But you'll be back out there soon enough." His dad nodded gravely, like his words alone would be enough to make it so. "This…being dependent, it's not you."

"There's nothing wrong with needing help." That was something else that his mom had said over and over, but it didn't seem to have sunk in for his dad. He didn't like the way his dad said *dependent* like it was a bad word. Even after his accident, his father had bristled at accepting help from the extended family and neighbors who had been eager to offer a hand. It had been one of the few areas of contention between his parents, as his mother had been much more tied into the community, always giving to others and helping out. Toby liked to think he'd inherited her outgoing nature, but he also still struggled with his dad's values, trying to not feel awful that he still needed assistance in many areas. "I mean, yeah, it would be nice to be able to shower on my own and drive again and stuff. But everyone needs help with something. Doesn't have to be a bad thing."

"Maybe." His dad sounded less than convinced, which raised fresh doubts in Toby's brain. Was that what he was doing? Being dependent on Reuben in a not-so-healthy way? Most days, he'd say no. He did what he could to help out around here, and Reuben seemed to go out of his way to treat him with respect. If he surrendered to Reuben anywhere, it was in the bedroom, which was private. But he couldn't deny that the past few weeks had battered his sense of himself as a strong, independent person who could take care of his family.

"This episode okay?" He needed a break from this heavy talk, away from his worries, especially worries about what would happen if he couldn't go back to work as fast as he wanted.

"Seen this one, but you'll like the twist." His dad made a go-ahead gesture with his hand. They passed a pleasant few hours with the show, and while just hanging out was nice, it wasn't as reassuring as he'd hoped as his head continued to churn.

Nell had brought over a stack of bills the other day, and they'd gone through them together best as they could, but there was no denying that they needed his income to return to pre-accident levels and soon. The workers' comp claim still hadn't started paying, and Annie was still dealing with red tape from the insurance company over the loss of the plane. Everyone seemed to expect the crash report to clear him of any deliberate fault, but he wouldn't rest easy until the official one was filed and the case closed. It wasn't uncommon for investigations to drag on weeks, even months or more, but the more time that passed, the more the uncertainty added to everything else weighing him down.

Reuben and Amelia returned in time to help with dinner. He had a strong feeling that Reuben had chosen today for the wildlife sanctuary visit to give him time alone with his dad, which he appreciated, but he also couldn't help the way his pulse surged at their return. Working to keep his smile from revealing too much, he rolled over to the kitchen.

"Was it fun?" he asked. This weird gallop in his chest at being near Reuben after time apart was getting worse, not better as the days passed, and he wasn't sure he liked it. Sure, the anticipation of the sex they might have later was nice, but he didn't like *needing* Reuben on an emotional level, especially not with his brain still all full of doubts he wanted to stomp. And he did like this, liked hearing about their day, liked simply being around Reuben in a way he couldn't say he'd had with other hookups and short-term flings.

"It was. The views on the drive there were worth it alone, and hearing from the caretakers was fascinating." Reuben retrieved a bottle of water from the fridge as Amelia kicked off her shoes.

"Someone could have warned *me* that it would be like school." Amelia had softened a great deal toward activities with Reuben, but she still had the same complaining streak that every teenager Toby had known had.

"You had fun, and you know it. I saw you smiling." Reuben gave her a pat on the shoulder that she didn't shrug off the way she might have a few weeks ago. "And wasn't that you begging to know when we can kayak again?"

"Being outdoors maybe isn't *so* terrible," she allowed. "And being on the water's kinda cool. But right now I'm starving. What's for dinner?"

"Dad brought halibut to share. Nell's making room in the deep freeze for this year's salmon catch," Toby said to her. "And we're doing baked potatoes because those are easy, and you can choose all your own toppings."

"Fun." Apparently not prepared to be patient, Amelia grabbed a yogurt from the fridge.

"How can I help?" Toby's dad asked, using the couch arms to help him stand up.

"You're the guest," Toby told him sternly. In reality, his dad's frequent dizzy spells made him a poor candidate for knife work or holding hot pots, which was why Toby or Nell did most of the cooking at home. Even him microwaving food was a worry. "And you brought part of the dinner. You've done your part. But you can come sit at the table, tell Reuben and Amelia about where to go next."

"I guess I could do that." His father made his way from the couch to the table using his walker.

"You need to be here when the physical therapist comes next," he teased his dad. "She can make us race. I think you'd probably win."

"Ha. Just practice." Never one for a ton of joking, his father's tone was dry. "Don't you switch to crutches soon?"

"When they clear my arm and leg for more weight bearing." Toby was looking forward to having the increased mobility of crutches or canes, but he tried not to sound too eager as crutches weren't an option for his dad with his balance issues.

"You want to season the fish?" Reuben arranged the

pieces in a large pan for the oven. "You're better at that than me."

"Sure." He turned his attention to the halibut and to working with Reuben, who had laid out the spices next to the pan. "Oh, you forgot—"

"Salt. Right here." Reuben handed him the shaker before he even got the words out. "Don't put too much—"

"Pepper on Amelia's. I know."

"You guys cook together a lot?" Toby's dad's head tilted.

"All the time," Amelia answered for them. "And yeah, it's like they share a brain or something. Cute."

Fuck. He could have done without that last observation. He'd had a feeling for a few days now that Amelia knew he and Reuben were more than platonic friends, but he really wasn't ready to have his dad and Nell figure that out yet. Not when he himself wasn't sure exactly how to define this thing they had going—it was unlike any fling he'd had before, and he enjoyed Reuben far more than most hookups. Enjoyed who he was around Reuben too—he'd never let go like this before with a partner on so many different levels. Sexually. Emotionally. Physically. But all that comfort seemed to vanish under his dad's watchful gaze.

"Tell them about taking us to the Homer Spit when we were little," he urged his dad, needing to quickly get the focus off him and Reuben. "Because it's fairly level, I'm thinking about going along when they try to bike it, see how far I get in the chair."

"You try doing it with a stroller, one kid in a backpack, and another who kept wanting to run ahead. Those were the days."

"Yup." Toby had always enjoyed the story of this

particular family outing, and he let his dad tell it, only interjecting to defend himself from time to time. He and Reuben worked on the dinner while his dad talked, and unexpected longing surged in him. He wanted more moments like this, wanted his dad to like Reuben and Amelia, and the depth of that wanting made his chest hurt. This wasn't supposed to be that serious. A summer fling, not a commitment, not a shared future. He didn't like caring like this, not at all.

Nell came rushing in after his dad had moved to talking about places Amelia and Reuben could try four wheeling. His dad's longing for the days when he and Toby had gone out on the ATVs together was clear, which made Toby have to swallow hard, but his dad did a good job of selling Amelia on trying it.

"I'm totally down on trying driving before I'm sixteen. Hey, Nell!" She beamed at Toby's sister.

"Hey. Your shirt looks great!" Nell was full of tales from her new job and chattered nonstop as she and Amelia arranged all the toppings for the baked potatoes. The oven timer dinged, and Toby's cozy feeling only intensified, people he cared about all gathered together.

"You're making me want a haircut," Amelia said as she took a seat at the table.

"Sure. Get your dad to say yes, and I'll see which of the stylists can work you in. Josie is particularly good with curly hair."

"Dad…" Amelia made exaggerated big eyes that had the whole table laughing, even Toby's dad.

"I suppose you can. It's your hair." Reuben gave her an indulgent smile.

"Win!" She fist pumped before turning her attention to the dinner.

The light mood continued as they ate, but as they were finishing, Nell's face turned more thoughtful. "I've been thinking about your specialist appointments coming up."

"Oh?" Toby tried to keep his tone neutral.

"It's not *bad*. I'm just worried about doing that many hours of driving all on my own. You know how I hate long drives, and I'm worried about leaving Dad—"

"Who doesn't need looking after." His dad pushed his plate away. "It's a day, Nell. Surely you can both trust me to live without you."

"I can do it," Reuben said smoothly. "We could use another stock-up trip in Anchorage anyway, so I don't mind the drive."

"You've done too much already." Toby's dad frowned. "We can work something out."

"Annie?" Nell's gaze darted between her dad and Toby, clearly torn about how to best get her way and still keep the peace. "If you ask Annie nicely, maybe she could fly you? Go with you? I mean, she's already agreed to look in on Dad—"

"It's no trouble," Reuben said in his take-charge voice, the one Toby associated with him getting stuff done. And in other circumstances, he liked that voice, very much, but right then it grated. "It'll be a nice adventure, right, Amelia?"

"Do I have to? I *hate* doctor's offices. And my stomach hurt the whole drive here, all those twisty roads. How about I stay here?"

"How about not." Reuben's stare would melt a glacier and make a polar bear quake, but all Amelia did was sigh heavily. "You're fourteen. And it's an overnight. No."

"I know! We'll trade!" Nell smiled broadly. "Amelia can stay with me. We'll go through some more of the fabric in the garage, do her hair. It'll be fun. Like when Han was still home."

"I'm not sure..." Reuben's eyes narrowed.

"That way we're doing you a favor and you're doing us one. Even." Nell had years of experience in appealing to the way their father thought, but Toby wasn't sure Reuben, who seemed to take great pride in his generous spirit, would follow the same logic.

"Please, Dad! I haven't had a sleepover in forever! Please!" Amelia made more of the pleading eyes, which worked far better than any Nell logic at softening Reuben, who exhaled sharply.

"I guess it's not the worst plan," he allowed.

"Thank you!" Amelia and Nell wore matching grins, but Toby's dad continued to frown, even once they'd moved onto cleaning up. And he was even quieter than usual as Nell gathered their stuff.

"I'll see you out." Toby rolled toward the door, keeping pace with his dad and his walker until they were out on the porch and he could ask, "You okay?"

"I don't like being indebted to that man." His father stopped at the porch rail.

"Reuben's a friend."

"Friend? He's closer to my age than yours, I'd bet."

"Pretty sure you've got like twenty years on him, Dad. And you were that much older than Mom. I've heard the stories." When his father's frown deepened, he realized how that sounded, so he quickly added, "Besides, I've always had friends of all ages."

"It's not just age. He's too rich."

"Now you sound like me." Nell rubbed Dad's shoulder. "And yeah, he's an out-of-towner, Tobes. Unlike

Dad, I'm happy to let him do us a favor, but just don't go getting attached."

"Or reliant," his dad added firmly. "Being *friends* is one thing, but a man handles his own business. You know that."

"Yeah," Toby said weakly, because really, what was he supposed to say to that? His dad had said similar things many times over the years. There wasn't going to be any changing his mind that accepting help didn't make someone weak. And Toby wanted to view himself as strong. Independent. Able to function on his own. He got what his dad was saying. He, too, hated needing Reuben for favors.

But when they were alone, just the two of them, it didn't feel like a trading of favors at all anymore. Damn his dad and Nell for tarnishing that connection, making it seem like something sordid. It wasn't like they had a future beyond this summer anyway, but it rankled that they couldn't see what he saw in Reuben and that he couldn't share how important Reuben had become to him without majorly rocking an already unsteady boat. And it made him doubt himself, doubt what he'd been feeling the past few weeks. Was this simply him taking the easy way out? Or did they have something real together? And if it was real, did it even matter?

Chapter Fifteen

Reuben hung back, let Toby see his family out on his own, but he couldn't shake a general feeling of unease. The dinner hadn't been a rousing success despite Nell's and Amelia's good moods about their plans. Paul didn't like him. It rankled more than it should've, mainly because family was so important to Toby, and like a teen with a crush, Reuben would have liked to make a good impression.

And his uncomfortable feeling only grew when Toby stayed out on the porch long after Nell and their father had left. Despite the post-dinner hour, the sun beat down on Toby's dark hair, cast a halo around his head. Reuben still wasn't used to the late sunsets here. Even by the time Amelia headed up to her computer game, the light had barely started to fade because the sun wouldn't set until around midnight. And still Toby sat on the porch.

Unable to stand it any longer, Reuben grabbed two beers from the fridge and headed out to the porch. Toby had finished his antibiotics and had cut back to over-the-counter pain meds, so he'd been able to enjoy the occasional beer together. And Reuben had a feeling he needed one right about then. He didn't open by asking whether Toby was okay, not when it was pretty clear he wasn't.

"Thought you could use a beer," he said instead, holding out an open bottle, which Toby accepted with a nod. "Up for some company?"

"Not sure." Toby kept his gaze on the view of the hills as he took a long sip from the bottle. "I'm probably not the best right now."

"How about you let me be the judge of that?" Setting his own beer down on the arm of one the deck chairs, he moved behind Toby, started rubbing his shoulders.

"That feels good," Toby groaned. "Okay. You can stay. Especially if you keep that up. Man, do I love your fingers."

"Good." Reuben started by working out the knots in Toby's neck, digging in with his thumbs, the sort of steady pressure that he knew by now that Toby liked. "Nice as it is out here, if you come back inside, I can massage you right."

"Not sure I'm up for sex tonight." Toby's face contorted like it couldn't decide whether to offer a frown or an apologetic smile.

"I didn't say anything about sex." Not allowing himself to be put off by Toby's bad mood, Reuben kept right on rubbing. "We've hung out before without sex. I don't need that tonight. I'd be happy to just massage you for a while."

"Because you get off on that, right? Doing things for me?" Toby's tone was bitter even as he relaxed into Reuben's grip.

"It makes me happy to do things for you, yes. Especially things that I know make you feel good. And I've told you before that I neither need nor want orgasm as some sort of quid pro quo. Ever. So what's this about?"

"I just hate this. Hate not being able to do stuff I should be able to do on my own."

"Well, for what it's worth, I don't know many people who can effectively rub their own shoulders," he said lightly. "There's nothing wrong about needing a little help from time to time."

"You sound like my mom." Toby's voice was sad and far away.

"You must miss her a lot. I know I still miss mine. It's almost easier for me not to think about her, which probably isn't the healthiest."

"No, I get you. Because if you go there, if you let that pain in, it *hurts*. And I miss her most on nights like this. Like she should be here to hear about Nell's job and Hannah's medical school rotations. It's this…hole in our family, and I keep thinking I can plug it, but I do a piss poor job most days."

"Don't be so hard on yourself. You're doing the best you can."

"Yeah. But it might not be enough." His voice dropped to a bare whisper. "What if I don't heal as fast as I'm supposed to? Or completely? What if I can't keep up at work?"

"My own mother had a good saying for that. 'Don't go borrowing trouble.' There's no sense in dwelling on all that right now. You've got people who lo—*care* about you who would help. Annie. Your coworkers. Your friends. Nell. Me. If you need extra recovery time, so be it. You'll deal."

"I just hate being *dependent* on people." The way he said the word made Reuben think it wasn't exactly his own term. Something—or someone—had gotten into his head. "I'm supposed to be this independent guy."

"You can need help and still be independent. You're a smart guy. You know that. And just playing devil's advocate for a moment, even if your injuries were permanent, it wouldn't change who you are. You'd still be you—strong and funny and sexy and, yes, independent. Suddenly needing more help in certain areas wouldn't affect that."

"You really see me that way?" Toby asked softly.

"I do." Reuben dropped his hands to come crouch in front of the wheelchair so Toby could see how serious he was. "You are one of the strongest people I've ever met. How effectively your limbs work doesn't affect how I see you as a person. As someone I like and care about." He was going out into treacherous waters, confessing that last part, but it was true. He'd come to care so much about Toby, and it was killing him to see him so down.

"Is the opposite true though? Would you still like me if I didn't need help?" Toby sounded like he was trying to puzzle something out.

"I'm pretty sure I'd like you however I could get you," Reuben admitted. "I like *you*. I don't have some sort of… I don't know…rescue complex."

Toby made a noncommittal sound like he wasn't too sure but didn't want to press the point, instead mumbling, "I like you too."

"Then let me show you how much I like you, hmm? You're all kinds of tense, and there's only so much I can do out here." They didn't have neighbors in viewing distance, but he was also hyperaware of Amelia's window right above them.

Going quiet for a long moment, Toby's face scrunched

up, some sort of internal war going on before he finally exhaled. "Okay."

After handing Reuben his beer, he turned his chair toward the house, leaving Reuben to follow him to the bedroom. Not intending to leave until Toby was good and relaxed, Reuben locked the door behind them while Toby transferred himself to the bed. He pulled off his T-shirt before making a face.

"Hell. Don't think I can lie on my stomach. Fuck. I can't even do getting a massage right."

"There is no right way. Lay on your side." Setting aside their beers, Reuben helped him rearrange the pillows to support his legs and torso with one behind his neck and shoulders too. They'd cuddled like this a fair amount in the evenings, but this time, instead of spooning Toby, he sat next to him on the edge of the bed. He retrieved the lotion they now kept in the nightstand in a larger size for *reasons*.

"Thought you said no sex? Anymore I just have to smell that stuff, and I'm hard and thinking about your hand," Toby complained.

"I think you can deal. Think about my hands on your back not your dick." Reuben was determined to show him that this…whatever it was, was about far more than sex, and that spending time together didn't have to end in an orgasm for them to both be fulfilled. If Toby thought Reuben was only here for the sex, he hadn't been paying attention, and perhaps Reuben needed to try harder to show him that he needed a lot more than Toby's body. To that end, he started back on Toby's neck, spending long minutes working the tense muscles until a sigh rolled through Toby's body.

"My dad doesn't like you." The words came out with

a shudder, almost as if Toby hadn't planned to let them out along with the exhale.

"I know." Reuben had had a feeling that's what Toby's funk was about and had hoped that if he was patient enough Toby would want to talk it out. "And that matters to you. Is there anything I could do?"

"Halve your net worth?" Toby snorted as Reuben moved to his shoulders. "No. You're too…"

"Male? Jewish? White? Tall? Old?" Reuben tried guessing when Toby trailed off.

"All that plus the rich and not-from-here thing, probably, although I don't think he cares so much about the Jewish thing. Not sure on male—he's known I'm bi, but who knows? And I'm the one who digs your size."

"Good." A pleasant warmth swept up his face, same as it always did when Toby complimented his looks. But he liked knowing he turned Toby on because Toby sure did it for him. Even now, he was having to work to keep his touch more soothing than seductive, all the lean, tan muscles under his hands. He worked Toby's shoulders and upper arms with long, firm strokes that had Toby softly grunting.

"I can't change my bank balance, but I did work very hard to get where I am today. I'm not going to lie and say I'm not proud of my successes. But they're not all that I am."

"I know." Another long sigh from Toby as he wiggled in silent invitation for more rubbing. "I mean, I'm over thirty now. I shouldn't care so much what my dad thinks—"

"Of course you should. You love him. He's important to you. And because of that, he and Nell are important to me too."

"Why?"

"I meant what I said earlier. I care about you. Beyond the bedroom. You being happy is important to me. And I'm not going to take his dislike too personally, okay? You keep having him over, and I'll keep trying to make inroads, hoping he warms up more to me."

"This wasn't supposed to get so complicated," Toby groaned.

"I know." Reuben understood why he sounded so stricken even as the words stung.

"Flings aren't supposed to be so frustrating."

"Do you want to stop?" Reuben dropped his hands from Toby's back.

"No." Toby reached behind him, thumped Reuben's side with his cast-covered arm. "Can't stop. Not now. Not when…" He trailed off again, but this time Reuben didn't try to fill in the blanks as his own emotions clogged his throat. Finally, Toby took a deep breath. "Not when it's so damn good, you know?"

"Yeah. It is. I like this. I like *you*. But I don't want to hurt you either."

"You're not."

He had a feeling Toby was lying—they were both too deep into this thing now. Parting was going to hurt no matter what. And if Reuben was complicating his family relationships, well that couldn't really be glossed over either. But even knowing that, he too was powerless to turn back now, not when he needed this so much. He tried to put those feelings into the massage, tell Toby how much he cared, how he truly didn't want to hurt him, and how very much this thing was coming to mean to him too.

"Fuck. Melting into the pillows here." Toby yawned.

"Good. My whole intention." Reuben dropped a kiss on the back of his neck.

"Don't leave." It was a sleepy request, undoubtedly aimed at getting Reuben to doze next to him for a time, but it hit Reuben square in the gut, a low sucker punch of guilt, because he *was* going to leave eventually and it was going to hurt and there was no avoiding it.

"I won't." Stopping the massage, he gave in to the urge to stretch out behind Toby, hold him close. There might be no getting around parting, but damn if he was going to miss a single opportunity to stay right where he was.

"Dad? Are you ready?" Amelia called from the main room of the house.

"Coming." Reuben hurried up and hit Send on the email he'd been composing to an associate with a question. Despite being on sabbatical, as Natalie described it in official emails, he was still getting regular inquiries from those working with longtime clients, and he was happy to help.

At first he'd jumped with every incoming message, but now he tried to limit his replies to when Amelia and Toby were otherwise occupied. And he couldn't deny the strange churning in his gut with each email recently. It wasn't just the time difference and literal miles of distance. Felt like the guy who'd made all those deals was a different person almost, and there were days he didn't quite recognize himself in the mirror.

All the biking and hiking had him leaner than he'd been in a decade, which had earned him a good teasing from Craig and Leticia when he'd sent them some pictures Amelia had snapped, but it was more the inner calm that was truly alien to him. The guy in the mirror was settled, not relentlessly pushing forward, not driven by forces he'd never entirely understood. He'd only felt good with a full calendar and overflowing to-do list—proof of how needed he was. Here, though, the only pressing thing on the agenda driving him was the planned trip with Toby and Amelia to the Homer Spit. And he was needed not for his reputation as a closer, but for his ability to load the bikes and wheelchair and drive. Straightforward requirements that were easy to meet and weirdly satisfying.

The outing for the day was a four-mile asphalt trail at the base of the little curl of land below Homer that stuck out into the bay. It was a great day for a drive—bright blue sky with puffy white clouds hanging over the dark mountains in the distance. A cool ocean breeze should temper the blazing sun, which was why Toby had decided to come along—his plan was to do a small portion of the trail in the wheelchair, but mainly sit and read and wait for Reuben and Amelia. They'd get a late lunch together at one of the restaurants along the Spit afterward.

"You sure this book is good?" Toby stuck the mystery Reuben had recommended in the little bag that Amelia had sewn for the back of the wheelchair. Reuben had been slowly working through the house's bulging shelves of suspense and mystery books, reading while Amelia sewed, first time enjoying fiction in years. And he'd discovered a particularly sarcastic private investigator hero he thought Toby might enjoy, especially with the high action component to the stories.

"Lots of explosions," he assured him as they made their way to the SUV.

"You want my tablet as a backup?" Amelia asked Toby. "I'm bringing it just in case."

"I'm probably good, but thanks." Toby smiled at her before transferring to the passenger seat of the car. Amelia had softened considerably toward him since the sewing lessons, and Reuben remained amazed at the transformation in her. She was fast amassing a box full of creations to mail to Natalie.

"I wish we had the horses from yesterday, not the bikes again." Even Amelia's complaints had less of an edge these days. Toby had arranged for the son-in-law of his boss to take them on a trail ride with some other tourists, and Amelia had taken to the horses the same way she had kayaking, asking all sorts of questions, and begging to know when they could go again.

"Some of the girls at your high school may own horses," Reuben said as he pulled out of the driveway. "I bet if you asked, your mother might be able to arrange for lessons there for you."

"I don't want to think about school." Amelia thumped her head against the seat back, her scowl occupying Reuben's rearview mirror.

"Then don't." Toby's voice was light, interrupting before Reuben could make things worse with Amelia. "Plenty of summer left. I've been thinking of asking Nell if she'd like to leave Dad with me when she goes fishing next, maybe take you with her. I'll warn you now, it's hard work. Nothing like one of the boating tours or something—the sun beats down on you, your hands and legs get sore, and it's likely to be a long day."

"And fish guts?" Amelia sounded both impressed and repulsed at the same time.

"Lots of those too. But it's also fun. There will be

other kids your age fishing with their families. It's not uncommon to see four generations of Athabascan families fishing together. I've got lots of great memories of being your age, out with family, fishing or hunting." Toby sounded fond, the way he always did when talking about his childhood, and Reuben found himself strangely wistful listening. "There's always a big gathering in May as fishing season starts to open for the year—fishing is very social around here. There's even fish camps for the kids."

"Sounds fun. If Nell's going, I'm in." As usual, even if fish guts were involved, if it meant seeing Nell, Amelia was all for it. "Tell me more about when Nell was little?"

Toby launched into a story about Nell eating an entire jar of smoked salmon on her own, and the easy way he handled Amelia's questions made Reuben's insides warm. He liked listening to the two of them, loved the easy way Toby slid from his story to telling Amelia about an upcoming arts festival where she'd be able to see projects made by others who sewed and crafted, keeping her talking the whole drive to Homer Spit.

Right as they found a parking spot in the crowded lot full of other tourists, his phone chimed with an email alert.

"Gonna get that?" Amelia sounded resigned, slumping back in the seat, already pulling out her own phone.

"No," he said, surprising himself with the assertiveness of his response. It was probably a reply to his earlier email, and a few weeks ago, he wouldn't have thought anything about making Toby and Amelia wait while he checked his messages, replied to what was undoubtedly something that only *felt* urgent. And the fact that Amelia so readily assumed that he'd put the email first was sobering. He didn't like thinking of all of the birthday parties and family dinners he'd interrupted for work, some of it necessary and some of it more him simply unable to disconnect.

I don't want to be that guy anymore. Resolved, he pocketed the phone. They'd be back at the house soon enough, and whatever it was could wait until he wasn't in the middle of a day out.

"Let's go," he told the other two. The relatively flat trail stretched in front of them, plenty of bikers, hikers, dog walkers, tourists, and other wheelchair users enjoying the absolutely epic view of the snowcapped mountains across the bay. Scrubby bushes lined the trail, but there were not many trees to interrupt the panoramic vista. He and Amelia walked the bikes alongside Toby until he found a viewpoint near a cluster of small shops alongside the trail.

"Think I'll wait here for you guys to return, and then we can eat over there." Toby gestured at a restaurant designed to look like a small lighthouse.

"Sounds like a good plan." Reuben headed off with Amelia. Biking was so much easier now than it had been that first day, but it wasn't only his muscles that had changed. His heart had too, something he couldn't deny as he looked back over his shoulder at Toby, who was already absorbed in the book.

"Wait," he said to Amelia, pulling up short on the side of the trail and fishing out his phone.

"Your email? Really?" Her shoulders drooped, disappointment clear in her eyes.

"No, not that. I want a picture." And he did, in the worst way. And not just any picture—he wanted *this* one, a candid of Toby, a reminder of this seemingly ideal morning, of how Toby and Amelia had joked on the way here and of how Reuben felt when he looked at him. Memory of the previous night's sex was still fresh in Reuben's mind too. They hadn't had sex the night Toby's family had visited, but they'd made up for it last night, making out and stroking off until they were both limp and sweaty in each other's arms. The sex he'd remember for sure—it would probably fuel his solo exploits for years to come—but it was the quiet moments like this that he feared losing. Would he remember the crease of Toby's forehead when he read? The size of his hands relative to the paperback? His little smile, the real one, not the charming one he flashed the world, but the one that was just Toby, smiling for himself? The exact blue of the morning sky?

He wanted it all, and he snapped several pictures in a row. He got it now, why people collected snapshots and souvenirs—trying to hold onto something so precious it couldn't even be named. And it was probably a losing bid against the frailty of memory, but sometimes one simply had to try, had to have something to take away from a perfect moment.

"You like him," Amelia said softly. "Like more than a crush."

"Yeah." Reuben couldn't lie to her or himself any longer. "I like him. More than a crush."

"You'll miss him." Frowning, she kicked at some stray pebbles. "Maybe I will too."

"Yeah. We will." He didn't have a good answer for her. He was going to miss Toby, miss this place, miss who he was here, who Amelia was, the little not-quite-family they'd made, the three of them. But he was Reuben Graham, professional closer, the guy who could always find a solution, get a deal done. There had to be a way to save them all from the coming pain, and he was determined to find it. Because not only could he not lose Toby, he also didn't want to lose the self he'd only begun to rediscover.

Chapter Sixteen

"I'm so excited!" It was possibly the first time Toby had seen Amelia anything other than groggy first thing in the morning. But here she was, bouncing on her toes as Reuben filled the travel mugs. Toby had X-rays early in the afternoon, an appointment with the orthopedic specialist later, then in the morning one with the neurologist to make sure he wasn't having any lasting effects from the concussion. Which he wasn't, but he couldn't control the feeling of dread that rose whenever he thought about the impending trip.

"We know. But just FYI, Nell's not usually a morning person. You may have to chill while she wakes up."

"I'm not a *kid*. I don't need entertaining." She huffed. She was probably extra excited to see Nell after their fishing trip had been such a success. She'd arrived back with stories of some of the kids she'd met and sung Nell's praises for days after. Nell had promised to show her the finished smoked fish on this visit, and surprise, surprise, Miss Picky Eater had decided she loved salmon since Nell did. "And I've got my sewing machine and my laptop. I'll be fine."

"Our house's internet is slow." Why he felt the need

for all these warnings, he couldn't say, but the flutter in his stomach went beyond unease over the doctor visits.

"Toby. Stop. I'm going to have fun." Determined tilt to her chin, she collected her sewing machine case and backpack and headed toward the SUV.

"Not too late to make her come with us," Reuben said in a low voice.

"No, it'll be okay." Putting his backpack on his lap, he made his way to the door. "Not sure why I'm being weird."

"Maybe because things have been…interesting?" Reuben's mouth quirked as he followed.

He was being diplomatic—the past few weeks hadn't thawed Toby's father any, but with every night, every shared meal, every long talk, Toby sank deeper into the quicksand that was his tangled emotions about Reuben. He loved the nights when his dad and Nell were over, had loved grilling some of Nell's catch for his dad with Reuben's help, but couldn't help yearning for his dad to see what he saw in Reuben.

"Yeah. Guess that's it." He let Reuben help him into the SUV. Reuben was an old pro by now at muscling the wheelchair and walker into the back. They'd had a number of fun day trips together as a trio, and while simply being out of the house was a pleasure, it was the time together that he'd come to treasure most. Watching Reuben light up when fishing, seeing his pleased grin at the end of a bike ride, observing his growing relationship with Amelia—it all added to the experience. And as much as he ached to get back to being active himself, he'd treasure these memories.

Amelia kept up her excited chatter on the drive to his home. As they pulled in, another source of discomfort revealed itself. He didn't like seeing his house through Reuben's eyes. Oh, he knew Reuben was way too good-mannered to say anything. But there was no denying that the faded brown building was small and humble. Battered wood siding. Roof that probably needed replacing sometime soon. Small windows. Ramp leading to the front door that didn't match the rest of the property, not that there was anything resembling a cohesive design with the two metal outbuildings chosen for their durability, not looks. A swing set his dad had built for the girls that Toby still needed to dismantle sat between the house and the sheds. Driveway that could use fresh gravel. It wasn't awful, but it was clearly a modest family home, not a vacation paradise. The main value was the land, and that was what Toby fought so hard to protect and keep for the girls and his dad.

Inside the rooms were small with mismatched furniture—all pieces his mom had loved, but probably not what Reuben and Amelia were used to. The living room seemed even narrower than usual with Reuben looming behind him. His dad was in his usual recliner by the TV, documentary already on. A bleary-eyed Nell greeted them at the door with coffee mug in hand. She directed Amelia to take her stuff upstairs to the room at the top of the stairs that Nell had shared with Hannah back when Hannah lived at home, then turned to Toby.

"Do you have a minute before you need to hit the road? Could I talk to you?" Her eyes darted between their dad and Reuben.

"In the kitchen?" he guessed.

"That might be best."

"Go ahead. We've got time." Reuben settled himself on the narrow sofa as Toby rolled toward the kitchen, which was behind the living room, but he didn't stop until he was at the dining area, out of sight and earshot of the others. As soon as he was even with the table, he saw the reason for Nell's summons.

"Bills?" he asked, gesturing at the papers and envelopes covering the table. "We can go over them when we're back tomorrow. Or is there something that can't wait?"

"Han called. She doesn't want to worry you—"

"You guys keeping secrets, that worries me plenty."

"It's not *secret*. Just she's worried about meeting all the fees and expenses for the fall, even with her scholarships. She says it's been tight all summer for her, and she was making noises about delaying for a term."

"No. Absolutely not. Neither of you are taking a term off. I'll be back flying, and I'll get Annie to give me all the hours she can."

"My stupid college has fee increases for fall." She sank into one of the wooden chairs. "And we've got a stack of bills from your accident coming due. The co-pays are going to kill us."

"I'll handle it." He kept his voice firm, not wanting her to share the doubts that plagued him. "In the meantime, if Han needs money, make that a priority—I don't want her doing anything stupid like skipping meals to save money. You remember how to auto-transfer to her account?"

"Yeah. You're below the minimum you told me to not drop below though."

"*Fuck.* Sorry. Send her something small anyway. We'll work it out."

"Yeah." She didn't sound convinced, which was okay because he wasn't either. Damn it. He'd known money was going to be an issue heading into fall, but why did everything have to come due all at once? He might have something coming to him from workers' comp through the state, but the wheels for that were barely creaking. Nell had helped him do the forms, but the insurer was taking its sweet time deciding whether he was an employee or a contractor. He supposed he could ask Mr. Bigshot Lawyer out there for help with figuring out the workers' comp stuff, but he was loath to even think about asking for that kind of help. Hell, even mentioning his money worries wasn't going to happen. He could handle this on his own, same as he had for years now.

"Don't tell Dad, okay?" he said to Nell. "No need to get him worked up about money."

"I won't." Nell quickly gathered up the papers littering the table. "I'll make a pile for us to go over when you're back. And you'd better go now, get on the road. And rescue Reuben from Dad."

"Oh yeah." He'd almost forgotten about leaving the two of them alone, but when he made his way back to the living room, a minor miracle had taken place and they were talking without his dad glowering.

"See that's why they needed reinforcements..." Reuben trailed off as Toby approached the couch.

"Ready to go?" he asked.

"Yes. We were watching a great documentary on World War I strategy." Reuben gave him an encouraging smile, one he tried to return but probably fell short, thanks to his black mood.

"Drive safe," his dad ordered as Reuben stood up. "Thanks for the rec."

"I told him about a documentary on the streaming

service I saw an ad for," Reuben explained. "Looked good."

"You should tell me how it turns out," he said to his dad, who was standing as well, apparently determined to see them out.

"Maybe." The set to his dad's jaw said that he'd been simply being polite and had no intention of taking advice from Reuben. Oh well. One step forward there, two back. They moved toward the door, Reuben telling Amelia goodbye and issuing a flurry of last-minute reminders.

Back at the car, Reuben helped him out of the chair and into the SUV, something they'd done dozens of times, but it felt different with his dad watching from the front window, face obscured by the blind. *A man handles his business.* Damn it. He couldn't risk either his dad or Reuben finding out about the money worries. And he needed these appointments to go well in the worst way, couldn't afford a single setback.

At least they had sun for the drive to Anchorage. Or rather at least the sky had sun. Reuben had the dark thundercloud that was Toby riding beside him. They passed the first stretch of the drive with Toby fiddling with the stereo, seemingly unable to land on a station to match his mood. He kept shifting around, but shot down Reuben's few attempts at talking.

"Are you comfortable enough in front? If your leg needs—"

"I'm fine." Toby's voice was just short of a bark, then he softened it. "Sorry."

"Nell have bad news for you?"

"It's nothing." Toby looked out the window, where

an expansive vista of the pass greeted them, green and lush. Since it was a weekday, traffic was fairly light, at least by Reuben's east coast standards although Toby had already had muttered things about the line of RVs in front of them and mentioned how heavy tourist traffic was since it was fishing season.

"We're friends, right?" Reuben wasn't giving up so easily this time. *Something* had happened back at the house, he was sure of it. Toby had been quiet on the drive there, but seeming more nervous than bad mood. The house reminded Reuben a bit of his family's apartment growing up—small but well loved, with pictures everywhere. Little Toby and Nell and the other sister growing up through the years. A smiling dark-haired woman with Toby's eyes featured in many of the pictures, and Reuben's chest had gone tight at the realization that she was probably Toby's mom. Handmade quilts and blankets were draped over the back of each chair and couch. Paul had occupied an older recliner that brought to mind the ones Reuben's father and bubbe had favored. For once, they hadn't been doing too badly at small talk while Nell and Toby had been in the kitchen. And whatever Nell told him had left Toby in this uncommunicative funk. "If something's going on with you or your family, you can talk about it."

"It's fine." Toby's already defined jaw was hard enough to sharpen knives.

Well, okay then. Toby wasn't going to open up to him, which smarted. He'd thought they were better friends than that, especially after this many weeks. Resigned, he let Toby switch the music yet again. At least the drive was spectacular even if the company was sulky. He especially loved the section after the mountain passes when

Turnagain Arm of the Cook Inlet came into view. Because they made such good time to the outskirts of Anchorage, they had plenty of time to stop for food before Toby's X-ray appointment.

"So, tour guide, what would you like to eat? We never did get much breakfast." Reuben could have asked the car navigation system for places and might have been assured a more upbeat answer, but he figured it was worth a try.

"There's a diner I like that's not too far from the medical complex. Decent coffee, which you probably need after the drive, and good pie. Kind of a retro vibe."

"Sounds fine." Reuben let Toby tell the car where to navigate to and easily followed the busy road to a low-slung red brick building with cheerful blue and white sign. Parking was a surprising challenge—he'd forgotten somehow during his weeks on the peninsula that Anchorage was an actual city, one with city problems like slow traffic lights and one-way streets and tight parking spaces. Luckily, there were no steps, so negotiating the uneven pavement with the wheelchair wasn't too difficult.

"Man, they better approve me for a walking boot and crutches today. I am *done* with this chair."

"You'll listen to the doctors," Reuben reminded him before he could think better of it.

"They better listen to *me*." Toby was clearly spoiling for a fight, what with his tight shoulders and glower.

But Reuben refused to be goaded into a pointless argument, and instead followed the young server to a table in the middle of the room. She removed a chair for Toby and gave them colorful menus that featured skillets—large portions of eggs, meat, biscuits and gravy served on a large cast iron skillet. He was intrigued enough to order one with eggs and steak, but Toby only got a piece of chocolate cream pie.

"Are we not feeding you enough desserts?" Reuben asked after they ordered. "Amelia has this crazy idea that I need a do-over birthday. With a cake. I don't think I need anything, but if you want to get some cake mixes when we stop at the store tomorrow..."

"Maybe." Toby shrugged, then managed a small smile. "If Amelia says you need a cake, you need a cake. She's got pretty decided opinions on stuff like that. Let her do something nice for you."

"Says the guy who has a hard time with that concept," Reuben teased. "But yes, some cake wouldn't kill me. And she does like to boss me around, doesn't she?"

"Gee, I wonder where she gets that from." Toby smirked, and finally it seemed they were back on decent footing, talking about Amelia and her sewing projects and her opinions on everything from food to movies to board games that she still steadfastly refused to try. They chatted more easily once the food came.

"Are you sure you don't want some of my meat or eggs? Biscuit?" Reuben broke his giant biscuit in half. "This is a ridiculous amount of food."

"I'm good." Toby shrugged. "Kinda...hyped about the X-rays, I guess."

"I can understand that. We'll just make sure to have an early dinner." He tried to offer an encouraging smile. "And hey, no Amelia, so we can order something she wouldn't try."

"There's a Turkish place we can either order from or go to. Ditto a ramen place. I bet you'd enjoy either." Toby seemed to be slipping back into tour guide mode, and while that made for more pleasant conversation, the shadows of his mood from earlier still lurked in his eyes.

And when the server dropped off their check, his frown made a reappearance as he reached for it.

"I've got it." Reuben tried to take it from him.

"No." Toby's voice was back to clipped tones. "You always get everything. You already put the room for tonight on your card. And I just… I can't, okay? I just can't."

Ah. Reuben got it. It was a pride thing for him. Which was understandable even if frustrating. Reuben was used to paying for dates and friends, and Toby paying, especially when he knew money was a worry for him, didn't sit the best with him either. "Can we split?"

"No, it's my turn." Eyes hard, he stared Reuben down.

"All right. If we're going to do the taking turns thing with paying for dates though, that means I get dinner tonight. You can do tomorrow's breakfast if you really want to."

"I do. And this is a date?" Toby's mouth quirked in an adorable way that made Reuben want to kiss him, even in the middle of the crowded diner. He wouldn't, of course, but his body thrummed with the awareness that they'd be alone all night in a hotel room together later.

"I would think we'd qualify as dating, yes." Reuben tried to tell him with his eyes about those plans for that evening and to remind him that any two people who saw each other naked this much would be reasonably assumed to be dating.

"Point taken." Some of the frustration in Toby's eyes was replaced with heat. "And we should probably head out."

They stopped at the cashier so Toby could pay, and

Reuben didn't miss his look of relief when the card went through. Damn it, why couldn't he just let Reuben take care of it? Reuben had been that guy with more pride than cash once upon a time, but now he was in a position to help, and he hated that Toby wouldn't let him.

The medical complex was a sprawling collection of buildings, none terribly tall, but occupying a sizable footprint. Toby's independent streak continued as they made their way from the parking structure to the radiology department, and he tried to wave off Reuben's offer to push the chair. He managed for short distances with his casted hand, but longer ones remained challenging. And painstakingly slow. And again, Reuben only wanted to help.

"I've got it." Toby glared at him. "We've got time, but walk on ahead if I'm too slow for you."

"Of course not. We'll go at your pace."

Finally they reached radiology, and it wasn't long before an earnest young woman in scrubs came to collect Toby.

"Is your…dad coming back with you?" she asked, head tilting as she considered them.

"Not my dad. Just a friend," Toby said with a harsh laugh.

Fuck. Was Reuben really that much older? He guessed he was, but he hadn't really thought about how that would read to others. But it wasn't the woman's assumption as much as Toby's reaction that stung. Toby's fast denial was another small rejection to add to Reuben's pile of little hurts on the day. Hadn't they just established they were dating? He understood why Toby might not want to be public with their relationship, but he didn't have to like being dismissed like this.

"I'll stay here," he said before Toby could. "Unless you want me to tag along?"

"Nah. I've got this." Toby's answer didn't surprise Reuben, nor did him letting the pretty woman push the wheelchair, but Reuben still felt a heavy cloak of frustration and helplessness wrapping around him.

Damn it. He wanted this to be real. Wanted to be a real, true partner for Toby. Wanted to be everything he needed. Wanted Toby to see that potential. Not for the first time, he wondered if there were limits to how out Toby was—would he ever be comfortable introducing Reuben as a boyfriend? Acting like a couple in public, not just the bedroom? Letting his family know they were together? Reuben simply wasn't sure and had a feeling that Toby's insistence on calling this a fling was his way of avoiding those same questions.

And more than anything Reuben wanted the stupid expiration date on this *fling* to evaporate. He had no clue how he was supposed to return to his ordinary life after this, how he was supposed to reconcile these intense, awfully permanent-seeming emotions with the temporary nature of their connection. But he was more resolved than ever to find some sort of solution. Some sort of future. Because hell if he was ready to be dismissed and forgotten.

Chapter Seventeen

The last time Toby had X-rays, he'd been drugged up and rather out of it. He'd expected this visit to be rather straightforward, but instead the process was surprisingly complicated with the tech needing a lot of different views of the leg and arm. And the casts came off for better pictures, which should have been a huge relief after weeks with them on, but instead felt strange with limp, rubbery limbs that didn't work as expected. The weight of the casts was gone, but the weight of his fears and doubts only increased. He'd lost so much strength and muscle mass already. He needed far more help moving around and getting into position than he liked, flopping around like an ungainly seal as the X-ray tech had him move this way and that.

And of course, she couldn't tell him what she was seeing, saying that the doctor and radiologist would have to consult.

"But you're doing an awesome job!" Her voice was the sort of fake cheery that Toby hated. He did enough of it himself with clients, but he liked to think he was less obvious about faking enthusiasm. "Just a few more pictures."

A few more turned out to be more like another fifteen minutes, but at last she returned him to Reuben, who was studying his phone.

"Hey. Haven't seen you with that thing in a while." He'd been harsh earlier, both with the bad mood and being uncomfortable when the clueless tech labeled Reuben as his father, and he tried to make amends with a friendly tone.

"Yeah. I'm still in the loop on several things at work, but I try to limit the email time, especially when you and Amelia are around."

Work. Oh yeah. That was right. Reuben had a real life that wasn't here, a real life with real work that he'd be returning to in just a few weeks. Fuck. Toby did not want to think about that right then, didn't want to imagine a fall and winter without Reuben. Definitely didn't want to think about Reuben back to his workaholic ways, Amelia off at boarding school, and Reuben spending nights with someone who better fit that lifestyle, someone slick and stylish and loaded.

Pocketing the phone, Reuben stood. "On to the doctor appointment now? Bit weird to see you without casts."

"Yeah. They're probably putting something back on—splints or a walking boot or whatever. But it's nice to feel air again. Oh, and you need to push. Tech said not to use my hand or leg without the cast until I see the doctor."

"No problem." Reuben easily maneuvered them to the building that housed a lot of the specialists, and eventually they reached the waiting room for the orthopedic surgery practice.

And *wait* was the operative word as his appointment time came and went. Eventually, Reuben dug his phone back out.

"More email?"

"No." The back of Reuben's neck and ears turned pink, which was fucking adorable on such an otherwise authoritative guy. "Amelia finally got me on her game. I'm managing a colony now, apparently, and the app keeps reminding me to check the terraforming equipment and stuff."

"Let me see?" Toby leaned in. Talking about the game was far easier than confessing his money worries or talking about how weird his arm and leg felt without the casts on. And it served to cut some of the tension that had plagued them, which was Toby's fault for not wanting to talk. But talking was *hard.* Hell, even admitting to himself that he didn't know what he was going to do with all the mounting financial pressures was difficult. He didn't like not having a ready solution.

By contrast, the game was a fun distraction, and by the time a medical assistant called his name, Toby had the app on his own phone, hogging up his limited memory space and dinging him with alerts about short supplies on the border planets. He'd almost forgotten his discomfort about the coming appointment, but all that rushed back as soon as the doctor bustled into the room. A short man with a balding head, the doctor had an officious attitude that immediately put Toby on edge. He'd seen him in the hospital on his rounds and hadn't liked him much then either, but as long as he had good news, Toby would put up with the grandstanding.

"Mr. Kooly, good to see you again." The doctor shook his hand. "Good to see my handiwork coming along."

"It's healing then?"

"Well…" Plucking at the legs of his no-doubt-pricey

dress pants, the doctor sat on the rolling stool in front of
the exam table. "Maybe not quite as fast as we'd like."

"What do you mean?" Bile rose in his throat. He
couldn't take any bad news, and the doctor's switch into
serious mode had sweat pooling on his lower back. "I
get a walking boot and crutches, right?"

"Not quite yet." The doctor held up a hand before
turning to the computer on a nearby counter, bringing up
some X-rays on the monitor. "The arm is looking good,
and we'll go down to a removable splint for that. However, a month or so is still pretty early for healing a leg
injury of this nature. We're not talking about a simple
fibula fracture. The tibia bears far more of the weight
burden, and then you had the knee and ankle damage
on top of it. We're going to put you in a cushioned boot
today, but I'm going to say you're not ready for much
weight-bearing. And still twenty-four hour wear—it's
not quite where I'd like to see it for removing the boot
or arm splint for showering or sleeping."

"And crutches?"

"I'm prescribing a scooter-walker—one that has a
kneepad to keep the weight off the injured leg. And
we have to think about your arm, whether it's ready to
support the weight of the crutches. It's ready for a rigid
splint, but it's not one hundred percent either. It can be
a goal of physical therapy to get you on crutches over
the next few weeks, but I don't want to see you going
to full-time crutches quite yet and risk a setback on the
arm. You need to slowly work up strength again."

"So no driving yet, either?" Toby scrubbed at his
hair, trying to think of something that could be salvaged
from this news.

"No, not yet—that would be weight and pressure on

the leg that I don't think you're ready for. And driving with a boot is a challenge under the best of circumstances." The doctor's frown deepened. "Right now, you're in the middle of the reparative phase of healing—too much weight bearing too soon could double your overall healing time. I know the temptation is to want to get right back to walking and driving, but being patient now will save you time in the long run."

"I don't have time," Toby all but growled. "I need to be back at work—"

"Well, that's what the workers' comp is for." The doctor said it with a careless shrug like that money was simply a given and like Toby was being unreasonable pushing to get back to work sooner. Toby would bet money he didn't have that the guy had never found himself lost in a bureaucratic nightmare of endless forms and delays. "We'll get you back to work, but it's going to be another two to three weeks before we upgrade to weight bearing. And it's really not uncommon at this stage for us to say to hold the status quo a little longer. We need to make sure another surgery won't be needed—"

"Another surgery?" Dread made his limbs heavy, made it hard to not slump on the exam table with the weight of everything pushing down on him.

"Well, we can't rule it out yet. But stay off it, focus on patient healing, and I'm hopeful. Another surgery would by necessity add more time to the healing process."

"Yeah," Toby said weakly. Left unsaid was the expense of another surgery. It wasn't only lost time. Toby simply couldn't afford more co-pays. Which meant that he'd need to follow orders about not putting weight on the leg, but bitter, bitter disappointment gathered in his stomach, clogged his senses.

The doctor had more to say, but the roar in Toby's head made it hard to concentrate on what he was saying as he examined Toby. Then an assistant came in with the casts and he was strapped back in. In theory, these casts were lighter than his last ones and the fact that they were technically removable was nice, but in reality, they felt heavy as anchors, tethering him to the earth, keeping him from the sky where he belonged.

"Almost done. We'll get you back out to your ride, no worries." The cheerful assistant trimmed excess off the Velcro straps.

His ride. *Reuben.* Fuck. He'd been deliberately trying to not think of him while the doctor delivered his verdict. His recovery time would now push up against Reuben's leaving date. But more than logistics, he didn't like how much he needed Reuben right then, needed him to say that everything would be okay, needed his distraction and reassurance both. He wasn't supposed to be needy like this, was supposed to be able to weather bad news on his own. But hell if he felt up to the task, not with everything on the verge of crumpling down around him.

Devastated. It was the best word Reuben could think for the look on Toby's face as one of the medical assistants wheeled him back into the waiting room, new giant plastic gray boot on his leg with a half-dozen or more Velcro straps and a similar black contraption on his arm. Both were serious, heavy-duty looking casts, and the hard set to Toby's mouth said he wasn't at all impressed by his new accessories.

"Bad news?" he asked gently, moving to take over for the medical assistant.

"I've got it from here." Toby waved him off before nodding at the pretty woman in cranberry scrubs. "Thanks, Maria."

"No problem, Mr. Kooly." Her light laugh as she lingered a minute too long said she wouldn't mind flirting a little, maybe getting Toby's number. And Reuben supposed a better guy than him would point that out to Toby as they left her to make their way to the elevator. But while Reuben might only have him a few more weeks, he wasn't giving him up a minute before then, and he didn't share well. So, he just hit the down button and waited for Toby to start talking.

"I have to come back in two weeks or so." Toby thumped his head against the elevator's back wall. "*Another* trip. I was really hoping he could release me to a doctor in Homer or something, but no. I'm a special, complicated case and…." He trailed off with a frustrated growl. "I fucking hate this."

"I'll bring you. It's no problem. We'll bring Amelia—she can deal—and we'll see some touristy stuff in addition to your appointment. It'll be—"

"Don't you dare say fun," Toby warned.

"I was going to say fine," Reuben lied. "It'll be fine. We'll still be here to help you out. Is that the main worry? Logistics?"

"I wish," Toby said as the elevator opened for the first floor. He started to roll forward, then abruptly stopped once clear of the doors. "Fuck. Not used to this new arm cast. Keeps catching on the wheels. Supposed to be an improvement, but it feels worse."

"Do you want to go back up? See if they didn't fit it right?"

"They did. Probably gotta get used to it. I'm just… fuck. So fucking frustrated." It was the most Reuben had heard him curse outside of the bedroom, and he wasn't sure what might help. He settled for rubbing Toby's shoulder.

"I can see. I would be too. You've had a day. X-rays. Casts off. Casts on. New configuration to get used to. More doctors tomorrow. Could you let me get us to the car while you decide what food goes better with the drink you've totally earned?"

Looking away, Toby worked his jaw muscles before giving a mighty sigh. "Fine. Push away. Sorry that I'm being...difficult."

"You're not." Another lie because it had been a frustrating day to say the least, but Toby was under tremendous stress, and Reuben couldn't fault him too much for the bad mood.

"Yeah, I am." Toby laughed, then shook his head as Reuben started pushing him in the direction of the signs pointing to the parking structure. "You sure we're dating? I'm pretty sure that even *I* wouldn't want to date me, way I've been snapping at you today."

"Well, luckily you're not me. And yes, we are. And yes, I do want you, even a little cranky."

"Just a bit." Toby gave another rueful laugh.

"So what was the bad news?" Reuben tried asking again. "Return appointment because it's not healing right?"

"Something like that. It's just not happening as fast as they had thought. They want to wait before I start putting weight on the leg, and they want me to go slowly with crutches. Like super slow. And I've got a prescription for a new type of walker—"

"Which we'll pick up," Reuben said smoothly before Toby could come up with a reason to not.

"I'm not supposed to be bummed about any of this because apparently setbacks like this are common, but *man*. I didn't want this. Not now."

"I know." Reuben navigated the parking structure to the row where he'd left the SUV.

"I just… I need to forget about all this." Toby's voice sounded weary as Reuben helped him back into the car, and his expression was almost pleading, what with the big eyes and slack mouth. "Can you help me do that?"

Some last piece of Reuben's heart that didn't already belong to this man despite his best efforts pulled loose from his chest. He had to swallow hard before answering. "Yeah, I can do that."

"Good." Toby's eyes fluttered closed as Reuben shut the door for him, and he didn't open them as Reuben climbed behind the wheel.

"Here's what we're going to do," Reuben said decisively. If Toby needed someone to take charge, then he absolutely was the right guy for the job. "We'll get the new walker from the medical supply, then get food. You don't look up for going out, so I'll call in a to-go order for the Turkish food and some beers for us to pick up on the way to the hotel."

"Okay." The solemn way Toby drew the word out suggested that he was trusting Reuben with far more than just their dinner order.

While Reuben was never one to back away from a challenge and didn't doubt he could give Toby what he wanted, the trust still humbled him, made him want to try that much harder to be what he *needed*.

They managed the walker pickup without Toby needing to get out of the car. Sensing that Toby didn't need to be bothered with too many choices, Reuben ordered for both of them while Toby continued to pretend to doze. And it was a pretense—Reuben knew by now what Toby's real sleeping face looked like, how his breathing sounded, how the tension left his body. Right then, Toby's breathing was too shallow and his body far too tense for Reuben to believe he was actually sleeping, but he also wasn't going to force Toby to interact if what he needed was to check out from the world. He left Toby in the car while he ran into the Turkish place and collected their order which smelled amazing, redolent of spiced meat and fresh bread.

"Okay, now I'm hungry." Toby managed a small smile as Reuben handed him the order to hold.

"Good."

The hotel was nearby, and once in their room he opened a beer for each of them and spread the food out on the L-shaped desk.

"Think you ordered enough?" Toby laughed.

"I figured a selection would be nice," Reuben shrugged. In truth, he'd been thinking of how Toby had skipped real food at the diner, probably out of a need to save money, and Reuben already had a plan to suggest leftovers in the morning. He might understand Toby's pride's but was also all for reducing the burden on Toby for his turns.

He wasn't surprised when Toby helped himself to large portions of rice pilaf and kebabs, adding to Reuben's theory about him actually having been hungry earlier. Knowing better than to point that out, he took his own plate to the chair, which he pulled next to Toby, who was still in his wheelchair, balancing his plate on the edge of the desk and attempting to eat with the new hand cast. Reuben flipped on the TV.

"Thanks." Toby nodded at the TV. "Not up to much talking, sorry."

"I figured." Bypassing the news, Reuben settled on a quiz show.

"Practicing for the retirement home?" Toby teased, mirth still not reaching his eyes.

"Yup." Reuben made no apologies as he smiled back. "I got baklava for desert. Bigger piece to you if you guess more answers than me."

"You're on." Toby might be in a funk, but he was still the same competitive guy down deep that Reuben liked so much. And he was surprisingly good at the word games, easily beating Reuben by the end of the episode and the end of their heaping plates of food, which had been surprisingly first class. Despite Toby bragging about the rich food scene in Anchorage, he never would have expected to find better Turkish food here than he'd had in New Jersey, but the kebabs had been perfectly seasoned and tender, the rice fluffy and buttery, and the bread yeasty and ideal for soaking up the sauces.

"You've done this before." He gestured at the credits for the TV show as he cleaned up their plates and served the dessert, giving Toby the bigger piece as promised.

"Guilty as charged. Dad liked this one for a while after his accident. The occupational therapist suggested he watch it, and I ended up watching some with him when I was home. So maybe it's not *only* an old people show."

"Gee, thanks." Reuben faked indignation to get another smile out of Toby.

"Hey, you're the one who's always going on about how old you are. I'm just agreeing with you." Toby took a generous bite of his pastry. "Damn. This is amazing."

Reuben was pretty sure that the amazing part was the look of rapture on Toby's face as he licked sugar from his lips, but he focused on Toby's other comment, unable to tell how serious Toby had been. "Well, I am." Losing the joking tone, Reuben tried to meet his eyes. "Honestly though, does it bother you that I'm so much older? Does it make a difference?"

"Since we're apparently dating now and stuff, I guess that's a valid question, but no. I've told you, you're hot. And apparently I've got a silver bear fetish thanks to you. And it's sorta…"

"Yes?" More interested in the conversation than dessert, Reuben set his piece aside for later.

"I know I shouldn't like it, but I kinda dig your…experience. Your ability to take charge of a situation. You make me…comfortable, weird as that is to say."

"It's not weird. I like that I make you feel like that. And who says you shouldn't like it?"

"I'm supposed to be able to handle my shit." Toby's face turned stony.

"And you can. You do. You're one of the strongest people I know. But you've also got a lot on your plate. It's okay to not just need help, but to enjoy having someone to share the burden with. Liking the chance to let go occasionally doesn't make you weak."

"Maybe." Toby's mouth pursed and he didn't sound convinced, so Reuben reached over, gave his shoulder a squeeze. Sighing, Toby relaxed into the touch. "And I *do* like letting go with you. A lot. I just hate the rest of everything right now. Hate asking for shit. *Needing* help."

"I know." He continued to rub Toby's shoulders. "How about you just shut off that part of your brain for the night? You said you wanted me to help you do that. Let me."

"Yeah." Shutting his eyes, Toby stretched so his head could fall back against Reuben's arm. "That would be nice. I just want a shower, another beer and to get seriously fucked. Not terribly picky about the order."

"Shower we can manage." Reuben checked the bathroom. "There's a flip down shower stool."

"Cool." Toby rolled up behind him. "I meant the other part too. If you really want to help…"

"I do," Reuben assured him as he rolled up his shirt-sleeves to help with the shower. "And getting you off is absolutely on the agenda."

After tossing his T-Shirt to the ground, Toby stared him down, grabbing Reuben's hand to pull him closer. "I. Want. To. Get. Fucked. Not a massage. Not us jerking it together. Fucked. You said you want to give me what I need, and I need that."

Swallowing hard, Reuben tried to calm his racing pulse and quiet the urge to ask Toby if he was sure. He hadn't forgotten Toby saying he'd never cuddled or slept next to a guy before Reuben, and he had a feeling this might be uncharted territory for him, but he also wanted to honor Toby knowing what he wanted and being brave enough to ask.

"Okay." He knelt to brush a kiss across Toby's forehead. "Okay."

Chapter Eighteen

Toby exhaled hard as soon as Reuben agreed. His heart clattered against his ribs, a pack of untamed sled dogs racing around his insides. Damn. Saying that aloud had *not* been easy, but he knew Reuben by now, and he could almost see him plotting some sort of post-shower massage to help Toby sleep. Which was nice and all and Reuben *was* incredibly good at relaxing him that way, but it wouldn't do what he really wanted, which was to not fucking think. To tell his worries to shove it and just *feel*. Some people used alcohol or drugs for that purpose, but for him, sex had always been the best, quickest, cheapest high. And sometimes, sweet and slow, like Reuben had introduced him to, was exactly what he needed and wanted. But other times, a guy just wanted it fast and mind-obliteratingly hard.

Even as he got the shower ready, Reuben was still looking at him like he expected Toby to change his mind any second.

"I want this. Condoms in my wallet. And I know perfectly well you packed the lube." Too much lotion mess had led to Reuben producing actual lube a while back, which was good, because Toby wasn't letting logistics get in the way of getting fucked. He wriggled out of his shorts. If there was one blessing to his injuries, it was that they hadn't occurred in the dead of winter. At least he could get by with a bare minimum of clothing.

"You've done it before, then? Liked it?" Reuben's head tilted, and Toby, who had been prepared to lie, found yet again that there was nothing he could hold back from this man.

"Sort of. Pegging and fingers count, right?" Toby grinned as Reuben knelt to help him cover the casts with one the cast covers he'd apparently picked up at the medical supply place. Damn man really did think of everything.

"Well, it's not exactly the same." Done with covering the casts, Reuben helped him transfer from the wheelchair to the shower chair.

"I'm aware of that. Which is why I want to try it. With you. And I know it's more complicated with my injuries, but I'm not sure when I'll get another chance with someone I'm as into as you." Truth be told, he was more into Reuben than he'd been anyone else in his life, but he wasn't quite ready to confess that. And yeah, his experience with other guys had been a lot of hasty blowjobs and furtive make-out sessions with clumsy handjobs, but that didn't mean he hadn't thought about this. Often. But it wasn't what people seemed to want from him in bed, and voicing the desire wasn't easy, even now, with someone he trusted as much as Reuben.

"I'm into you too." Reuben's mouth quirked as he passed Toby the soap. "And I'm not going to ask again if you're sure, but I just want to say that I don't need fucking. I've had relationships where that wasn't on the table and been just fine. This isn't something you need to do for me."

"Maybe I need to do it for me," he admitted. Even though they hadn't discussed it before, Reuben simply exuded the vibe of someone who loved fucking and who was probably very, very good at it. And honestly, the fact that he hadn't pushed was part of why Toby felt comfortable enough bringing it up. Perversely, Reuben not asking had him wanting it more, wanting to prove that he wasn't too fragile for fucking. Prove something to himself too. What, he wasn't exactly sure, but some part of himself needed this on a level he didn't really want to closely examine.

As Toby washed, Reuben unbuttoned his shirt and neatly set it on the sink counter. "I'm going to do a fast rinse after you."

"Darn. And here I thought you were just providing me with some eye candy." He made a point of ogling Reuben in decent lighting for once—it was usually dim in his room late at night when they fooled around, and Reuben really did deserve to be appreciated. Big broad shoulders, powerful back muscles, fuzzy chest, pale pink nipples. The whole package was just tasty. *Oh. Good idea.* Crooking his finger, he motioned Reuben closer. "Lose the pants and come here. I want to try something."

Reuben's mouth quirked up but he complied, stepping out of his pants, revealing even more deliciously fuzzy flesh in his strong thighs and legs, and his seriously jacked cock made Toby shiver in the best way. Stepping into the shower, Reuben splashed himself with the water spray.

"Okay I'm here."

"Closer." Toby steered him closer with his left hand. "See, I think I can…" He trailed off to demonstrate, angling himself so that he could lick Reuben's plump cockhead. He'd never been much on subtlety when it came to oral, relying more on sheer enthusiasm than skill, but from Reuben's sharp intake of breath, he could tell the direct approach was working just fine.

"I thought you wanted…"

"This. I want this." He sucked in as much of Reuben's cock in as he dared and used his fist on the rest, setting a slow but deliberate rhythm. He already knew that Reuben had amazing powers of restraint, which made it all the more gratifying when Reuben muttered a stream of curses under his breath and leaned against the tile wall.

"You get me off this way, and I'll take twice as long with you." Reuben's tone was a warning, but Toby only pulled back long enough to laugh.

"Not exactly a threat. I like the sound of that." He licked at the underside of Reuben's cock, loving the heavy vein there that wrapped around the shaft.

"You won't." Reuben was clearly trying to be stern, but the waver to his voice told Toby he was getting somewhere. "Because *you* aren't coming until I say. And I intend to make you work for it."

"Bring it on." Now they were talking. This was exactly the out-of-his-head sort of sex Toby was craving, Reuben going all bossy on him, taking over, threatening to push his limits.

"All right. You want me to come?"

"Mmm." He hummed his need around Reuben's cock, not letting up on the suction.

"Gonna have to let me take over if you want that. No more teasing."

Teasing? Toby hadn't been teasing—he'd been working for it. But then Reuben snaked his hand down to gently cradle Toby's face, and his stomach wobbled. This wasn't how things usually went.

"I can't deep throat," he admitted, pulling back, both to talk and to see if Reuben if would let him.

"Not asking you to. Just let me drive. Trust." Reuben stroked a thumb over Toby's lips before repeating the gesture with his cock. The way they were positioned, Toby needed to use his left hand on Reuben's hip to steady himself, and not having a hand on Reuben's cock made him nervous in a way where his body couldn't seem to decide whether it was turned on or not. Then Reuben slowly thrust forward, cock slipping over Toby's tongue, and his own lust surged, cock jumping. Okay, sexy. This was sexy. Scary and sexy at the same time, letting Reuben have the control, knowing he could decide to push Toby's boundaries but trusting him to not.

Reuben, however, rewarded his trust with slow, shallow thrusts that only gradually picked up speed, never going deeper than Toby could handle. And he still had a lot of freedom—the ability to use his tongue on the underside of Reuben's cock, the chance to vary the suction, the power to urge his on with his hand on Reuben's hip. Even so, this was still very clearly Reuben's show.

"That's it. It feels so good." Reuben's breath came faster now. "Show me how much you like this."

Without waiting for his brain's permission, a moan escaped his throat. Yeah, he liked this. A lot. He sucked harder, trying to convey that with his lips and tongue. Speeding up, Reuben continued to stroke his cheeks and jaw, a tender counterpoint to his aggressive thrusts.

"Want my come? That what you want?"

"Yeah," Toby gasped as Reuben pulled back enough to let him get a breath. "Please. Want to taste it."

He had a bit of a thing for messy sex and right then, he craved—*needed*—Reuben's come, wanted it on his skin and his tongue, wanted it any way Reuben wanted to give it to him. And with that awareness, the giving up to what Reuben wanted, the high he'd been seeking slammed into him. His cock throbbed and his muscles burned from holding the awkward position, but his spirit soared.

"Close. Going to let me go fast?"

Toby moaned his agreement, even as Reuben's thrusts started to lose some of their finesse, things getting sloppy, exactly the way he wanted them, having to chase Reuben's cock with his mouth to keep up, blocking everything out other than the burning need to get Reuben off.

"There. There. Take it. *Fuck*." Reuben's voice dropped several octaves as salty come flooded Toby's mouth, making him need to swallow fast, but not fast enough to prevent some from dribbling out of his mouth. Fuck, yes. The multiple sensations were almost enough to make him come with nothing more on his cock than air and increasingly tepid water.

"Hell. That was…" Reuben shook his head, releasing a shaky laugh. "Unexpected. You're too damn tempting."

"Good." Toby used his tongue to swipe at the come on his face.

"Your turn, but you better be prepared to *work* after that little display." Reuben's deliciously stern tone was back, and Toby couldn't hold back his grin.

"Yes, please." It kind of sucked that he couldn't make a run for the bed to prove his eagerness, make Reuben chase him, that instead he had to be patient, wait for Reuben to quickly soap up and rinse in the rapidly cooling water, then wait for him to hand Toby the towel and help him transfer back to the wheelchair. But the wait was also good, made his pulse thrum like waiting in line for a show to start. Whatever was coming, it was going to be *good*.

Finally out of the shower, Toby had to deal with the soggy cast covers which was a bit of a dick-wilter.

"Damn casts. Ruin all spontaneity," he grumbled, body still reminding him that while Reuben was all loose and post-orgasm smiles, *he* hadn't come yet.

"Oh, I'll show you spontaneous." Reuben laughed wickedly as he dried himself off and followed Toby back to the bedroom. Man, he really did like this side to Reuben, the effortlessly bossy and commanding and sexy-as-fuck side. Reuben stopped to collect the condom from Toby's wallet and the lube from his bag and tossed both on the closest bed.

"Can't wait."

"On your side will be easiest." Reuben raided the other bed for pillows, arranging them around Toby as he settled in the middle of the bed. He knew by now exactly how Toby liked the pillows for lying on his side, and that small amount of caretaking threatened to undo Toby, made emotion rise in his throat. Ever considerate, Reuben even draped the pillow closest to Toby's cock with a towel. He lay on his left side, using pillows under his arm and leg casts. It wasn't exactly a sexy position as it was closer to sprawled starfish than come-hither sexy lounge, but it was comfortable, and as he slept like this most nights, it was a position he knew he could hold while Reuben did whatever torture he had in mind.

He'd expected Reuben to spoon him, maybe even

flip on the TV, take some time to recover before they got started on round two, but instead, Reuben stretched out facing him and pulled him in for a long kiss. They'd had all sorts of kisses so far—sleepy, aroused, friendly, about-to-come, satisfied—but this one was different, had a potential to it, a sort of charged energy. Reuben managed to both kiss like he hadn't just climaxed and like they had all night. Reuben smelled like hotel soap mingled with his usual high-class herbal scent that Toby was beginning to think was less hair product or after-shave and more intrinsic Reuben.

They kissed for long minutes, Reuben taking him from anticipation to needy to a different plane, one where he was floating along, all sensation and light, content to see what was coming next. It was the same high he'd felt in the shower when he'd let go of every-thing other than Reuben and the moment. And perhaps Reuben had been waiting for his contented sigh, because as Toby melted into the pillows from the kisses, Reu-ben growled. He swept his hands up and down Toby's torso while they kissed, dipping lower to palm his ass.

But the touch was less prelude to fucking and more possessive accompaniment to their increasingly hungry kisses, which continued with more leisurely touches until Toby felt like he was holding a fistful of helium balloons like a cartoon character about to lift off on nothing more than hope and good feelings.

"How do you do that?" he asked breathlessly as Reu-ben let him up for air.

"Do what?" Reuben leaned in to nip at Toby's neck.

"Make everything disappear. Make me all…floaty." He lacked the ability to explain what the assault on his senses was doing to him, but he wanted Reuben to know how much he liked it. Needed it.

"Floaty is a good start." Reuben's chuckle rumbled through Toby, warmed places he hadn't even realized were chilly. He sat up, and Toby instantly craved the return of his nearness. "But let's see if we can improve on it."

With far more dexterity than Toby would have predicted, Reuben moved to the other side of Toby, dropping kisses on the back of his neck. Having a feeling where Reuben's mouth might be headed, Toby tensed.

"You don't…uh… I don't need…" He floundered for how to point out that he neither required nor wanted a ton of prep or buildup.

"Floaty, remember?" Reuben rubbed his shoulders, touch soothing. "You let me decide what you need. Tell me if you don't like something, but let me be in charge."

"Okay." It was hard to keep up a protest with Reuben's hands working their usual magic on his muscles. He still craved a hard and fast fuck, but the good feelings he'd collected so far helped him stay patient. And when Reuben started again with the kissing of his back, he relaxed into the contact. Reuben scooted lower, nipping at Toby's ass. He had to swallow back another round of objections because he hadn't had a partner rim him before, and a strange mix of anticipation and trepidation gathered in his gut, along with a healthy dose of "you shouldn't want this" self-talk.

But that lecture evaporated when Reuben licked down his crack, new sensations firing all along his nerve endings even before Reuben touched his rim. And when his tongue flicked *there*, he couldn't hold back a whimper.

"Please."

Reuben hummed appreciatively before attacking Toby's rim in earnest. And if Toby had expected some version of what he'd attempted with partners before himself, tentative explorations and light teasing, he'd vastly underestimated Reuben, who devoured Toby's ass like he was starving for it, like he was determined to light Toby up from only this. His stubble dragged against Toby's skin as his generous mouth took Toby apart. He rimmed like he kissed—like a guy who utterly loved what he was doing and who was confident enough to own that. And the more he licked and sucked, the more a deep need gathered inside Toby. Forget floating. He'd gone from happy, lazy cloud to burgeoning star, all coiled energy and pulsing need.

"Fuck me." His dick was so desperate for friction that he rubbed against the pillow, terry cloth of the towel dragging against his sensitive nerve endings, as Reuben continued his all-out assault. "Fingers. Cock. Not picky. Fuck me. Need it."

Reuben's muffled laugh was his only reply, but the *snick* of the lube bottle opening made Toby exhale with relief. He'd figured that Reuben would replace his mouth with his fingers, but instead he started a duel assault, rubbing circles while he continued to lick and flick until Toby was rocking back against the pressure of his finger.

"Come on, come on. Give it to me."

"Impatient." Reuben shifted back, pressure of his fingers intensifying. Toby liked the sensation of being penetrated, liked the initial resistance and burn, then the rush as his body yielded. And he loved that Reuben had gone straight to two fingers—he was more than ready and loved that intense fullness as Reuben worked them deeper. Pleasure gathered in his tensing limbs and lower back, everything waiting for—

"*That.* Oh fuck. That. I need that," he babbled as Reuben connected with his gland.

"Like it?" Reuben worked him in long, lazy thrusts, stretching him on upstroke before going deep again.

"Want to come."

"This way?" Reuben managed to sound almost disinterested, but the brush of his hard cock against Toby's leg said otherwise. "Or wanting something else?"

"Smug bastard," he gritted out. "Fuck me. Now."

"Now, now, that's not sounding very…floaty."

"Screw floating. Need it too bad. Need you," he admitted in a rush.

"You've got me." Reuben stroked his thigh before sitting up, handling the condom. Fuck. His cock was *big*, and for the first time in this whole enterprise, Toby knew a moment of hesitation. As if he sensed Toby's unease, Reuben leaned over him to kiss near his ear. "Okay? Tell me what you want."

It was less sexy order and more concern, but the gruff tone grounded him, reminded him what he did want— Reuben. Wanted Reuben's voice in his ear. Wanted Reuben's bulk surrounding him. Wanted Reuben in him. Wanted to block the world out, including his own nerves, and just feel, even if that meant letting go of his own expectations. Because maybe that was it—his need scaring him even more than Reuben's monster dick. The cock he could handle. Coming apart at the seams, not so much. But when he let himself have this, let himself wallow in his craving and his need, it just felt so damn good that there was only one answer.

"You. Want you. Fuck me."

"Oh, I will." Reuben straddled Toby's lower leg, a position that let him line up his cock as he loomed over Toby. Apparently not in the same rush as Toby, he teased, tracing Toby's rim with his slick, condom-covered cockhead, rubbing firm circles until Toby was panting and pushing back.

"Now. Now. No—" Toby broke off with a low moan as Reuben finally pushed forward. And okay, this was more stretch than he had had before. It burned, but behind the discomfort, the familiar high of penetration lurked, made him rock back, seeking more. And *more* was the operative word—more stretch, more fullness, more high, more sensations. More of everything.

"Doing okay?" Reuben asked, but Toby could only give what he hoped was an encouraging moan as reply, beyond speech now. When he'd thought about fucking with a guy, most of his fantasies had involved fast and hard, the sort of imagined brutal breakneck pace that worked when he wanted to jerk off quickly. But he should have known by now that Reuben wanted nothing to do with a fleeting fuck. Instead, Reuben set a slow rhythm that made up for its lack of speed with unerring accuracy, gradually going deeper and deeper, grazing Toby's gland with each thrust. And unlike the quick fuck of his dreams, this one consumed his soul, demanded far more from him than orgasm, required that he let go on a level he hadn't before.

But when he did, when he released the last moorings on his self-control, let himself moan for it, let himself meet each thrust, he *flew*. Not floated. Not exploded. *Flew.* And just like in a plane, it was addictively freeing, the endorphin rush hard to describe, even as he knew dangers lurked, but he couldn't dwell on those then, not when it felt so good. Not when he was fucking *flying*, living from one moan to the next.

"God, you're so hot." Reuben drew a finger down Toby's side. They were both sweating now, bodies slapping together. "Want to come?"

Did he? Toby honestly wasn't sure anymore. Coming would be awesome, but it would also mean the end of this…whatever you called it when fucking became a reckoning. No, not reckoning as that would be him alone, a solo flight. This was something different. Something shared. And oh, that made everything better. Reuben's body pressed against his. Face flushed, eyes bright, quaver to his voice that said he wasn't quite as cool and collected as he liked to appear. If he too were flying high on this, then yeah, Toby wanted to come, wanted to see and feel Reuben go too, wanted to see what new heights they could reach together.

"You too," he managed. "Come too."

"I will." Reuben grabbed the lube and drizzled some on his palm before fisting Toby's cock. Seemingly effortlessly, he matched the stroke of his hand to the thrust of his hips. Slow, but steady. Firm. There. A gradual build that was no less devastating for the deliberate pace. He alternated been focusing on his own gathering pleasure and watching Reuben's face as he struggled to maintain control. Every moan and gasp from him felt like a victory, added another thrill.

"More," he gasped. "More."

"Yeah." Reuben surprised him by almost immediately complying, hips snapping faster, strokes going deeper, pressure against Toby's gland increasing with every thrust. His unerring precision confirmed every suspicion Toby'd had about Reuben being good at this.

Coming with something in his ass was always different, the way the pleasure pooled in unexpected places, spread out, less mountain hike to a sharp peak and more exploring hills and valleys as tension quietly increased until climax became inevitable. But even as his balls tightened, his body hung out on the edge for what seemed an eternity.

"Come on," he urged. Reuben losing control was what he needed, the missing piece that would push him over. "Need you to come too."

"Close. Fuck. Want you…"

"Yeah. Me too." He groaned, not sure either of them was making sense but beyond caring.

"Together," Reuben demanded, thrusts coming swiftly now, rapid bursts of bliss that spiraled Toby closer. *Together.* Yes, he could do that. Would do that. Together they could do this, could do anything. And flying on that feeling of invincibility, his body shuddered, orgasm starting in his neck and abs, muscles quaking even before his cock started spurting.

"Fuck. *Toby.*" Reuben pushed deep, and Toby swore he could feel his cock pulse. His ass spasmed in delicious aftershocks that wrung him dry. And just like a perfect flight, the landing was soft and sweet, a gradual returning awareness of his limbs, of the bed, of Reuben pulling out and collapsing behind him, pulling Toby close.

"Never want to leave," Toby mumbled as he rested his head against Reuben's shoulder. He didn't mean the bed—eventually, the need to shower and to move to the less rumpled bed would win out. But this moment, this moment right here. He wanted to stay here forever, bask in what they'd been. What they'd made, together. All of it together. He didn't want to leave this moment, this man, this version of himself that he barely recognized but that felt more real than anything that had come before. Reality tickled the edges of his consciousness, but he pushed it away, wanting to wallow here as long as he could.

Chapter Nineteen

Reuben half expected an awkward morning or at least the return of Toby's black mood, but he was pleasantly surprised by Toby snuggling deeper into his embrace when his phone alarm went off.

"Don't want to get up," he mumbled.

"I'll hit snooze." Not wanting to let go of Toby, he fumbled for his phone on the nightstand one handed. If not for Toby's doctor's appointment, he'd be more than happy to try for some wake-up sex, but barring that, he'd settle for another few minutes holding Toby.

"This sleeping all night together thing...pretty awesome." Despite his plea for more sleep, Toby blinked and stretched against Reuben, who was still spooning him. They'd cleaned up with a second shower the night before, then cuddled in the other bed with a mindless movie until Toby had fallen asleep with his head pillowed on Reuben's arm. Damn perfect.

"It was." Reuben dropped a kiss on the back of Toby's neck. "Honestly, we can probably get away with this back at the house. Maybe not the loud sex, but sleeping together's fine. Amelia's figured out that we're more than friends, and I don't think seeing me emerge from your room is going to scar her."

"Probably not. She's really cool with it, you think?"

"As cool as a fourteen-year-old who doesn't want to see 'mushy stuff' can be, yeah. I figure all kids are mildly grossed out at the notion of their parents as romantic beings, but despite her grumblings, I think she genuinely likes you."

"Good. It's mutual. She's a good kid, and truth be told, far easier than Nell was at that age." Toby stretched again and sat up. "Let's get her that cake mix when we go the store."

"The big box store probably only has cake mix for twenty."

"More leftovers for me." Toby grinned, no trace of yesterday's darkness.

Had Reuben known that fucking might have that effect on Toby, he would have suggested it sooner. He didn't need fucking but couldn't deny really liking the act, liking the closeness and intimacy of it. And there was also something nice about having waited, about having the weeks of friendship and affection to draw on, making the experience that much deeper and richer. And hotter. Reuben simply couldn't remember hotter sex, and definitely couldn't remember the last time he'd gone double. The second orgasm had hurt in the best way possible, leaving him a pile of singed nerve endings and little else. But now, restored by sleep, his body surged with the sort of energy only sex like that could provide.

"Speaking of leftovers, there's plenty left from last night. How about we pretend to be hungover college students and have dinner for breakfast?"

"Sure. Does that mean breakfast for dinner then? Better put pancake stuff on the list if so."

It was the sort of domestic exchange any couple might

have as they planned their day, but it still lightened Reuben's heart, made him wish for things he wasn't sure he could have. Savoring each moment, he tried to memorize little things like Toby's laugh as he dug into a plate of leftovers, his blissed-out expression as he declared baklava better than donuts, and his comfort at hanging out naked in the bed, covers discarded. Not nearly so cozy with his own nudity, Reuben dressed before eating, making sure Toby got the lion's share of the sweet stuff.

Toby's mood seemed to deflate on the way back to the medical complex, but luckily the wait for the neurologist wasn't long. He emerged only a short time after the medical assistant had taken him back, which Reuben hoped was a good sign.

"How was it?" he asked cautiously.

"Not bad. Says I've recovered well." Toby's grin held a lot of relief. "Says I should be good to fly and drive as soon as my leg and arm cooperate."

"That's excellent news." Reuben smiled at him as they made their way out. He knew from other remarks that Toby was a little nervous about flying again, but bringing that up right then didn't seem prudent. "You've earned cake to celebrate for sure."

"Hey now, the cake is for *you.*" Toby laughed. "Store now? Is it bad I'm kind of looking forward to driving the motorized cart?"

"Take your fun where you can get it."

At the store, watching Toby attempt the cart was entertaining, his obvious enthusiasm at being more mobile infectious. Filling the big cart Reuben was pushing took far longer than it needed to, Reuben trying to indulge Toby's enjoyment at being out of the house by going up and down each aisle. It was the sort of warehouse store that had plenty of things other than food to distract them. Back home, Reuben had groceries delivered, and neither Natalie nor Dan had been the "let's shop together" type, so this shared time was something of a novel pleasure.

"You need that cookbook." Toby pointed at a display of books where one advertising thirty-minute dinners was prominently displayed. "Expand the menu from burgers and chicken."

"Hey, I've got you for variety. Even Amelia likes your chili and fish," Reuben protested even as he tossed the book in the cart. Toby had been predictably reluctant to add things for himself to the cart, like the brand of chips that only he liked, so Reuben was more than happy to take any suggestion of his.

"Yeah, but I'm not going to be around forever." Toby picked up another book to examine the back cover, already moving on, but the joke hit Reuben like a well-aimed dart. He didn't want to think about cooking for himself back in his condo. Didn't want to think about it not being the three of them, Toby giving him tips and joking, Amelia making requests. There had to be a way to make that future less bleak, and he was determined to find it.

"Should we get Nell something as a thank-you for watching Amelia?" he asked to distract himself from dour thoughts. "And maybe Amelia something too…"

"Who are you and what have you done with Mr. No Souvenirs, not even pictures?" Toby laughed, but his eyes were serious.

"Given him a lot of perspective." The truth slipped out easily. "Soon she'll be at school, and I won't have her to spoil so easily." *Or you.* And there he was, back at unhappy thoughts of how quickly the summer was passing.

"You're a cute dad." Shaking his head, Toby drove his cart over to a display of cosmetic sets, various lotions and potions and makeup items in colorful cases. "Nell doesn't need anything, but get one of these for Amelia, and you can do one for her too, say they were a two-for-one sale or something."

They spent far longer than they needed to debating color combinations before they settled on which sets to get. And on the way to the checkout, he added an Alaska Grown sweatshirt for Amelia that Toby said was a hot item, trying to force himself to feel upbeat about it keeping her warm at school in the fall. Knowing the total bill was likely going to be eye-poppingly big, he sent Toby ahead with the car keys to return the motorized cart. When he emerged, Toby was already in the passenger side of the SUV.

"Bugs me that I can't help you load up." Toby's frown was back as was the grumpy set to his shoulders.

"Hey, you helped just by being along." Reuben stowed the last of the groceries and slid behind the wheel.

"Does this count as a date, then? Because I'm thirsty. I can get coffee for us on the way back to the highway, if you want?"

Reuben wasn't particularly thirsty, but he had a feeling this was Toby's pride again, so he nodded. "Sure. Gotta get you your hourly sugar fix."

The line of cars at the drive-thru was predictably long and slow, and by the time they had their drinks, it was already getting on toward noon.

"Good luck with making up time." Toby pointed at the map displayed on the car's console. "Looks like traffic is backed up on the highway too. Not uncommon this time of year, especially if there's an accident or something. I'll text Nell, let her know we're running behind."

"Guess we had too much fun shopping."

"Yeah." Toby sounded more resigned than upbeat. "I wasn't thinking about the time. I hope everything's okay back home."

"I'm sure it will be fine," Reuben reassured him. Really, though, how much trouble could Nell and Amelia get into? And Toby absolutely deserved fun, deserved a few hours when he wasn't burdened by family worries and whatever else that was going on that he wouldn't tell Reuben about. Reuben wasn't going to apologize for giving him a break. Even if it meant a small delay, Reuben trusted that things would work out, but the defiant tilt to Toby's jaw said that he didn't believe him. Oh well. Reuben would simply have to prove him wrong.

Toby drummed his fingers on the dash, staring out at the endless string of barely moving cars in front of them. They'd had the exact same view of mountains on the left, inlet on the right for well over an hour now, crawling forward, taking well over double the time to make it past Portage. Even telling Reuben the story of Beluga Point, an important Athabascan site, hadn't been enough of a distraction.

"My kingdom for one of our planes about now." Toby sighed, checking his phone for the hundredth time. Still no reply from Nell. He wished he could shake the dread that something was wrong. Reuben was undoubtedly right that there was no reason to worry. Nell had seemed increasingly responsible lately, and Amelia was a smart kid.

Even Reuben's usual boundless patience seemed

taxed, his mouth a thin line as he clenched the steering wheel. "I've been in awful New York and New Jersey traffic, but man, this is brutal. At least at home, my Le—*car* has satellite radio, and I've usually got an audio book on reserve. Or I'm able to take a business call from the car."

Toby had to smile because Reuben had totally been about to name drop a pricey car and stopped himself. But one couldn't completely erase the high-powered guy from his wheeling-and-dealing ways.

"Admit it. You're totally one of those drivers having heated discussion with your hands-free call, gesturing alone in the car, closing big deals from the freeway."

"I've closed a few that way." Reuben's tone had a fondness to it that made Toby's teeth clench. Part of Reuben *did* miss that life, no matter what he said, and Toby would do well to remember it.

"Tell me about your place." He needed details, needed to picture Reuben living this other life, the one Toby had no part of, the one he'd be going back to. "Close to the office, I bet?"

"Oh, you do know me well." Chuckling, Reuben turned down the radio they were both ignoring anyway. "Yeah, it's walking distance. Natalie and I had a place in the suburbs, but I hated the commute, so letting her keep the house was an easy choice. It's a loft condo."

"See, I knew it was a bachelor pad. And judging by your taste, it's probably tricked out."

"Well, I don't know about tricked—it's modern, exposed brick and stainless accents. I was too busy to do any decorating myself, so I let Craig—he's one of the friends supposed to come on the trip—recommend a decorator friend. They did a nice job. I'd say it's comfortable, but I don't spend a ton of time there." Reuben's tone was thoughtful and more than a little distant, as if he was trying to puzzle something out. "Nice bathroom, though. You'd appreciate the shower and the water pressure. Hot tub on the balcony, which yeah, I guess would make it a bachelor pad in your book."

"Sweet." Toby wasn't really considering what he'd think of the place, more concerned with picturing Reuben in this environment, putting him firmly out of reach in some starched and pressed suit, glass of wine in his hand, not the beer he usually shared with Toby. Some suave date in the hot tub on the balcony, glittering lights of a city below.

"Big bed. You could come see." Reuben shrugged, but his voice was too careful for this to be a completely casual observation.

"Me? What the heck would I do in New Jersey?" Nowhere in his imaginings had Toby seen a place for himself. Reuben might not be joking, but he might as well be for how realistic this suggestion of his was.

"See me." Reuben managed to sound wounded. "Get the tour of my shower and hot tub. Maybe sightsee for real some if we decided to leave bed. I'd say it would be a break from fall or winter for you, but we get snow too."

"Sorry, snow's a deal breaker." Somehow Toby managed to keep his tone light.

"I'm serious." Traffic still barely crawling, Reuben reached over, patted Toby's thigh. "You could come visit."

"No, I couldn't. I'm going to need every hour Annie can give me as soon as the doctors clear me," he admitted. Mentioning money sucked, but it was easier than trying to explain how uneasy he was at the prospect of seeing who Reuben was back in his glitzy real life. "Winter *is* usually our slow time, but airfare would be killer."

"I'd pay, of course." Reuben said it as easily as if they were discussing groceries, not what would likely be hundreds of dollars. Toby'd researched fares before for clients—he knew how expensive cross-country flights could be.

"No, you wouldn't. I pay my own way." Toby had to work to not sound pissed, because he was a little. He did *not* need some sugar daddy paying his way to go visit for what would undoubtedly be a sex-filled reunion weekend. And for what purpose? What could possibly be served by him agreeing to go visit? It would just make it harder to make a clean break, make them miss each other that much more.

"You've got a November birthday—don't deny it because I heard Nell teasing you about it. You could think of it as a birthday present from a friend. And I really would like to see you again. We could have fun. All kidding aside, I'd love showing you the city."

That vision flickered again—Reuben in a suit with a glass of some expensive wine that Toby couldn't pronounce in a sleek condo that belonged on some TV drama show, and he tried to place himself there, tried to see a space where he'd fit with Reuben's fancy lawyer friends, fit with the bustle of a big urban city. Nope. Couldn't do it.

"Not a city person," he said at last. "Even Anchorage feels too big to me sometimes, so noisy and everyone in a hurry. I've never been farther than Seattle a couple of times."

Some of the light dimmed in Reuben's eyes, and his

face hardened, but his voice stayed level and upbeat. "There are other options—"

Buzz. Buzz. Toby's phone vibrated loudly in his lap, a quick succession of incoming message. Cell reception could be spotty in the mountain passes, and they must have just hit a signal.

"Sorry. I should—"

"Go ahead. Look." Finally some frustration had crept into Reuben's voice, proving the man wasn't completely made of granite. And really, Toby should finish the conversation about him visiting, firmly kill any idea of this thing continuing beyond Reuben's time here. But he was a giant chicken and flipped his phone over. Five new messages? What the fuck? Even before he opened the first message from Nell, his pulse started roaring like a De Havilland prepping for takeoff.

Dad fell. We weren't home. I'm so sorry. So sorry. Found him when we got back. Couldn't get him up myself. Ambulance guys here now.

Heart—hell, his entire damn chest cavity—in his throat, he read the next message. *Ambulance taking him to hospital in Homer. A & I following. I'm sorry.*

The third message was from Hannah. *Nell just messaged me. Sorry I was with a patient. Is Dad okay? Message me back!*

Message four was from a nosy neighbor trying to be helpful who had seen the ambulance and message five was from Annie. *Just got message from Nell. Got a situation with a plane here, but going to try to meet her at the hospital. Heard about the highway accident delaying traffic too. Don't worry! I'll update you.*

"Fuck. Fuck. Fuck." Toby beat his head against the headrest. Traffic was sort of moving again. Still not regular speed though and nowhere near as fast as he needed. He needed to be in Homer *now*, not five hours from now or whenever the traffic finally let them.

"What?" Reuben asked. "What's happened?"

"Dad fell." He quickly summed up the text messages for Reuben. "Can we meet them in Homer? You can collect Amelia, and Annie or Nell can bring me back at some point."

"Of course we can. And no, I am not going to just drop you off." Reuben sounded upset at the very idea. "I'll stay until we know more, see what else might be needed."

"We can handle it," he said curtly as he banged out a fast reply to Hannah telling her to stay put and that things would be okay. Hell, he felt bad enough that Nell had apparently felt it necessary to text everyone they knew, including Annie. He hoped Annie's work thing was nothing serious. Last thing he needed was the business to be having problems. He needed his job in the worst way now. And Annie wasn't his only worry. Next thing they'd have Hannah flying down if he didn't do some fast texting and that was the last thing they needed. That done, he sent another text, this one to Nell, reporting that he and Reuben were on the way.

On way. Traffic still backed up. What the hell happened???? You weren't there??? What the actual fuck, Nell?

The reply came a lot faster than he'd expected. This is Amelia. Nell gave me her phone to hold while she drives. Don't get mad at her please!!! It's all my fault. Several weeping emojis followed this pronouncement.

We went to get my hair cut. I'm sorry. Don't yell at Nell!!!! You're being mean.

Oh fuck. Now he'd apparently cursed out a fourteen-year-old. A fourteen-year-old whose father he was sleeping with. And now that same teen was *pissed*. This wasn't good. He'd always had something of a short fuse where Nell was concerned, and now it was biting him in the ass.

Sorry, he texted back. Didn't think about you having the phone. I'll be nicer, he lied, because he was still planning to interrogate Nell the second he saw her. But, yeah, he could moderate his tone. Just tell Nell that your dad and I are on the way, and my boss Annie may be too.

Another quick reply came in. Fine, but you better be nicer. I don't know what my dad likes about you anyway.

Ouch. Like seriously, *ouch*. That stung. As if he needed another reminder that Reuben had no business thinking about anything beyond this summer. Now Amelia hated him, and he felt like a first-class heel, one who definitely didn't deserve a guy like Reuben.

"Any news?" Finally coming to a passing, Reuben used it to get around a row of RVs.

Your kid hates me. With good reason. But he didn't share that, instead muttering, "No. No news. Don't even know how badly he's hurt. Nell's driving."

"We'll get there. It will be okay."

"You said not to worry, that nothing bad would happen, and you were wrong. So excuse me if I'm not so sure." Apparently not even Amelia's text lecture could completely extinguish his temper. And he knew he wasn't being fair, but he couldn't seem to help the frustration that was seeping out.

"I'm sorry." As usual, Reuben didn't take the bait. Damn the man and his even-keel psyche. "Maybe what

I should have said is that I'll do everything in my power to get us to the hospital. And that we should try to have a positive attitude until you know more about what happened."

"Thanks. Sorry I snapped. It's not your fault we got the late start—I was having fun shopping. I should have watched the clock more. Should have known Nell would pull something like this."

"You're allowed fun. And this may not be Nell's fault. Or yours. Sometimes things happen even if people are right there—Amelia split her lower lip falling at her fourth birthday party with ten adults right there."

"Yeah." He exhaled for what felt like the first time in a half hour or more. "You're right. I'll try not to leap to conclusions."

"Good. We'll get there. See? Traffic's picking up." Reuben punctuated this observation by deftly passing another slow-moving car. In addition to whatever accident had slowed things on the way to the peninsula, the height of fishing season had provided its usual glut of cars hauling small boats, jeeps with dipnets hanging off, vans packed with families out for their limit and tourists both.

But Reuben was right. They *would* get there. And then Toby would sort this whole mess out. Leaping ahead to things like who was at fault and ambulance co-pays wouldn't help anything, and besides, what mattered most was that his dad be okay.

Please let him be okay.

Chapter Twenty

The remainder of the drive to Homer was tense. Used
to east coast traffic, Reuben did his best to shave off
time, but there was a limit to how fast he was willing to
go, especially on winding roads, and the last thing they
needed was a speeding ticket or an accident. Toby spent
most of the drive alternating between being absorbed in
his phone and griping about slow-moving RVs and losing his phone reception.

"Any news?" he asked when Toby's phone dinged for
the first time in forty-five minutes.

"Nell and Amelia are at the hospital now." Toby
sounded marginally more positive than the last time
Reuben had asked. "He's being sent for tests. Biggest
worry is possible concussion. There's also a chance that
it wasn't one of his usual dizzy spells. It could have been
a stroke or something like that, so they're doing additional tests and blood work. Nell says he's alert though
and complaining up a storm, so I'll take that."

"That's good. Conscious is really good news." Reuben tried for an upbeat tone, but memories of late-night
dashes to hospitals for both his parents were taking up
way too much mental real estate. He tried not to think
about loss, both in the past and that which was yet to

come. It was a little startling that he'd invited Toby to come visit. But parting had been on his mind all day despite his best efforts to forget how little time was left, how much he did not want to say goodbye, and those worries made it hard to stay in the moment. Life could change so damn fast, and there were no guarantees. Too bad Toby wasn't amenable to visiting, had so thoroughly shot down the possibility that they could keep this thing they had going.

Fuck. It sucked, caring so much about Toby and wanting him happy and knowing the best thing for both of them might also be the hardest thing he'd ever done. Letting Toby go was going to *hurt*, but he was determined to make every moment until that point count. And that meant helping Toby through today, not letting his hurt at Toby's reaction to the invitation cloud his ability to be supportive.

"How are you doing?" he asked Toby. "Not too stiff? Hungry? You should probably think about eating something."

"I'm stiff, but I don't want to stop to stretch. Or eat. We can get something at the hospital. I just want to get there."

"I know. I'm trying. We're about to pass the turnoff for our place, so I figured I'd ask. I'm worried about *you.*"

"Thanks." Toby offered a crooked half smile. "I'll be okay. And this isn't our first rodeo with dad falling."

"No?"

"No. It's been ten years since his initial accident. He's had any number of complications and hospitalizations. That's why I come down so hard on Nell, which I know isn't the best."

"You're a good big brother," Reuben said gently. Toby told him all the time that he was a good dad, so he figured he could repay the favor. Because Toby really was, even if he did have a temper sometimes, and maybe he needed to hear it.

"I'm really not. Anyway, he's got a history of not wanting to ask one of us for help with something, then overdoing it, and hurting himself. And I understand him even better after this summer—he just wants to do stuff for himself. Hates needing help. And cognitively, he made a remarkable recovery. It just sucks that his balance and physical challenges didn't do the same. So he wants to do things that his body won't let him, and sometimes that frustration leads to accidents."

"It must be hard with you traveling for work?"

"Yeah. I try to do most of my traveling in the summer when Nell's home or when she can come down for the weekend, or I'll get someone else to check on him, but it's always nerve-racking. When Mom was alive, it was easier, that's for sure. She worked from the house on her sewing business and was able to be his primary caregiver."

"I saw her picture when we dropped Amelia off. She looked nice. Kind. And a lot like you. I know you're having a frustrating day—"

"That's putting a fancy spin on it. Shitastic more like."

"Shitastic day. Anyway, I think she'd be proud of you, of all you do for your dad and the girls."

"It's not enough." Toby thumped his head against the headrest. "This whole damn summer, I've dropped the ball. Stupid fucking plane crash."

"I'm sorry." Reuben swallowed hard because it sounded awfully like Toby was regretting meeting him.

"It feels a little like it's my fault. Maybe I should have canceled along with Craig and Leticia. Or shouldn't have spent so long fishing that morning."

"Hey. You needed that fishing time." Toby shot him an apologetic look. "It's not your fault. Shit happens. Shitastic days even. And I know you by now, you always want to fix things, but sometimes things just suck."

"And sometimes it's just a matter of it taking the right combination of assets—people, resources, time— to solve what seemed broken."

"You can't fancy lawyer your way out of everything."

"Watch me." Reuben was determined—*committed*— to solving Toby's problems, both the ones he knew about and the ones Toby was only alluding to, which almost surely involved money. But first he needed to get them to the hospital, which was another forty-five minutes or so beyond the turn that led to their place. Toby's attention returned to his phone, so Reuben focused on the road for a while.

"Hell." Toby shook his phone as Reuben followed the GPS directions into Homer. Eyes wild, he looked ten coffees' worth of jittery. "Nell's not answering messages. I'm not sure where to go when we get there. I know the basic hospital layout, but not sure if he's still in the ER or what."

"We'll figure it out. And no news probably just means bad phone reception or she got busy talking to someone."

The hospital was small compared with the sprawling medical complex in Anchorage, but the low building was surprisingly modern in design. Reuben helped Toby into the wheelchair, noting for later how stiff Toby seemed after the hours in the car. He wished the hot tub was an option, but maybe they could make do with a hot shower and massage. The admissions clerk working the front desk directed them to the room, which was down a long corridor.

"Dad!" Amelia came flying at him before they even reached the room, surprising him with a rare hug. "Oh, Dad, I was so scared! And it's all my fault!"

"I'm sure it wasn't."

"It's because Nell took me to her salon to get my hair cut. We were gone too long." She gestured at her hair, which was indeed shorter and fluffier, curls more tamed and less frizzy than usual. New earrings dangled from her ears—similar in style to the ones Nell had shown them earlier in the summer.

"It looks nice. And these things happen. No one should be mad at you."

"He's mad at Nell." She glared down at Toby, an alarming amount of fire in her eyes.

"I'm sorry. I texted without thinking. I'm not really mad at either of you, promise," Toby said as Nell emerged from one of the rooms. Shaking her head, Amelia didn't look convinced, but stepped back so that Nell could give Toby an awkward one-armed hug.

"I'm sorry, too." Nell's eyes were red. "We were in a hurry this morning to get to my stylist friend while she still had an opening. I should have done a better of job of making sure Dad had snacks laid out. Apparently, he got dizzy when he went into the kitchen and fell reaching for something in the pantry. He hit his head on the edge of the counter on the way down."

"It's okay." Toby's mouth twisted as he sighed. "How is he now?"

"Cranky. He's just back from more tests. They still haven't ruled out a stroke of some sort, but they decided to admit him for observation while they ran the tests because he does have some concussion symptoms. Come see for yourself. Lights are low because they were hurting his eyes. Annie's still not here—dealing with something at work, but she's been texting me for updates. As has half the Peninsula."

"Well maybe if you hadn't told them all first…" Frustration gave Toby's voice an edge Reuben wasn't used to hearing from him.

"I was *worried*."

"I know. Sorry." Toby rubbed the bridge of his nose, and Reuben ached to be able to do more for him. They all followed Nell into a dimly lit double room with an empty bed near the door and Toby's father sitting up in a hospital bed with a white cover draped over him. Paul had an impressive gash over his temple with what looked to be fresh stitches in it.

"You made it." Paul addressed Toby as he approached. Reuben hung back with Amelia by the curtain.

"There was terrible highway traffic the whole way back from Anchorage. Big accident."

Paul made a noncommittal noise like that excuse might not be good enough for him. Reuben wanted to speak up, but in a rarity for him, wasn't sure what he could say that wouldn't make things worse for Toby.

"How are you? Really?" Toby rolled close enough to touch his dad's arm, and Reuben felt his flinch away from Toby all way in his own heart.

"Fine. Hot. Room's a bit crowded. Any chance I can get you alone without your…*friends*?" The way he spat *friends* made it clear he'd considered several other less nice labels.

"Uh…" Toby cast a helpless glance at Reuben.

"That's fine. Amelia, let's go for a walk." He wasn't ready to leave Toby on his own here, but staying wouldn't help anything either. Hell, he probably shouldn't have followed Toby into the room—he hadn't been thinking fully. However much it bugged him that Toby's dad didn't like him, he wasn't going to be the asshole who tried to come between them. He stepped forward to quickly squeeze Toby's shoulder. "Text or call me if you need anything."

"Sure." Toby didn't even glance in Reuben's direction as he nodded.

As he headed to the hall with Amelia, for the first time in a long time, he felt lost, floundering around without plan. He wanted to solve everything for Toby and his family, but he wasn't sure how to do that, especially if Toby wouldn't let him in. Maybe this had started as convenient summer fling for Toby, but it had never been that simple for Reuben—he'd had jumbled emotions where Toby was concerned since even before the crash, the aftermath only intensifying his complicated feelings. And now it was so much more than simply sex, and he could only hope Toby felt the same way.

"Sorry. Didn't mean to bring a circus, but you didn't need to snap either."

"They don't need to know all our family's business." His dad's mouth was a thin, hard line. "And I need a favor."

"Of course. Anything." He couldn't really argue with his dad not wanting to air personal things in front of Reuben because he felt similar, keeping his money worries to himself the past few days. But he also couldn't help a guilty pang—Reuben wasn't just another friend or acquaintance, he was… Well, Toby wasn't exactly sure *what* yet, but important in a way he didn't want to fully examine, especially not then with worry about his father clouding everything else.

"Tell the doctors to stop with all these tests. You've seen me fall before. I'm fine. No stroke. They're talking about some sort of MRI with contrast, and I don't need that. Nell can take me to my healer. I don't need all this fuss. The bill…"

"We will deal with the bill," Toby said firmly, even though his brain was flipping the money panic switch already too. "You'll listen to the medical staff. It *could* have been a stroke—you're getting older, you know, and you've already got several risk factors."

His dad snorted at that. "Getting older. Ha. Like that boyfriend of yours? What's *he* at risk of?"

"He's not—"

"I might be hurt, but I've still got eyes. I see the way you look at him. Saw the way he touched you just now. And you're grown. You handle your business as you see fit, but you don't need someone like that hanging around."

"He's a good guy," Toby protested. "And he's not *that* old."

"Yeah, he kind of is," Nell interjected, totally not helping. "But he's hot for a sugar—"

"Stop. Both of you." Working to not raise his voice, he stared them down, not sure which he was more frustrated with. "Whatever else he might be, he's my *friend*. Who's been incredibly good to—*for*—me this summer. And returning to the actual point of this conversation, you're getting whatever tests the doctors want."

"Fine. But don't say I didn't warn you about the bills."

His father ended by fumbling with the controls for his bed, reclining himself, clearly trying to send a message that he was done with Toby.

"I'll handle the bills," Toby promised. *Somehow.* "You going to try to rest now? Did they say sleep was safe for you?"

That earned another snort. "Like to see them try to keep me awake. Just tell the nurses' station that I'm resting. You two go on now. I know you're itching to fight, and I don't wanna hear it."

"We're not going to fight," Toby protested weakly, because chances were high his dad was right. But he still hated being dismissed like this, following Nell out to the hall like a kid sent to bed without dessert.

"Excuse me." Nell stopped a passing nurse in teal scrubs. "Is Mr. Kooly in room 31 okay to sleep? He says he's tired, but they said he could have a concussion."

"I'll check on it," the nurse promised before bustling down the hall, leaving him and Nell staring at each other.

"Well?" Nell leaned against a railing that ran along the wall. "Are you going to let me have it?"

"The haircut couldn't wait?" He slumped in his chair, shoulders suddenly too heavy for his spine. "Wait. Don't answer that. He's fallen before on my watch. I'm just being mean, like Amelia said."

"She's not wrong." Nell studied one of her silver nails. "But I am sorry. Especially about the ambulance. I kinda freaked when I saw the blood, and then he was still dizzy, and even with Amelia helping—"

"Stop. You shouldn't feel guilty about calling 911. It's not your fault that ambulance co-pays are ridiculous." He scrubbed at his hair because even if it wasn't anyone's fault, the bill was still going to fucking suck. "And hey, what's another bill at this point, right?"

"I have a plan about that." Looking away again, she bit her full lower lip.

"I can already tell I'm not going to like it."

"I'm not going back to college in the fall." She looked back at him, square in the eyes, daring him to disagree.

"What? No. No, you are not quitting school over a few bills. That I will handle. You just have to trust me, Nell." His voice did an embarrassing crack on Nell's name, anger and fear and hurt working together to strangle his vocal chords.

"No, you have to trust *me*. I hate school. Hate it. I can't pick a major, hate writing, hate the teachers, hate the pretentious students who have all these plans while I'm still struggling to pass the basics."

"It'll get easier." He reached for her hand, but she didn't take it.

"No, it won't. You just haven't been listening to me this summer. I love my job. I know it's silly stuff to you, but I love hair and makeup. She cried a lot of it off, but you should have seen how happy Amelia was with her makeover before we found Dad. Just getting the right cut made such a difference for her."

"She does look nice," Toby allowed. "Grown-up. Reuben's going to hate that."

"Reuben can deal." Nell rolled her eyes. "And anyway, that's what I want to do. Hair. For the first time I'm excited about something. So I'm going to take the fall off, keep working reception, maybe pick up a second job, save up for doing cosmetology school in Anchorage. Maybe by spring…"

"Beauty school isn't *college*. Mom wanted you to do college. Four-year degree. I promised—"

"*Tobias*. Quit being a stuck-up prick. Just because you had to leave college behind doesn't mean the rest of us have to pay the price for *your* lost dream. I don't think Mom would have hated the idea of beauty school. And you're not Mom. You're never going to be Mom. So stop fucking trying. Just *stop*."

He felt like his chest cavity was caving in, a shoddy roof in February finally succumbing to the snow burden, years and years of trying and trying finally catching up with him. It hurt. It fucking hurt so bad that he had to rub his chest, make sure it was still there, intact, that it was just his soul that Nell was breaking, one well-placed blow after another.

"I can't." His voice broke again, stupid nonworking thing. "I *promised*. And you have to think of your future. Not a few bad months of bills. Or classes you hate. Your future—"

"How about yours?" she countered. "Bankruptcy sound good to you? Because that's where this is headed if we can't get our heads above water. So, yeah, I'm done with school. For a lot of reasons, but mainly because we need— Oh, hi, Amelia." Straightening, Nell's whole demeanor changed, and Toby swiveled his head to find Reuben and Amelia right fucking there behind him. And sweet hell, how much had Reuben heard? Judging by Reuben's somber, concerned expression, too fucking much.

"We're kind of—" He opened his mouth to tell Reuben that he needed more time with Nell, but she cut him off.

"Done here," Nell said brightly. "Did you guys find

if the coffee place is still open? A, you want to see if we can track down mochas or a chocolate bar or something?"

"Yes!" Amelia sounded only too happy to leave Toby alone with Reuben.

Nell was walking away before he could even send her a "we're not done" look. And Reuben's eyes flashed cool speculation that said he was only too happy for the chance to interrogate Toby.

Well, fuck this. Fuck his life. And he was done having his life fall apart in the middle of a hospital hallway, nursing staff passing back and forth, undoubtedly curious to see what the next installment of the hallway drama would bring. He rolled toward a waiting area, not pausing to see if Reuben was following. If Reuben wanted a piece of him, he could fucking take a number.

"How bad is it?" Reuben took the chair closest to Toby in the blessedly abandoned seating area.

"Nothing I can't handle." He didn't play dumb, but he also wasn't about to go volunteering shit either. "We'll be okay. Nell is just being dramatic and looking for an excuse to flake out on school."

"School's expensive. And you've got her and Hannah both. And the medical bills…" Reuben let out a low whistle. "But you did get workers' comp, right? That helping any?"

"There's a holdup with that. Not even sure I understand what they're saying, but I'll figure it out—"

"You could let me take a look. I *am* a lawyer. I might spot something."

"I'll figure it out." He was being stubborn, but he just could not stand the thought of Reuben rescuing him right then, even from paperwork.

Reuben let out a mighty sigh. "And the rest of it? Your dad needs more help than Nell can provide. And it sounds like you're snowed under by bills. Let me help out. Get someone from a home health place for your dad. Take care of the worst of the bills or at least make sure Hannah's school is set for the fall."

"I don't need your money. You're always so quick to solve everything with a few dollar bills. But that's not what we need here."

"Oh? Seems to me a cash infusion is an easy solution." Reuben's voice was infuriatingly light, not taking the barb Toby had tossed out. "One I have and am freely offering."

"We don't do charity. Or pity."

"It's absolutely not pity." Reuben held up his hands. "But it doesn't have to be a gift. It could be an interest-free loan. We could even draw up a paper agreement if that makes you feel better."

"It doesn't." Toby ground out the words between clenched teeth. "I can't take your money. Even as a loan or what-fucking-ever you want to call it."

"Why not? We're dating, right? This is what couples *do*. They help each other out in times of need."

"We're not that kind of couple." As soon as he said the words, Reuben recoiled, face going pale. Fuck. Toby was being harsh, but he couldn't seem to moderate his words. "And it's *because* we're sleeping together that I can't take your money. It would feel like… I dunno…*payment* for services rendered. Dirtying up a casual fling. I know I sleep around, but I don't barter for it."

"You really think that? That I want to pay you for sex?" Reuben's voice was a harsh whisper. "And I think we both know this has gone far beyond casual fling now.

I want to help you, same as I would any partner. I respect you—respect your independence and pride especially. This isn't me wanting to compromise you or… *dirty* things up. I care about you. This is me wanting us to be a couple, a real couple, one that helps each other out in hard times."

Reuben's words were like little darts, stinging Toby's already abraded skin. He wanted to believe him in the worst way, but one truth remained inescapable. "We're not a real couple. You can pretend all you want, but you're leaving in a few weeks, going back to your life. Real couples don't have an expiration date."

"I meant what I said earlier—I want you to come visit. I'm not ready to end this thing, not by a long shot."

A noise halfway between laugh and scoff escaped Toby's throat. "So I come visit—thousands of miles— for a sexy weekend. That you pay for. And that makes us a real couple? Nah, man. That just takes something that should be DOA and puts it on life support. I give it, what? A visit? Maybe two. And then you're back at your fancy life and I'm back here, and the last thing either of us need is some…paperwork hanging over our heads as you move on. Because you will."

"I don't have to." Reuben reached across, grabbed Toby's hand. "Moving on doesn't have to be inevitable. Ask me to stay."

"What?" Toby had to blink, make sure Reuben was still in front of him, earnest expression on his face. "No way. That's crazy talk."

"No, it's not," Reuben insisted, squeezing Toby's hand. "You know I've been wrestling with what to do with the buyout offer. Amelia's about to go off to school.

Me staying here, at least part-time, isn't that unreasonable. And it would let us give this thing a real chance."

"No." A cloud of fear replaced all the indignation in Toby's gut. "I can't let you do that. You can't give up your life for a *fling*."

"You keep saying that word, but I don't think it means what you think it means. Flings don't finish each other's sentences like Amelia is always teasing us about doing. Flings don't care like this. I know. I've had flings, and this is the opposite of casual. What I feel for you isn't going away. And before you protest, I know that you feel it too. I know you care."

"Doesn't matter what I feel." He couldn't deny what Reuben was saying, but hell if he liked it. Or rather, he liked it too much, wanted this to be real, wanted Reuben's care and concern. But he couldn't have that, couldn't *let* himself have it. And he absolutely could not let Reuben give up everything for him. "I'm not asking you to stay."

Reuben dropped his hand, slumped back in the chair. "Because you don't want me to stay. All this talk about how inevitable it is that I'm leaving and that this thing is ending—this isn't just about you not wanting to take my money. You don't want to be a real couple, don't want a future together."

Toby bit down on the protest that wanted to break free from the confines of his mouth. Reuben was wrong—Toby didn't want Reuben to leave. But he had to stay quiet, had to let Reuben do the best thing for himself, and that thing was not Toby.

"See?" Reuben gestured, indicating Toby's silence. "Admit it. It would be easier for you if this ended. You're scared to have it be anything other than temporary."

"You calling me a coward?"

"No." Reuben's voice softened. "Just pointing out the obvious. You're resisting every idea that could let us have a future. And I think it comes down to you not wanting that future or at least not wanting it enough to try. And I get it. I do. Us together for real would mean you being out in a way you haven't been before. And your family doesn't like me, doesn't approve, and that's even harder than just the logistics of being openly in a same-sex relationship."

"People know I'm bi," Toby protested, even though there was some painful truth to what Reuben was saying. It wasn't just pride keeping him from agreeing to Reuben's nuts plan of him sticking around. "And Dad's stuck by me over that—some people we know aren't the coolest with it, but he's never given me crap about who I sleep with."

"Except me. You can't deny that him not liking me grates on you, makes it harder on you. And maybe this is me being selfish, trying to force you into a future you don't want or need."

I need you. The words refused to come out, trapped behind a wall of wanting Reuben to do the right thing for himself, not give up his fancy life for an injured, broke bush pilot. And much as he hated to admit it, not upsetting his dad was a bonus to forcing Reuben to see the ridiculousness of what he was proposing.

"Quit focusing on stuff that doesn't matter. What you're saying—you staying here, that's not you truly wanting a future together either. You're just looking for an excuse. You've been in knots all summer over the buyout deal. Swooping in to rescue me and my fucked-up life, that's a smokescreen for you not wanting to deal with your life and hard choices. You want me to ask you to stay so that you have a reason to choose one way or the other. And I'm not going to be your excuse. You want a project. Something to rescue. And that's not going to be me."

"I want…" Reuben shook his head as he trailed off, then inhaled sharply as he seemed to come to some sort of conclusion. "Maybe it doesn't matter what I want. I know you think I've got this…rescue complex. But I want a partnership. Equals. However, if you can't see that, if you can't want that, if you can't trust me to know my own mind, maybe this isn't what I thought it was after all."

"It was a distraction for you. A fun one, for both of us, but it was a distraction from things you don't want to deal with right now. And eventually, you're going to realize that, going to see that this isn't what you truly want. And I am *not* going to let money complicate that end game for you. Or let you do something permanent like moving that you'll regret in six months. So no, no I am not going to ask you to stay. Or take your money." He tried to make his voice final, even as his heart hammered and his eyes burned.

"Fine. If that's that what you want." For the first time, Reuben sounded truly angry. Which had been Toby's whole intention, make him mad enough to stop with the ridiculous offers, but his anger still hurt, a bandage ripped off too soon, his skin tender and raw and not ready for this. Despite knowing this was the right thing for both of them, he hated the retreat he could feel from Reuben, the way his anger signaled the end of all their closeness and companionship. Hated himself for hurting Reuben. Hated wanting—*needing*—Reuben. Misery blanketed him, all the anger and hurt knit together in an impenetrable fabric around what was left of his heart.

"It is. And I think you should go." Each word was a struggle, but it needed saying. "Let me handle my shit myself."

"No. That's not necessary. I'm not kicking you out or anything like that. We've got a few weeks left and—"

"I just need space. We both do—can't do that thrown together, hormones and emotions clouding our judgment."

"But it's your place too. Where will you go?" The hurt in Reuben's voice was even harder to take than his anger had been.

"It's not my place. Never was," he lied to save them both the pain of repeating this conversation again in a few days or weeks. Admitting how very much like home the vacation house had felt wouldn't solve anything. "And for tonight at least, I'll go back with Nell. If dad's here, I can sleep in his room. I'll work something out."

"I don't like this—"

"There you are!" An exasperated-sounding Nell came around the corner, carrying two cups, trailed by Amelia who was also carrying dual cups. "We brought you guys some coffee."

"Thanks," he said, as much for the interruption as the drink. "Reuben and Amelia are heading out," he said to Nell, willing his plan into existence, trying to not look at Reuben's stricken expression.

If he looked too hard, he was going to lose his nerve, going to apologize for being so harsh, going to beg for another chance, going to end up going back to Reuben's place, Reuben's bed, and that would solve absolutely nothing. There was no future for them. Reuben deserved better, deserved the life he'd built for himself back east, and no way was Toby going to ask him to give it up. Not for him. Not when his life was such a mess. Not when he had so little to offer. And not when it would be so easy to take Reuben's help, too easy to let him take over, solve things that Toby needed to handle on his own. Even if it hurt, even if it fucking burned, even if it felt like his chest wasn't going to survive this latest strain, he was going to let Reuben go, going to let him walk out of here, going to make sure neither of them looked back.

Chapter Twenty-One

"Did you and Toby break up?" Mercifully, Amelia waited until they were in the car to ask him that. Her voice wasn't unsympathetic either, surprisingly gentle.

"I'm not sure." He didn't want to lie to her or brush her question off, but he also honestly wasn't sure what the hell had just happened. Things had gone from a straightforward offer to help Toby with money to a spiraling argument that jumped from money to him offering to move to Toby shooting down all of it. And it had ended with the dreaded "I need space" cliché, which yeah, probably meant they had broken up, if there had been anything there to begin with. He'd been so sure there was, that Toby was feeling the same depth of emotion he was, but after the easy way Toby had seemed to dismiss him, he was no longer certain. Resting his head on the steering wheel, he took a long inhale. "I guess so. He's going home with Nell tonight."

"Is it because of me? Because I said he was mean?"

"No." Reuben had to laugh at her earnestness because the alternative was to let himself get choked up. "It's not your fault. None of this is. Not Toby's dad falling or us fighting or anything like that."

"Okay." She settled into the passenger seat, buckling up. "Because he's not *that* bad."

"I'm sure he'd appreciate the compliment." Each light word was work as his speech and limbs felt weighed down, as if a grizzly were sitting on him, making it hard to concentrate. Only thing he wanted to do was figure out how to solve the Toby situation, but he had Amelia to think about, couldn't sit here beating his head into the steering wheel indefinitely. Knowing she was counting on him to not totally fall apart, he put the car in gear and told the GPS to head back to the vacation house.

There were limits to how much conversation he could take so he flipped on the music. But that turned out to be almost worse than trying to explain what had happened to Amelia as each song reminded him of Toby. Upbeat songs made him think of lying on the bed, laughing at something stupid on the TV, bodies touching, soaking in each other's nearness. Love songs brought to mind every romantic moment, every kiss, every touch. And mournful songs did the last thing he wanted and made him dwell on his growing list of losses. The weeks he was supposed to have with Toby. The places and things they wouldn't get to visit and do. The meals they wouldn't share. The autumn in New York visit. The future together that he'd seen only the barest glimpses of and still wanted desperately.

"If you flip the station one more time, I'm gonna scream," Amelia warned as they approached the turn-off for their place.

"We're almost home." He turned the stereo off altogether. "When we get there…"

"You need to be alone and all broody. I get it. I'm gonna check in with my game. It's been a long day."

"I was going to say we should eat something, but yes, that too. Thanks. You're the best." And she really was, not pushing him to talk and heading upstairs with a bag of carrot sticks and container of ranch dressing as soon as they entered the house. But then that left him alone, truly alone, with his feelings.

Fuck. How had things gone so badly? He spent some time putting away all the groceries, and even that made him all sappy, the memory of the fun they'd had just that morning resonating in each purchase they'd made together. And it had been *together*—it didn't matter who actually paid. They'd worked together as a team, planning meals, getting surprises for the girls, and discovering new things about each other. Why did Toby's pride have to make him so stubborn? Because Reuben had the ability and desire to help, it seemed so straightforward to him. Why couldn't Toby see it that way?

Groceries organized, he bypassed the beer Toby liked in favor of a glass of wine. Funny how he'd hardly touched the stuff all summer. After a quick stop to change into swim trunks, he took the wine out to the hot tub on the deck, another thing that hadn't been used very much since Toby couldn't and Reuben much preferred spending evenings with him. But Toby wasn't here now and Reuben's bad mood was, so he indulged himself.

But as he contemplated the view of the trees and hills, light only just starting to fade, all he felt was even more alone, not the least bit relaxed. Was Toby right? Was he just looking for a distraction? He didn't think so—what he felt seemed so potent and real. When he offered to stay, he'd surprised even himself, but it also felt so damn *right*. Like they'd been working toward that moment all summer and all he needed was the least encouragement from Toby to make the choice to do this for real.

But Toby hadn't given him that. Hadn't wanted what Reuben had to offer. Not money. Not proximity. And fuck but it hurt. Scalded his skin, finding raw places that hadn't stung in years, long-held wounds. His mother resisting his help. Natalie telling him to stop trying to fix everything. Dan saying he liked him better angry and hard. Maybe the problem really was Reuben. Especially where Toby was concerned—he couldn't erase the age gap, couldn't delete his gender or bank account or whatever other factors went into Toby's reservations. And hell if he knew how to solve any of it. Instead, all he could do was stay in the hot tub longer than was strictly prudent, letting dusk fall around him. When he went back into the house, he had to fight against the urge to creep into Toby's room, see if the bed in there smelled like him. Like them. Lay there and see if what they'd had felt real, try to make sense of his muddied feelings.

Nice as it sounded to wallow in his sorrow, he pushed that urge down. He wasn't going to invade Toby's space like that, even if he wasn't actually in it, wasn't going to let himself get that emo. Instead he turned for his own room and welcomed the sleepless night in front of him as penance for all that had gone wrong, all his failings.

However, somehow he did doze in the small hours of the morning, and he woke up to the smell of coffee and pancakes. For a heart-stoppingly wonderful second, he thought Toby had returned, then he heard the clang of a pot and Amelia cursing at herself. Nope, he wasn't that kind of lucky, not today. He pulled on some clothes and went out to rescue Amelia from whatever nice gesture she'd dreamed up.

"Breakfast? You don't have to do that," he said as he helped himself to a cup of coffee. And for once, it wasn't hair-curling strong. "But this is good. Nice job."

"Followed Toby's tip about measuring." Her cheeks turned rosy. "Thought I'd surprise you. I was going to bring it in on a tray, like Mom and I did that year for Father's Day when I was little, but you woke up."

"Sorry." He had to swallow hard around the sweetness of the memory. "That's awfully nice of you."

"I had an ulterior motive." She stuck out her tongue while she concentrated on flipping a pancake. "I need you fed for our hike."

"Hike?" Reuben asked. She pointed at the fridge, and sure enough the calendar of activities he'd made with Toby had a hike penciled in, a trail they hadn't tried yet. But while Amelia had grown a lot more enthusiastic about trying new stuff, hiking still wasn't her personal favorite, and he had to rub his eyes, make sure he wasn't still dreaming. "You want to hike? Today?"

"Yup." She pushed a plate his direction. "Eat up."

He took a tentative bite. "You're not planning on shoving me off a cliff, are you?"

"Dad!" She put her hands on her hips. "I'm trying to be *nice*."

"I can tell. And I appreciate it. But it's not necessary. I promise I'm going to be okay. I've had breakups before." And he had, but none ached quite like this. But he wasn't telling her that, not when she was being so sweet to him.

"I want to hike. Please." Her chin jutted out, same as it had as a toddler when he'd been powerless to deny her then too.

"Okay, okay, we'll hike." It wasn't like waiting around all day for Toby to call would serve any of them any good anyway. But a few hours later, hiking shoes on, July sun beating down on them, he was reconsidering that logic. The trail near Sterling and Skilak Lake apparently offered an impressive view after a steep section. He tried to keep Toby's warnings about bear preparedness in mind as they started out. They hadn't actually encountered a bear up close in their hikes, but he also wasn't eager to change that fact.

Much as he was grateful for the distraction from his brooding, the trail's tight switchbacks and rapid climb took all his concentration. Amelia, however, sprang from rock to rock, nimble and agile now, a completely different girl from the complaining creature she'd been at the start of the summer. Simply watching her was a pleasure equal to the views.

"You can slow down," he suggested, nearly sliding on a jagged rock. "We should pace ourselves."

"*Dad.* Come on. It'll be worth it."

A dry wind whipped at their clothing the higher they climbed. The curvy lake beneath them was a pristine blue, contrasting with the deep green of the gentle hills surrounding it and the black of the mountains farther in the distance.

"We made it." Amelia beamed at him at the summit, whole valley spread out before them. They'd passed other hikers on the way up, but they were alone here at the top.

As he inhaled the crisp air, a deep peace settled over him, one that made his troubles with Toby feel surmountable and small compared to the vastness before him.

"This was a good idea," he told her as she lounged against a boulder. She'd been right—the hard work of the climb had totally been worth it.

"Good." Unlike like most days lately, she was makeup free, and he had to admit he liked her freshly scrubbed like this. But she seemed weirdly nervous all of a sudden, biting her lip. "You like it here, right? Like a lot?"

"Yeah, I really do." Despite everything that had happened, it was hard to deny his deep connection with this place, especially with a one-of-a-kind view surrounding them.

"I need to tell you something." Looking down at her dusty shoes, Amelia took several shallow breaths.

"Okay." Reuben willed his voice to stay neutral, not to leap to any conclusions, even as the back of his neck prickled. She'd clearly brought him here for a reason, and his gut churned with several awful possibilities.

"I don't want to go boarding school in the fall."

He exhaled hard, relief that it was something fixable coursing through him. "Like you're nervous about going? Worried about fitting in?"

"No. Like I don't want to do it at all. Don't want to live in the dorms. Don't want to be with all girls. Don't want to be away from *you*."

"Me?" Reuben had never thought of himself as much of a draw, especially given how reluctant she'd been at the start of the summer. He'd figured he was the lesser of two evils to get out of camp, but not someone she really *wanted* to spend time with.

"Yeah. I like hanging out. I like cooking together with Toby and going on the trips he plans like the kayaking and the horses, and I like coming back to a home, not a dorm…"

"Honey." He had to take a deep breath, steel himself. "If this is about me and Toby, I'm honestly not sure we're going to be able work things out. He doesn't seem to want the same sort of future I do. So I can't promise you more time with him, much as I wish I could. And if that's your motivation for not wanting to go to school, I'm sorry, but I'm probably going back to New Jersey. Back to my condo and work."

God, he hated how just the thought of his loft and work weighed him down like a winter coat in July. He was supposed to love his job, had spent the start of the summer chomping at the bit to get back to it, but something had changed in recent weeks where he was dreading, not anticipating being back in the office, dealing with office politics. Not even the thought of seeing friends like Craig and Leticia was particularly enticing, and that was sobering.

"But you love it here." Tears welled up in her eyes, and she slumped against the rocks. "And I do too."

"It's been a vacation. But we can't be on vacation all the time."

"Why not? Why can't I go to high school here? I met those kids fishing—they seemed nice. Not fake nice like the girls at my old school, but actually nice. And fun. I love Toby and Nell's stories about their schools. Why can't this be our real lives too?"

"Toby doesn't want me here." God, it killed him to admit that out loud.

"So?" She frowned even deeper. "If you want to be here and I want to be here, what does that matter? He's not the only person out here, I'm sure."

"I don't want someone else." And he truly didn't. He wanted Toby. Wanted his smile, his body against Reuben's, his laugh, his companionship. Wanted the self he was around Toby too. The easy guy who read novels and watched superhero shows and tried new recipes and forgot about his email. The guy who laughed and cared and loved. Oh fuck. Did he love Toby? Or maybe the better question was how could he not? How could he feel all this and it not be love?

"So you say now." Amelia rolled her eyes. "But, I'm serious. I don't want to do boarding school. And it's taken me weeks to get up the courage to tell you, so please listen to me."

"I'm listening." He grabbed her hand, squeezed. "And I appreciate you being so brave and honest with me. But your mother has her heart set on you going to her alma mater."

"But you get a vote too, right? You guys have joint custody for a reason." Her voice was close to full-on wail now. "And I should get a say too. I want to stay with you. Here or back home even. Just don't make me go away."

Pulling her into a hug, he held her tight. "I won't, okay? We'll work this out. I want what's best for you. Always have."

"I want the best for you, too," she said, muffled against his shoulder.

"Thanks." Brain buzzing, he held her closer. What was best for him anyway? He'd been so focused on what was best for others—Amelia, Toby, even Natalie and the firm. Yesterday, when he'd offered to stay, that had all been about Toby, giving Toby what he thought he needed. But what did Reuben need for himself? What would make him happy? Fulfilled? It felt selfish, thinking in those terms. And honestly, a little scary, prioritizing his own needs, not having those of others to fall back on to excuse his decisions.

Inhaling deeply, Amelia's fruity shampoo clogging his nose, he looked out at the lake again, the way it was

perfectly placed against the horizon, glittering like a diamond set in the ring of the hills. Like a promise of everything good in this world, far removed from petty worries
and depressing news cycles and meaningless choices.
And he might not have all the answers he needed, but
he did see where he'd screwed up with Toby, offering
what Reuben assumed was best for him, not stopping
to consider what either of them actually needed. And
maybe the same was true with Amelia. God knew he'd
messed up enough there with assumptions and misguided efforts.

"You might not want to live with me full-time. I
haven't been the best dad to you over the years. I mean,
we tried to give you everything, but I wasn't around
enough."

"Don't be ridiculous." She pulled away to stare up
at him, looking and sounding so much like her mother
that he almost had to do a double take. "I mean you're
not wrong about being a total workaholic. But I don't
need some TV-show perfect dad. And I didn't need the
best schools and nannies and stuff like that. I just need
you. And I want to live with you because you listen to
me and you give me space when I need it and you're not
afraid to admit when you're wrong."

"Thanks. I have been trying." It hadn't escaped his
notice that nothing she'd listed had to do with his money
or status or even his time. It had to do with energy. The
effort he'd put into their relationship this summer. She
needed his presence. And hell, Toby was right that he
was too fast to try to solve things with money. He'd
been guilty of using that as a shield for years, because
real emotional work was hard and involved a level of
humility that didn't come naturally to him. It gave him

the same sort of distance that focusing on the needs of others did, kept him from true vulnerability.

"I can tell." She gave him a tentative smile. "But I have to be honest. I haven't wanted to go away to school all year. It took me a while to get brave enough to tell you, but talking to Nell helped, seeing her get brave enough to tell Toby that she doesn't want to go to a four-year college. If she can be brave enough to go for what she wants, then I can too. And even if we hadn't done all the bike rides and kayaking and fabric store trips and day tours, I still wouldn't want to go. It's just not what I want for me."

For me. And there he was back at the question of what he wanted most for himself. Amelia was being so brave, asking for what she wanted most, what she needed, being willing to go for it even if Reuben wasn't fully up to the task. Could he be the same type of brave? Go for what he most wanted in life? *Why should it matter?* Her earlier question still rang in his ears as well. Why should it matter what others thought, including Toby? Or Natalie for that matter. If he wanted something, truly wanted it, why shouldn't he take the leap and fight for it?

"I hear you. You don't want to go. You're right that it should be your decision, but I'd like it if you did stay with me instead of going away to school." Admitting that he had a preference made his voice raspy, like a rusty door that didn't open very often. But he figured she might need to hear that he did want her around. And he needed to say it, needed to practice admitting that he did care. "However, your mom is going to freak out. Be prepared."

"I don't care." The stubborn tilt to Amelia's face was back, and her eyes hardened. "I want what I want."

Me too, kid. Me too. But he didn't voice the thought aloud, instead pulling her in for another hug, hoping with everything he had that they both got what they wanted. Needed. *Deserved.*

Chapter Twenty-Two

"Why does today have to be so complicated?" Nell stirred some coffee into her sugar and milk, turning the concoction the barest hint of brown. For himself, Toby was having a big travel mug, black and Amelia-level strong as he had barely slept the night before. He'd missed his big bed back at Reuben's place, missed having Reuben in it. Nothing smelled right here and endless thoughts of whether he'd made the right call sending Reuben away were hardly comforting bedmates.

"It's not *that* complicated. Look, I'm sorry that you're stuck playing taxi. I know how much you hate driving. But my work is on the way to Homer, so it's not like I'm asking you to go that far out of your way."

"Yeah, yeah. I guess I can say hi to Annie or something." She'd been in a bad mood ever since Toby told her about Griffin's phone call asking if he could take a look at a problem he was having with a plane. Apparently, that was what had kept Annie from visiting yesterday. One of the planes was having trouble, and they'd been waiting for a part to arrive, and now it had, but Griffin was still having issues with it. Because of Toby's crash, the fleet was still down a plane, so Annie needed this one functional as soon as possible. And if

Griffin, who was usually a magician when it came to cranky engines, was having problems, it had to be bad. And likely there wasn't going to be much Toby could do that he hadn't already tried, but there was something nice about being asked and the reminder that he'd have a job waiting for him once his body decided to get with the healing program.

Nell had been largely quiet on the drive home the night before, not bringing up Reuben, but he'd known that peace wouldn't last. She waited until they were on the road, him unable to do more than sit with his teeth on edge at her driving.

"So did the sugar daddy break up with you or you with him? Because I've been wondering all night. And I figure you're too banged up to cheat..."

"People break up for reasons other than cheating." Funny how pressing a worry that had been at twenty, and how little a one with Reuben. He might have all sorts of reservations about a long-term relationship with the guy, but he didn't doubt for a moment that Reuben would be faithful. And that was as much detail as he was giving Nell, who would probably tell him to take Reuben's money while continuing to crow about how right she'd been about their relationship dynamic.

"Sure. Like I broke up with a guy once because his sighs sounded like a coffeemaker."

"That's not why you break up with someone either." He tried to think whether Reuben even *had* annoying habits other than the whole thing about wanting to rescue Toby. He liked the way Reuben sounded, his voice, his mannerisms. Hell, he even liked the way Reuben cut his food into precise bites and chewed like each mouthful was meaningful. *Fuck.* He had it bad. He had to remind himself that he only dug his take-charge presence when it wasn't trying to take charge of Toby's life...

"This guy did it all the time." Nell drove at a speed better suited for an aging Winnebago than Toby's SUV. "And I renew my offer—I've got friends who think you are super cute and who would enjoy taking care of your cranky ass while you finish recovering."

"No thanks. Focus on the road." He tried to think of a fate other than death worse than having a twenty-year-old amateur nurse with a crush hanging around. Besides, he didn't want a rebound relationship. He wanted...

Reuben. His hands clenched with the force of missing him so hard. But he wasn't going to *get* Reuben, for a whole host of reasons, including that he wasn't what Reuben truly needed. He cared about Reuben too much to saddle him with all his burdens, even if he could bring himself to be okay with taking Reuben's help.

And it wasn't only Reuben that he had a problem with accepting help from. Watching Nell wrestle with the wheelchair made his stomach churn, a feeling that didn't get better when Griffin came walking over to help.

"We brought a walker too. I can lean on that in the hangar." It was weird, being back here after so many weeks away. The small collection of hangars and outbuildings had been his second home for nearly a decade, the little lake where the active floatplanes were docked as familiar to him as his bedroom back at his dad's house. His brain kept noting little differences—fresh coat of paint on one of the sheds, Griffin's hair more styled than usual which probably meant River was back in town or on his way, flowers in the window of Annie's office that hadn't been there before. As they passed the office, Nell ducked inside to say hello to

Annie, leaving him and Griffin to continue to the hangar, Griffin carrying the walker for him.

"So was it your mom's idea to call me and make me feel useful, or do you actually need my opinion?"

"Way too busy around here to be stroking your ego," Griffin teased in the dry way he had. They'd worked together for years now, and while they'd never been the sort of coworkers who hung out together off duty, he considered him a friend same as he did Annie, who was also Griffin's mother. "I need this plane to pass inspection. We need to replace the one from the crash, and refurbishing this one was our best bet."

And there it was, another smack of guilt slamming into him. It didn't matter how many times people told him that the crash wasn't his fault. He still felt terrible, still had the dreams where the plane was plummeting and he couldn't stop it. It was knowing that he was letting people down that was the worst—Annie and Griffin needed that plane. He needed the job. Reuben had needed a good pilot that day. He was *supposed* to be a good pilot. He wanted to be back out there more than anything, but he'd be lying if he didn't admit that the doubt crows kept coming calling.

Once in the hangar, he switched to the walker to approach the parts Griffin had laid out on a tarp on a workbench, studying the collection of items and letting Griffin talk him through the problem.

"Did you try flipping the part? Like flip it, rotate ninety degrees, and then try easing it in to see if it clicks in then." It was the only thing he could think of that might help.

"Let me see…" Working methodically, Griffin lined up the flipped part. *Click.* The snap echoed through the hangar. "Fuck it. That worked. Why didn't I see that hours ago?"

"Eh. Sometimes you need a different perspective."

"Yeah, but I dragged you all the way here for a five second fix." Griffin shook his head. "Hate wasting your time."

"It's not wasting my time. I'm happy to help. I've been cooped up so long it's good to feel useful again."

"Yeah, but I'm supposed to know this shit." Griffin scrubbed at his hair, messing up whatever style he'd been going for.

Happy to help. Why was it okay for Griffin to need help and Toby to want to assist him, but not okay for Reuben to offer him help? Toby wasn't quite sure what the answer was, but he had a feeling his own misplaced assumptions were playing a role. Like Griffin, he assumed he was good at certain things and didn't want to need help, didn't want to show weakness. But wasn't weakness a part of life?

"You can't be perfect all the time," he joked, but he meant the words as much for himself as Griffin. Maybe Griffin wasn't the only one who needed a fresh perspective.

A rustle sounded behind them, and he swiveled the walker to discover River, Griffin's boyfriend, in the doorway. Griffin's entire presence transformed, face softening, eyes going warm, shoulders relaxing, and this…lightness rolling off him, as if he couldn't hold back the tidal wave of his happiness.

"You're back." Griffin quickly crossed the hangar, meeting River in the middle. "Drive was clear? You made good time."

"Drive was fine even with the tourist traffic." River

clutched Griffin's biceps, staring up at him like they were the only two people left on the planet. "God, I missed you. I can't wait to see the cabin progress, but I wanted to stop here first."

"I'm so glad," Griffin said gruffly. And then Griffin, king of the stoic expression and he who kept his private life under strict lock down prior to last year, surprised the hell out of Toby by kissing River. Hell, he probably startled River too, judging by his adorable squawk as Griffin claimed his mouth.

I want that. What would it be like to have someone waiting on him like that? To have someone that happy to see him? To be that in love? And wasn't that the real question. What would it be like to be as crazy in love as the two of them clearly were?

Wait. Images bombarded his brain. Reuben betting him for the bigger piece of baklava. Reuben joking in the kitchen. Reuben's face contorted with passion. Reuben's eyes wide at a particularly gorgeous vista. Was Toby in love? Was this what love felt like? Like his left arm had been removed, like something had hollowed him out, left him empty and wanting and unable to even reach for what he needed most. If this misery was love, he wasn't sure he wanted any part of it.

But then his eyes returned to Griffin and River who were still so wrapped up in each other that they hadn't spared a glance for Toby. For every ounce of misery Toby felt, they radiated back pure joy. This was the flip-side of love's ability to hurt, its potential to transform embodied. Prior to River, an air of loneliness had followed Griffin around, and he seemed content to spend his life in this hangar, cranky and distant. Clearly something had changed.

Toby wished they were slightly better friends, the sort who might talk about these things, then he could ask what the hell he'd done to get so lucky. How did a guy change so much? *He took a risk.* Toby knew that much at least because he'd covered a few flights for him. Griffin had chased River down, fighting for him. And if this sort of happiness was the payoff, it was no wonder he'd taken the risk.

Feeling like the worst kind of voyeur, he cleared his throat as he transferred back to the wheelchair. "I…uh… I'm gonna go find Nell."

"Okay. Thanks for the help. I'll bring your walker to your SUV in a minute." Voice rough, Griffin barely looked over at Toby as he made his way out of the hangar, and Toby was certain more kissing was about to occur before Griffin made good on the promise. Sure enough, he looked rather rumpled with a bruised mouth when he met them at the car a short while later.

Jealousy over what Griffin had and what Toby had let go kept him quiet on the drive to the hospital. Could he be Griffin-level brave? Did he want to? Would the risk be worth it for him? For Reuben? For them? Hell. He simply didn't know.

The doctors had ruled out a stroke for his father, and he was ready to go home when they got there, already grumpy even before they hit the halfway point.

"Your music hurts my head," Dad complained to Nell from his place in the front seat.

"Fine." She flipped the stereo off. "We could always talk instead. Toby broke up with his sug—*friend.*"

"My private life is not up for gossip." Toby leaned forward from the backseat. "Focus on driving. Dad probably wants to sleep."

"*Dad* is right here. And that's good, son. Good call. He's not what you need."

But maybe he is. Toby bit back a groan. Some part of him had wanted Reuben. Needed him even. Needed Reuben, needed his caretaking, needed his support and enthusiasm. And that same part of him liked all of that, reveled in all Reuben could offer, even as other parts of him rebelled, long-held beliefs lecturing him about what he could and could not need and enjoy.

"Well other than his money. We sure could use that," Nell interjected before Toby could decide how to answer.

"No we couldn't. Men like that always have strings. Keep track of every favor. Know who owes what," his dad lectured.

"He's not like that." And really, Reuben wasn't. He was the most generous person Toby had ever met, and Toby believed him when he said he simply wanted to help. The problem wasn't with Reuben's motivation. "He's a good guy, and he genuinely cares. I wish you guys could see that."

"You sound like you're still hung up on him." Nell's voice was light, but the truth in her words slipped under his skin. He sure as hell wasn't over Reuben, wasn't sure he *wanted* to be over Reuben. He'd had flings before where being over and done with felt like a relief. But that wasn't the case here at all, instead it felt like he was letting go of an essential part of himself, not just Reuben.

"You'll get over it," his dad added, but Toby wasn't sure at all, and he stayed silent the rest of the way to the house.

Once home, he started in on a plan he had hatched with Nell earlier.

"So what we're going to do, is we're going to stock

the area next to your chair with snacks. Water bottles. Chips in baggies that we're going to measure out. That way you don't need to get up as much and you don't need to be reaching for things in the pantry."

"I'm not a *kid*, needing something like that. I can do for myself." His father glared at him from his favorite chair, frown deepening as Nell brought in a storage shelf they'd cleared off earlier.

"I know you can, but Nell and I want to help you."

"If you wanted to help, you'd stop taking so many tourist trips. And she could stop going out every chance she gets with those friends of hers," his dad complained.

"We need my job. And Nell's young. I've been too hard on her as it is. Let us make it easier on you when we're not here. We're also going to get you an alert necklace—"

"I don't need a damn beeper around my neck."

Toby had been trying hard to stay patient and calm, unlike past arguments, but his control kept slipping the grouchier his father became.

"Yes, you do. Why won't you let us help you? And you're the same with neighbors and family who want to help." While it was true that his mother's side of the family had been bigger and more active, his father wasn't without relatives who cared, but something in him had always stood apart, doubling down on his belief that he should handle his own problems. He knew that belief had caused his more social mother pain, and he was only now seeing how it had impacted his own value structure. "You chase everyone off."

"I don't want to be a burden," his father shot back.

"You're not." Toby gentled his tone again. "We love you and we only want to help. That's all."

Click. Something slipped into place in his brain even as his dad harrumphed and looked away. As surely as the part had slipped into position for Griffin, stark clarity rammed into Toby's consciousness. *Love you. Only want to help.* Did he really want to be like his dad, thirty years down the line, biting off the heads of people trying to help him, continuing to believe that accepting help made a person weak? And was he really going to walk away from love because of pride? Looking at his dad, he could see so clearly the burdens of pride. The way he never wanted help, even from the neighbors and extended family. He was glad that his dad had taught him to be his own person, taught him to take pride in hard work and his ability to provide, but he didn't want to spend the rest of his life shackled to an ideal when he could have had a real partnership instead.

His eyes flicked to one of the dozens of pictures of his mom in the living room. There were no guarantees in life. Some people only got one shot at love, one shot at that kind of partnership. And others like Griff took risks with their hearts, with their pride even. Toby knew now what kind of guy he wanted to be. And he could only hope it would be enough.

"I'm going to call her." Amelia hopped from foot to foot as they exited the SUV back at the vacation house after their hike. "It's late back east. I can't wait much longer."

"You should let me do it." Reuben needed a shower and possibly a nap, but he wasn't going to leave Amelia dealing with Natalie on her own.

"I need to do this." Stopping moving, she gave him a surprisingly hard stare. "Sometimes people need to do things on their own. Even if it sucks."

"I know. I get that." And he did. A few weeks ago, Reuben would have insisted she let him make the call, lay the groundwork with Natalie for her. Trying to solve all her problems the way he had wanted to solve Toby's. But that approach wasn't the best. He needed to work on letting people stand on their own more, so he nodded. "I'm going to be right in the kitchen, okay? I'll start thinking about dinner. You can come get me if you need me. And, honey, it's okay to change your mind. You won't hurt my feelings if you talk to Mom and decide to try school anyway."

"I'm not going to change my mind." Again with that stubborn tilt to her face. God, she could look so much like both Natalie and Reuben's mother at the same time that it was almost spooky. "But thanks."

"Anytime. I'll be here." Not up to anything too taxing and still hoping for a shower, he put a freezer lasagna in the oven. He figured they could have that and a bagged salad and call it good. Rather than head to the shower while Amelia was still on the phone outside, he flipped channels on the TV, looking for anything that might be a distraction from how tangled up he still was about Toby and now Amelia too. He hadn't had any luck at that when Amelia came back in, eyes puffy and red, and held out the phone.

"She wants to talk to you."

Flipping off the TV, he took a deep breath and did not say that he'd told her this would happen. She'd needed to be the one to tell Natalie, for whatever reason, and maybe he didn't have to fully understand in order to support her and love her through this. So, he pulled her in for a tight hug before taking the phone, whispering in her ear, "I'm proud of you. Go on upstairs."

"Reuben?" Natalie was already worked up as soon as he picked up the phone. "What's the meaning of this? She says she's not going to school in the fall? *My* school. There's a window seat in the library with my mother's name above it. Her mother has a tree in the courtyard there as well, and the *only* reason Amelia got in at all is because she's a triple legacy. God knows it wasn't grades or extracurriculars last year for her, unless you want to call that computer game of hers a hobby."

"She's taken up sewing here. We're mailing you a package in a few days with some things she's made for you. You'll be impressed." He said the last part loud enough for Amelia to hear on her way upstairs, and she turned and gave him a tentative smile before ducking into her room.

"Sewing? What's she supposed to do with that?"

"I'm not sure. I don't think she knows yet either. Just let her have fun."

"Fun? Like her 'I'm going to live with Dad and we're not even sure where yet, but we'll figure out a school' plan? That sort of fun?"

"Yes. Look, I know this is hard for you. You loved boarding school. But Amelia's not like you. She had friend issues all last year, apparently, and says the randos online are better than her real-life peers. She's not the popular kid like you or the athletic leader like me. She's her own person now, and that person has unique needs."

"Randos? God, you even talk like her now. What she needs is the third best private school in the country. Everyone cries their first few weeks. *Everyone*. She'll buck up."

"I don't think she should have to. I'm on her side on this one."

"So I gathered. Do you have a custody lawyer lined up? Because when we agreed to joint custody, this is *not* the sort of triangulation I envisioned." Natalie's voice had gone cold and hard.

"I don't need one." Reuben could match her tight syllable for tight syllable. "You still want me out at the firm? You want me to quietly take the buyout, no negotiating or haggling? Then I want Amelia to get what she wants here."

"You're holding our child hostage because you don't like the idea of leaving the firm? You're asking me to choose between a school that I know will be good for her and a course of action I know is the right one for the firm? You're a bastard."

"No, I'm giving you a choice." He used his take-no-prisoners voice that he hadn't needed in weeks here. "Choice A is we resolve this amicably, and everyone gets something they want. Choice B is yes, you can expect a battle. But you know as well as I do that she's old enough that the court will listen to her opinion too. A prolonged custody battle isn't guaranteed to go your way."

"Or yours," she tossed back. "You can expect to hear from my attorney."

"Guess I'll need to keep right on working at the firm to afford mine. You think on that," he said right before she cursed and ended the call.

"Fuck. Fuck. Fuck." He did some cursing of his own. He hated fighting with Natalie, knew she did love Amelia, and hated that either she or Amelia were about to be bitterly disappointed. And if he could only pick one to bolster, he'd pick his kid, but that didn't mean he was heartless toward Natalie's position. They'd had a lot of years of amicable friendship between them, and even if the marriage had been ill-fated, he still cared about her. But Amelia had to come first here.

"I'm taking a shower," he yelled up to Amelia. "Listen for the oven timer."

Maybe if he showered long enough, the world would make sense again. The Amelia thing was fraught with uncertainty, and his head still swam with uncertainty over Toby. He knew now what he wanted, but the getting it… Fuck. The getting it was going to suck. He wasn't giving up though. Amelia was counting on him, but more than that *he* was counting on himself too, counting on him to be brave and, yes, a little selfish and go after what he most wanted.

Chapter Twenty-Three

"Thanks. I owe you big," Toby said to Nell as they arrived at Reuben's place.

"I'll help you get the chair out, but I'm not sticking around to see if he takes you back."

"That's okay." Toby tried to project a confidence he wasn't sure he felt. But Reuben would want to talk, right? At least that much? It had only been twenty-four hours, so Toby had hope that Reuben hadn't hardened entirely toward him. "If he kicks me out, I'll call Griffin or something, go stay at Annie's tonight while I figure stuff out."

"That's probably the better plan." Mouth twisting, she gave him a frustrated look as they got the wheelchair out of the SUV. She hadn't been at all happy that he wanted to go talk to Reuben in person. However, some things were better handled face-to-face. On the phone, it would be too easy for Reuben to hang up on him. At least this way, he'd have to listen.

"I know you and Dad don't like him much, but I need to do this for me, okay?"

"I don't *dislike* him. I like Amelia a ton. I think he's nice enough. Just too old for you, not really your type at all."

"Why don't you let me worry about my type? And

his age?" He couldn't deny that Reuben was outside his usual, but maybe that was part of his appeal—whether it was his age and experience or simply his personality, something about him worked for Toby like nothing else ever had.

"Okay. And for what it's worth, I think Dad will come around eventually—he doesn't hate Reuben specifically as much as not liking rich outsiders and not liking him for *you*."

"I hope you're right, because I'm not giving up on this without a fight."

"I hear you. And good luck. Hope you know what you're doing." Chair set, she headed back to the SUV, clearly intent on leaving even before he entered the house.

"Me too." The door was probably unlocked, but he knocked anyway, pulse jumping around like a heavy metal guitar soloist. Amelia answered the door, which didn't calm him any. "Hey. Your dad around?"

"Maybe." Her mouth twisted. "I'm still mad at you."

"I know." He supposed he better get good at apologies in a hurry. "I was mean to Nell. And I apologized to her, but I'm sorry you had to see that. I was mad and scared about my dad, but I still shouldn't have lashed out like that."

"And my dad?" She gave him an eagle-eyed glare that felt like it saw to his soul.

"That too. I came to talk to him. Make things right."

"He was *sad*."

"I'm sorry. I didn't want to hurt him. I just... I needed to think. Get my head on straight."

"Well, it better be straight now. And he's in the shower, so you'll have to wait." Holding the door open, she finally let him in the house. "And I'm making him cupcakes. You better not ruin that."

"I won't." He hoped he could follow through on that promise, not accidentally steal Reuben's appetite with another argument. "Can I help?"

She considered him for several long moments as if she was trying to decide how to appropriately punish him for hurting her dad. "Okay. You can put the wrappers in the pan."

Grateful to have something to do with his hands, he followed her to the kitchen area and did as she directed. Tongue sticking out the same way it did when she sewed something difficult, she followed the directions on the box of cake mix he and Reuben had bought. Man, had that been only yesterday? Felt like he'd lived lifetimes since then.

"It's chocolate so set the timer for a little less than the box says," he advised as they finished filling the muffin cups. "Better underdone than over."

"Fine." She slid the tray into the wall oven, next to the lasagna, which was looking almost done. "At least you got a huge jar of frosting. I'm not sure how to make that."

"It's not hard. My mom made all our birthday cakes from scratch. I'll show you sometime."

"If Dad keeps you around, maybe," she said ominously.

"If Dad what?" Reuben came into the kitchen, head damp, feet bare, wearing a faded T-shirt and baggy shorts, and looking so good that Toby's next breath got all tangled up with the force of wanting him. Reuben stopped short as his eyes landed on him. "Oh. You… uh…"

"Amelia let me in," he said quickly. "But I can go. If that's what you want."

"He helped me make cupcakes," Amelia added quickly, surprising the hell out of Toby with her support.

"That's good." Reuben licked at his lower lip, eyebrows knitting together. "And no, I don't want you to leave. We should…" His gaze flickered around the room, landing on Amelia, and Toby got the message that he didn't want to have this out in front of her.

"Can you watch the cupcakes?" Toby asked Amelia rather than give Reuben a chance to get out of talking. "And maybe take the dinner out too? Your dad and I are going outside."

Reuben blinked, then straightened. "Yeah, that's not a bad idea."

After Reuben slipped on shoes, Toby headed outside, pausing at the edge of the single step for the deck. "Can you help me down?"

"Sure." Reuben helped him navigate the step. "I take it we're going for a stroll?"

"Well, I'm going for a *roll*." Even Toby's laugh was nervous as he followed the little path that led to the sleepy paved road at the end of the driveway. He didn't figure they'd get that far, but moving even at this creeping pace was better than staying still, getting lost in Reuben's face, trying to figure out what to say.

"You came back. Was it for your stuff or to make the cupcakes or…" Reuben sounded breathless despite their slow progress.

"Or. I wanted to talk. Helping Amelia with cupcakes was a bonus. And it wasn't her idea, me coming here. I… I did a lot of thinking today. And last night, honestly. Didn't sleep well."

"Me too. I missed you."

Reuben's admission loosened the twisted muscles in Toby's chest, made it easier to breathe. "I missed you too. Nothing felt right back home."

"Nothing felt right here without you either." Reuben stopped near a tree and looked down at him, earnest expression in his eyes. "And then Amelia hit me with a bombshell today, and I really wished you were here to talk it over with. I think I've gotten too used to hearing you tell me I'm a good dad."

Toby had to laugh because he was supposed to be the one worried about being too dependent, not Reuben. "You are a good dad. I'm sure whatever she said, you can deal."

"She doesn't want to do boarding school in the fall."

"Whoa. Your ex is going to freak."

"Yeah, she did. But that was only part of what Amelia said. The other part was that she wants to stay here in Alaska. And that made me realize what a disservice I did to you, demanding that you ask me to stay. I can't stay somewhere simply because someone else wants it."

"Yeah." Toby's throat was thick, clogged with what felt like layers of felted emotions. "You can't. I can't be the reason you stay or go. But I could have admitted how much I want you to stay. Not to guilt you, but so you'd have all the facts. But you're right. In the end, it has to be what you want. What you need. Even if that's not me."

Admitting that last part made his hands tremble, but even with everything he'd realized in the past twenty-hours, he still firmly believed that where to live and whether to pursue a future together had to be Reuben's call and couldn't be something driven by guilt or pity. An evening breeze whipped through, ruffling their hair.

"I don't want you to resent me," he added when Reuben stayed quiet.

"I wouldn't." Reuben's reply was slow, almost as if he were still thinking it over. "You *are* what I want. Absolutely. I've lived a lot of years, had a number of relationships, and I've never felt for anyone what I feel for you. And I probably should have said that yesterday. That I want you whether or not you want my help with your problems. I'm not in this to rescue you. Hell, if anyone's getting rescued it's me."

"How do you figure that?"

"I was working myself to death. I had a terrible relationship with my kid. Was stuck in a less-than-ideal work situation because of my pride and because I had no idea who I'd be without work. Then the plane crash happened and everything changed for me."

"That was a near-death experience, not *me*." Toby studied the gravel on the shoulder of the road.

"Maybe some of it. But other parts were you. Through watching you, I rediscovered how important family is— or at least should be. And when you'd tell me that I'm a good dad and to keep trying with her, I believed you. Also I'd pretty much given up on finding a relationship despite really liking having someone. But you showed me that maybe it was a matter of having the right someone and not so much me being crappy at relationships. You gave me back the part of me that loves having people around to care about."

"You do love to take care of people."

"And that's not a rescue thing," Reuben added. "I know you think it is and I'll admit that I love taking care of people. You. Amelia. Other people in my life. And maybe I'm not the best at letting people solve their own problems. But I don't *need* you to have crises. I just need you. And if that means letting you stand on your own—"

"Standing is still a little challenging these days." Toby couldn't resist teasing because the alternative was admitting how tight his chest had become again.

"Sorry. Not the best metaphor. But I do understand now where you were coming from last night. You need to handle certain things yourself. And my money isn't always going to be the answer to problems. It's not for Amelia—she wants me, not my ability to pay her tuition."

"I want you too," Toby admitted softly.

"Thanks." The tips of Reuben's ears turned pink. "She needs my energy. And that's what I should have offered you first. I do want to help you, but in whatever way that *you* need it most, whether that's my time or whatever. But it has to be what you need, not what I think you need."

"I'm honestly not sure what I need. But I could have been more open to discussing it with you, coming up with a plan, letting you help more. I've heard my whole life that a real man handles his shit, doesn't rely on others, puts in hard work alone, and it's hard to let go of that." A rare car was coming, and Toby rolled to the side of the road.

"I get that." Stepping closer, Reuben squeezed his hand. "For what it's worth, you are strong. And independent. And I lo—*like* that about you. Very much. Your independence is a big part of the appeal for me, not something I want to take away."

"I know." Toby had to look away again because the emotion in Reuben's eyes was almost more than he could bear. "There's probably a compromise where I can let you help without feeling like you're taking over."

"I don't always have to take over," Reuben protested. "I thought we made a pretty good team."

"Yeah, we did. I like doing stuff with you. I like being with you." This time he was able to meet Reuben's gaze, try to convey how serious he was.

"I like that too. And that's why I do want a future with you. Not a fling. A future," Reuben said firmly.

"I do too, but I don't want you throwing away yours or Amelia's simply so we can have a chance of working out."

"Oh, I think it's more than a chance." Reuben's conviction further eased the tension in Toby's shoulders. "But that's what I've been thinking about all day— what's best for *me*. And Amelia, of course, but for myself. What sort of future do I want? What's best for me? And I keep coming back to you. And this place." He gestured at the scenery around them—the towering trees and green hills. "I like who I am here. I like who I am around you. With you."

"I feel like this is where I should say that you can have me even if you go back to New Jersey. We could work the distance out. Somehow."

"Your family is here. Your heritage. Your job." Reuben shook his head. "No, I'm not asking you to give that up. I've got a loft that never really felt like a home, a job that wants me gone, and my only real family is Amelia now. And I know your dad drives you crazy sometimes, but he's still your dad. I'm never going to ask you to give up him or your sisters."

"Thanks. I'm still not sure how I feel about you staying," he confessed, twisting his hands in his lap. "It's such a big step. And I'm going to try to do a better job of letting people help, but I can't guarantee that I won't fuck up again."

"Maybe you don't have to be sure right this second." Reuben rubbed his shoulder. "Maybe neither of us do. I'm still not sure what's happening with Natalie. I could be in for a custody battle, and much as I don't want it to, that would impact things."

"So what then? What do we do now?"

"Right now?" Reuben smiled, wider than he had since Toby arrived. "We go and eat cake and try to trust that things will work out the way they're supposed to."

"I can do that." Toby returned the grin, trying to quiet the twitch in his back muscles that said they still had a ways to go between being on the same page after their argument to getting anything resembling a happy ending.

Forty-eight was way too old to be acting like a seventeen-year-old who couldn't wait to get his crush alone, but that was pretty much where Reuben found himself during dinner with a surprisingly chatty Amelia. The talk earlier had helped, yet he'd be feeling a whole lot better if he could get his hands on Toby.

"I'm glad you guys aren't fighting anymore," she said as she handed out the cupcakes. They were too sweet by half—the premade frosting almost cloying and they were well past done, but making them had been important to her, so he tried to drown his with a glass of milk. Ever the sweet tooth, Toby seemed far more forgiving of the dessert, taking two.

"I'm glad we're not fighting too." Toby caught Reuben's eyes, and his private smile sent warmth zooming to all Reuben's parts that were already counting down until bedtime.

"Good. My mom will just have to deal." She nodded emphatically.

Crap. At least half of Reuben's good mood evaporated. "Honey. Even though Toby and I talked things out, that doesn't mean there aren't more challenges ahead. Your mom may still be a major issue—"

"You didn't tell her about Toby, did you?" Amelia frowned, censure flashing in her eyes.

"It wasn't entirely relevant," Reuben blustered, not looking at either of them.

"I don't get it. I want to be here. You want to be here. Toby wants us here, right?" Her voice dared them to object.

Across the table, Toby seemed to shrink back into his chair. Outside he'd seemed committed to some sort of future together, but he'd also confessed his mixed feelings about Reuben moving here. As a result, Reuben was reluctant to make any firm plans with Amelia until he and Toby talked more. But he was also curious about Toby's reply.

"I…uh…" Toby's gaze turned to his cupcake, scrutinizing it like it might have the answers. "Yeah, it would be nice, but reality… Your mom… Your dad's job… Whether or not you guys are really up for a dark Alaska winter. Even if you love it here in the summer, lots of people struggle with winters. A ton of variables for you guys to weigh, you know? I'm trying hard not to be selfish here."

"You're not," Reuben said quickly. "I like knowing you want us here, even if the logistics seem hard."

"See?" Amelia smiled archly. "We all agree."

"I wish it were that simple." Toby's answering smile had an undercurrent of sadness to it that made Reuben nervous. Maybe it didn't matter how much the three of them wanted a future if Toby didn't believe in it.

"It is." Amelia's voice was as firm as Reuben with a team of underlings. "No more future talk right now, though. Do you guys want to see my latest colony? I modded their terraforming equipment. Nothing's impossible if you have the right cheat codes."

That made both him and Toby laugh as Amelia dug her laptop out of her backpack, apparently oblivious to how badly Reuben wanted Toby alone. But it had been a trying few days for her too, and maybe she simply needed extra attention. Trying to be understanding, he let her walk them through the game until finally she professed her tiredness.

"Guess I'll shower and read before sleep." She yawned.

"Good idea." Toby's gaze met Reuben's again, and the heat there comforted some of his dancing nerves. Perhaps this would work out after all.

"Night." Reuben gave her a fast hug. "Think I'll watch TV with Toby for a while."

"Uh-huh." She rolled her eyes before scampering up the stairs.

"Please tell me the TV is only for noise distraction," Toby said as they entered his room.

"Absolutely." Happy to be on the same page at last, Reuben flipped it on and clicked on the first thing the remote landed on—some sort of cooking show. He adjusted the volume before following Toby to the bed, waiting for Toby to transfer himself before he stretched out next to him.

"I'm sorry if Amelia was rather pushy." Lying almost-but-not-quite touching, he luxuriated in his nearness.

"She wasn't." Toby's half smile belied his words. "Wish it were as easy as she wants."

"Me too. And maybe it can be." He rolled closer, needed to touch Toby in the worst way, even if it were just the brush of their arms and thighs. On the TV, the chefs were bickering about portion sizes, which was funny because fuck potatoes, Reuben was dying for a heaping helping of Toby. "We care about each other. We'll make it through the logistics."

"Yeah." Toby still sounded distracted, to the point where Reuben couldn't feel good about kissing him like he was desperate to.

"What's wrong?" Caution made his voice more wavery than usual.

"Nothing." Toby shook his head, then laughed. "Okay, okay. Trying to get the courage to ask you to take a look at my workers' comp stuff tomorrow. Part of my whole 'get better at asking for help' thing. I haven't gotten any money yet from the claim and was wondering what the deal is."

"I'd be happy to." And he was, voice too bright because he was relieved that it wasn't Toby reconsidering them making up.

"Good." Some of the tension leaving his body, Toby finally closed the last gap between them, scooting into Reuben's waiting embrace. Someone laughed on the TV, further cutting the strained mood they'd had going all evening. "And I'm going to go nuts if you don't kiss me soon."

"That I can definitely do." Reuben didn't waste any more time before claiming Toby's mouth. He tasted like too sweet chocolate and everything Reuben remembered. Soft lips. Warm mouth. *Toby.*

And Toby's groan matched his own as their tongues met. He knew by now exactly how Toby liked being kissed, but it also all felt brand-new again, like he was discovering fresh ways to stoke the fire for both of them. Sweeping his hands up and down Toby's torso, he nipped at Toby's mouth, learning anew that Toby liked little acts of aggression, the scrape of teeth, the clutch of hands, the demands of growls and insistent tongues.

"More." Rolling, Toby tried to tug Reuben on top of him, but Reuben resisted.

"Careful. Don't want—"

"Please. You won't hurt me. I want to feel you on top of me. Turns me on like crazy."

Powerless to deny him, Reuben complied, but kept the majority of his weight on his forearms and tried to avoid jostling Toby's leg cast. Kissing in this position always felt more intimate, unleashed something protective and primal in him that made the kisses longer. Sweeter. Hotter. And yeah, he could agree with Toby that feeling his hard cock against his own was a turn-on. It had been years since he'd come in his pants from little more than pressure and making out, but Toby's drugging kisses quickly had him closer to the edge than he liked, and he tensed, trying to hold back his arousal.

"Come on. Let me feel you. Quit being so cautious. Let go." Toby pressed on Reuben's back, trying to pull him closer. The part of Reuben that worried held back, still hyperaware of not wanting to squash Toby, but the other part, the turned-on-like-crazy part slowly won out as Toby sucked hard on his tongue and slid his hands under Reuben's shirt.

"Not fair," he groaned, body taking over and thrusting against Toby.

"Yeah. Like that." Toby bucked up to meet him. "We haven't done it this way yet, and I wanna."

"Yeah?" Reuben's voice was a low growl he scarcely recognized.

"Uh-huh. Wanna kiss you until I fall apart. Until we both do. Because I missed this. Missed you. Missed what I feel when I'm with you like this."

"Tell me," he demanded, needing these sweet, needy words as much as the kisses.

"Safe. Warm. Protected. Like it's okay to stop thinking about what things mean and just *be*. Like I can be myself with you, all of me."

"You can. I like you. All of you." He shoved Toby's shirt up, needing more skin. There were other words he wanted to say, permanent words, words he wasn't supposed to feel yet but couldn't deny any longer. Scary words. Words that Toby might not welcome. Or return. So, he kept them to himself, tried to put them into his kiss, into the movement of his body against Toby's.

"Too many clothes. Want to feel you." Toby yanked Reuben's shirt. He sat up for a moment, so that they could both scramble out of their clothes, meet again skin-to-skin. He was less cautious now, settling more firmly against Toby, who groaned as their bare cocks collided for the first time. "Fuck, yeah."

"Missed you too. So much." Reuben kissed him like he was medicine, like his soul might wither and die without this man, without this moment, without this meeting of their bodies. He rocked against Toby, body knowing what it wanted. Needed.

Toby's cock was hot against his own, damp tip dragging against Reuben's skin. And there he was, back on the edge. Usually, he needed more friction, needed the satisfaction of getting the other person off first, but a rising drumbeat of arousal swept him along.

"Wanna come." Toby broke away from the kiss to moan, hooking his left leg around Reuben.

"Do it." Dipping his head, Reuben nibbled on Toby's neck and collarbone, continuing to thrust against him. Toby met him motion for motion, head thrown back, breath coming in harsh gasps.

"Fuck, you are so sexy."

"Pretty sure that's my line." Even Reuben's laugh was strained. "And you are. Feel so good."

"Let go. Let go," Toby panted. "Really go. Wanna feel it."

At first, Reuben wasn't sure he could, wasn't sure how to deliver what it was Toby was seeking. Letting go hardly came as easily to him as giving pleasure did. But then Toby tugged him back up for another kiss, tongue fucking its way into Reuben's mouth, teasing him until Reuben took over, chasing Toby's tongue back to his mouth, setting an insistent rhythm with both his mouth and body. His control slid, a mantle slipping off his shoulders, inch by inch until he truly was bare to Toby, nothing left except need and want.

"Come for me," he ordered, holding Toby closer as he thrust harder, loving the rub of their cocks together.

"You. First," Toby countered, bucking against Reuben, hand on his back urging him on.

"Close. Fuck, I'm close." His mind wasn't sure what to make of the tsunami of sensations bombarding him, the pleasure he couldn't hold back especially when

Toby whimpered, a soft, needy sound that wrapped itself around Reuben's balls.

"Do it." Toby's back arched, and that did it, the slight increase in pressure against his cock tipping him over until the last of his control was gone and all he could do was thrust wildly, ride his orgasm out. Toby pulled him in for a breathless, sloppy kiss, giving Reuben his moans as he too came, splashing warmth between their bodies.

"Fuck." Reuben tried to roll away, but Toby didn't let him.

"No. Mine. Stay."

"Okay." He was done protesting, all the fight and worries fucked out of him until all he could do was gather Toby close, hold him like this was all he'd ever need. And maybe it was. Maybe right here was the only place he'd ever truly belonged. All he knew was that he'd do anything to protect this, to keep Toby feeling safe and protected and *his*. He might not have all the answers, might not know what came next, but he knew that he wasn't giving this up without one hell of a fight.

Chapter Twenty-Four

"We should bring Toby's family the leftover cupcakes," Amelia declared as she loaded the dishwasher with the breakfast dishes, distracting Toby from the laptop he and Reuben were huddled in front of at the dining room table.

"I…" Toby wanted to see his dad, make sure he was doing okay after the hospital stay, but he wasn't sure how showing up with Amelia and Reuben would go over. However, it was going to have to happen eventually. Talking with Reuben last night had gone a long ways toward making him more comfortable about seeking a future together—and the world-rocking sex hadn't hurt either. However, logistics, fucking logistics, kept clogging his brain. Wanting wasn't the same as *having*.

"Nell likes chocolate. More than Dad." Amelia shot Reuben, who'd declined the offer of cupcakes for breakfast, a mock scalding look. "I want my work appreciated."

"Maybe," Toby allowed, if only because he couldn't endlessly spin his wheels. The only way to go from wanting something real with Reuben to having it was to try, hard as that was, logistics and all.

"I can stay in the car if that helps. I'm not looking to

be a wedge between you and them." Reuben's voice was patient as always, which helped.

"Thanks." He gave Reuben what he hoped was a grateful look.

Reuben tapped the laptop screen. "Back to this. You've got a clear claim, and they're doing what government agencies love to do and trying to grasp at straws for reasons to deny. But if you get Annie to type up a written explanation of your employment agreement— the fact that you get a base salary plus bonuses for the long trips and tips, that will make a difference."

"I hate asking her for help," he groaned. "She's already holding the job for me."

"From everything you've said, she's a good boss. This is part of being a good boss, doing the paperwork that gets you what you need during your time off."

"Yeah, she is. It's more that I hate needing favors."

"I know." Reuben rubbed his shoulder. "No one likes workers' comp claims, but this is part of the process. Now, I'm making you a list of everything you'll need to dispute the claim. They haven't formally denied you yet, which helps. These requests for extra information happen fairly frequently from what I understand."

"Thanks." Toby couldn't help the sweat that kept gathering in the small of his back over needing Reuben's expertise. "This is probably a far cry from the multimillion dollar deals you're used to working on."

"This is the part of the work I've missed—coming up with an action plan to solve a problem."

"See? You don't really want to be retired." Sadness joined the dread to settle over Toby again. Much as he professed a love for it here, Reuben wasn't really cut out for this life.

"No, I don't." Reuben surprised Toby with his ready agreement, making Toby's shoulders tense further. "And honestly, while my savings are comfortable, I intend to live a good long life, and not sure I've got forty-plus years of living expenses built up. But I am at a point where I can call my own shots, pursue passion projects. The way I figure it, I can do some consulting from here, using existing contacts, while I build up the sort of small corporate practice that would make me happy. I've already been investigating getting licensed here, whether I can take advantage of reciprocity rules—"

"Because of course you have." Toby had to laugh because there was little Reuben did without going full steam ahead. "You really want a small practice? No giant deals?"

"I think I do. Someone very wise told me it wasn't too late for me to be one of the good guys."

"Someone wise, huh?" Toby had to smile as he remembered their conversation while stranded all those weeks before.

"Yeah. And I think I'd enjoy working smaller deals, hands-on, helping small businesses."

"And you really think you can do that here?" His heart clattered, scarcely daring to hope that there was something approaching compromise that would let Reuben be Mr. Hotshot Attorney and let Toby have what he wanted most too.

"I don't see why not. Plenty of businesses here need transactions work, and I'm not without contacts or the reputation to take on some consulting contracts to bridge the gap."

"So we *are* staying?" Amelia sounded downright giddy as she came back to the table. Toby had forgotten she was still downstairs. Much as he wanted things to work out for him, he wanted only good things for her too.

"You're turning down an amazing school," he felt honor bound to remind her as Reuben typed away on the laptop. "The schools here are smaller, not as well funded as some fancy private school. And you haven't seen a winter yet. It's easy to want to stay in the summer." He'd seen that with other tourists before—falling in love with the area during a summer vacation, only to pull up stakes at the first hard winter.

"I love snow," she said with the enthusiasm of someone who hadn't actually had to navigate it beyond days off from school. "I do. I love winter."

"It's not just the cold and snow. I meant what I said yesterday—it's the darkness that really breaks people, even more than the snow. Both of you might end up hating that part."

"And we might not. Much as I've loved the outdoor stuff, I've still got plenty inside to occupy me, and I want to try. How will we ever know if this might have worked if we don't try?"

"Good point." Toby offered her a smile because she did make sense, and that was why he'd come back to apologize to Reuben yesterday. How would he ever know what might have been if he wasn't brave enough to try? To fight for it? And he really liked how she said *we*, like she and Reuben and he were a team of some kind. "You never know, you might take to cross-country skiing the way your dad took to fishing."

"I'll try it." Her easy shrug was miles from the sullen teen who had first arrived with Reuben. "And if we get cold—"

"Trust me, that's a given," he teased.

"Then I'll sew quilts. Like how your mom did for your family."

"That's awesome." His throat was suddenly four sizes too small for the amount of emotion welling up. "She would have liked you, you know? None of the three of us took to sewing like you have. I think she'd be glad to know that some of her material and stuff went to a good home."

"Would she like Dad?" Amelia did have a way of cutting right past any pretense to the heart of what mattered. Giving her the consideration she'd earned, Toby took a moment to think, really think about her question. Reuben glanced up from the computer too, clearly curious about Toby's response.

"Yeah. I think she would have. Eventually, at least. She told us over and over that she only wanted us to be happy, and your dad makes me happy, so yeah, I like to think she would have liked him. And you. You make me happy too."

"You're as bad as Dad with sappy stuff lately." Amelia's cheeks went as pink as Reuben's cheeks. "I'm going to need to blast a bunch of asteroids later just to make up for all this *feeling*. I'll be glad when Mom comes around, and this can all be settled."

Toby wished he shared her certainty that everything would work out. But as he reviewed the list Reuben had typed up of concrete steps to take with his workers' comp claim, he tried to channel her confidence. She was right—the only real course of action was to try. To hope for the best and simply try to have the future he now wanted. And he saw that clearly now. He wanted a partnership with Reuben—a real one with giving and taking and helping and receiving. He wanted to take care of Reuben and be taken care of in return. Someone to share a life with, ups and downs. All of that.

But even knowing that didn't make it easier a while later when they took the cupcakes to Toby's dad and Nell. True to his word, Reuben returned to the car after helping Toby out.

"I'll wait here. You'll want to talk to your dad," he said as Amelia dashed ahead, eager to show Nell the makeup sets from Anchorage.

"Yeah. I'll invite him for dinner later in the week too. Give him more of a chance to come around."

"Good plan." Reuben squeezed his hand. "This will work out. Promise."

"Trying to believe that." He tried to give Reuben a smile before heading into the house.

"We brought you cupcakes," he said to his dad who was in his usual chair. "Amelia made them, so be kind to her."

"She's not a bad kid. Nell seems taken with her." His dad sized him up with the sort of stare that used to make Toby quake in his sneakers back as a teen. "So that's it then? You're with him now?"

"He's got a name. Reuben. And yes, we are. You've known I was bi—"

"Not about that." His dad waved Toby's explanation away, even if his screwed-up mouth said that maybe it was at least a little about that. "Annie's Griffin's done well for himself. That flashy writer guy he's with—not sure about him either, but it's not his gender. Outsiders. You can't trust them to stay. Writer guy's going to get a wild hair to move on one day, leave Griffin in the lurch. And next thing we know *you'll* be on the east coast, see you on holidays if we're lucky."

"It's not going to happen like that," Toby protested. "He wants to move here."

"So he says now." His dad shook his head. "I don't buy him as long-term potential for you, not unless he's taking you from us. Sorry."

"Well, I do. He's what I want." Just saying the words out loud made Toby's heart beat faster. "I like him. Like really *like* him. He makes me happy. Happier than I've been in years."

"That's my fault." Shrugging, his dad looked away.

"What? No, it's not. What are you talking about?"

"Told you yesterday. I hate being a burden on you and Nell. Feels like you lost years taking care of me."

"There's no one I'd rather take care of. Seriously." They weren't huggers, and despite helping him in the shower countless times, Toby didn't usually go out of his way to touch his dad, but this was important, and he gave him an awkward pat on the arm. "You've been listening too much to Nell. She likes to act like I'm carrying some sort of…angst over leaving college. But you and Mom? Helping out? I don't regret any of that."

"Thanks." His dad's eyes were shiny when they finally turned back toward Toby. "Still. I've been damn stubborn. I want you to look into what my insurance covers. Maybe get Nell some help. Home health care."

"That would help. And I know she'd appreciate that. But it's not going to change my mind about Reuben—he's not trying to take me away from you guys. That's not why he makes me happy."

His dad snorted like he wasn't so sure. And since Toby wasn't even going to allude to sex or romance with his dad—Amelia wasn't the only one keen to keep sappy stuff out of family spaces—he struggled to explain.

"I like who I am around him," he said at last. "And I like who he is too. I think maybe we help each other be better versions of ourselves."

"I like the old you just fine." Sighing, his dad surprised him by returning the arm touch. "But I've said before. You're grown now. If this is what you want, what makes you happy, then I'm not gonna tell you different."

"Thanks." He supposed that was as good as he was getting from his family at the present. And it was enough. Because they did mean the world to him, and he couldn't imagine life without them in it. But he also wanted the freedom to pursue a life with Reuben. A future. See where this connection they'd found led. It felt a bit like hiking an unfamiliar trail without a map or compass, but he was working on feeling excited, not dwelling on all the ways this could still go wrong. After all, some trails led to spectacular places, and he'd never know if they didn't try.

"You're doing it!" Reuben cheered from his position next to Amelia in the line of chairs ringing the physical therapy area at the place in Homer. A few days ago, Toby had a follow-up appointment in Anchorage and received a lighter walking boot cast with the all clear to start weight bearing and working with crutches. His arm was still in a light splint, which made the crutches awkward for him, but he was trying his best to follow the therapist's directions, and Reuben was determined to applaud Toby's each and every accomplishment.

"It's harder than it looks." Sweat beaded up along Toby's hairline and his dark eyes narrowed as he concentrated on the next step. The past few weeks since their fight had flown by, days spent exploring and cooking and getting hooked on Amelia's game, and nights spent loving. And worrying, but that part was more private, his own internal drama over not knowing exactly what the future would bring. To Toby and Amelia, he tried to project nothing but optimism.

"Go, Toby, go!" Amelia looked up from her phone. "You get ice cream afterward for sure."

"Any flavor you want." Reuben tried to tell him with his eyes that he'd properly reward him later as well.

They were all going out for lunch after Toby's appointment, then stopping at Toby's work so he could check in on the plane Griffin was restoring, which was scheduled to go up on a short test flight later that afternoon. It wouldn't be long until he was back on duty, at least in a limited capacity. Time was marching on, the summer coming to an end, and Reuben was more sure than ever that this wasn't a fling, that this was real, and his feelings for Toby had only deepened. Too bad that so much was still unsettled—

Buzz. As if his phone could read his muddled thoughts, it buzzed insistently in his pocket. *Natalie.* He'd been waiting for this call all morning.

"I'm stepping outside," he whispered to Amelia.

"Okay. Tell Mom that I still haven't changed my mind." Amelia's head shake made her look far older than fourteen, worrying over Natalie's next move taking its toll on her too. She'd had a wonderful time at a local arts festival, more convinced than ever that she wanted to stick around here. From kayaking to horses to ATV driving, she'd really opened herself up to a world of new experiences, and more even than enjoying the activities himself, Reuben loved watching the changes in her.

For his part, Reuben had engaged in many long discussions with Natalie that hadn't gone anywhere. She seemed determined to wait them out, banking on their return, acting like they'd both change their priorities once back east. And that wasn't happening, so round and round they went, like a badly executed game of chess. And after weeks of stalemate, they'd finally agreed to do a video chat the next day with a custody mediator, trying to avoid the sort of lengthy custody battle that was looking more and more inevitable.

"Natalie?" Reuben picked up on his way out of the building, going to the short sidewalk outside the physical therapy practice which was located in a small, aging strip mall. He paced toward a one-hour photo place.

"One year." Natalie's voice was sharp and crystal-clear, reception surprisingly cooperative for once. "You get one year."

"Pardon?" Pausing by a message board littered with paper flyers, he tried to follow her declaration.

"I don't want to air all our business in mediation. And the firm needs an answer to the buyout question ASAP. I simply can't afford to let this drag on and on."

"It's not fair to Amelia either," Reuben added, pulse speeding up, hope rising that perhaps Natalie had found the compassion he knew was in her.

"That too." Little click-click sounds signaled she was drumming her manicured nails against something. "I thought I was a *good* mother. Thought I'd raised her… Oh, never mind. Guess it doesn't matter now."

"You are a good parent." Despite all their differences, Reuben didn't doubt that she cared. "But part of parenting is learning to parent the kid we actually have, not the one we think we should have."

"I get that." She gave a defeated-sounding sigh. "And

I'm trusting you that this is what she needs right now—living at home with you, going to public school. But I don't want to concede all four years of high school right now. One year. We'll look at her grades, adjustment, behavior, needs, etc. at the end of the school year. And I get all school breaks, since you seem determined to carry through with this insanity of settling in the literal Arctic."

"I think the one-year plan is reasonable." He avoided the temptation to explain that the Kenai Peninsula wasn't actually in the Arctic Circle, but he was too close to getting a concession from her to risk pissing her off again. Amelia wouldn't like the plan, but it was better than a long custody battle would be, and Reuben could admit that he too was curious how she'd actually do in public school. It could be that she'd be ready to try the boarding school by the end of the year, and he wanted to be open to that possibility. "And of course, I'll sign whatever you want to email over about the buyout. No haggling, as we agreed on. If you can trust me with Amelia, I'll trust you to not screw me over on the terms."

"I am trusting you. And I hear you've been putting feelers out about some consulting work. Sounds like you won't be idle long. But I never thought of you as the small solo practice type."

"Neither did I," Reuben confessed. "But strangely I'm energized. Excited by the freedom and what I'll be able to do."

"Are you sure that the excitement isn't just infatuation?" She knew about Toby from previous conversations—there hadn't been any point in keeping the fact that he was seeing someone from her, as it would have come out eventually. "With both the state and this guy? It might wear off, you know?"

"I know. But I don't think that's going to happen. He's the real deal. I…" He took a deep breath. Maybe if he got used to saying the words, he'd be able to get them out when they really counted. "I'm in love with him."

A strangled cough sounded behind him, and oh fuck, Amelia was right there, Toby next to her, balanced on his crutches, both of them with wide eyes and slack mouths.

"Hell."

"He's right there, isn't he?" Natalie sounded delighted by this turn of events. "How about you tell Amelia to call me later? In the meantime, I'll start on the paperwork for all this. And not going to lie, part of me wishes I were there to watch you talk fast."

"Bye, Nat. And thank you. Avoiding mediation is good for all of us."

"Yay!" Amelia did a little dance right there on the sidewalk as he hung up. "No mediation tomorrow? She's agreed?"

"She said that you can have this school year with me, and then we'll reevaluate. Your grades will play a role. And before you tell me again that there's no way you're changing your mind, I think this is wise."

"I'll take it." Continuing to grin broadly, she walked backward toward the SUV. "And I'm gonna get in the car now and plan my lunch order. Take your time."

"So, that's good news." Toby stepped—or rather lurched—forward, still not the steadiest on the crutches. "I'm sure you'll still have to go back and pack though."

"And get the loft listed with a Realtor," he confirmed. Behind them, green hills met a perfect aquamarine sky. Yeah, he could give up his loft for this, no problem.

"Sure you want to do that?" Toby's head tilted, mouth moving as if there was more he wanted to say.

"Yup. Not only do I want to free up the asset while I adjust to my new budget, but it's simply not who I am anymore. It never felt like home. No matter what, it's time for a change."

"No matter what, huh?" Toby still sounded uncertain, like he was working something out in his brain. "You mean like if we don't work out?"

"We're going to work out." Reuben was determined to will that proclamation into existence, even if he had to believe enough for both of them. He knew Toby *wanted* that future and understood why the believing part didn't come as easily to him. The wanting was the important part, and every kiss, every touch, every long look and longer conversation assured him that Toby did care for him. "And I know you heard what I said—"

"To get Natalie off your back," Toby interrupted.

"No. Because I mean it." He forced his voice to stay firm, not quaver like a teen looking for a prom date. "I'm in love with you. And I know that you might not be ready to hear it, and that's okay."

"Not gonna deny that it's a little freaky." Toby offered him a crooked smile. "But if I've learned anything else this summer, it's been a reminder that life is short and that there are no guarantees. My parents thought they'd have forever. Then it seemed certain that she'd outlive him. But life has its own plans. And look at us. We could have easily died in the crash. I *would* have died on my own. This summer really has all been about second chances and what we do with those chances."

"Yeah. That's exactly how I feel, especially about time with Amelia too. Like I got a second chance there to get it right with her. And I got this chance with you, and I know it's big and scary, but I'm not going to run from my feelings."

"Me either. I mean it's not like I can run that fast these days anyway." Toby laughed, eyes meeting Reuben's. "This is real for me too. Not a fling. I'm glad you're staying because I'm falling too."

"Good." Reuben rolled his shoulders, muscles loose for first time in days, future worries lifting.

"Can we get ice cream now?" Toby chuckled again. "Because I'm really wanting to kiss you, but your kid is staring at us so I'm thinking I better settle for the ice cream."

"I'll make it up to you later," Reuben promised. And he would. He'd prove to Toby that his trust and patience weren't misplaced. He'd show him with his kiss, with his body, with the words that didn't always come easily that what he felt was genuine and true. That this was love. And a love like this was more than worth any uncertainties. This was something worth building around. Worth celebrating too. "Let's get you that treat."

For him, though, he had all the sweetness he needed as long as he got to keep this man right by his side. Everything else would work out.

Chapter Twenty-Five

December

The lake glittered beneath Toby, a frozen diamond dancing in the last of the day's sun. With a four o'clock sunset, he'd needed to make good time coming back from a winter wedding tour, dropping his happy clients off in Anchorage, and continuing on home himself.

Home. Such a different concept now than just a few months ago.

His approach for landing was textbook, and the conditions couldn't have been better, but his pulse still skittered. He was probably always going to carry a little extra anxiety from the crash with him, quadruple checking everything, monitoring the weather like his life depended on it—which it did. But even with nerves, there was still nothing like being back in the air on a day like this, coming back satisfied from a great group that been a lot of fun to take around. And even better, the San Diego-based group had tipped generously, setting him up well for some holiday present shopping.

Amelia had informed them with her usual directness that she intended to celebrate both Hanukkah with Reuben and Christmas with her mother over the school holidays and that presents would be welcomed for either holiday. Nell too had things she had her eye on, and while they'd never been particularly celebratory as a family, he liked the idea of doing nice things for her and Amelia. And Reuben. Who was hard as hell to buy for, and thinking of present ideas had been a nice distraction from the lonely nights while he was with the tour group. But he'd finally come up with something that might work, and now he had to tune out distractions, focus on his landing.

Landing with skis was always a challenge, but it was one he welcomed as he glided in. Hell, he was simply happy to have been able to be back at work, helping Griffin and the rest of the crew swap the floats for skis, putting to rest the long season of his recovery and starting a new one where he was back at almost full strength.

His leg told him when weather was coming, and he continued to need to be careful to not overdo things, but he felt stronger with each day.

"How was it?" Bundled up against the wind, Annie greeted him as he exited the plane. She'd shown tremendous trust in him, letting him take the planes out and putting him back in the tour rotation. While she was never one to be particularly emotional or demonstrative, she did seem to be watching him closer these days, sort of like an aunt might. Thanks to Reuben, he'd come to appreciate having people to worry over him, and he gave her a wide smile as he saw to the plane.

"Not bad. Great tippers. Pleasant couple. Totally in love with nice guests along. Smooth flights."

"Ah. Totally in love, huh?" She gave him a knowing smile. "Think you can tell Griff all about the benefits of winter weddings? His sisters would love to plan something…"

"Hey now, feels like we just had yours. And somehow, I don't think Griffin's the wedding type."

"You're right, of course. Not even River might be enough to make him change that much." She laughed, gray braid shaking. "And you?"

"And me what?"

"They could plan something for you. We consider you family too. Maybe for when Hannah's home?"

"I don't need a wedding." His ears in his hat went all hot and tingly.

"Yet." Smiling broader, she walked him back to the office. "You still trying to make that event? Better scoot. And drive safe!"

"I will." And because he did have somewhere to be, he made sure that everything was in order and headed for his old SUV, which still smelled vaguely of Nell's perfume. Once his workers' comp back pay had come in, he'd been able to help her get a used car with good four-wheel drive, which she used to get to work at the salon and a second job at a diner.

He wasn't surprised to see that car as he pulled into the parking lot for the high school, her emerging looking model-perfect as usual in a silver puffy coat and pink and silver hat.

"How weird is it to be back at a high school?" Nell gave him a fast hug. "I parked three times, just trying to make sure I wasn't on the line and wouldn't get some teacher complaining at me."

"You're a good friend for coming. She's going to be thrilled."

In the end, Amelia had ended up going to high school

in Homer rather than the smaller high school Toby and Nell had gone to, but Toby and Nell had both been here for their fair share of athletic events growing up.

"You made it!" He turned to find Reuben behind them, huge smile on his face. The parking lot was full of other families going into the school, so Toby settled for a fast hug that only left him wanting more later. "Man, I missed you. Good trip?"

"Eh. It was okay. Missed you too. Cute wedding. Now Annie's got wedding fever. Poor Griffin."

"Weddings *are* fun." Nell's eyes sparkled as she bit her lip. "You know what would *really* freak Dad out—"

"No," he said firmly before she could put Reuben on the spot. She'd warmed up considerably toward Reuben in the past few months, seeming to delight in thinking of him as Toby's big rebellion. Reuben helping her investigate which beauty school would be the best fit hadn't hurt either. And she got far too much enjoyment from watching Toby's dad try to navigate this new reality. But even Dad was doing better—less grumpy, letting neighbors and extended family along with some home health care ease the requirements on Nell and Toby. In some ways, their relationship was stronger now, less tension.

"What *no*?" Nell batted her eyes. "You know it's coming. You guys are so stupid in love it's not funny. Just get it over with."

"If that's not a ringing endorsement of marriage, I'm not sure what is." Reuben laughed and ushered them both into the building. However, his eyes caught Toby's and there was something there, a sort of speculation that made Toby's toes curl inside his boots. "And just for the record, I like weddings."

"Didn't you already get one?" Toby teased. "Sure you want all that paperwork a second time?"

"I didn't get one with *you*," Reuben tossed back, almost too casually, eyes still serious. "And you're worth any amount of paperwork."

We'll see, Toby said with his eyes because they'd had the out-loud version of this talk a few times.

"Aww. See, you guys really are too cute." Nell linked arms with both of them and dragged them toward the auditorium. Once inside though, Toby untangled himself so that he could sit next to Reuben, who was fishing out his new camera.

"Look at you." He bumped Reuben's shoulder. "That's almost nicer than Griffin's."

"Should be. It's what he and River recommended." They'd had them over to dinner recently, like a real couple in their real house with their real friends, because Reuben liked to socialize and so did River, who had opinions on everything from decorating schemes to menus to cameras. "I can't wait to send pictures to Natalie."

"Where's that guy who couldn't be bothered with pictures?"

"Think I left him stranded on an iceberg." Reuben laughed, then whispered, "Shh. I think they're about to start."

The drama class's annual winter performance was an endearing mix of poetry, monologues, skits, and even some stand-up comedy, along with reminders about tryouts for the spring play and pleas for more parent volunteers. And in a skit featuring a *Grinch* parody, he made sure to note the fabulous makeup and costumes of the participants, because he was sure he'd be quizzed later right down to the ruffles on the nightgowns. The Grinch herself towered over her Whoville residents, resplendent in a repurposed green evening dress and expertly evil makeup. And when she cackled, audience in the palm of her red-tipped hand, Toby knew beyond a doubt that Amelia had found her people. She'd worked weeks on the costume and makeup plans—even more than on her lines. And definitely more on this than the upcoming final exams for the term, but seeing her beam like this was worth all her moaning about geometry.

Discreetly, he took Reuben's hand, gave it a squeeze. He'd done a great job at seeing what Amelia needed to well…be *Amelia*. And he'd been the one to sit through the last week of frantic rehearsals while Toby had been out on the tour, so he'd more than earned some sort of reward later.

"She looks so happy," he leaned and whispered as they all applauded.

"I hope the pictures show it."

"I'm sure they do." He knew Reuben was a little worried about what might happen after this year, but after months of him telling Toby to trust in the future, Toby had finally started repaying the favor. "It'll all work out."

After the performance, there were cookies in the library, and it didn't take long before Amelia, still in costume, found them.

"How was it? How was it?"

"You were fabulous, honey." Reuben gave her a big hug. "I can't wait to show you the pictures later."

"You look amazing," Toby added.

"You did make it!" Her smile seemed to increase in wattage when it landed on him. "One of my friends looked out and said my dads were here—"

"Your *dads*?" Nell blinked rapidly.

"Well, yeah." Amelia's cheeks turned pink and she talked faster. "That's what they call Toby and Dad. My dad and my other dad. They're not mean about it or anything. And he's still *Toby*, but—"

"It's okay," Toby cut her off before she injured something. "I don't mind. Let them call me what they want. As long as you're cool with it."

"I'm cool," she mumbled, looking down at her red high heels. "You're on my emergency contacts and everything now. Might as well make your bonus-parent status official."

"Oh, this is *perfect*." Nell's eyes did the sparkly thing again that made Toby's neck prickle. "I love it. Your two dads. And yes, let's make the bonus-parent thing official. Think you'll be able to sew matching vests?"

"My mom, Toby's Dad, and all the haters would *freak*." She grinned like this was the most optimal outcome. And maybe, just maybe, it was.

"Let's do it," Nell declared.

"I'm pretty sure one of *us* needs to do the asking, not you," Reuben said with a chuckle.

"Then get on that," Amelia said, playfully pushing him toward Toby.

"I just might." Reuben winked at Toby and warmth spread all the way up his chest. Now he *really* couldn't wait to be alone later. He was going to have to act quick if he didn't want to be the one upstaged.

It was all the way dark by the time they made it home after dinner with Nell. Reuben really did like her and her influence on Amelia, but he'd been counting down all damn day to this moment. Glass of wine for him, beer for

Toby. Lights low and TV softly droning on. Dog, who'd arrived a few weeks before Thanksgiving, a large mutt of indeterminate breed and age who'd shown up one day at the bottom of the driveway without an owner to be found, dozing on his bed in the corner. The humans' king-size bed piled with fluffy comforters facing the gas fireplace with a nice view of the night out the large picture window.

But the only view he was presently concerned with was waiting for Toby to emerge from the shower. Many things had sold him on this house—the spectacular view of the mountains from the great room, the house's friendly red color, isolated two acre lot, good school district for Amelia, third bedroom that made a nice home office for him—but he had to admit that the second he'd seen the fireplace in the master, he'd mentally put Toby in front of it and that had been that and he'd started talking prices and closing dates.

And the firelight was every bit as wonderful as he'd pictured, dancing off Toby's damp skin and hair as he finally came in from the attached bathroom. The dog briefly looked up, snorting softly at the sight of his favorite person, then resumed dozing.

"Come here," he demanded, patting the comforter next to him. "And lose the towel."

"Gee, you'd think it had been a month, not four days." Toby laughed as he complied. "Thought you had a dog to let out and emails to check. Eager much?"

"He was fast. And I finished the emails. And yes, eager. Very." Reuben pulled him close. His consulting work, along with a couple of local clients, was indeed keeping him busy, but if the past six months had taught him anything it was when to set the phone aside. "Not being able to kiss you at the school was torture."

Neither of them was much into PDA, and they were still feeling their way forward with the area, but damn had he wanted to kiss Toby senseless the second he'd seen him in the parking lot. But there was nothing stopping him from doing it now. Dipping his head, he claimed Toby's mouth, swallowing his surprised gasp, reacquainting himself with Toby's taste and feel. Business travel was simply going to be a fact of life for both of them, but that didn't mean he couldn't appreciate each homecoming to the fullest.

"Love you." He pulled back long enough to stroke Toby's sharp jaw. The words came easier these days, but they still weren't something he tossed off without thinking, without *meaning*.

"Yeah, me too." Toby leaned in for a fast, soft kiss. "Missed you." The glancing contact wasn't nearly enough, and Reuben tried to roll to his back, taking Toby with him, but Toby resisted. "Wait. Wanted to talk first."

"Oh." Reuben sat up, trying to shove aside his lust to actually listen and trying not to let rising dread get the better of him.

"Between Annie, Nell, and Amelia, it feels like the whole world has gone wedding crazy."

"Yeah. I thought Amelia's comment about having two dads was cute though," he said cautiously. "They're just teasing because they want us happy. And we *are* happy, right?"

"Yeah, we're happy." Toby smiled, but his voice sounded oddly nervous. "The two dad thing, though, that's a big responsibility. I don't want to let her down."

"That makes two of us. But you won't. She loves

you, and you're great with her. I didn't put you down as her emergency contact at the school and doctor's office lightly. I love watching the two of you together. Vet's office has both of us down too. And you know I'm in this for the long haul."

"Yeah."

"And irrespective of what others want, I want—"

"No." Toby held up a hand.

"No?" Reuben had to blink. That was a rather firm rebuttal, and he hadn't even gotten the full sentence out.

"No, you do not get to be the one bringing this up again."

"I don't?" He still wasn't entirely following Toby. "You seemed willing to at least entertain the idea—"

"I *am*." Toby made a frustrated noise. "But everyone, you included, seems to think that you need to be the one doing the asking."

"Ah. I see," Reuben said, even though he still didn't quite. "And you don't like that?"

"I don't like the assumption that it's something that I need to be talked into. Like I'm the reluctant one. Because maybe that was true for a while, but it's not true now. I don't need some…big gesture to convince me to make things more permanent."

"You don't?" Reuben thought of the long list of ideas he'd been considering and discarding. And yeah, he'd been guilty of thinking like that.

"No. And I was going to wait until whichever day you're doing the Hanukkah presents for Amelia, but I don't want to miss my shot." Reaching over, Toby cast around in the nightstand drawer until he came up with a small velvet bag. "I got you something in Anchorage. At first I figured I should come up with some sort of contract—you know, impress my big shot lawyer."

"You don't have to do that. Trust me, I'm plenty impressed." Reuben's pulse pounded like he'd been hiking a steep grade for hours.

"But in the end, I went all boring cliché." Upending the bag, he revealed a gold ring with some sort of engraving on it. He held out, and Reuben accepted it with shaking fingers. Closer inspection showed that the engraving was a series of fish forming a circle.

"Fish?" Reuben had to blink and hold the ring up to the light.

"Well, you know. I caught you." Toby offered him a crooked smile. "And I'm not saying *soon*. More just *yes*—yes, it will happen, and yes, I want it as much as you. I know you need to wait and see what Natalie does at the end of the year—"

"I don't think she's going to be a problem, but even if she—or something else—was, I wouldn't let it stand in the way of having a future with you. You're part of my life now. We're going to make this work. I'm saying yes too."

"And see, that's exactly why I got you this. For a lot of months you were the one doing all the believing. Then lately, you've been worried—don't deny it."

"I have been, but it's more about hoping that Natalie sees how well-adjusted Amelia is here than about doubting our feelings for each other. And I'm still not happy about you insisting on paying something for rent and half of the dog's vet bill. It made me worry that you still see this as something temporary."

"I don't, but I do want things fair. That's probably not going to change. I can't let you pay for everything. But I can trust you with my heart. With my future. And contract or promise or whatever you want to call it, I want this permanent. I mean, we've got the house, the dog, the kid. Hell, we even had something resembling a dinner party. Why not make it official?"

"My thoughts exactly." Reuben turned the ring over in his palm, still marveling at it, at Toby really, truly wanting this and everything it symbolized. "And I vote sooner rather than later, but I'm happy to wait too. You doing this—it means everything to me. *You* mean everything to me."

"Same." Toby leaned in then, and Reuben's fingers curled around the ring, keeping it safe as they tumbled backward on the bed together. And as their mouths met, he knew he'd do everything in his power to keep Toby safe, to safeguard his precious heart and not let him regret the gift he was giving Reuben. In his kiss, Reuben tasted forever, tasted everything he'd craved for years, never knowing what he was missing until this man found him. Saved him. He'd protect Toby's heart with everything he had, because Toby really had given him everything he'd never known he needed. And now the only thing he needed was this man, this moment, this future stretching out before them.

* * * * *

Author Note

I did extensive location research for this book and tried hard to be as accurate as possible. However, minor liberties were taken for the sake of story arc, and any inaccuracies are entirely my own. If you're inspired by this series and want to take a journey of your own, there are several tourism companies like the one Toby works for, and I'm so grateful to the wisdom I found from these tourist resources during my research. Reuben and Amelia had a great deal of fun exploring over the course of the book, and I so enjoyed discovering all the different adventures they could have. Our national and state parks, especially in this region, are true treasures.

Acknowledgments

The editing journey on this one was more extensive than some of my projects, and I must salute my tireless editor, Deb Nemeth, who always manages to help me find the heart of the story. I appreciate her so much. And the rest of the Carina team is pretty darn awesome too. I am so grateful to all those behind the scenes. A huge thank you to my agent, Deidre Knight, who believed in this project from my first excited ramblings, and to Carina Press for giving it a splendid home.

This book couldn't exist without my amazing writer friends. Edie Danford kept me sane during a difficult draft. Carmen, Shay, Erin and Karen provided me with amazing Alaska resources and invaluable beta feedback. I know this book is stronger because of you guys, and I'm forever grateful. Wendy Qualls is my plotting buddy, and Layla Reyne keeps me sane with writing sprints and friendship. Thank you to all my friends so much for being there. I cannot name you all, but you enrich my life so much.

I also have the best readers in the world. My reader's group, Annabeth's Angels on Facebook, provides joy for my life in ways I never could have imagined. Thank you to all my readers, all around the world. Every mention, share, like, retweet, word of mouth, purchase, note, and other types of support mean the world to me. Thank you to my readers for taking a chance on this new series and new adventure with me!

Finally, thank you to my friends and family who love me and stand by me no matter what. I'm only able to do this because of you. A big thanks especially to my family who put up with a very harried writer during this one and who probably heard far more about Toby and Reuben than they ever wanted to. You're the best.

Coming soon from Carina Press and Annabeth Albert

*When a set-in-his-ways park ranger must spend the
winter snowed in with a free-spirited newbie volunteer,
neither is prepared for the flare of attraction,
but turning snowbound passion into something
lasting may be their greatest challenge.*

Read on for a preview of

Arctic Heat

*book three in Annabeth Albert's new
Frozen Hearts series.*

Chapter One

Come for the snow. Stay for the ranger porn. Owen couldn't help his smile as he surveyed the large Department of Natural Resources meeting room. He was really here in Alaska, doing this after it being little more than a daydream for so long. Happy shivers raced up his spine. His fellow volunteers were mainly fresh-faced college kids and retirees, but he lingered over the uniformed rangers near the front, trying not to stare but probably doing a miserable job of that. Because *wow*. These guys made drab green and khaki downright sexy with their broad shoulders and generous muscles and rugged jawlines.

The orientation was for new winter state park volunteers like Owen, who would spend the season living in remote locations to assist rangers and other paid employees. Experienced rangers would be educating them on everything from avalanche risk to generator operation and state land use regulations. Some returning volunteers and rangers were there for the CPR and first-aid certification refreshers, chummy people who obviously already knew each other and laughed and joked as they helped themselves to the coffee station set up at the side of the room.

He was scoping out the people he might be assigned to work with, and one particular man who stood by himself kept catching his attention—a uniformed ranger who had a few years on him, probably putting him at forty-something, just shy of "silver fox" and firmly in "yes, please" territory with his strapping build and iconic good looks. The DNR ads for the volunteer positions would undoubtedly get triple the response if they slapped this guy's picture on the materials. Hell, if winter in Alaska wasn't already on Owen's bucket list, one glimpse of those steely blue eyes might have done the trick.

He was hoping to be assigned to work with some cool people, since he'd be in close contact with only a handful of people on a regular basis, and he knew from experience how important team chemistry could be. He'd take anyone easy to get along with, but man... Talk about chemistry. Ranger Blue Eyes took the frisson of anticipation thrumming in Owen's gut and transformed it into something warmer and more intimate. And damn wasn't it nice to feel that sort of attraction again, after all the nagging worries that it might be gone for good.

Owen wasn't particularly vain, but he was damn observant, and he'd caught those eyes looking his direction more than once. Sure, part of it was undoubtedly that Owen had misjudged and overdressed in a nice button-down and dress pants and stuck out in the room filled with khaki, flannel, and denim. And maybe some of it was that he was one of only a couple of Asian people in the room. Maybe the guy was simply curious, but Owen had transformed *curious* into *interested* more than a few times.

And because Owen was nothing if not a man of action, he took his tea, orientation packet, and notepad

closer to the guy, trying to come up with a good opening on the fly. However, before he could speak, a broad-
faced woman with dark hair clapped her hands at the
front of the room.

"All right, let's go ahead and find seats. We'll be getting started in a few minutes, so get your coffee now!"

His ranger prey immediately took a chair, and there it
was, Owen's chance to spend the next few hours basking
in hot ranger vibes. He was in perfect position to slide
into the chair next to his dream guy and offer him his
best smile and—*fuck*—slosh hot tea. That part had not
been planned at all, and judging by the man's glare, the
intrusion was hardly welcome.

"Oops. Sorry! Are you okay?" Owen passed him a
napkin, resisting the temptation to dab at the guy's damp
uniform pants himself.

"I'm fine." The ranger continued to frown as he
soaked up the tea, which had splashed both his pants
and the desk arm of the chair. "It'll dry."

"I'm not usually so clumsy. I'm Owen. Owen Han."
Carefully arranging his stuff first, he stuck out a hand.
"I'm new here."

"I figured." He took Owen's hand, which was as
warm and firm as Owen had hoped. And the tiny smile
that tugged at his mouth was almost intoxicating in its
endearingness. "And I'm Quill Ramsey. Not new."

"Figured." Owen tried another smile, this one hopefully not too flirty but still inviting more conversation.
"Nice name. Not sure I've heard that one before."

"Eccentric mother." The way Quill said *eccentric*
suggested relations between him and his mother were
strained. "Apparently she circled all her favorites in the
book, then picked at random."

"That's kind of cool, actually. I'm named after the high school teacher who made my parents work together on a class project. Moms, right?"

"Yeah." Quill's tone didn't exactly encourage more talking, but Owen was nothing if not friendly. And persistent. His sister the therapist called it aggressively extroverted, and she wasn't entirely wrong.

"So, are you helping with the presentations or here to get recertified in the first-aid stuff?"

"Both." Quill's mouth quirked in something close to a grimace. Owen dug his voice—low and deep, Western without the twang. The he way he spoke like there was a tax on each word made Owen feel like he'd earned a gift when Quill continued. "Didn't realize I'd let my CPR lapse—we had support staff changeover in our field office, but still, I should have known. And yeah, since I'm here, Hattie talked me into leading the discussion about avalanche risk awareness." He gestured in the direction of the woman at the front of the room before his eyes swept over Owen again. "Not that all of you will need that lecture. You interning here in the home office? Heard they were getting a few folks in finance and business relations."

Owen had to bite back a groan. He really should have gone more outdoorsy with his wardrobe choice instead of "need to make a good first impression." He well knew he looked young, but he was beyond tired with reading as a college-aged twink instead of professional adult. And maybe he had been in finance once upon a time, but he was bidding that life good riddance. "Not a business intern. I'm thirty-six. I'm scheduled to winter in Chugach State Park."

"That so?" Quill blinked, and Owen kind of liked

knowing that he'd caught him off guard. Good. Maybe he could surprise him in other ways too.

The ranger's mouth moved like he wanted to add more, but Hattie clapped her hands again and called their attention to the podium. As she began her welcome, which was accompanied by cheerful Powerpoint slides, Owen couldn't resist another glance over at Quill. His assumptions might be irritating, but he was everything Owen had always imagined an Alaskan ranger would be. Damn. He really needed to find out where he was stationed stat, because Owen would like nothing better than to be snowed in with those biceps and those intense eyes. Talk about a dream winter.

Thank God the too-chatty newbie wasn't going to be Quill's responsibility. Someone else would have to keep him alive until spring, because this guy was a popsicle waiting to happen. It wasn't just his wardrobe choices that were more suited to the accounting department—his carefully styled dark hair and hipster glasses said he was the sort of high maintenance that never meshed well with the hard, often grueling work of winter parks management. At least he had the sort of build that might be able to keep up—surprisingly muscular arms and shoulders on a lean body. It had actually been his build that Quill had noticed first, his uncanny resemblance to a certain state champion butterfly swimmer who Quill had obsessed over a million lifetimes ago.

But that was then, and here and now Quill couldn't get distracted. He was here as a favor to Hattie, not to get caught up in any fresh eye candy. Besides, if the guy's build had pulled one memory loose, his voice and re-lentlessly friendly demeanor had hearkened back to another, reminding Quill a little too much of JP, who'd had that similar "never met a stranger" thing going on that Quill had never fully understood. He'd never figured out why some people enjoyed filling a perfectly good silence with inane questions. He had colleagues for twenty years without ever needing to have a deep chat or fill in personal details. He liked working with competent individuals, appreciated hard work and a positive attitude, but mainly he enjoyed his autonomy, liked the days that passed without ever needing to make small talk or figure out the sort of social niceties that had never come naturally to him. God, he hoped they didn't assign him a talker for the winter. That was the last thing he needed.

Also not natural? Sitting through long meetings. God, he felt like he was back in college again, sitting through a lecture he didn't need, fighting the urge to find something else to occupy his attention. The margins of his agenda called to him, the siren song of white space needing filling, but he wasn't twenty anymore and he wasn't going to let his colleagues catch him doodling. He could make it through some boring introductions and reminders that he'd long since memorized. So he kept his pen firmly capped and tried not to let his attention wander too much to the newbie, who was leaning forward, attention fully on Hattie, occasionally jotting a note in the small red leather notebook with a bullet-shaped silver pen. His good taste in accessories spoke to a certain level of income and comfort that Quill didn't usually see from the seasonal volunteers.

Owen had a way of biting his lip when he wrote that directly challenged Quill's resolve to let in zero distractions. The guy's eagerness really was strangely compelling, and Quill had to resort to making subtle hash marks with his department-branded pen to keep from staring. He was beyond relieved when Hattie declared a break after she and a ranger from Kenai finally finished a presentation on department regulations and policies.

Quill made his way to the front of the room because he might be antisocial, but he wasn't *that* much of an asshole friend. "You're doing great," he told Hattie as she clicked around on a laptop, setting up the next topic. "All settled in? How's Val?"

"Val's okay. Still fighting morning sickness, but we're on track for a March delivery. Having a house again is such a novelty. I think I'm driving her nuts with all my plans for the nursery."

"Good for you." Quill tried to mean it. It wasn't Hattie's fault that her on-again-off-again girlfriend had shocked them all with a proposal and a serious case of baby fever. Now Hattie had a desk job, a baby on the way, and for the first time in fifteen years, Quill had to face a winter without his best friend, his right-hand person. She understood Quill like few others, gave him the space he needed while still being a positive, helpful presence in his life. And instead of giving their office another ranger to replace her, budget cuts meant that the department in all its wisdom was bringing in a winter caretaker volunteer for the Hatcher Pass area that was Quill's primary jurisdiction.

"It'll all work out." Hattie squeezed his arm. "For you too. Change is good for all of us."

Quill had to snort because if there was one thing he hated, it was change. Give him the same brand of boots, the same turf to patrol, the same menu, and the same friends, and he was a happy ranger. The change from Hattie to someone new had had his back stiff for weeks now, tense with worries over who they might assign him and how they might get along—or not.

But he tried to keep his voice upbeat for Hattie's sake. "Says you. So, which of these is our person? Or people? Did they give us a couple?"

"Ah. About that." Hattie shuffled a stack of papers next to her laptop, looking away. "Your caretaker's been delayed. We're trying to reach her by phone, find out what the problem is. She's a recent college grad and seemed super promising. But one way or another we'll have something worked out for you by tomorrow at the latest."

"Fine." His back went from tense to rigid. Fuck. More uncertainty. There was plenty else Quill wanted to say, chiefly that he didn't want to winter with someone who'd skipped the training. And that a recent college grad was undoubtedly too green to start with. But this was Hattie and she was trying her best with her new position, and budget cuts and unreliable people weren't her fault.

"You're up next. Try not to scare them too much with winter weather risks. Smile."

"Hey. I'm not that scary." Presentations were a part of the ranger job, but he'd typically let Hattie handle a lot of the tourist education duties because yeah, it wasn't his favorite thing. And he supposed he did tend to come off as a bit dour, covering his nerves at talking to a crowd with warnings and reminders.

"Yeah, you kind of are." She shook her head, but her voice was laced with affection. Turning her attention to the crowd milling about the room, she directed people back to their seats, then introduced Quill in the sort of glowing terms he'd let only her get away with.

His stomach did the weird quiver it always did before

public speaking, something he tried hard to ignore. He wasn't the shy kid who hated being called on anymore, and despite his unease, he was prepared with picture slides of different dangers. Twenty winters in, he knew his stuff, and he tried to remind himself of that as he got started.

Stupid tips about eye contact and imagining the audience in comical situations had never worked for him, so he focused on the back of the room as he explained the risks unique to Alaskan winters. However, his attention kept drifting to Owen Han and his earnest expression and shiny pen moving across his page of notes. Surprisingly, something about his concentration settled Quill, made his voice surer and stronger, made him feel like he was speaking directly to Owen instead of the room at large.

Of course Owen, like a good chunk of the audience, was ill prepared for what lay ahead. Even people with a lot of snow experience in places like Minnesota had trouble grasping what an ever-present danger avalanches were.

Quill took his time with lots of pictures and patient explanations, trying to keep in mind what Hattie had said about not scaring people, but he needed them to understand the often harsh realities. It was a rare winter when he didn't see at least one fatality, usually from a human-triggered avalanche, and he was determined to do his best to make sure that none of the volunteers ended up a grim statistic. The more he spoke, the more comfortable he became, but he was still relieved when he reached the end of his slides.

The audience had some good questions, including one from Owen about avalanche beacons. Despite the whole resemblance to JP thing, Quill liked his voice, which had more than a hint of California to it—casual vowels and easy confidence. Too much confidence really, assuming that technology like the beacons were foolproof.

Quill explained their limitations, but he wasn't terribly surprised when Owen caught up with him again in the line for lunch.

"So why tell backcountry visitors to get beacons if they often fail to make a difference?" Owen asked, notebook out, which really was rather adorable. And smart, taking this training seriously. Made Quill respect him that little bit more.

"Well, they *can* save lives, but everyone in your group needs one, not just a few designated persons, and you need to practice with them. Most people skimp on the number of beacons or they never practice, so when disaster strikes, they're not prepared. Beacons don't substitute for preparedness. And some people use them as an excuse to get overconfident or take risks, and that's also problematic."

"So practice is key." Owen jotted down notes in a crisp, precise handwriting.

"Also, not to get too gruesome on you, but a certain percentage of victims will die from hitting trees and rocks on the way down. The beacons only work if you survive the ride."

"Ah." Owen's skin paled as he considered this fact. "Makes sense, I guess. And you did a great job, laying out all the dangers."

"Thanks." Quill's neck heated as he wasn't sure what to make of the praise. Lunch was a simple buffet of sandwich fixings, chips, and cookies, but the line in front of them was slow as people took forever deciding. He supposed it was only polite to try to keep the conversation going. "Have you been around snow much yourself?"

"Well, I grew up in the Bay area, so not much snow there. But I worked at a Lake Tahoe ski resort a couple of winters in college. Summers too. And I've been on other ski trips. I like snow," Owen said with the sort of authority of someone who'd never had to deal with months on end of the stuff.

"That's good." Quill wasn't going to be the one to burst his bubble, but volunteers like Owen had a tendency to not make it through their first real winter. Loving snow wasn't the same as being able to cope with the dark, frigid days that defined an Alaskan winter. But he'd promised Hattie he wouldn't scare the volunteers, so he simply added lightly, "Being able to ski will definitely be a plus for you."

"I hope so." Owen gave him another of those near-blinding earnest smiles. And such was Quill's luck that the guy had deep, movie star-worthy dimples, which had always been kryptonite for him, even more than public speaking was. They made heat bloom low Quill's gut, made the rest of the line seem to fade away. The dimples were probably part of why Quill had initially placed him as being younger, but up this close he could also see subtle smile lines around his eyes that said he was indeed on the wrong side of his twenties.

This close also meant that he could smell the guy's crisp aftershave—a clean, modern scent that probably cost more than Quill's boots, but hell if it didn't combine with those dimples to utterly disarm him.

"The line moved." Owen's smile this time was more crafty, like he'd figured Quill out and intended to exploit that knowledge.

"Thanks." Quill grabbed a plate and the nearest two slices of wheat bread. Owen might be nice and hot as hell, but he was also dangerously distracting. And Quill knew better than most how deadly even a few moments of misplaced attention could be. The smartest course of action would be avoidance and to thank his lucky stars that he wouldn't be snowed in with those dimples.

At least Hattie's person wasn't likely to pose the same sort of temptation that Owen did. His gut churned again. He really did need all this uncertainty settled. And if he felt some regret over moving away from Owen as he took his food over to sit near Hattie, he stomped it down. He had a job to do, one that didn't leave room for much else, and that was simply how it was.

Don't miss
Arctic Heat *by Annabeth Albert,*
coming September 2019 wherever
Carina Press ebooks are sold.

www.CarinaPress.com

About the Author

Annabeth Albert grew up sneaking romance novels under the bed covers. Now, she devours all subgenres of romance out in the open—no flashlights required! When she's not adding to her keeper shelf, she's a multi-published Pacific Northwest romance writer. The #OutOfUniform series joins her critically acclaimed and fan-favorite LGBTQ romance #Gaymers, #PortlandHeat and #PerfectHarmony series. To find out what she's working on next and other fun extras, check out her website: *www.annabethalbert. com* or connect with Annabeth on Twitter, Facebook, Instagram, and Spotify! Also, be sure to sign up for her newsletter for free ficlets, bonus reads, and contests. The fan group, Annabeth's Angels, on Facebook is also a great place for bonus content and exclusive contests.

Emotionally complex, sexy, and funny stories are her favorites both to read and to write. Annabeth loves finding happy endings for a variety of pairings and particularly loves uncovering unique main characters. In her personal life, she works a rewarding day job and wrangles two active children.

Newsletter: http://eepurl.com/Nb9yv.

Fan group: https://www.facebook.com/groups/ annabethsangels.

We hope you enjoyed reading

ARCTIC *wild*

by

ANNABETH ALBERT

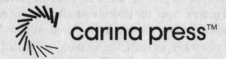

Connect with us for info on our new releases,
access to exclusive offers and much more!

Visit CarinaPress.com

Other ways to keep in touch:

Facebook.com/CarinaPress

Twitter.com/CarinaPress

CarinaPress.com/Newsletter

New books available every month.

Everything's bigger in Alaska.

Big scenery. Big danger. Big emotions.

Gorgeous, sweeping vistas and deep,
complicated feelings pair with life-and-death
situations in Annabeth Albert's Frozen Hearts trilogy,
pitting men against nature.

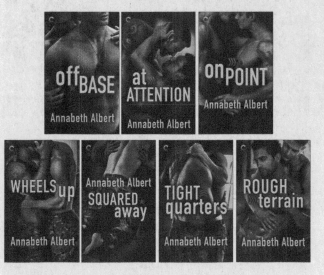
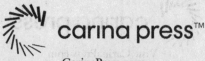

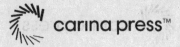
carina press™

Introducing the Carina Press
Romance Promise!

The Carina Press team all have one thing in common: we
are romance readers with a longtime love of the genre. And
we know what readers are looking for in a romance:
a guarantee of a happily-ever-after (HEA) or happy-for-
now (HFN). With that in mind, we're initiating the
Carina Press Romance Promise. When you see a
book tagged with these words in our cover copy/book
description, we're making you, the reader,
a very important promise:

**This book contains a romance central to the plot
and ends in an HEA or HFN.**

Simple, right? But so important, we know!

Look for the Carina Press Romance Promise and one-click
with confidence that we understand what's at the heart of
the romance genre!

Look for this line in Carina Press book descriptions:

*One-click with confidence. This title is part of the **Carina Press
Romance Promise**: all the romance you're looking for with an
HEA/HFN. It's a promise!*

Find out more at **CarinaPress.com/RomancePromise**.

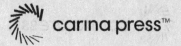